05109

# GRAVE DOUBTS

GRAVEROBBERS

# GRAVE DOUBTS

## A Quin and Morgan Mystery

## John Moss

A Castle Street Mystery

DUNDURN PRESS
TORONTO

Project Editor: Michael Carroll
Copy Editor: Barry Jowett
Designer: Erin Mallory
Printer: Webcom

**Library and Archives Canada Cataloguing in Publication**

Moss, John, 1940-
    Grave doubts : a Quin and Morgan mystery / by John Moss.

(A Castle Street mystery)
ISBN 978-1-55488-405-6

    I. Title.  II. Series: Castle Street mystery

PS8576.O7863 G73 2009        C813'.6        C2009-900106-3

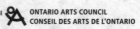

We acknowledge the support of **The Canada Council for the Arts** and the **Ontario Arts Council** for our publishing program. We also acknowledge the financial support of the **Government of Canada** through the **Book Publishing Industry Development Program** and **The Association for the Export of Canadian Books**, and the **Government of Ontario** through the **Ontario Book Publishers Tax Credit program**, and the **Ontario Media Development Corporation**.

Care has been taken to trace the ownership of copyright material used in this book. The author and the publisher welcome any information enabling them to rectify any references or credits in subsequent editions.

*J. Kirk Howard, President*

Printed and bound in Canada
www.dundurn.com

Dundurn Press
3 Church Street, Suite 500
Toronto, Ontario, Canada
M5E 1M2

Gazelle Book Services Limited
White Cross Mills
High Town, Lancaster, England
LA1 4XS

Dundurn Press
2250 Military Road
Tonawanda, NY
U.S.A. 14150

*For Beverley Haun*

## *chapter one*
## Hogg's Hollow

---

$W$inter in Toronto is a prolonged confrontation with street-blackened slush and ice-laden winds, punctuated at intervals by thick snowfalls of breathtaking beauty. This year, as the winter backed into spring with sullen unpredictability, David Morgan became increasingly restive, sometimes morose, despite the distraction of his various passions.

Morgan currently specialized in tribal antique carpets from Persia, as he persisted in calling Iran. He could not afford to buy the carpets he admired and dragged his partner, Detective Sergeant Miranda Quin, into myriad rug merchants on their travels about town. She had a better eye for colour and design and the dealers tended to address her, rather than him. She sometimes explained they weren't married, they were cops. This made dealers nervous — unnecessarily, since their profession was homicide.

Miranda enjoyed these carpet excursions, but Morgan had recently developed a competing enthusiasm that puzzled her: handcrafted furniture by settlers who tried to disguise local softwoods with paint. She knew how succeeding generations added layer upon layer in various hues until the baby boomers came along, bought cheap, and furiously stripped back to the original wood. The patina of ancient colours was now a rare mark of authenticity, good taste, and very high cost. The word *Canadiana*, which Morgan used as if only he knew what it really meant, made her nervous. She preferred the mellow warmth of old pine, newly refurbished. In Miranda's mind, authenticity gave way to aesthetics; she connected more with the present and he with the past. Morgan assured Miranda she was wrong.

Her partner's restlessness when they were not immersed in murder paradoxically focused his mind. It also darkened his mood, especially when snow persisted as the nights grew shorter and the days were long. As for Miranda, her natural optimism was affirmed by adversity. A lull in their caseload made her nervous. They both needed something to happen. What, she had thought, could better distract him from seasonal affective disorder — which seemed to pursue him from season to season — than the gruesome discovery of desiccated corpses behind the walls of an old house, locked in a lovers' embrace?

A winter mosquito hovered above David Morgan's book as if a bit of punctuation had fluttered off the page. His gaze shifted from the flow of words as he pushed an open hand through air until instinctively his fingers closed and ground against his palm. He turned his hand inward to examine the insect remains and was disconcerted when the force of his breath made them airborne again.

Puzzled by his own cruelty, Morgan set his book down and leaned back on the sofa, staring up into the loft of his Victorian postmodern condo as if he were looking for something. When the natural light faded and the gloom overhead turned to darkness, he began to pace the perimeter of the room in measured steps. The haze of evening filled his window, pierced by sleet-rimed branches hovering darkly over the rooftops of neighbours across the street. He paused and turned on a table lamp, which cast a dull, luminescent wash across the glass.

Picking up three photographs from the coffee table, Morgan walked to the switch on the brick wall and flicked on the overhead. The front window flared into a huge mirror and he could see himself poised awkwardly at the edge of the room, holding the pictures as if they were notes for a speech.

He doused the lights and the city returned, layered and receding like a Turner montage.

Morgan did not have to scrutinize the photos; their content was inscribed in his mind. They were police shots from a crime scene. Miranda had dropped them off just before dusk.

He had been immersed in his Folio Society edition of *The Persians*. She had come to the door and, smiling ambiguously, offered him a manila envelope and shuffled back down the icy walk, negotiating her footing one step at a time.

"Come in out of the cold," he called after her.

She leaned against her car, waiting. Her eyes flashed brown and green and golden in the evening light. She shook her head slowly from side to side and her auburn hair took on the rippling hues of the evening sky.

Framed in the open doorway, he removed photographs from the envelope and held them aslant to the light.

"These are cheerful," he shouted.

She waved and climbed into her 1959 Jaguar XK 150, British racing green — she had only put it back on the road at the beginning of the week, anticipating good weather.

"Where're their bloody heads?" He waved the photographs in the air as if he could conjure the missing parts.

"That's the point!" she called through an open window. The Jag's engine roared mischievously. He repeated his question with a mute, exaggerated mouthing of the words. She swerved the car out into ruts of unplowed slush. He watched as it slithered down the street until she was out of sight.

The pictures were recently taken, but the bodies were historical artifacts. Wearing early Victorian clothes. Regency? Possibly. He would have to check it out.

Miranda was whimsical, but not capricious. There would be an explanation. A male and female, decapitated, bodies entwined in a macabre embrace — perhaps there was something in their symbolic rapport she wanted to share.

Morgan shrugged, trying to be indifferent. People didn't shrug their indifference when there was no one to see them, he thought.

They had worked together in homicide long enough they were inured to the grotesqueries of death, but murder fascinates. You start with a corpse and work backward, he reflected, until the victim's demise is the inevitable outcome of what you've unearthed. A metaphysical inversion: you turn the quest for the meaning of life on its head. You search for the meaning of death.

Morgan stood still in the gloom of the lamplight, contemplating the pictures in his hand. When he had closed the door after Miranda disappeared, he had determinedly reinserted himself into the travails and triumphs of ancient Persia. Minutes later, his concentration broken by the arbitrary execution of a mosquito, unaccountably alive in the wrong season, he found himself on his feet, motionless, irritated by his desire to resist whatever it was she was up to.

He wheeled about and strode into the glare of the kitchen. Taking a beer from the fridge, he returned to the living room, flicked the lights on full, and settled into the wingback chair he had years ago released from captivity at a thrift shop on Jarvis Street and had been meaning to have reupholstered ever since.

He spread the photographs across the coffee table and leaned forward to examine them, trying to avoid his own shadow. Then he sat back, keeping the pictures in his peripheral vision, and as the hours rolled by he opened his mind to a montage of images: images of sex and death, of Upper Canadian pioneers, of Darius, Xerxes, and the invasions of Greece, all scudding through at random velocities.

The photographs offered three perspectives on the same tableau. One was from across a room that was evidently in the process of demolition. It showed a sizeable cavity or closet that had been revealed where rotting plaster and clumped layers of wallpaper were sheared from a wall, and inside on the floor there was an ominous rumple of shadows. In the next picture, taken from the doorway of the hidden closet, the bodies of a man and a woman lay closely together, and somehow, paradoxically, they seemed chastely intimate.

In the third, the bodies had been removed to the larger room and were laid out on display for the camera, still with their limbs entwined. On the back, pencilled in Miranda's handwriting, were the words, "Catherine Earnshaw and Heathcliff."

Curiously, nothing was noted about the missing heads.

Morgan turned the other two pictures over, but they were blank. It was getting late. He telephoned her anyway. A sleepy voice answered.

"Morgan?"

"How did you know it was me?"

"Who else?"

"It's only eleven —"

"— forty-five."

"Talk to me," he said.

"Did Heathcliff have a first name?"

"Miranda?"

"I thought you'd be interested."

"Possibly."

"They're still at the scene," Miranda said. "Headless. The superintendent wants forensic anthropologists to see them *in situ*. But tenured scientists don't work the night shift."

"Whoever moved them must have already looked for the heads. They shouldn't have been moved. Amazing they didn't come apart."

"They're frozen in an eternal embrace, Morgan. Like sculpture, flesh turned to bronze."

"I hope someone has the imagination to bury them like that."

"In the Yorkshire dales?"

"Maybe the English won't take them. They've got enough old stuff already."

"They took the Elgin Marbles!"

"The Parthenon looks better without them. Less cluttered."

"Good night, Morgan."

"Oh, no! No way. We're going up there."

"Come on!"

"We're going headhunting; I'll be over in fifteen minutes."

"Morgan, go to sleep."

"You wouldn't have offered the temptation if you weren't prepared for the consequences."

He could hear her smiling.

"How do you know, *up there*?" she said. "Up where?"

"They're wearing town clothes but the room is country."

"Keep going."

"See the fragments of plaster?" he continued as if she had

the photographs in front of her. "They're dangling on horse-hair from hand-split, swamp-cedar lath. You can see the crown moulding is local design, wood not plaster, and the baseboard is original. Upper Canadian, transitional farmhouse. Too bad they can't salvage it. I'd say we're talking about somewhere on the northern margins of early Toronto — before 1834 when it was still Muddy York — up around Hogg's Hollow, east off Yonge. Within hearing distance of Highway 401."

"Sometimes you're fun, Morgan. See you in half an hour. Bring coffee."

She hung up the phone and rolled over, pleased with herself. She had almost fallen asleep, waiting for his call. She knew, for all Morgan's interest in pioneer cabinetry and oriental rugs and exotic fish and Arctic exploration and Easter Island and language acquisition and the history of ideas, that nothing got him going like an unresolved murder. And if they were absorbed in a mutual interest, her own disposition unaccountably mellowed.

She stretched languidly. Morgan would be closer to an hour getting there. She had time to enjoy the warmth of the room before preparing herself against the penetrating dampness outside. He refused to buy a car and trudging through accretions of icy slush from the Annex over to Isabella would take its toll. He would be late, chilled to the bone, and grumpy. Grumpy was different from morose. She could laugh at grumpy, and he would laugh back.

She was wearing only a T-shirt and men's boxers. One of the advantages of a condo over rental is that she controlled her own thermostat.

Miranda had lived in the same place as a student. When she returned to the city after three years in the RCMP, she discovered the building was being converted to private ownership and snapped up her old apartment. Partly it was for nostalgia — the reassurance of familiar terrain — and partly it was her fondness for varnish on the balustrades checkered by time, worn marble stairs, paned windows, and porcelain fixtures. Consistency was the hobgoblin of little minds! Someone said that. Probably Swift or Pope. It sounded eighteenth century-ish.

She thought of herself as "urban contemporary," perhaps because she grew up in a village. Morgan was raised, impoverished, in Cabbagetown, just south of where she lived now, back when it was in transition to becoming an upscale address. He was a gentleman by nature not birth, and endearingly unkempt, but not shabby.

Her intercom buzzed.

"Morgan?"

"Yeah?"

"You're here so soon."

"I took a taxi."

"You never."

"I did. Are you going to let me in?"

"Did you bring coffee?"

"Yes."

She buzzed him in, then unlocked her door.

She was in the bathroom, dabbing sleep wrinkles out of her face with icy water, when he called from the kitchen.

"Do you want milk in yours? I asked for double-double but they're both black with no sugar."

"Good," she mumbled, applying lipstick as a token gesture. "Help yourself. I'll stick with black."

She walked out into the kitchen.

"You look good when you're sleepy; very ethereal."

"Like the ghost of Catherine Earnshaw. Brunettes can't be ethereal; we're alluring."

"Seductive."

"In your dreams, Morgan."

She did look attractive, rumpled. Sometimes he was very aware she was a woman.

"Doesn't that make you think of erectile dysfunction?" she said.

"What?"

*"Wuthering Heights."*

He grimaced.

Once, in this same apartment, they had made love. He remembered, looking at her now, that it was good, but they never tried it again.

"Let's go," he said. "We can drink these on the way."

"No, just a sec, I need milk to cool it down. What's it like outside?"

"The usual."

"Cold, wet, and the sky is radiant?"

"Glowing putrescence, like a painting by Turner. Let's go."

In Miranda's car, they reviewed what they knew about the case. It wasn't their case but they were already committed. It wasn't anyone's case, really. It was a matter of historical interest, not criminal justice.

Miranda asked Morgan to dig her cellphone from the depths of her purse and call headquarters to let them know what they were doing. His own was, inevitably, battery-dead and in his sweater drawer along with anachronistic cuff links and a gold, hardly used wedding band.

"We happened to be in the area," Morgan explained to Alex Rufalo, their superintendent, and after a brief exchange dropped the phone back into her bag.

"We're not the only ones who work late," he said.

"We're not working, remember?" She paused. "Rufalo went home before I left. There must be something up to bring him back in. The office as sanctuary, no?"

"Yes. Maybe."

Miranda pulled the Jag up in front of a nondescript frame house, sliding roughly against the curb as she parked.

"Damn slush," she said. "This is the address. There's a patrol car down the street. A light in the upstairs window. What do you think? Doesn't look like much."

"This'll be it."

"Okay," she said, getting out of the car. Despite the telltale light in the upper window, a book-cover cliché foreshadowing dread and doom, the place looked deserted and remarkably ordinary.

As Morgan clambered awkwardly from the low-slung car, he expounded. "Ontario country vernacular. Storey and a half, steep gable, central hall, symmetrical design; Georgian with early Victorian pretensions. God forgive the aluminum siding. It's clapboard underneath."

"You figure so?"

"Yeah."

They dumped the dregs of their coffee out onto the icy snow but, without any place to leave them, held on to the cups. They knocked on the door and waited. Morgan scrutinized the blank wall overhead, trying to estimate where the arched transom would have been. As a practical concession to warmth, it was probably covered in about the same time as the surrounding farmland became housing tracts.

The door opened and a uniformed policewoman stood squarely in the middle, backlit by a dull glow from the kitchen.

"Yes?" she said. The woman did not seem intimidated by late-night callers at a murder scene.

There was a moment of awkwardness as she waited for an explanation, which Miranda found pleasing, knowing they were not automatically assumed to be police.

"Officer?" Miranda did not recognize her. "I'm Detective

Sergeant Quin, this is Detective Morgan."

The woman nodded without introducing herself. "You're a sergeant too, I imagine," she said, glancing at Morgan, then back to Miranda. "I wasn't expecting anyone just yet. Are you coming in?"

"Please," said Miranda.

The policewoman led them through refuse and rubble into the kitchen. The kitchen itself was bright and hospitable.

"I've got some coffee," she said. "You might as well use your own cups. I've been letting it steep to counter the smell."

"It doesn't smell," Morgan observed. "It's just an old house. Smells like burnt coffee."

"I'm surprised you're alone," said Miranda. "I'm surprised the stove's working."

The woman shrugged. "Wrecking crew left the power on. Most of the wiring's been stripped, or at least the fixtures. Some rooms are dark, others not. Like a bad horror flick, without the music. They're all bad, I guess." She indicated the location of the desiccated lovers with an upward nod. Her features softened for a moment. "Those two aren't very good company; they're sort of into each other. If it wasn't for the missing parts, they'd be kind of sweet."

"Sweet?" Morgan said. "They're dead."

"The dead in one another's arms, Detective." He waited for her to finish her thought, but that seemed to be it. She gazed into his eyes without smiling.

The woman poured them coffee. Miranda liked her; she warmed to anyone who could serve coffee that smelled so rank without an apology. Morgan was wary; her confidence seemed almost a reprimand for assumptions about her uniformed status.

They sat at the grey Arborite table, sipping. The woman was young and, despite the androgynous uniform, attractive. The coffee was execrable.

"It's not necessarily murder," said Miranda. "It could be a third party honouring their dying wishes. A ghoulish accomplice; except what would he — or possibly she — have done with the heads?"

"Could have been separate acts," said the policewoman. "They could have died embracing; then someone stole the heads for souvenirs and sealed the remaining remains in the wall."

"'The young in one another's arms,'" said Morgan, delivering the phrase in quotation marks, catching up to her previous statement.

"Yeats. He wasn't talking about dying, Morgan. He was talking about sex." Miranda cast a conspiratorial glance at the young policewoman.

Morgan began compiling a list of doomed lovers in his mind, from Hero and Leander to Sean Penn and Madonna. Himself? No. *Doomed* elevated something that was simply sad.

The young woman seemed in no hurry to show off her charges, and for Miranda and Morgan it was a matter of pacing.

"So where're you from?" Morgan asked.

The officer flushed with anger. Miranda blanched. In an immigrant society you never ask people of colour where they're from. You either know, or it's not your concern.

"I'd guess southwestern Ontario," Morgan blithely continued. "Down past Waterloo County — that's where Miranda's from. Do you have a name?"

"Naismith. My family is from Halifax. Africville. Until they tore it down. I thought you were figuring maybe Jamaica. Dat girl, man, her come from de islands?"

The Caribbean cadence was derisive, but Morgan wasn't sure if she was mocking him or herself. That was the point, thought Miranda.

"Africville? United Empire Loyalists."

"Good stock, as they say in the people trade. We pre-date the Loyalists. Freed-men, before the Revolution, when Halifax was still called Chebucto by the Mi'kmaq. But I grew up within sight of Detroit; we're not from Africville anymore."

"And went to the University of Windsor," said Morgan, trying to connect.

"The University of Western Ontario. Where I was rushed by the African Club, the Afro-American Student Coalition, the West-Indian Association, the Moorish-American Movement. La Societé Franco-Afrique, you name it."

"Nothing Canadian?" said Morgan, unsure whether that was a good thing or bad. That is the point, thought Miranda. It was both.

"Nothing Canadian *and* black; they were mutually exclusive. I could be professionally black or honourary white. That was it! I was in demand socially by every white group on campus so they could pretend we were exactly the same."

"Cursed by the colour-blind," said Miranda.

"You've got it," said the young woman. "If you think invisibility is a bitch, try being the object of tolerance."

"So," Morgan asked, carefully, "is Toronto — the most cosmopolitan city in the world, as they say — any better?" He was fascinated by how much attitude she revealed, and how little was shown of what she actually felt.

"Well, sir, here I'm an ethnic minority. Before I was just a minority. You tell me."

Blowing steam across the top of his coffee, Morgan lapsed into personal reflection. He had never been invisible but he had certainly been isolated. By choice? Is it ever by choice?

Listening to the silence, Miranda realized that from the moment the front door opened she had been aware the young woman was black. She had admired her dark complexion, her gleaming hair, her bold face. Miranda was suddenly uncomfortable, knowing she would not have catalogued the features of a white officer unless the person was either extremely homely or outrageously beautiful.

Their eyes connected and for a brief moment each woman looked into the depths of the other, each at a loss as to what was revealed.

"What have you done for a toilet?" Miranda asked. "I see most of the plumbing is gone."

"Haven't had to. But I figure I'd just go outside."

The two women pushed at the back door, ratcheting it open against the drifted snow, and Miranda stepped out. She was back before the officer had even poured herself a refill.

"That," said Miranda, "was not pleasant."

"But quick," said Morgan.

The two women chatted for a while, sitting at the Arborite table, nursing their coffees. Morgan, standing, leaned against a counter, grinding his soles on the floor. He sat down. The women tried to open their conversation, to make it inclusive, but he only listened, and periodically glanced at the ceiling, trying to envision the macabre scenario overhead.

Miranda looked at her partner over the rim of her cup. She felt almost sorry for him. Delay somehow relieved his guilt for wanting to subvert professional disinterest and plunge into the Gothic depths of what promised to be a really good story.

"I'm going up," he finally announced, rising to his feet again.

The muted groan of his chair against the battered linoleum startled them. A faint moaning echo reprised as the other two slid out their chairs and joined him shuffling through rubble as they made for the stairs.

*chapter two*

# The Room Upstairs

D emolition had been arrested in its earliest phase, although the place must have been deteriorating through seasons of freezing and thawing for years. Thick layers of wallpaper had peeled off in great patchwork swathes, revealing plaster that looked pulpy or had crumbled away. Horizontal strips of hand-split cedar showed through gaps where a salvaging contractor had retrieved old fixtures and woodwork. The stair railing was gone, but the wood trim hadn't been touched yet.

As they spread out on the dilapidated stairs to distribute their weight, Officer Naismith explained how salvagers had discovered the hidden closet. In prying a hanging cabinet from one of the bedroom walls, a crowbar smashed through the pulpy plaster and revealed an unaccountable cavity. It wasn't so odd in a larger house for an awkward space to be covered over — Morgan knew that — but it was unusual in a cottage like this. They didn't build in closets; they would have used armoires and dressers, or pegs on the wall. There might be the occasional odd architectural nook. Covered over, it would be forgotten in a generation or two.

"Here we are," said Officer Naismith as if conducting a tour. "The largest bedroom, no less."

"It's still pretty small," Miranda observed. Then, moving forward, she gazed downward. "Oh, my goodness, they look so in love!"

The room filled with a hushed silence.

Officer Naismith was quietly jubilant. Morgan smiled enigmatically. Miranda's lack of professional propriety or affected indifference seemed a genuine relief. Candour from Miranda was not always forthcoming, especially in front of colleagues.

Miranda stifled what might have been laughter or a sneeze, the officer started to giggle, Morgan scowled. But the grisly scene, while eerie, was not oppressive. Death seemed so long in the past, solemnity was no more obligatory than grieving over displays at a waxworks museum.

Morgan kneeled to scrutinize the skin on the back of the male's hand. Leaning forward, he nudged the body and jumped when the hand seemed to flinch.

"My goodness," he said defensively. Not swearing was a modest perversity in a world where obscenities vied with profanities to displace more thoughtful expletives. "They're light as a feather. I hardly touched him." He fingered the man's sleeve. "This material is incredibly well-preserved. It's stood up better than its occupant."

Miranda squatted down opposite, examining the woman's clothing.

"What a lovely dress," she noted, glancing up at the officer then back at her partner. "Satin and lace, and there's no sign of a struggle, no bloodstains. It's a bit odd, Morgan. There's no blood on either of them."

She eased around to look at their severed necks.

"Clean cuts, by someone who knew basic anatomy," she observed. "Even if they were dead, there should have been residual blood. They must have been dressed like this after they were decapitated."

"They don't seem to have shrunk very much," Morgan said. "The frock coat seems a little big, maybe. Her dress is right on."

"How come there's no collateral degradation? You'd think their flesh would meld with the materials, that the cloth would show signs of decay."

"They must have been sealed up virtually airtight in the heat of the summer," Morgan observed. "I suppose the flesh would dry out before rot had a chance to set in. I don't know; it seems a bit strange."

Morgan took a pen from his pocket and probed into the dark folds of the frock coat, retrieving a signet ring that had slipped from the man's wizened finger. He held it up to the light.

"Masonic. It has the same pyramid capped with an all-seeing eye that's on the American one-dollar bill."

"Is it really?"

"Yeah. Take a look the next time you have one."

"I know what's on their dollar bill, Morgan. It's the ring: I'm surprised it's a Mason's ring."

"How so?"

"Because. Look what's in *her* hand," Miranda unclasped the fingers carefully so as not to break them off and revealed a small, gleaming crucifix on a length of fine gold chain.

"She'd have trouble wearing anything around her neck."

"It's an unlikely combination," Miranda said, ignoring his quip. "A Roman Catholic and a Mason. I wonder if that's why they're like this."

"Dead?"

"In the romantic posture. Doomed by love — destroyed by a righteous father?" "What do you think, Officer Naismith?" Morgan asked. "You haven't said anything."

"I was just watching the masters at work," she responded.

Morgan suspected she was being ironic.

Miranda smiled, rising to her feet.

"I'm Miranda," she said, holding out her hand awkwardly. They had already passed the level of intimacy where exchanging first names seemed inane. They shook hands with whimsical formality.

"Morgan is Morgan. He has another name but keeps it a secret."

"I'm Naismith."

"Naismith Naismith," said Morgan.

The woman laughed. "Well, you're Morgan Morgan."

"David."

"Rachel."

"And I'm still Miranda. So what do you think, Rachel? What's happening here?"

"I really have no idea."

"Yes you do."

"Do I? Well, I doubt it's her father who did it. I think they've been set up as a sentimental paradox."

"A paradox?" said Morgan.

"Intimate lovers; but headless, their identities erased."

"Subversive," said Miranda.

"Do either of you know 'The Kiss' by Auguste Rodin?"

"Yes," said Miranda.

She summoned to mind the enduring embrace of bronze lovers. One of the most famous portrayals of romantic passion ever conceived, bigger than life, highly erotic, the caught moment of absolute love.

"Yeah," said Morgan. "The plasters were at the ROM exhibition last year."

"Did you read the fine print?" Rachel Naismith asked. "Beside the display?"

They felt a little truant; both looked inquisitive.

"The story behind 'The Kiss' is intriguing," she continued. "Once you know it, the sculpture changes. It literally turns from dream into nightmare, a diabolical vision of sensual entropy —"

"Sensual entropy! I like that," Morgan exclaimed.

"Translation, please," said Miranda, not in the least embarrassed for not knowing what the officer meant. "You honoured in art history, I take it."

"Yeah, art and art history."

Morgan took it on himself to explain Rachel Naismith's esoteric phrase, perhaps to prove he understood. He seemed oblivious to the possibility of appearing pedantic.

"Entropy is a measure of inefficiency, say in an organism or engine where heat is wasted rather than being transformed into energy. A perfect trope for suspended passion."

Rachel smiled, indicating she liked Morgan, pedantry and all.

"That's more or less where I was going," she said. "Rodin apparently had Dante in mind when he sculpted 'The Kiss.' There's a passage in *The Divine Comedy* about lovers locked in a perpetual clinch, having been dispatched *in flagrante delicto* by the woman's husband, who was the man's brother. They fetch up in Hell, an inferno of their own making. Sentimental inversion: they are doomed to hold the posture of their passion forever."

"That's what 'The Kiss' is about?" exclaimed Miranda.

"That's what Rodin apparently had in mind. It was supposed to be part of a tableau of Heaven and Hell; it was his unfinished masterpiece."

"Beauty becomes horror," Morgan mused in quiet astonishment. "And horror becomes beauty."

"Becomes, both ways," Miranda offered.

He looked at her quizzically.

"Beauty becomes, transforms horror; beauty becomes, complements horror. Change, no change."

Miranda sometimes spoke in a kind of syntactical shorthand. He nodded approval. She turned to Officer Naismith, who seemed to be playing with the verbal permutations in her head.

"You're right," Rachel Naismith continued. She wasn't sure who was right about what. She lapsed into silence, apparently not wanting to sound like a gallery brochure or an academic treatise.

Miranda gazed at the ghastly sensuality of the corpses intertwined at their feet, who now seemed part of something infinitely more sinister. Rachel's comparison was anachronistic, of course. These lovers had been here long before Rodin translated Dante's words into sculpture. But they certainly embodied an unholy paradox. Beneath the sad drape of their clothing, the absolute stillness of articulated limbs conveyed a haunting absence of life. But, as Rachel had suggested, without heads, they were not individuals. The true horror, Miranda realized, lay in the extinction of their personalities.

Morgan had seen one of the original marble versions of Rodin's sculpture in the Tate Gallery when he lived in London after graduating from university. The plaster at the Royal Ontario Museum seemed more real, though, perhaps because it was shaped by the hands of the master, and the stone and bronze versions were done in large part by artisans. Or perhaps it was because London was another life.

Miranda pictured "The Kiss" in her mind. Although she had only seen the plaster, she now imagined the image in bronze. The lovers were naked; the bronze seemed alive, flesh trapped in illimitable torment. "I like it better, knowing the story," she said. Unable to resist sounding like a brochure herself, she continued, "It anticipates the age of irony and the death of romance."

"Oh," said Rachel. "I thought romance was dormant, not dead."

"Only for some of us," said Morgan. "For these two it's the other way around. Death *is* romance."

"From the ring and the cross, I'd say they were doomed from the moment they met," said Miranda.

"Some lines aren't meant to be crossed," Rachel proscribed with an edge in her voice.

Miranda looked over at Morgan but his attention had shifted to the small cabinet leaning on its side near the gaping wall. It was three shades of bluish-green, with a diamond pattern on the door and an exposed bottom shelf between scooped sides. Across the top was an exaggerated cornice, a minor oxymoron of comic austerity.

Anticipating her query, he explained. "It's a Waterloo County hanging cupboard, mint condition — it might have belonged to your ancestors. German vernacular, Pennsylvania Dutch, made a couple of generations after they'd resettled as Loyalists. What's unusual, really, is that salvagers had to rip it out with enough force they opened the crypt."

"It seems out of place."

"It is, in a sense. There couldn't have been much of a market this close to town for country furniture. I'm guessing people, here, travelled up to Berlin, a century before it was renamed Kitchener, way before trains, to visit relatives or take the mineral waters in Preston. The cabinet is small enough to be brought back by wagon or carriage. Wagon, I'd say, given the modesty of the house. But why was it attached so securely, and why wasn't it painted over with the rest of the woodwork?"

"Listen!" said Miranda. All three held their breath.

"There's somebody downstairs," she whispered. "It's either ghosts or forensic anthropologists! I thought academics slept through the night...."

The clatter and absence of voices seemed ominous, until a hauntingly beautiful woman suddenly appeared in the doorway, followed by a man with quick eyes and a portly physique. Morgan, Miranda, and Rachel Naismith exchanged amused glances, while the dead stirred uneasily as floorboards beneath them shifted from the combined weight of the living.

"Good to see you," said the woman with a tired smile, while the man moved directly to the bodies on the floor as if courtesy were superfluous.

"We're the investigating anthropologists," she explained. "That is Professor Birbalsingh." She nodded toward the man hunkered over the corpses, examining them like specimens. "I'm Dr. Shelagh Hubbard from the Royal Ontario Museum."

Miranda introduced Morgan and the officer, and then herself as an afterthought. The woman nodded at Rachel, then took Morgan's hand and her countenance warmed from weary to sleepy. She was very blond. Surprisingly, when she took Miranda's hand, the sensuality did not subside. This woman has a sexual relationship with the world, Miranda suspected, wondering whether Rachel received short shrift due to race or, more likely, to her status in uniform.

"We got an evening call from police headquarters. Somebody named Rufalo," the woman continued with a congeniality that was apparently meant to counter her colleague's brusqueness. "It sounded intriguing. Professor Birbalsingh phoned me several times through the night. He couldn't sleep for thinking about it, and I couldn't sleep without disconnecting the telephone and putting my bid for university tenure in jeopardy. So here we are."

"Me too," said a voice from the stairs. "I wouldn't miss this for the world."

Ellen Ravenscroft, the medical examiner, stepped into the room, forcing the other four to realign themselves in relation to the bodies and the man on his knees who was engrossed in the details of wizened flesh and uncommon apparel.

"Surprised to see you two here," said Ellen.

"Just ghoulish curiosity," said Miranda. "It's not official."

"Not official?" Rachel Naismith exclaimed. "You've been drinking my coffee! And you're tourists! For me, it's a crime scene."

Miranda introduced her to Ellen Ravenscroft. The two women did not exchange courtesies, beyond nods of recognition for their professional roles.

"I'm surprised they'd send a medical examiner on a case like this," said Miranda. "I'd have thought the academics had it covered."

"If it's dead and there's a chance it was human, it's ours," Ellen responded. "Just a formality, love, so I can fill out the papers."

"No autopsy?"

"Not likely," she said. "Excuse me."

Morgan watched with admiration as the ME shunted the academic experts aside and squatted down to examine the bodies. "I'll take a look here before you two start messing about."

Professor Birbalsingh rose to his feet, harumphing with indignity, eyes flashing, muttering something about forensic anthropologists, but said nothing more. He hovered like a raptor tracking its prey until Ellen Ravenscroft glowered up at him and muttered "forensic pathologist trumps anthropologist," backing the professor away.

"Did the police get pictures?" she asked.

"Yes," said Officer Naismith

"That's what brought us here," said Miranda.

"Okay, let's just see what we have —"

"Be careful with that," snapped Birbalsingh with a vehemence suggesting he was not used to his authority being usurped, especially by a non-academic and a woman. "It is a very fine cloak. You do not want to cause it damage. These are very good clothes."

Without turning around, the ME announced, "I am Dr. Ravenscroft, coroner's office. Who are you, love?"

"This is Professor Birbalsingh from the University of Toronto," said his colleague. "I'm Shelagh Hubbard, cross-appointed from the ROM. We're the forensic anthropologists here by request."

"By request? Well, isn't that a treat. They let you off campus. I went to York, myself."

"For the suburban atmosphere, I presume."

"You do, love, you presume," she said, standing up. "The real York, as in Yorkshire. Not the nether regions of Toronto and certainly not the 'New' one — the five boroughs on the Hudson."

"So, what do you see?" Miranda interjected to restore professional decorum, although Rachel and Morgan had been enjoying the repartee.

"They're thoroughly dead." Ellen Ravenscroft seemed to triumph in a declaration of the obvious. "Their heads are missing. I'd say that's about it." She nodded gravely. "They're all yours, Professor Birbalsingh, Dr. Hubbard. If the heads turn up, kindly inform someone."

"Anyone in particular?" Miranda asked.

"I've got my doubts about the heads," said Morgan. "They weren't in the crypt, so they're probably converted to dust."

"Well," said Miranda, "apparently a conversion was called for."

There was an awkward pause; then, remembering the cross and ring, Morgan chuckled and as soon as he did Rachel Naismith recognized the joke and chortled to herself. Ellen seemed indifferent to missing the point.

"I'm out of here, my friends. Give me a call, Morgan. We'll talk about missed opportunities. Good night, Miranda. Good night, Officer."

And almost as an afterthought she said over her shoulder, "Good night, forensic anthropologists. Let me know if you find anything." And, finally, with a fading sigh, "Do call me, Morgan."

Miranda rolled her eyes at her partner as Ellen Ravenscroft disappeared down the stairs. He looked away, he squinted back at her, mouthing an indecipherable phrase.

"What is it you're trying to say, Morgan?"

He shrugged.

"Do you two want more coffee?" Rachel asked.

"Definitely not for me," said Morgan.

Shelagh Hubbard stood up. "I'd like some coffee, if you wouldn't mind, Officer. It couldn't be worse than I make myself."

"You'd be surprised," said Miranda.

"Would he like some?" Rachel asked, nodding in the direction of the portly Professor Birbalsingh, crouched over his headless victim. "I've got lots. It's been steeping all night."

"I think he probably would," said Dr. Hubbard. "Both black, no sugar."

"That's good," said Rachel. "I didn't bring extras."

"Milk and sugar are necessities," said Morgan, who preferred double-double, and had no intention of enduring more of the poisonous brew.

"Only for those who can't do without."

"That is a tautology," he said.

"Yes it is," she said, reassuring him.

She walked out of the room and suddenly there was thunderous clatter as if the stairs had collapsed. Miranda was closest and through the door in an instant, calling Rachel's name.

Rachel waved from the gloom in the downstairs hall.

Miranda heard an embarrassed scramble behind her and wheeled around to see Morgan and Shelagh Hubbard jammed in the doorframe, in a comic simulation of the grotesque embrace on the floor. Miranda rolled her eyes and returned her attention to Rachel, who was waiting.

"You okay?" Miranda called. "What the hell happened?"

"It was only a loose step," Rachel answered. "I skied my way down. You take care, any of you, coming down after me." She craned forward to see the couple in the doorway frozen in place by their futile attempts to avoid pressing flesh.

Morgan and the anthropologist disentangled themselves and receded into the room. Miranda followed.

"I see you two are becoming quite friendly," she whispered to Morgan, looking at Shelagh Hubbard.

The woman was preternaturally attractive; her pale skin and light blue eyes and long blond hair, pulled tightly against her skull, made her seem otherworldly, but not ethereal; less ghostlike than deadly.

Shelagh Hubbard bent down to exchange words with Professor Birbalsingh. He was closely examining the remnants of dried flesh at the collars of each corpse, something that held his interest more than anything the living could possibly offer. He nodded assent.

The woman took out her cellphone, explaining that since the cadavers had been inappropriately disentombed, they were vulnerable. She did not explain how or to what. Rapid deterioration, Miranda supposed; airborne bacteria, diseases of the dead. They needed to get the bodies to the lab at the university as soon as transportation could be arranged. Ambulance or hearse? Miranda wondered. Neither seemed quite suitable.

With the medical examiner gone, the forensic anthropologists were in charge. The police function was to offer assistance, guard the remains, and bear witness to the irrevocability of death. It was time, Miranda thought, for the ghouls to go home. She glanced at Morgan and saw that he was gazing at Dr. Hubbard, perhaps savouring the effects of their fleeting embrace. The woman was wearing perfume, Miranda realized; a subtle scent but inescapable. She had dressed for the occasion.

Miranda considered the implicit judgment about disturbing the bodies. Almost certainly the uniforms who answered the call had moved them only enough to identify the problem. Normal procedure would demand nothing be disturbed. But at some point, as Morgan had suggested, time intrudes and evidentiary materials simply become artifacts.

Morgan was lingering. He had a genuine interest in forensic anthropology. Little was revealed, however, by observing the mental activities of the two academics, who were scrutinizing and registering from their specialized perspectives. This must be how we appear, he thought, prowling the scene of a crime — cerebral and disengaged. He chuckled at the image as he admired Dr. Hubbard.

Miranda coughed throatily, seemed to listen for something elusive, then coughed again. Then she announced, "I'm going to scream."

Morgan looked puzzled, tolerant.

She shrieked wickedly in variable pitch.

A racket from downstairs was followed by thumping footsteps, and Officer Naismith sprang through the doorway, her semi-automatic clasped in both hands. Everyone froze.

For a moment even the bodies seemed part of an allegorical *danse macabre*, with Rachel cast in the role of Death.

Then the tableau collapsed in laughter, much to the officer's annoyance.

"Sorry," Miranda said. "I should have warned you."

Rachel looked down at her Glock semi-automatic, summoned an indignant smile, and tucked it back in its holster.

"Bang bang," she said.

Good recovery, Morgan thought. He regarded Miranda with bewildered affection, and waited.

"Listen," Miranda said. "You can hear the emptiness."

Nice, thought Morgan, imagining the music of the spheres.

"I noticed when we were in the kitchen — I've never figured out why people say the word *echo* to hear an echo. I wonder what they say in Chinese."

She had their attention.

"Okay," she said. "Listen."

She called, "Echo-echo-echo."

They could hear a faint reverberation in the walls.

"There's a laundry chute," she said.

Yes, Morgan thought. You can hear emptiness if you know what to listen for.

"I remember the laundry chute in my grandmother's house," Miranda explained. "We'd holler up and down, and when they covered it over because they were afraid we'd climb in you could still hear where it was through the walls."

Morgan picked up a crowbar from the floor next to the hanging cupboard. He walked along the main supporting wall, tapping. They could hear chunks of plaster skitter behind thick layers of paper and sift between the lath down into the hidden depths.

He stopped and looked out in the hallway. There was a brace at eye level supporting a brick chimney that rose into the attic — all that remained of an abandoned heating system when stovepipes had snaked through the different rooms during the winter. Beneath the brace a thickening in the wall. Morgan rapped on the protrusion. There was a hollow thud.

He went back into the bedroom, aligned himself precisely, and smashed the back of the crowbar against the wall. Shards of layered paper scattered, plaster flew, and lath shattered. Professor Birbalsingh muttered unhappily.

Once a hole appeared at laundry-chute height, Miranda stepped forward and tried to peer into the cavity. Choking on the dust, she pulled lath and plaster away with her bare hands. Morgan interceded with the crowbar. Rachel Naismith helped, and soon they had an opening big enough a person could reach in up to the shoulder.

Morgan set the crowbar down, preparing to explore, but Miranda shunted him aside.

"This one is mine," she said. "What'll you bet there's a board jammed across to stop things falling through to the cellar."

She extended her arm fully down into the hole, grimaced as she made contact with something, and carefully lifted her arm out of the chute. Her hand was entwined with long tendrils of human hair. Suspended from the hair was the mummified head of a young woman, skin taut against the skull, lips drawn in a haunting grimace, membranes in her eye sockets catching fragments of light.

"Morgan," she said. "Could you get the other one?"

Morgan tried to look in but his own head cast a shadow. He reached down, blindly, careful not to rip his flesh on splintered lath, and suddenly flinched. Steeling himself, he grasped the short-cropped hair of the remaining skull. He pulled it upwards and through, into the room.

Miranda was still holding the woman's head cradled in the crook of her arm. Without exchanging words, both of them carried their grim loads over to the bodies.

Professor Birbalsingh and Dr. Hubbard stood aside while Morgan and Miranda kneeled and propped the heads against the necks from which they had been severed.

When they rose to their feet, the floorboards shivered and the heads lolled to the side. The detectives smiled shyly at each other. They had at least made a gesture to acknowledge the victims had once been alive.

Taking his cue from Miranda, who seemed quite pleased with herself but ready to leave, Morgan announced, "Well, folks, our work's done here. It's time for us to call it a night." He felt strangely uplifted, as if the pieces of a lingering murder investigation were finally coming together, and at the same time he felt cheated, knowing it wasn't theirs.

Birbalsingh grunted as he manoeuvred his soft body to get a better perspective on the male. Hubbard was opposite, hovering over the woman. It was as if they had divided the victims according to gender.

She looked up at Morgan, then at Miranda, then back at Morgan.

"Goodnight, Detectives," she said.

Miranda sensed strain in the woman's smile. Possibly the police had overstepped their bounds in retrieving the heads. Perhaps in placing the heads they had undermined procedural objectivity by performing their small ritual of empathy and defiance.

Miranda didn't much care. She was ready to go home.

Rachel Naismith saw them to the door.

"Thanks for dropping in," she said.

"We'll do it again, sometime," said Miranda.

The two women exchanged a quick embrace, while Morgan walked by himself toward the car.

Miranda caught up and, slipping on the sidewalk,

grabbed his arm to recover. He walked her to the driver's side. Morgan stood back and waited until she pulled away from the curb, but he still got an icy soaker as he climbed in beside her. It had been an adventure; they both felt somehow winter was over. They drove into the darkness, at its bleakest just before dawn.

## *chapter three*

## Cabbagetown

---

The heavy wet snow that accumulated during the night made Yonge Street treacherous. Morgan sat back, white-knuckled, fatalistic but hopeful as Miranda negotiated her way through ruts of turgid slush and gave wide berth to a blue-beaconed truck spewing sand that bore down on them from the other direction near Eglinton. It was the only vehicle they encountered on the desolate streets all the way to the Annex. She was a good driver, relatively speaking, and fervently protective about her car. She would deliver him safely to the door for the sake of her vintage Jaguar.

Weird and wonderful, he thought. Her devotion to the car, like her commitment to her teenage ward, Jill Bray, was a perverse response to heinous crimes. It was astonishing the satisfaction both had brought to her life. She would never have purchased such a car on her own; nor would she by choice have begun parenting with a feisty and resilient survivor of horrific abuse, a child-woman whose story strangely mirrored her own. The car was an act of defiance; Jill was an affirmation of love.

When she pulled up in front of Morgan's condo, he echoed his invitation of the previous evening. "Do you want to come in?" As if to make it more enticing, he added, "Until the streets are cleared? For an early breakfast?"

She looked as if she might be considering it.

"If you want to sleep, I'll take the sofa," he said.

"That clinches it," she responded. "I'm off. I want to sleep through the day in my own bed. You know what I was thinking?"

When she turned to address him, the indigo instrument lights cast her features in an eerie pallor. She looks sculptural, he thought. Her face is like alabaster in moonlight.

"I was thinking about Heathcliff and Catherine."

"I'm not surprised," he said.

He was tired, but sat back against the leather of the deep bucket seat.

"Don't relax too much. But it just crossed my mind while I was driving: *Wuthering Heights* was published in 1847."

"You know that why?"

"You're not the only one who stores away bits of esoteric information." She paused. "I looked it up."

"Never give away your sources."

"Okay, we have two people. We assume they were lovers —"

"Assume?"

"Maybe it was a macabre joke and they were famous for hating each other. Anyway, there they are, posed like Heathcliff and Catherine, post-mortem. Only *Wuthering Heights* hadn't come out yet."

"And?"

"And nothing. It just means no one was emulating Emily Brontë."

"Same with Auguste Rodin. 'The Kiss' was a century later. But what about Dante? *The Divine Comedy* was written five centuries before the murders took place."

"That's stretching it, Morgan. Our culture-conscious killer would never count on someone getting the connection, and certainly not cops." Miranda found the notion that police don't read, listen to music, enjoy art, attend theatre, or cook like gourmands extremely irksome. It did not bother Morgan. "Maybe the way they're posed is not an allusion to anything, just inspired depravity."

"Inspired depravity!"

"I sort of feel guilty they've been disturbed," she said. "Don't you?"

"Not really. They've been locked out of time; now they're back in."

"That's very profound, and sad."

"Let's say the former and call it a night."

"G'night, Morgan."

"Phone if you work it all out. If you see Jill, give her my love. And thanks for the ride."

She waited until he unlocked his front door, which years ago he had lovingly painted with fourteen coats of midnight blue. It gleamed a putrescent brown in the reflected light of the city at dawn. Miranda shuddered and drove off, giving a reckless beep on the horn. She was suddenly so exhausted she could hardly guide the car through the ruts, and she concentrated on the promise of a warm bed with fresh flannel sheets.

Morgan closed the door. He was thinking about Rodin's sculpture. While he got ready for bed he pondered the problem, if it could be considered a problem. How can there be such discrepancy between an artist's intent and the accepted response to his art?

As he lingered in front of the bathroom mirror, he envisioned "The Kiss" in its various manifestations: plaster and terra cotta and marble and bronze. An image of the desiccated corpses in Hogg's Hollow intruded but was displaced by the full-size plaster maquette he had seen with Miranda while they were playing hooky from work at the ROM. It was a ghostly white apparition in a room full of chalky anatomical figures on their way to more permanent representation in metal and stone. A ghost among ghosts.

Catching sight of himself reflected amid the images shunting through his mind, he relaxed and briefly attended to the mundane necessities of brushing his teeth and washing. He lifted his pyjamas, black moose strolling on a red background, from a hook on the back of the bathroom door and walked stark naked up to his bedroom where he stood, shivering, lost again in contemplation.

He was so tired, nothing made sense, and after becoming thoroughly chilled he put on his pyjamas and climbed into bed. He curled around himself and breathed deeply, lifting the covers for a moment to let a defining burst of cold air penetrate his cocoon, then he sealed them snugly around his shoulders and almost immediately drifted into a deep slumber.

Morgan awakened to the insistent ring of the telephone. He picked up the receiver on the night table but there was only a dial tone. Maybe he had dreamed it was ringing. Light rising from the window downstairs indicated it was midmorning, but he was not interested in getting up.

He rolled over on his back without looking at his watch or the alarm clock on the dresser and drew the covers close. He had tried an eider-down duvet someone once gave him, but preferred the weight of thick wool blankets, which seemed to modulate their proffered warmth according to his needs, rather than smothering him with the indifference of feathers.

Snug, breathing the cool air of the room, he tried to reconstruct his last dream.

Inevitably, it evaded coherence. There were images of wizened corpses entwined as intimately as their clothing allowed, of skulls with their features contorted into the tight grimace of mockery at the fears of the living, of plaster and bronze torsos and severed limbs, of flesh mounded and shapeless, waiting to be formed into bodies. There was a diorama contrived at Hogg's Hollow with meticulous care to convey mystery, and a confusion of intent and response. There were intimations of genius, and no question about murder. Heathcliff, Rodin, romantic love, death ...

"What are you thinking about, David? Where is this going?"

Corpses beheaded, enclosed in an airless crypt, the death of romance. He said nothing.

"Turning death into metaphor isn't murder, David. Perhaps murder preceded, but the display is romantic. Don't you see? Get rid of the heads, let the bodies embrace. It is passion over reason, David, as it should be."

His wife was leaning across a kitchen table, challenging him. He had not seen her in a dozen years and they had been divorced even longer. He knew he was in a dream. He felt defensive. He roused himself, trying to wake up.

"Stay here, my darling. Don't leave me. We can work this out together."

He stifled an answer, refusing to give her presence validity.

"Don't you love me? Do you love me?"

He had no answer.

"Talk to me, David. Tell me about loving forever. Show me the perfect kiss. How delightful, David — an eternal instant. How abysmally sad."

He tried to find her eyes, but they were empty sockets. Her lips were tightly clenched but the voice was clear and unnervingly familiar.

"Two heads, David, kissing forever. It's all in the head. Reason over passion, don't you see? Drop two heads down a chute, no telling what they'll be up to, perpetually falling. Didn't you ever wonder about heads in the guillotine basket? Between decapitation and the end of consciousness, did they exchange glances? What secrets and jokes passed among them, David?

"Was that our problem, David? Minds and bodies didn't come together? We couldn't tell secrets from jokes!"

Morgan spoke at last and his voice was like thunder.

"I do not love you, Lucy...."

The sound of his words resounding through the loft awakened him. He rolled over and stared at the ceiling, inconsolably lonely.

Thoughts gathered of the ring and the crucifix and gradually filled the emptiness. Did the conjunction of such potent talismans lead to death, or was death merely the prelude to staging the scene in anticipation of eventual discovery? What variables were manipulated for our benefit, he wondered, and what for the author's own? And what were the gratuitous contributions of history, of time passing? He could have no way of knowing our ways of seeing, so far in the future.

Morgan tried to reconstruct the character of the killer. That seemed the key to understanding his crime. It would have taken considerable strength to manhandle the corpses, even if they had been killed and prepared on the premises, which seemed probable. He would have had to understand something of carpentry and plastering. It's unlikely a woman of the day would have known these things, but an observant male might be familiar with the procedures without himself being in a trade.

Given the killer's morbid imagination, combined with meticulous patience and sanguinary determination, he must have been fairly mature — most likely a British immigrant, as were most of his neighbours — and literate. He would have grown up reading the Graveyard Poets in England, or at the very least been an aficionado of Italianate novels like *The Mysteries of Udolpho*. His tableau has all the elements. But it is a Gothic mystery in reverse: it invites a kind of archaeological speculation rather than fostering terrors and suspense.

The cabinet! It had been placed over the sealed opening of the crypt; it had been bolted to the wall. Like an ostentatious padlock on a hidden door. It invited discovery, exposure of the secrets it purported to conceal. This was a flourish of the criminal mind, fiendishly confident, taunting posterity.

Morgan had come full-circle: character and crime were inseparable.

He was fully awake now, but not rested. After getting up for a pee, he settled back under the covers. It was a day off and a Saturday. The two didn't always coincide. He thought he might walk over to the old neighbourhood later on, if the sidewalks were cleared. It had changed profoundly, yet it was still called Cabbagetown, and here and there he could see remnants of when it was a sprawling, working-class slum.

On the margins it had degenerated into a needle park of prostitution and derelicts. But in the heart, among the designer townhouses transformed from dilapidated tenements, he could see a familiar wall or a window, and suddenly he would be back with his dad, walking him to the streetcar on the way to school, or racing around corners and churchyards with other kids, pretending they had bikes.

Morgan smiled at the ceiling. He did not think of himself as having a deprived childhood. Fred and Darlene did what they could. They were in a subclass now known as "the working poor." His dad was employed at the Toronto Transit Commission streetcar yards and his mother picked up seasonal jobs, usually around Christmas when she could get work in restaurant kitchens, and in the summers when she did housecleaning for people in Rosedale away at their cottages.

He did not actually know what his father did with the TTC. Whatever it was, it was the same job he started with forty-five years before retirement — the same job he so desperately missed for the following three years until he died. Some of his friends at his wake said that he died of a broken heart.

He was not present at his own wake. Darlene waited until he was buried before she invited a bunch from the yards over for beer and sandwiches, along with their wives, most of whom she had never met.

His mother had her own friends. They were denizens of Cabbagetown, like herself, proud of their British heritage, narrow-minded and loving. Children were the focus of their lives, and as the children grew up, the women grew fat and smoked as if tobacco were oxygen, and many of them drank. He shrank from his generalization, knowing how close it was to the truth.

Morgan surprised his teachers and puzzled his parents by staying in school and by winning a scholarship to the University of Toronto, and even more by accepting. The only one not surprised was Morgan. At seventeen he knew he was smart. He knew his parents were smart as well, and that made him bitter. Whenever he purged himself of esoteric facts over dinner, they were indulgent, if sometimes baffled. But when he explained to them the most complex aspects of high-school science or the arcane intricacies of literature and history, they immediately understood.

Not that they talked a lot, especially to each other. For the most part Darlene and Fred lived parallel lives in a mean environment and conversed mostly through their son. When I left, he thought, they had nothing to say.

He moved into a grotty room on St. George Street close to campus. His most intimate associates were a band of mice whose presence he entertained with grudging congeniality. After catching one in something called the Mouse Motel and watching it lurch about, trying to free its feet from the gluey substance on the miniature floor, he abandoned all thoughts of extermination, kept his food securely stored, and occasionally bought the mice cat kibble for treats.

In the summers he worked at high-paying roughneck jobs in the north, and while he visited his parents from time to time he never again stayed overnight. By the end of his four years as a student, he had almost fallen out of the habit of visiting them altogether. In the winter of his last year the three of them got drunk in a squalid familial gathering he never wanted to repeat.

He didn't tell them about graduation. At the end of the summer he left for Europe in search of a personality that would bring the disparate parts of his being together. After two years he came back. His father died soon after his return, and his mother died a year later.

Morgan's mind teamed with small images of a world gone forever. He could smell the tobacco scent of his mother making corned beef and cabbage, her hair wisping down over one eye. He could hear the tired stomping of his father coming up the front steps, see himself running to the door to meet him. He could feel the safe embrace of his bedroom, listening to the television drone downstairs while reading about dinosaurs or space travel or pyramids, and later, as he got older, about cultural theory and quantum mechanics.

Morgan pulled the covers close around him; he was homesick.

The telephone rang and he answered it and again there was only a tone. He must have been asleep. He was not sure if it had actually been ringing or if he had dreamed himself awake.

He dialled Miranda's number. A sleepy voice answered.

"Did you call me?" he asked.

"Who? Morgan, no, I'm asleep. And I will be again if you'd go away. I'm gonna hang up."

"You've never hung up on anyone. You couldn't."

"Wanna bet?"

Click.

Well, anyway, he thought, it wasn't her calling. He lay back and waited. After a few minutes, the telephone rang; this time it was real.

"Morgan?"

"Yes."

"Was it anything important?"

"What?"

"Your call?"

"No."

Click.

He looked at his watch. It was ten-thirty.

He got up, showered, and dressed. After a large breakfast to compensate for the lack of sleep, which included more than his usual ration of bacon and several extra pieces of toast, he settled onto the blue sofa to read. He fingered the book on Persian history without opening it. It was a bit of what Miranda would call "a snare and a delusion" — a 1985 reprint of a nineteenth-century text, with a new, tooled cover embossed in gold, not published to be enjoyed but to be admired.

He filed the book on a shelf and retrieved his Saturday *Globe and Mail* from the turgid slush on his stoop. It was the only paper he had delivered — his weekly fix of news, commentary, and culture. Not necessarily light reading, but an eclectic diversion for a couple of hours.

Morgan always read the paper sequentially, from front to back. Miranda declared she had never encountered such absurdity. No one reads newspapers in order. They weren't even designed that way. Sometimes he was intentionally perverse.

On page ten he came across a short article headline BONES OF CONTENTION. Cute, he thought, then blanched when he realized the story was about their doomed lovers at Hogg's Hollow.

How on earth did the paper get the story in time for the morning edition? It had to have been called in, but by whom? Headquarters? Highly unlikely. The coroner's office? They never release information unless in the aid of an inquest. Certainly not Miranda. He and Miranda avoided publicity — it interfered with their work. Even though as a team they were a minor legend among their colleagues for eccentric efficiency, they had managed to avoid the kind of celebrity that subsumes individual cases in a running account of the detectives who solve them. It would not have been Officer Naismith. That left Dr. Hubbard or Professor Birbalsingh.

It was no surprise, then, that the forensic anthropologists were mentioned by name, each spelled correctly. Everything else in the article was tantalizingly macabre, yet intriguingly vague. This account was fed to a desk reporter by someone in sufficient authority to be credible and skilled in the art of public relations. It was not presented as a crime story but as an historical curiosity. The readers' empathy was encouraged not for the victims but for the scientists involved in resolving their identity — scientists whose determined expertise would unlock the secrets of their morbid embrace.

Annoyed by the *Globe* article, Morgan grabbed his coat and set out for Cabbagetown. As he walked along Harbord

Street into the heart of the U of T campus, he tried to stabilize the source of his ire, which hovered somewhere between
amused irritation and genuine anger. The publicity was pro-
prietary, a declaration by the forensic anthropologists of
ownership. Good for them; damn their sense of entitlement.

In front of Hart House, he stopped to dump snow
from a shoe, balancing precariously on one foot. He stared
intently at a gritty lump of ice. His father had taught him the
secret of balance, how to put on socks in a standing position:
fix your gaze on a particular spot and the wavering stops.
His father taught him to splash cold water on the back of
his neck in the morning to eliminate grogginess, to spit on
his shoes for the final polish, to savour the taste of authentic
ginger beer, to discriminate among newspaper comic strips,
to use chopsticks, to blow his nose without a tissue — snort-
ing through one nostril at a time, pressing the other — when
no one was watching.

Morgan looked around at the architectural disson-
ance that skirted University Circle. Nothing had changed in
twenty-two years. In this season, the buildings looked bleak,
the flowerbeds were like burial mounds, and the shrubs were
tangles of dried sticks or clumps of bedraggled green. After a
night of sleet, followed by a cold turn that left the air crisp, the
sky an intense winter blue, and the white a translucent gathering of all the colours in the spectrum, the snow-covered lawn
glistened in comical contrast.

The main door into the anthropology laboratories was
locked but Morgan called building maintenance on a campus
emergency phone and when someone showed up he flashed
his badge and was admitted without being asked for an
explanation. He was not expecting so much activity behind
closed doors on a weekend, as he searched for the forensics
lab — graduate students at their Sisyphean labours, earning

their meagre stipends. Time off, he surmised, is for faculty —
unless they have just been presented with disentombed cadavers in pristine period dress.

A slightly manic young man in a lab coat directed him to
the location of Professor Birbalsingh's newest project, chuckling
as he walked off in the other direction. Morgan had attended
graduate school for a week before dropping out to study crim-
inology at a community college. With a novitiate's grasp of academic procedures and obligations, he felt a tenuous connection
to the young man's vaguely demented detachment. For years he
had imagined returning to university, with the idea of eventually teaching. He knew that his brain was too restless, however.
He liked having a mind with a mind of its own.

He pushed the door open without knocking and entered
a room that, despite the gruesome paraphernalia, was quite
unlike Ellen Ravenscroft's austere aerie in the heart of the city.
Death, here, was not an end in itself, as it was at the morgue.
It was an object of conjecture, subsumed by the conventions
of an academic discipline. While cool, the room was almost
cheerful. The blinds were only half drawn. Dust motes swirled
in sunlight reflected from the snow outside. The bodies,
which were lying on autopsy trays, had been separated and
stripped of their clothing. Both Dr. Hubbard and Professor
Birbalsingh were intent on the male at the moment. A graduate assistant was meticulously cleaning plaster dust and debris
from the hands of the female on the adjoining table. On a
stainless-steel counter behind them, a wooden box the size of
a valise sat ominously.

Before his observation of the scene could be considered
a covert activity, Morgan coughed to announce his presence.
The professor didn't look up and the student focused more
intently on her work, but Shelagh Hubbard turned around
and, recognizing who it was, smiled warmly.

"Sorry to bother you," Morgan said.

"No bother," she answered. "The Inquisitive Detective," she declared, as if it were a title. "You couldn't resist."

"Actually, I wanted to know about the newspaper story."

"The newspaper?"

"There was a write-up in the *Globe* this morning, with just enough detail to promise a follow-up. I assume you were the source, Dr. Hubbard."

"Shelagh, please. We're not formal around here."

Her eyes swept the room, then she nodded in the direction of the naked bodies and whispered, "Except for him, the Obsessive Professor."

"I heard that, *Miss* Hubbard."

"He is disciplining me, detective. I am 'doctor' at the museum, 'professor' at the university, and 'Shelagh' to my friends. I am '*Miss*' only when proclaiming my marital status or incurring the wrath of my mentor."

"Shelagh, the story?"

"Didn't they mention you? I'm so sorry."

"To get into the early edition, you must have called before you got to the scene."

"A romance doomed to endure beyond death. It seemed opportune —"

"Or opportunistic."

"If you'd prefer. In museums and anthropology, he or she who hesitates doesn't get the grant. Shape the story and the money comes in — a straightforward equation. We're not curing cancer here; we're recovering the past."

"Isn't it beyond recovery, by definition?"

"We illuminate the past from a present perspective — is that better? Isn't that what you do, as well, in the detecting business?"

Morgan smiled.

"You haven't been here all night, have you?" he asked.

"We have," said the stolid professor, without looking up.

Shelagh Hubbard glanced at her mentor, then addressed Morgan. "I virtually dictated the story from the way Professor Birbalsingh described it. I was precise — perhaps a little inventive, but not dishonest."

"And yet, surprisingly vivid," said Morgan.

"Read carefully, Detective," said Sheila Hubbard with a modicum of pride. "You'll find mostly the piece is about atmosphere, the grotesque in our midst, death at the doorstep. It's tabloid melodrama, upgraded for the *Globe* with good grammar and compound sentences."

Morgan regarded the woman with a begrudging admiration. She was not about to apologize.

"And the clothes," he asked her, shifting direction. "They seem remarkably well-preserved."

"They are museum quality," she said, and she smiled enigmatically. "I'm hoping we can spruce them up a little and steal them away from Professor Birbalsingh for the museum's permanent collection."

The graduate student came over to where they were looking down at the articles of clothing laid out on a table. "I'm betting they were put on after mummification occurred," she said.

"Impossible," said Dr. Hubbard. "The drying-out process took place because they were sealed into an airless closet, Joleen. They may have been dressed after they were dead, but their crypt was clearly undisturbed until we opened it yesterday."

The graduate student did not appear intimidated, nor particularly dissuaded, but said nothing. Morgan considered the implications of a lengthy delay between death and the *memento mori* tableau. He wondered: was the arrangement meant to inflict humiliation on the dead? To provide grisly satisfaction for the killer? To symbolize the transcendence of love for the lovers' accomplice? To taunt posterity with an impenetrable mystery?

Shelagh Hubbard had rejoined her colleague, and the two of them huddled over the headless corpses, conferring in whispers. The graduate student lingered beside Morgan. He introduced himself.

"And where are you from, Joleen?"

It was his favourite question, the way others will ask a stranger, What do you do? or, How do you like the weather? He needed to know where people were from. He was so completely a creature of one city, it connected him to the larger world.

"Cabbagetown," she said. "That's right here in downtown Toronto."

"I know where Cabbagetown is," he said quickly, staring at her for a moment, trying to place her within the social spectrum — tenement or townhouse?

"Working class, poor," she declared, as if reading his thoughts. She was neither defiant nor ashamed; it was like saying she was brunette or a woman. "And what about you?"

"The same."

"What are you two on about?" asked Shelagh Hubbard, turning around as if she were coming up for air.

"Common ancestry," said Joleen with a laugh.

"Common heritage," Morgan amended. She was of Chinese extraction — Morgan hated the brutal and trivializing term, "extraction." They were both from Cabbagetown.

"Joleen, eh? Did your parents ever go to Nashville?"

"When your last name is Chau and you don't live in Chinatown, you get called 'Joleen.' It's about trying to fit in, avoiding the ethnic thing."

"You draw from a counter-ethnicity," said Morgan, rolling the name Joleen through his mind with a country cadence.

"I like that," said Shelagh Hubbard. "You could have been an academic, Morgan, the way you make up your own jargon. There'd be a publication in that: 'Crossing Over: Second-Generation Immigrants and Counter-Ethnicity in Naming Their Offspring.'"

"I'm seventh-generation, actually," said Joleen.

"I'm from Vancouver, myself," said Dr. Hubbard, as if her declaration made sense. "We'd better get back to work," she continued. "We can't leave everything to Professor Birbalsingh. You can watch along if you want, Detective."

"The clothes," said Morgan. "How did you remove them?"

"Very carefully. The limbs articulated with gentle persuasion. Hers were easier than his."

"They didn't have underwear on," said Joleen. "She didn't even have bloomers."

"They weren't invented yet," said Dr. Hubbard.

"Open-crotched culottes. Whatever. She wasn't wearing anything under her petticoats. Neither was he — no underwear under his trousers. The frock coat is fine worsted but his pants are a really coarse twill. You can bet they didn't get dressed like that on their own."

"The clothes are as valuable as the lovers themselves," Shelagh Hubbard observed.

"I doubt they would have agreed," said Morgan.

Shelagh Hubbard smiled enigmatically.

"And the bodies?" he asked. "They'll be examined and recorded and then shelved, I suppose."

"We really should get back to work."

"What are we looking for?" he asked.

"We? Anything at all. The cause or causes of death. They might have died separately. You could help us track down their identities, Detective. Not that it really matters, but it might give us insight into why they were killed. I doubt we'll ever know by whom."

"It matters. Without names, they're generic," Morgan observed. "Without a story, they're artifacts."

"I think you'd make a better poet than professor," said Joleen.

"Thank you," said Morgan.

"We're looking for anomalies," explained Shelagh Hubbard. "Discovery through difference: what is out of place, what distinguishes these individuals from others, who are they now? As bodies, they're generic, yes, but as artifacts they are a present phenomenon, one which we need to study, Mr. Morgan."

"Sorry. Carry on, by all means. I'll just take a peak in the box."

"Those are the heads. I think it would be better if you left them alone for now. We need to examine them in laboratory conditions."

"We're in a laboratory," he said as he lifted the top off the box. The heads had been carefully arranged side by side, protected from sliding about during transportation by a black, velvety material that bunched up between them. He instinctively reached down to suppress the material so that they could seem more together.

Shelagh Hubbard placed her hand on his arm, trying to draw him back. "These must be considered scientific specimens. If you don't mind."

"I do, actually." He pulled away. Unsure whether he was joking or trying somehow to restore a little of their lost humanity to the dead, he said, "The least we could do is set the box up on its side so they can observe what they're missing." He could hear Joleen suppress a giggle.

"Don't be absurd," said Shelagh Hubbard. She fixed her gaze on Morgan with an intensity that made him shudder. She seemed able to turn her allure on or off like a wilful chameleon. Her pale eyes had taken on a predatory lustre and the death's-head appearance of her high cheekbones, accentuated by her blond hair pulled back tightly against her skull, seemed suddenly, dangerously exciting. In spite of his better judgment Morgan felt drawn in, wanting vaguely to please her, uncertain what was required.

She stood unnaturally close. He tried to hold his ground. He thought he felt the curve of her breast against his chest as she turned slightly to the side. She turned again, and this time there was no mistake. She was using sexuality as an instrument of intimidation. She leaned into him. He flinched, then to her surprise he pushed forward, pressing his body against hers. For the briefest moment they stood torso to torso in an armless embrace. He could feel her breasts, both of them, the tight roundness of her belly, her upper thighs. He did an instant inventory, then she turned and stepped away as if nothing had happened.

Morgan looked down into the box. "Her lips are sealed," he said.

"Death has a way of doing that," said Shelagh Hubbard.

"No, I mean it. They're sewn shut." He pointed to a thread barely visible among creases of wizened flesh.

"Not an uncommon funerary practice," she said.

"Let me see that," said the professor, who suddenly appeared beside them. Ignoring prescribed methodology he unceremoniously picked up the woman's head by the hair and carried it over to an examining table to get a better look under the bright illumination. He plunked it down close to the stump of her companion's neck. For a moment the professor seemed confused. Then he took the head in his hands and moved to the other table where he set it in place above the woman's own body. He's not immune to the subtle proprieties of death, thought Morgan.

Morgan bent close to observe as the professor used a spatula and a small scalpel to pry between the lips and sever the threads. Her lips were drawn tight against her teeth, but with the thread gone, they shrank back and her mouth opened a little to the light. Morgan leaned closer.

"Oh, my goodness," he gasped in astonishment.

Professor Birbalsingh fixed his gaze on the woman's mouth. Without saying a word, he pulled back the leathery flesh of her lips. She had a remarkably good set of teeth. He gently forced them apart. He stood upright but said nothing. He glanced at Morgan in affirmation, then shifted his line of vision and seemed to become absorbed in something outside the windows.

"Well now," said Morgan. "I'm afraid I'll have to ask you to terminate your inquiry, professor."

The graduate student sidled closer to the centre of attention, smiling at some private joke.

"Could I use your cellphone, Joleen?" Morgan asked. "I need to call the coroner's office, police headquarters, and my partner in crime."

"What on earth?" said Shelagh Hubbard as if she were about to protest. Professor Birbalsingh remained silent.

"People her age always have cellphones," Morgan explained.

Ignoring him, Shelagh Hubbard moved forward, and for a moment seemed to lose herself in the revelation of what appeared to be glistening composite fillings in the dead woman's skull. Slowly, her posture stiffened and, avoiding Morgan's gaze, she too looked out the windows into the middle distance, perhaps observing the lost possibilities of a research grant and easy tenure.

Morgan felt strangely elated, vindicated somehow, although he had been as beguiled by the simulations of antiquity as the experts. The case was now under his jurisdiction; a case and not just a case study. But he also felt oppressed: what had appeared to be a quirky historical windfall was now a genuine tragedy. This was no longer about death — it was about dying.

"Oh, my God," said Joleen Chau, standing between the cadavers, "I've never seen a real dead person before!"

## *chapter four*

## Isabelle Street

---

Miranda was luxuriating in the warmth of her over-heated apartment, lying in on a leisurely Saturday off work. She rolled over languidly, shifting the flannel sheet off and away, and stretched until her muscles tingled through every part of her body. She arched against the bed, feeling wonderfully lithe and sexual, emotionally vague, intellectually drifting, like she had been making love for hours.

Damn it, she thought. I wish I could remember my dreams.

Suddenly, a loud thumping on the door wrenched her out of her reverie. My God, she thought. What's Morgan doing here at a time like this?

It had to be him. The building superintendent would have knocked deferentially, and the few people she knew in neighbouring apartments would telephone first. He must have slipped past the security door. She looked around for a robe. In movies there is always a dressing gown within hand's reach of the bed.

The hell with it, she mumbled to herself. I pay the heating bills, I'll wear what I want. By the time she got to the door, she was having second thoughts. What if it's Girl Guides selling cookies, or Jehovah's Witnesses? She glanced at herself in the full-length mirror. She was wearing an oversized T-shirt and nothing else. She looked good. If it's a couple of fresh-faced Mormons, I might let them in.

It was Morgan.

Through the peephole he looked grotesquely distorted. He was leaning so close, all she could see was the smile. His version of the Cheshire Cat; he had done it before, with full explanation. She opened the door. His face become solemn, then shy.

"I love your outfit," he said.

"Come in, Morgan."

She turned and walked barefoot into the living room as if she were wearing heels.

"What on earth are you doing here," she asked. "It's the middle of the night, my time, and I was having lovely dreams."

He plunked himself down on the sofa, admiring the full length of her legs before her lower half disappeared behind the kitchen counter. He had kicked off his snow-drenched shoes in the hall but he was still wearing his sheepskin coat.

"It's two in the afternoon," he announced.

"It's not."

She put on the coffee and came back around the counter, still feeling a little flirtatious, even though it was only Morgan. She walked across to her bedroom door, swaying her hips just enough to set the lower edge of her T-shirt astir. He peered into the fluttering shadows and immediately glanced away.

"Why don't you take your coat off and get comfortable," she murmured in a sultry voice as she turned to face him.

"No hurry." He seemed to be searching for something to say. "I was with you when you bought that T-shirt."

"Oh, yeah."

"Yeah," he said, giving her his most inscrutable smile. Not out of *Alice in Wonderland*, she thought. It's his Buddha smile. No, his post-coital Mona Lisa smile. No, his Jesus smile — endearing and infinitely dangerous.

He smiled so seldom, but when he did he had a range she found thrilling.

Still in the doorway, standing in opaque silhouette with the daylight from the bedroom behind her, she asked, "What are you doing here, anyway? It's too early for a gentleman caller — or too late."

They both smiled.

"It must be business, except you seem cheerful."

"Do you want to get dressed?"

"Do I need to?"

"Yes."

"Oh, dear."

She walked through into her bathroom, leaving the doors open.

"Has this got something to do with the boss working last night?"

He followed her as far as the bedroom door; then, leaning against the frame, he admired the play of shadow and light as she attended to her tantalizing ablutions just out of sight.

"I think he's had a fight with his wife."

"You mean there's no city-wide disaster? He's just hiding out?"

"Yeah."

"His wife's a lawyer."

"Yeah."

"Lawyers should only marry lawyers, and cops, cops."

"How do you figure?"

"A functioning lawyer is adversarial —"

"What's an unfunctioning lawyer?'

"I've known a few."

"Yeah," Morgan said, remembering one in particular she had dated a couple of years ago. Another lawyer, ineffectual and lethal, occupied a more sinister place in their recent past: he of the Jaguar, of posthumous infamy.

"At least with two lawyers, they understand the rules."

She turned on the shower.

He raised his voice.

"I'm not sure what that means."

"What?"

Splattering water drowned out his words, but not hers.

"About the rules," he shouted.

"Stand where I can hear you, Morgan! The shower's steamed up — you couldn't see me for looking."

He stopped at the bathroom door. She was wrong; she was absorbed in washing and her body was revealed in waves as water sheeted against the glass door. It was full and lean, the body of a mature woman in splendid condition. He remembered her from the night they made love; she had seemed almost girlish then. He backed away and sat down on the chair by her bedroom window.

"Can you hear me?" she shouted. "Where'd you go?"

"I'm here."

She shut off the water and for a moment there was silence.

"Why do you think lawyers have all the power, Morgan?"

"Because they know the law."

"Because they know its limitations."

Morgan thought about that.

"The rest of us live in moral chaos," she continued. "And we grasp at the law to make sense of it all. Not lawyers. They don't give a damn about sense and morality. That's why so many of them are politicians; they want order — they're inherently fascist. Think of the utter stupidity of 'yes' or 'no' answers in the witness box. There are no 'yes' or 'no' answers."

"Now you're sounding like me."

"I could do worse."

Suddenly she was at the door, wrapped in a towel.

"Get out of here, Morgan. The lady is about to get dressed."

He regarded her with mild exasperation, got up, and ambled back to the living room.

Cops should marry cops, she had said. Given her splenetic response about lawyers he decided that was not something to pursue.

"Aren't you curious about why you're being hauled into action on a day off?" he asked.

"Well, let's see," she said. "Since it isn't a major metropolitan catastrophe, and you seem in a rare good mood, I would say it has something to do with our lovers last night. Am I right?"

He stood in the middle of the living room, still in her sightline, hands in his pockets, with his back to her, slouched in a waiting posture. He still had on his sheepskin coat, although it was unbuttoned and hanging loosely on his shoulders, rather like a cape, she thought. He was lean and muscular, more with the air of a soldier than an athlete: a man comfortable in his body who carried himself with the pride of a combat survivor.

"Am I right?" she repeated.

He shrugged equivocally, knowing she was watching him.

She let her towel drop and stood naked in her bedroom doorway, barely two steps away, amused to think that if he turned around she would be righteously indignant.

"Get dressed," he said. He knew what she was doing. Senses especially acute in the moment, he had heard the towel slide against skin to the floor.

She suddenly felt vulnerable and foolish. She mimed a posture of exaggerated modesty, stuck out her tongue in Morgan's direction, and retreated.

Miranda strapped on a shoulder holster over her blouse and tucked her semi-automatic into place. She put on a loose jacket and walked into the living room where her partner was still standing, as if he were holding a pose.

"Okay, Morgan," she whispered in a burlesque of sensuality. "I'm packin' heat. Let's go."

She kissed him impulsively on the cheek as she walked by.

"I don't think you'll be needing that," he said.

She took off the jacket and holster and put her Glock in her purse.

Miranda sometimes carried her weapon, and Morgan seldom carried his. She liked the feeling it gave her of being a little bit dangerous. He liked the sense of relinquishing power, of playing danger against wit. They had talked about this several times, each accusing the other of subverting gender stereotypes, in deference to Freudian principles they both abhorred.

Miranda was surprised when they walked out of her building to find that Morgan had picked up a car from headquarters. "Okay, Morgan," she said, "this must be serious. You do not ever take charge of transportation. In our fair division of labour that's my job. You drive," she declared, as she slipped into the passenger seat. "And after this, lock the doors when you park. You'd feel like a fool if someone made off with a cop car."

Driving up Yonge Street, Morgan focused on manoeuvring through runnels of frozen slush. This late in the season, there wasn't even salt on the roads. The car lurched from rut to rut as he overcorrected, damning the shortfall on the city budget.

He was losing patience, waiting for her to ask again why they were back at work on a day off. She was resisting, certain that he would break by the time they reached Eglinton. One block south, the car caught an edge of ice and swerved. Morgan wrenched it out of the groove, eased it through a long skid, and let it slide to a stop smack against the curb.

"You drive," he said, and got out of the car. When they had exchanged places, he explained, without being in the least defensive. "You're better at winter driving than me. You enjoy it. I don't."

It was true, she liked to drive, even in bad conditions. He was not a nervous passenger, nor particularly a nervous driver, just not a very good one. Having grown up in a family without a car, he could never relate to men who measured their manhood by their prowess behind the wheel.

"If you do something, anything, just to prove you're a man," his father had said, "then you're not."

When he was eight years old, his father taught him to box. Not because it's a manly sport. "Hammering someone into unconsciousness, boy, that's nothing to be proud of. But the world's a tough place; you've gotta be tough to survive."

The boxing lesson came after a kid about ten years old had pinned Morgan down and cuffed him on the head until tears filled his eyes. He wasn't crying. It was an involuntary response. The kid wouldn't stop, so Morgan flailed wildly and landed a smack straight on the kid's nose. He broke his nose.

His father had been called in and had to take half a day off work. The boxing lesson was the only repercussion at home or at school.

His father made boxing gloves out of socks, folding one sock across the knuckles between layers over and under it, securing each makeshift affair with duct tape at the wrist.

"Make a fist, not around your thumb. Relax your thumbs," he said.

He got down on his knees so that he was the same height as his son. "Now let's see you punch. Punch me, David."

"I don't want to," Morgan said.

"Punch into my hand, hard as you can."

Morgan did what he was told. His blows met with little resistance as his father's hand gave way to the force. This wasn't like the kids fighting at school.

"What do they do?"

"They rassle. We don't really hit each other. Mostly we rassle 'til someone says 'Uncle.' Sometimes you have t'say 'Give.' Then they stop."

"And what if there's a bully who won't stop?"

Morgan didn't have an answer.

"Now try to hit my face," he said. "That's it, punch, punch, thrust, punch, break through. Good boy. Watch what I do."

To Morgan's surprise, his father parried against his gloves then slipped through his defence and hit him on the side of the chin. Morgan's hands dropped to his side. His father had never hit him before, and he had never even been spanked.

"Now hit me back, David. Come on, come on," he taunted.

Morgan watched his opponent's hands jabbing the air, waited, then struck. To his surprise, his small fist broke through his adversary's guard and landed square on his nose. His father reeled back on his knees, shook his head to clear the buzz, looked at his son through glistening moisture released by the jarring of his tear ducts.

"Damn me, boy. What the hell are you doing?"

Morgan was appalled. "I'm sorry, Daddy," he said. It was the only time he had ever called him that.

He wanted to hug his father, to forgive him for making him do it.

"Don't be sorry," his father said. Then to Morgan's surprise he started jabbing away at his son's instinctively raised fists. They were adversaries again.

"What's my name, boy?"

His father never called him "boy."

"Fred!"

"That's right, David. Know who you're fighting. Always know."

With sudden deliberation he reached through and landed a glancing blow against the side of his son's head, but leaving himself open, so that Morgan rolled with the punch and came up underneath with a solid blow to his father's chin.

"Good God, David. You're a little bugger."

Morgan stared at him sullenly, daring him to strike back. His father got up off his knees, rising to his full height. Morgan stared up at him. This was his father again.

"And never lose your temper. If you do, you've lost the fight."

When his father reached out to tousle his hair, Morgan flinched infinitesimally.

"Now get the hell out of here," his father said as he stripped off the socks from his son's clenched fists. "Go out and save the world from bullies."

Morgan remembered his father standing tall and powerful in the middle of the living room, but he also remembered the terrible sounds of him wheezing and coughing up tobacco-soaked phlegm as Morgan strutted out the front door.

While they were stopped at the Yonge and Eglinton intersection, Miranda glanced over to see if he was going to break. He seemed relaxed.

"Okay," she said. "Okay, tell me what's going on, Morgan. You win."

"Win what?"

"Whatever. You can't set the rules if you don't know the game."

"My goodness," he said. "You only coin clichés when you're riled up about something."

"Aphorisms. You can coin an aphorism. I'm not riled up."

"But you would like an explanation."

"No."

"No?"

"They're not old, are they! They're recently deceased. The whole thing was a set-up, wasn't it? A gruesome illusion, a joke? Right?"

"You've got it."

"You're kidding!"

"For sure."

"Is it our case?"

"It is."

"Oh, well done, Morgan."

"I dropped into the forensic pathology lab this morning."

"Because you had nothing better to do on a Saturday off?"

"I wanted to talk to Dr. Hubbard."

"Come on, Morgan. She's got cantilevered tits and Olive Oyl hair. Not your type at all."

"No?"

"She looks like a raunchy popsicle."

"I can't picture it."

"Morgan, if she ever let her hair down, her cheeks would sag to her chin."

He had never known Miranda to be so bitchy. She had good instincts, and she didn't hesitate to judge by appearance, but usually she was subtle. A cocked eyebrow, the trace of a smile. She was incisive but seldom unkind. And she was usually right. He, in contrast, saw neither what people wanted others to see, nor what they wanted to hide. He did not believe in the concept of self as a coherent entity. He saw personality as process, something revealed over time.

Often their conclusions converged, although his were less static than hers, and while they evolved slowly they were more open to revision.

"Is something bothering you?" he asked.

"Why?"

"You don't seem yourself."

"Do I ever?" she grinned. "I was looking forward to lazing in bed," she said. "Dreaming good dreams, spending a lovely while on my own." She continued to smile, without looking over at him. She had awakened blissfully distracted, like she had made love through the night, but her phantom lover had departed, and she could not remember his name. "So, what's going on?" she asked.

"We missed it. They missed it. The medical examiner missed it. We were royally duped — by a master of the macabre. It's all very Gothic."

"Damn it," she said. "I knew the clothes fit too well."

By the time he explained as much as he knew, they had pulled up in front of the house in Hogg's Hollow, which looked more dilapidated by daylight, somehow more sad, as if shunned by the neighbouring houses. There was a van parked slightly askew in the driveway. The name "Alexander Pope" in exquisite hand-script on the driver's door proclaimed the owner a person of profoundly good taste, either too modest to add a line declaring his profession or so confident it was not deemed necessary.

As they walked by, Morgan peered through the side windows and saw, lying in casual disarray, odds and ends of antique paraphernalia. There was a pair of hand-forged fire irons, were three or four swing arms from the inside of fireplaces, and a couple of iron pots and a kettle. There was a copper cauldron from central Sweden, an old import. There were cardboard boxes brim-filled with ancient nails, a brace of decoys, part of a dry sink, a box of door latches and hinges, and random lengths of painted pine. There were shadows and colours and contours Morgan would have loved to have explored. He was a natural at rummaging through obsolete treasures.

"The name's familiar," said Miranda. "A short poet; rhyming couplets; a gardener." What else, she wondered? "Didn't he say 'brevity is the soul of wit'?"

"No."

"No?"

"Shakespeare said that. Pope said 'Wit is the lowest form of humour.'"

"He must have been having a bad day. This is another Pope, I take it."

"This one lives in Port Hope. I asked him to meet us. I didn't think he'd be here already."

They paused at the door. Morgan's guest had obviously gone in.

"Do you remember? We talked about this guy in Yorkville."

"Last summer, in the coffee house. The architect."

"The ultimate expert in colonial house restoration and the simulation of rustic antiquities."

"'The simulation of rustic antiquities'! Sometimes you talk in quotations. Does he write poetry?"

"If you ask him nicely he might pen you a few short lines."

"Perhaps about corpses and crypts."

When they opened the door, standing immediately inside with his back to them was a man who in fact was exceptionally tall and quite angular. He was wearing a Fair Isle sweater that had once been a work of art and now threatened to disintegrate if he moved suddenly — which, by his current posture, seemed unlikely.

Without turning around, the man said, "She won't let me in, Mr. Morgan. This woman seems ready to draw her weapon and I'm not properly armed. Do you suppose you could help?"

Obscured by his lanky frame, Rachel Naismith was revealed by her voice. "Everything is under control, Detectives. He insisted on entering without authorization."

She edged around so that Alexander Pope had to step into the living-room rubble to get out of her way.

"He's tall as God, but not as convincing. I invited him to stand very still and he complied. Says he's here on your invitation. Refused to wait in his van."

"I saw no reason to remain outside," he said. "I'm assuming you outrank her, Detective Morgan. Do tell her to stand easy. I've never been at a crime scene before, but even here I would hope common civility applies." Morgan smiled. Here was someone totally comfortable with the persona he chose to project to the world, arbitrary as it was. His intonation and syntax were vaguely English, yet Canadian-born. In a few brief sentences he showed the residual inflection of a genuinely colonial sensibility. Once we were British, thought Morgan. Some still are.

Miranda gazed up at the man in admiration. Everything about him was authentic, she thought. His precarious sweater, his worn corduroy pants, his steel-toed workboots unlaced at the ankle, his three-day beard, and his unkempt steel-grey hair all went together with a fine eye for texture and colour. He held himself proud — he was immaculately clean, his clothes were well-cared-for, despite their deteriorating condition. He could have stepped off the pages of a women's magazine — the splendid model of an aging bohemian.

She looked at Officer Naismith, who was monitoring her observations. Alexander Pope had moved in the space of a foot or so from the policewoman's jurisdiction to Morgan's, gaining his freedom. "What are you doing here, Rachel? Have you been here all along?"

"Yes," she said. "I got triple shifted — I'm on my second time 'round the clock. Who is this guy?"

For no apparent reason, Morgan led Pope through the kitchen, where he mumbled something about avoiding the coffee, then back past the women out to the stairs, which they ascended one at a time. The lanky stranger had to stoop to avoid cracking his head on the stringer.

"C'mon," Miranda said to Rachel Naismith in a conspiratorial tone, "Let's see what our friend has to say for himself. And note: the bodies are not old! There's foul play afoot, as they say, and it's not ancient history."

"Wow."

"Yeah. Amazing, eh?"

"Then —"

"We don't know. Who they are, how they died, how they got sealed behind plaster, who did it, why, who wrote the script ... We don't know."

When they entered the room, Miranda was disconcerted to find the bodies gone. They were inextricably a part of the scene in her mind. Otherwise, the room was bright and airy, quite unlike the illuminated darkness of the night before. It seemed almost cheerful, despite the rubble and dust.

"Miranda," said Morgan, standing between her and the tall man, "This is Alexander Pope."

"I've always admired your poetry."

"Thank you."

"And this is Detective Miranda Quin. One *n*."

"Must be from Waterloo County. An Ontario Quin."

"And this is Officer Naismith —"

"Whom I have already met. Delighted," he said, bowing slightly. She regarded him warily, lifted her lip in a feigned snarl, and bowed in return. They shared a smile between them.

"The pleasure was mine, Mr. Pope. I've always admired your bulls." No one got the joke. "Papal bulls? Encyclicals? Pronouncements? Don't you hate that? It's been a long night."

"It is four-thirty-five," Alexander said. "In the afternoon. Saturday. March, I believe."

"If you want to go, Officer Naismith, we'll cover," Morgan offered. "You need some downtime."

"Hardly," she said. "But I'll heat up some coffee if you'd like. I've still got a bit left."

"No thanks," said the other three simultaneously.

"Now, Mr. Morgan," said Alexander Pope. "You said on the telephone there were anomalies here. You found two bodies in this closed-off closet, except for their heads, which fetched up in the laundry chute. I am to understand the dead couple were in an intimate embrace, rather in spite of mutual decapitation. I suppose there was a third party involved. Someone contrived what purported to be an ancient crime, but it seems it was not. And you want my opinion about what, precisely?"

There was a touch of the carnivalesque in the air. Pope was relishing his role as forensic antiquarian, Rachel was giddy from sleep deprivation, Miranda was distracted by lingering sensuality that refused to coalesce around particular memories or desire. And Morgan was happy. He had been drawn out of winter lethargy by a macabre spectacle so wondrously devised, where the anonymous victims were *dramatis personae* and the mysteries of death itself were on theatrical display.

The transition to serious work was abrupt. Alexander took out a Swiss Army knife and pried off a small slab of plaster from the edge of the hidden closet. He set the plaster on the floor and gently crushed it under the ball of his foot, then leaned down with surprising grace for such a tall and angular man and retrieved a few remnants of dust-dry powder and strands of fibre. He turned to the wall cupboard that was leaning against a pile of splintered lath, squatted down, and examined it closely. He smiled appreciatively, turned it over, and scrutinized the back, fingering the bolts that had been embedded in a stringer running between the studs of the original door frame. He drew a penlight out of his hip pocket and entered the closet, disappearing in the sudden darkness as he moved under the eaves. He emerged and walked over to the laundry chute, stuck his hand in with the flashlight, then squeezed his head through the restricted opening and looked down, then up. He extricated himself, rose to his full height, and smiled beatifically.

"Someone has done remarkably fine work," he pronounced. "There's a paradox, though. Everything has been meticulously contrived to seem in keeping with the age of the house. The plaster is a good imitation, slaked lime with horsehair binding, aged well, and layered with paint and paper. A lot of thought went into this project. The only woodwork that shows — the baseboard across the bottom where the door had been — is authentic. I assume the culprit took it from one of the other rooms. The filler, the paint, and the blending are spot on. But the inside of the closet has been sealed with a contemporary potion — Polyfilla, I expect.

"The lath over the sealed door and the chute must have been lifted from another room as well, even another house. It's all hand-split swamp cedar, but tacked on with old nails that have recently been cleaned. The chute, of course, was a rather ingenious dumbwaiter to bring wood upstairs for the fire. This house predates cast-iron stoves, which were evidently a later accoutrement. There is a fireplace here, hidden inside the gable-end wall. A stovepipe was later forced through into the chimney. Another goes up through the roof in the hall, above the dumbwaiter shaft. The chute was lined for laundry quite recently, possibly between the wars, and blocked off at floor level only in the last fortnight or so.

"It is an admirable counterfeit, all of this, but there is an intriguing anomaly, and that, Miranda — if I may call you Miranda — is the poetry you wanted. This fraud paradox-ically insists on being exposed — something hidden, a con-cealment, that yearns for revelation. This makes it a work of art. The whole project is designed for our appreciation, incomplete until it has been exposed.

"The key is the hanging cabinet: it was bolted in place, it is valuable. A salvager would be counted on to retrieve it. It would refuse to yield. The wall had to give way. The bodies were exposed not amidst rubble but in pristine condition — exactly, I imagine, as the killer intended. And there we are!"

Alexander Pope looked pleased with himself.

Morgan was excited by his articulate economy with words. The man was worthy of his namesake. Miranda was thinking, there is nothing poetic about murder, except in clas-sical tragedy, or in revisionist history, or perhaps in a psyche twisted by unspeakable suffering. She said nothing.

Morgan was thinking, this is theatre not poetry. But is the killer a brilliant and haunted dramaturge, or merely some wretched soul on the edge of events who has set a story in motion and is now waiting in the wings to see how it all turns out? Are we part of the audience or part of the action?

# chapter five
## Port Hope
---

For the next two weeks, Miranda and Morgan scanned missing-persons files, tracked down false leads, and despite an absence of DNA records, eventually established probable identities. They found that neither of the deceased had any connection with the derelict house, and no relationship with each other. The cause of their deaths had not been precisely determined, nor, due to their mummified condition, could the exact time of their demise be established, especially since both were missing for some time before anyone noticed. The man was a traveller from the States, and no one at his home office even knew he was in Toronto. He had an ex-wife who wasn't aware of his absence until a postdated cheque failed to be honoured, and who was the beneficiary of his modest insurance policy. He was Jewish and had never been associated with the Masonic Order. The woman was a fourth-year student at York University, ominously majoring in anthropology. She was from Liverpool, estranged from her family, had recently emerged from a dishevelled relationship with another woman, and was a Mormon, not Catholic as the crucifix implied. Her former girlfriend, an agnostic, was shocked by her death.

The papers ran with the Hogg's Hollow murders for a couple of days. Television coverage lasted only a few hours. When it turned out the dead were not actually lovers, the news media, following their prime directive to entertain, shifted attention to more accessible crimes and misdemeanours, where the blood was still warm and death was a thrill. The public appetite for horror was fickle. Without romance to keep the blood flowing, the story had the lasting power of a horror film, forgotten half way home from the theatre. It was as if the grisly events had actually occurred in the colonial past. They might have sustained interest for history buffs and the occasional misdirected forensic anthropologist, but otherwise seemed of likely concern only to police assigned to the case.

Miranda and Rachel Naismith became friends. One day when they were off duty they drove out to Port Hope in Miranda's Jaguar. Lunching in a family restaurant on Walton Street that had booth-side jukeboxes and grey-flecked tables and served real raisin pie, they felt the time-warped atmosphere bode well for their intended visit to Alexander Pope. They were both fascinated by the man's capacity to represent himself as being from an era that never quite was. Port Hope was the perfect setting for an adventure through time, straddling as it did so many periods in its diverse architecture and casual gentility.

The downtown area was Ontario vernacular, shorn of the garish paraphernalia of twentieth-century merchandising. Three- to five-storey red-brick buildings hovered close to the street, interspersed with the occasional civic edifice of quarried stone. Victorian cornices and casements, pediments and paint — all were revealed in parochial splendour, celebrating the town's pride in its historical past and aesthetic present.

Driving a circuitous route to Pope's place on the outskirts, Miranda and Rachel shared their admiration for old houses, from modest mansions topped with widow's walks to painted-brick cottages tucked behind white picket fences. Most of the older homes bespoke a lovely merging of civic responsibility, architectural self-consciousness, and horticultural vanity. It occurred to Miranda as they drove past a well-kempt cemetery that even the dead in Port Hope maintained decorum.

As curiosity began to seem an exercise in delayed gratification, they veered away from the town and after ten minutes of exhilarating lakeshore landscape they turned into a long driveway and drove up a hill to Alexander Pope's fine old house, which was set in brooding isolation behind a shrouding of foliage. The building itself was a marvel of austere congeniality on the outside, and conveyed the promise of esoteric pleasures within.

Waiting at the door on the side porch, which was partially enclosed as a shed, Miranda stared into the shadows beside them. There was what appeared to be the entrance to a wood-fired sauna. A stack of dry maple firewood. Various tools for gardening and building. A chainsaw. She felt the thrill of connection on seeing a couple of compressed-air tanks leaning against the wall.

He's a diver, she thought.

Alexander Pope was a man of wide-ranging pursuits, as well as of arcane skills, esoteric knowledge, eccentric apparel, awkward charm, and stellar lineage.

She was going to mention the scuba gear to Rachel but something in the other woman's muted excitement made her keep silent. The two of them were like teenagers calling on the mysterious boy in the big house who had just moved into the neighbourhood. When the inner door opened, they breathed deeply in unison, as if something magnificent were about to occur.

Alexander greeted them through the storm door like old friends. He recognized them instantly and invited them in. After brief chatter he gave them a tour of the house. He identified old locks, small cabinets, hinges, and latches, and with unexpected candour he showed them how to distinguish original sideboards and dressers and tables from reconstructions. He showed them replicas he had himself contrived, with meticulous attention to detail. Even hidden joints, places, and materials never meant to be seen, bore the artisan's signature devotion to successful dissembling.

Since the surrounding grounds were too soggy from the spring thaw to be negotiated, he explained the exterior of the house while they sat in front of the kitchen fire. He described how the Georgian lines were so well-served by painted wood siding made to represent ashlar blocks, which came to light when the layers of clapboard and aluminum had been peeled away.

On the outside, restoration had been scrupulously governed by Pope's desire for authenticity. Inside, he had taken liberties, moving or eliminating walls to achieve an airy yet intricate effect that allowed him copious wall space against which to display his country furniture.

All in all, Alexander Pope seemed to have eliminated the Victorian era. Everything around him had been made by, or honoured, the settlers from the Old World and up from the States who displaced native inhabitants in the area, or was unabashedly contemporary. The lighting was modern, not tacky reproductions of old lanterns and lamps, the plumbing and appliances were not coyly disguised. The panes in his twelve-over-twelve windows were rippled with age, although the glass had been set into newly built versions of old frames.

They sat on ladder-back chairs — brought up during the Revolution by United Empire Loyalists — at a harvest table from Ile d'Orléans before the fall of New France, with the robust patina of a dozen generations etched deeply into its broad, blackened boards, and drank instant coffee. It was better than Rachel's, Miranda thought, but not much. How can you ruin instant coffee? Perhaps it was never meant to be endlessly boiled.

Alexander Pope asked Miranda for a progress report on the Hogg's Hollow investigation, affecting a gravitas that Miranda found curiously winsome. Rachel laughed at him. He seemed not to notice. After eliciting particulars that from his perspective were extraneous, such as the identity of the victims and the finer points of their execution, he let the matter drop, cracked open a bottle of cooking sherry, and they spent the rest of the afternoon talking antiques.

Several times the possibility of murder as an art form arose, invariably embedded in a historical context, and drifted away amid talk of aesthetics and artifice, antiquities and architecture. They might have been in another time, or out of time entirely. It was a most pleasant occasion, thought Miranda as they drove back to Toronto, each woman silently savouring what they had shared.

The Port Hope foray occurred on the Saturday between Good Friday and Easter. Morgan had mysteriously taken his leave a couple of days earlier. He would only admit to a return date, later the following week. Miranda guessed he was heading south. The Cayman Islands, perhaps. That's where she had gone scuba diving several years back, living aboard a dive boat and earning Open Water and Advanced PADI certification. He had subsequently promised he would dive with her some day, although she wouldn't have held him to it. Knowing Morgan, she suspected he had snuck off to learn on his own so that he could keep up with her.

The visit to Alexander Pope was in some way related to her partner's absence, she suspected, although it had arisen in conversation with Rachel as simply a fun thing to do. She could not remember which of them first brought it up, but they had both taken it on as a pilgrimage — not to the man, but for the sake of the lovely odd values and grace he embodied.

Back at her desk the next week, Miranda was still annoyed with Morgan. The autopsy reports finally came in: they suggested both victims had died from a profound breakdown of the autonomic system, in all probability by protracted exposure to heat without adequate hydration — symptoms, according to the medical examiner's report, consistent with a slow death in the central Sahara.

Miranda shuddered. She phoned the medical examiner's office and asked for Ellen Ravenscroft.

"I enjoyed the report," she said. "Nice prose style; a touch ornate."

"Which report would that be, love?"

"The Sahara Desert. That was good."

"It was a particularly trying job. Onerous, very onerous. Have you ever been to Guanahuato?"

"Where?"

"Guanahuato. It's in Mexico. No, I don't suppose you have."

Miranda wondered why she had called.

"They put bodies on display in the Museo de los Mommias. There's a natural mummifying effect from the sand where the townspeople bury their dead. If no one pays the cemetery fees, after ten years the bodies are disinterred. The interesting ones go into the museum, the others are tossed out. It's electrifying, walking among them."

"Why would you do that?"

"Curiosity, love — about the poor sods who maintain the exhibit. Can you imagine working there? Like being a coroner's apprentice without the autopsies. I'm not much interested in a replenishing stock of dried-out corpses scavenged from reusable graves, despite my choice of professions, but when I was prying through the insides of your closeted lovers I couldn't help thinking about the state-employed ghouls of Guanahuato. You should visit sometime. They have an annual Cervantes festival."

"They weren't lovers."

"No, I expect they weren't. We found traces of mould on the male's skin. He'd been processed and placed on hold for a while before she came along. The poor thing had none on her at all, so they were probably encrypted as soon as she was prepared. Anyway, love, as I was working I recalled Guanahuato, bodies arranged for morbid amusement. It's a form of play, Miranda. Playing with the dead. Your killer is a fatalist with a warped appreciation for the absurdity of the human condition. Let's make death perform — it performs. You're looking for someone utterly lacking in empathy, someone who has an impoverished emotional life, inflexible religious beliefs, or none at all, and a fecund imagination."

"Thank you, Detective Inspector Ravenscroft. And the Sahara?"

"That was for colour. Guanahuato wouldn't have worked. You know why? I'll tell you why. Neither of your lovers was dead before the process of mummification began!"

"Oh, Christ!"

"A killer with a mind like the mind of God. You know the fall from Eden is all about making us live out our lives, knowing we're dying from the moment of conception. Not that I believe all that. Not the religious part. I'd say your murders are virtually incomprehensible from a mortal perspective. But so is life." She paused. "Medical examiners carry on conversations with the dead, you know. We're filled with deep thoughts. Let's get together. I hear Morgan's deserted you."

"He'll be back next week. I'll call."

"Do."

"Bye."

Miranda had no intention of calling, and Ellen Ravenscroft had no expectation that she would. Somehow, Morgan as an issue of playful contention between them had opened a minor rift. It was not so much that Miranda wanted Morgan as her lover — she was pretty sure she did not. But she did not want the medical examiner to have him, either.

Miranda at her desk was an uncommon sight. Superintendent Alex Rufalo noted her presence, looked at his watch, and chortled to himself. With Morgan away, she was spending more visible time in the office. Usually the two of them were off by themselves — freelancing, he called it; working the field. You never knew when they might turn up, day or night.

Aware of being watched, Miranda caught Rufalo's eye and smiled with what she imagined was non-invasive congeniality. She didn't want to pry but she wanted him to know she was there, if he needed her. Nurturing be damned, she thought, and went back to work. She was reading Morgan's inspired version of the Hogg's Hollow murders.

Rachel Naismith leaned against Miranda's desk, waiting to be noticed. She was in street clothes and carried a small pack or knapsack, as well as a purse. Miranda was intent on Morgan's account, which he had written up for her benefit as if it were a piece for *The New Yorker*. Without taking her eyes from the page, she said, "He writes more like Truman Capote than Dashiell Hammett."

"Are you talking to me?" Rachel responded. "Are you talking to me?"

"Yeah," said Miranda, sitting back in her chair. "He'd hate that. He'd much rather be Dashiell Hammett. How long have you been standing there?"

"Awhile. How long did you know I was watching?"

"Awhile. It's Morgan's report. He writes really well, but it's not exactly police-appropriate."

"You gonna change it? Do you want to go for a drink?"

"Yeah. This'll wait. The superintendent has other things on his mind."

"A messed-up marriage."

"Do you know him?" she said, glancing through Rufalo's door. "How do you know that?"

"He smiled at me," said Rachel. "He never smiles at uniformed officers. Not at the women."

"You're kidding."

"So, what I figure, he's got woman problems, he's in the wrong, he's compensating, trying to prove to himself he's not a chauvinist double-pig."

"Double?"

"He's a cop."

"How sixties. You're not in uniform now —"

"So he doesn't recognize me, which proves my point!"

"It does?"

"He's a man."

"He's a good man. A bit of a prick, but a good man," she said in a whisper. "His wife's a lawyer."

"I heard."

"So, let's go for a drink. This case is giving me the creeps."

"Weird, eh?"

"I feel like I'm in the middle of a play by Samuel Beckett, trying to make out what's going on in the audience." She liked that — the turn of phrase, a Morgan-like inversion. She wondered if he was diving.

"I played Estragon in a school production of *Waiting for Godot*."

"Some school," said Miranda.

"Some play. We had a great teacher. She insisted that if you know what the play means, you've ruined the play. She'd say things like that. To understand is to misunderstand. She was a superannuated hippy on the verge of retirement. It was funny and sad, and I never knew what the play was about, not even now."

"The fine line between madness and genius ..."

"There's no line at all. Let's get outta here."


When Miranda woke up, Rachel was naked in bed beside her. Without lifting her head, and with only one eye open, Miranda surveyed the situation. They were lying on top of the covers. Rachel was facing her, her head on the other pillow; she opened her eyes and smiled.

"G'morning, Detective."

Without saying anything, Miranda got up and went into the bathroom. She sat on the toilet with her arms propped on her knees and cradled her head between her hands. She was mildly hungover.

Rachel stood in the doorway, legs akimbo, arms folded beneath her breasts. Miranda looked up, smiled sheepishly. She had never been with a woman.

With calming deliberation, her eyes traced Rachel's body, starting at the long toes and slowly rising, exploring the deep colour of the woman's skin, sliding up past her trim ankles, knees, hard thighs, delving into the folds between her legs accentuated by the soft curly fringe of glistening hair, rising over her taunt stomach, her gently articulated ribcage and diaphragm, lingering on the sullen precocity of her small breasts, rising past her collarbone, which gleamed ebony through her skin, up the long neck to her chin, the full lips, the fine broad nose, the deep-set gleaming eyes, her face surrounded by a thick fringe of sleek, black hair. Is this woman my lover, she wondered?

Neither demure nor provocative, Rachel let Miranda survey her body. She said nothing. After a few moments she rose to her toes, lifting her entire form into an alluring and yet innocent pose, and slowly, softly, began to laugh. Miranda glanced away in embarrassment, then looked back, catching the vulnerability and strength in her eyes, and began to laugh herself. Two naked women, one sitting on a toilet, the other holding a statuesque pose. Miranda did not know where to go from there so she began to pee. This took them both to the edge of hysteria.

"Hurry up," said Rachel. "Now I've gotta go, too."

"Use the shower," said Miranda. "Don't be shy, girl."

Their laughter died out as Rachel stepped into the shower and closed the door, turned on the water, squealed until the hot water came through, and began to sing in such a low voice, the words and melody were inaudible.

Miranda brushed her teeth, handed a spare toothbrush over the shower door to Rachel, and after a few minutes Rachel opened the door and drew her in beside her. They began to soap each other with gentle exploratory gestures. Miranda wondered if perhaps the night before had been a prelude: she could summon only a vague recollection of sensuous well-being.

Rachel turned Miranda away and worked a lather on her back, then reached around with soapy hands to cup her breasts against her palms. Miranda relaxed against her and gazing down admired how fingers against flesh gleamed ebony and alabaster in the streaming water. One of Rachel's hands slid lower and her fingers splayed across the curls of Miranda's pubic hair, squeezing rivulets of foamy subs, but did not descend further between her legs, making no proprietorial assumptions. Miranda turned and surprised herself by arching away to hold Rachel's breasts one at a time, gently caressing them with suds.

Fascinated by her own lack of inhibition, she let her arms drop to rest against Rachel's hips and leaned forward, their bodies gently touching. Rachel's breasts pressed softly against Miranda's, which were a little heavier and, despite their similar heights, a little lower, and pressed into Rachel's diaphragm; they stood like that with the water streaming over them, passively rinsing. Their lips brushed against each other, foreheads touched, they tilted their heads to the side as if to kiss. Each cocked a leg slightly, pudenda pressed warmly against the upper thigh of the other. They did not move, feeling the intimate warmth of the pressure. They did not kiss. Somewhere in the mind of each there was the ambiguous image of Rodin's sculpture, and the remnants of last evening's discussion about undecidability in the works of Samuel Beckett.

Suddenly, the water went cold. They leapt from the shower, giggling, jostling each other through the narrow stall door. They did not dry each other off. Both realized their moment of intimacy had passed.

After Rachel left for work, wearing borrowed panties under yesterday's clothes, Miranda went back to bed. Gradually, she remembered sitting around in the living room drinking Bloody Marys after leaving the pub. She recalled how natural it had seemed, with Rachel staying over, the two of them walking into the bedroom, stripping to the buff like girls at camp, and climbing side by side into bed. Some time during the night they must have kicked off the covers.

Her hangover didn't amount to much but she was tired. She might have slept fitfully, being naked in bed with another woman. She was not in the least upset about compromised sexuality. She had no idea whether Rachel Naismith was a lesbian, or whether she herself was unexpectedly bisexual. Time would reveal all that. She was curious more than anything else. Miranda was comfortable with her own sexuality, if not with sex itself. If only she could get them together — sex and sexuality. She wondered if it were possible.

She remembered sunbathing beside the mill race near Waldron, the village where she grew up. She remembered the shadow of a man looming over her. The rest she forgot until he reappeared in her life, twenty years later, driving a Jaguar. The girl in the closet had a story of her own. But she died. Miranda could refuse to remain a victim; she could not.

They had talked late into the night, Miranda and Rachel. After meandering up Yonge Street, past shop after shop catering to bizarre sexual, psychic, and spiritual proclivities and the occasional outlet for mundane necessities like toilet paper and party balloons, they had found an anonymous trattoria and settled in for a surprisingly bad dinner with a nondescript bottle of wine. Afterward they each had a shot of grappa, courtesy of the owner.

Halfway back to Miranda's place, Rachel realized she had left her pack behind. When they returned to the restaurant, the proprietor was waiting inside the door with the pack in hand. He had not tried to call after her — maybe he had discovered it too late — but he was visibly pleased to find her in his debt.

"Officer," he proclaimed. "This is yours."

"I know it's mine, *paisano*. Did you find anything in it of interest?"

"Your uniform. That's how I knew it was yours."

"Or how you knew I was a cop."

"Yes, one of those two. Ciao, ladies. Good night."

As they walked along Isabella Street, Rachel argued persuasively that the man was a former Mafia boss in an RCMP witness-protection program. Miranda, having once been a Mountie, thought it more likely he was the illegitimate offspring of Prince Rainier.

Whatever the case, they agreed he was not a born restaurateur.

"I've only got V-8 juice. And some gin. Does that make a Bloody Mary?" Miranda called to Rachel from the kitchen.

Rachel answered through the open door of the bathroom. "It sounds wretched. Let's give it a try."

They settled onto the living-room sofa.

On the coffee table in front of them sat a large bottle of V-8, a bottle of gin, a salt shaker, and a bottle of Worcestershire sauce. Each mixed her own drink, Rachel licking the rim of her glass and dragging it through salt in the palm of her hand before mixing the gin and juice, Miranda shaking in enough Worcestershire to turn the liquid a muddy brown.

"I think," said Miranda, raising her glass in a mock toast, "this drink is a Bloody Mess."

"What do you suppose was going through the killer's mind?" said Rachel.

The two women were relaxed with each other. Conversation no longer needed to proceed through a logical sequence with appropriate segues. Each could say what was on her mind and connections were made through personality, not content.

"I mean, was it all for a diabolical show? Were the murders collateral damage? It was a thrilling display of pathological depravity — horror with an edge."

"An edge?"

"Of irony, I guess. It's very contemporary, isn't it? To make death a joke and a puzzle."

"Horror films are funny," said Miranda.

"They used to be scary. Think of *Nosferatu*, compared to *Interview with the Vampire* or the *Scream* movies, or *Freddie the 13th*."

"You've made a study of horror?" said Miranda. "Have you ever actually seen *Nosferatu*?"

"Only in clips, but whatever, the old films evoked our deepest fears. The new ones play to our vanity."

"Vanity? Like, you're frightened, but you understand why. We're back to irony."

"Death is the ultimate irony." Rachel said this as if she were quoting someone. "There was a directness in old-fashioned horror; it was the real thing. *Dracula*. Edgar Allan Poe, *The Mysteries of Udolpho*, *The Castle of Otranto*, even *Jane Eyre*."

"The real thing!"

"Where horror and terror converge." She paused. "When we are terrified to be alive."

"Wow, Rachel. That's scary. I'll take irony — with an edge."

Rachel seemed preternaturally composed as she discussed the Hogg's Hollow crime scene and related it to films and novels, showing an affinity for the ominous that Miranda found mystifying and strangely exciting.

"You're lucky, Miranda. You get to think on the job."

"All cops think. A traffic cop thinks. When I worked on Parliament Hill, striking in scarlet, I had to think."

"About what?"

"About security, about whether my hat was on straight,

about why I ever wanted to be a Mountie."

"Why?"

"Dunno. I wanted to be a cop. Morgan says it was for empowerment. He figures I was reacting to a subconscious sense of violation."

"Is he right?"

"Maybe."

Rachel sank back against the sofa cushions, waiting.

"There was a man; he was in one of my senior courses at university, much older than me. He may have ..." Miranda sat forward, took in a deep breath. "I was raped when I was eighteen. I never saw his face. I didn't know his name.... Maybe I did, I don't know. I made myself forget.

"I didn't connect the guy in my class with my assailant. Not consciously, not until last summer.

"At the end of the academic year, when friends were taking off for Europe or Thailand or preparing for graduate school — I had a scholarship to go on in semiotics, believe it or not — to everyone's surprise, including my own, I joined the Mounties."

"Morgan thinks you were trying to get away from this guy who was haunting your life?"

"Shadowing, not haunting. I didn't know he was there. Morgan thinks subconsciously I did. He thinks I was trying to take charge of my life. I don't even know if I believe in the subconscious. It's just a bunch of neurons in there and an infinite maze of electrical impulses."

"Tell me about your daughter."

"Who?"

"You've mentioned a girl. I thought maybe it was a custody thing."

"Jill? She's my ward. I've never had kids. You?"

"Not even an abortion."

Miranda was thrown for a moment, but saw nothing in Rachel's expression either to indicate morbid wit or incipient confession.

"Jill's fifteen, going on forty. And sometimes she's four. She's sweet and tough and smart. She's gone through a lot."

"And you?"

"I'm the administrator of her father's charitable bequests. I was his executor."

"Not the girl from the fish-pond murders?"

Miranda glared.

"I'm sorry," said Rachel. "That was thoughtless."

Miranda shrugged. Usually, she did not connect with versions of herself in the media, especially in stories as wildly exploited for gruesome perversity, despite all that went unrevealed. But Rachel's casual reference forced a vital connection between the trivialized account in the papers and her private and painful memories.

Rachel seemed to understand.

"It's so easy to lose track of the real people involved," she was saying. "Like the fifty-some prostitutes murdered in Vancouver. Maybe their bodies were ground up as pig food. People food? It wasn't until I saw somebody's brother weeping on television, suddenly the numbers, the macabre speculation broke down, those women, they were individual lives, each with her own terrible agony, dying her own special death. It's the Anne Frank syndrome. I understand more about the Holocaust, reading the account of a girl that ends just before her arrest, than from seeing the pictures of bulldozed bodies and reading statistics. I didn't even know Anne had died at Bergen-Belsen when I read her diary. The illusions of objectivity in historical texts or in tabloids destroy empathy. You know what I mean?"

Miranda stared at her, wide-eyed. Another person might

have just apologized.

"You talk to me," said Rachel. "You need to talk."

She reached across and put her hand on the other woman's knee. Miranda started to pull away, then placed her own hand over Rachel's and gave it an affirming squeeze that curiously translated through Rachel's grasp to her own knee, as if she were reassuring herself.

Miranda placed Jill at the centre of the narrative, merging public knowledge with confidential revelations; unsure, herself, about the lines between news and gossip and confession. She explained her connection to a wealthy recluse with a vintage Jag, and she explained Jill's connection to them both. She explained how she had been transformed by ghastly circumstances from investigating detective to Jill's guardian and the man's executor. She described horrors inflicted and horrors endured.

"But you cannot suppress evil for wanting," she said. "You can hide terrible things but you can't erase them. You can't forget just because you want to forget. You know what I mean?"

"Miranda, I do. I know exactly what you mean."

Miranda meant to ask Rachel to go on, but instead she pursued the dead woman in the closet. That seemed more real, for the moment, paradoxically, because Rachel was willing to listen.

"She died from dehydration," Miranda explained. "She felt her skin parch and shrivel, felt her insides decrepitate, felt her lips crack and her eyes bleed. This young woman, she was of no interest to her killer. Do you realize how rare that must be? Murder, not to end a life but to create death. It's beyond pathological. Almost satanic."

"Death as an act of creation! In that case, there will likely be more. Do you think so?"

They talked late into the night, then went to bed.

Miranda rolled on her side, staring at the indentation in the pillow where Rachel's head had been. She reached over and gently rested the back of her hand in the hollow. She could smell the fresh scent that lingered in the sheets, like the smell of leaves unfurling in the morning sun. She drifted into sleep, and an hour later awakened. She would call Jill at noon, when she was home from school, and see if she wanted to go out for pizza, maybe an early movie if the homework wasn't too heavy. They both liked movies.

## chapter six

## Rapa Nui

---

"**G**morning," said Morgan. "I'm back."

"I didn't know you'd been away."

Miranda mumbled, struggling to assimilate his voice into her scattering dream. She rolled over on her back and stretched. At least it was morning.

"I've been up all night. It's time you got out of bed," he said, as if there were a logical point. "I'm still at the airport; thought I'd check in."

"Thanks, Morgan. Where have you been?"

"Just got in from Sao Paulo."

"That's Brazil!"

"That's right."

"What were you doing there, for goodness sake?"

"Stopping over from Santiago."

"Chile!"

"Well done."

"What was in Chile? You are very strange."

"Easter Island. Santiago is the jumping off point for Easter Island."

"You're serious. You were at Easter Island."

"'On,' not 'at.' It's very small."

"Morgan, it's too early. Meet me on, or at, Fran's for breakfast."

"I'll meet you at Starbucks in an hour."

They both knew which Starbucks — the one over from police headquarters on the corner of College and Yonge.

"So, you've been away?" she said when she saw him.

He rose, kissed her on both cheeks, and slumped back into his chair. He had a large cappuccino waiting for her, with the saucer on top to keep it warm. His eyes were bloodshot and his hands swollen, but he looked content, like the cat, having swallowed the canary, who endured indigestion as a reasonable price for the pleasure.

"Tell me."

"Well," he said, "I got on an Air Canada flight at Pearson, heading for Easter Island. When I transferred to Varig Air in Brazil, I was travelling to Isla de Pascua. In Santiago, I boarded Lan Chile for Rapa Nui. And I landed on Te pito o te henua. All the same place. It was a magical journey. Did you ever read Leacock's *Sunshine Sketches*, where he gets on a modern train in the Metropolis, and transfers to an older train on his way to Mariposa as he travels back into another world defined by nostalgia and wit? I have just emerged from another dimension, defined by enchantment and mystery."

"You sound slightly demented. What on earth took you ... there?" Miranda gazed across the table at her partner, who was dishevelled, buoyant with enthusiasm. He was precious in her life, she wanted to tell him. She wanted to hug him and keep him invulnerable. "You are an idiot, Morgan. No one knew where you were."

"On Rapa Nui. That's what they call themselves, and their language, and the island. *Te pito o te henua* means navel of the world. It's not really a name; for a thousand years they didn't know there was anyone else on the planet. It's a geographical declaration."

"I wrote an essay on Thor Heyerdahl as an anthropological entrepreneur when I was in university."

"How very cynical. You were ahead of your time."

"Yeah, actually I wrote it in high school. '*Kon Tiki*: Boys at Sea.' '*Aku Aku*: Boys Still at Sea.' 'Indiana Jones: An Autobiography.' Whatever. Got an 'A.' Or should have."

"You ever notice how people ask about your travels so they can talk about themselves?"

"Yes, I've noticed that."

They sipped their coffees, each looking over the rims at the other. Miranda smiled, inhaled coffee, and, as she choked, slammed down her cup on the table. Morgan grimaced in sympathy. Her eyes watered, she tried to speak, she waved her hand to reassure witnesses that she was not about to expire. Everyone but Morgan looked away.

"Well then," he said. "Given this opportunity to say a few words, let me fill in possible gaps in your memory of Heyerdahl. Rapa Nui is about three thousand kilometres off South America, another three thousand from Tahiti. There are almost nine hundred *moai* — that's what the statues are called — and about three times that many people."

"Nine hundred," she mouthed in astonishment.

"Yeah, from three feet to sixty feet tall, not all completed. Every one is unique, like a signature — you know, the same and yet each version is different. They were created over an eight-hundred-year period."

"Sixty feet?"

"That one's still in the quarry at Rano Raraku. I spent a

lot of time out there."

He talked on and on, and Miranda was spellbound. Eventually, it was Morgan who exclaimed, "It's time we get back to work."

"I was working while you were away, you know. The world didn't hold its breath in your absence. Things happened."

"What?"

"Not much. Do you want a ride home? Maybe you should run up and let the superintendent know you're back."

"Is he still living there?"

"Just about. I think he's taken a room on St. George. It's a negotiating strategy. She threw him out, you know. The rumour is he was *not* having an affair."

"No!"

"Apparently she got tired of buying the toilet paper and pepper."

"Of course."

"That's my theory: if you don't keep track of the toilet paper and pepper, you're not sharing responsibilities, you're just helping out."

"I manage to run out of both on a regular basis."

"Exactly. And she was so busy being a lawyer, a wife, a housekeeper, and society matron, and a mother, neither of them noticed he was mostly just being a cop."

"You know all this, because ...?"

"A friend of a friend has an informant who works out at her gym."

"Ah," he said. He forgot to tell her about Rongorongo for sale in the marketplace. He would; she'd ask. A written language no one could read; she was executor of her assailant's estate and he had owned an incised tablet the size of a paddle blade filled with indecipherable glyphs. It was worth a small fortune, certainly more than her vintage Jaguar. Maybe she wouldn't ask; maybe she would assume Morgan would tell her anything new he might have learned, if he had learned anything new. They both knew he couldn't resist.

Without asking, Morgan ambled over to the counter and ordered two more cappuccinos. Miranda followed him with her eyes, sure other women were doing the same. There was something about the way he moved — a shambling self-assurance — the way his clothes looked worn in and not worn out, the crooked smile, the way he combined intensity with nonchalance.

She looked around the Starbucks interior. There were five other women; several of them, oddly enough, were looking at her. She was glad he was home.

After they checked in with Alex Rufalo, she drove him home. When he emerged from the bathroom, clean-shaven, hair combed, wrapped in a towel, he appeared almost normal. By the time he descended from the loft after dressing, he already seemed slightly unkempt; his hair looked windblown, although God knows there wasn't much air moving through his apartment, and his clothes, while clean, were already rumpled. All signs of exhaustion had left his face; he looked refreshed and relaxed. He sat on the blue sofa since she was comfortably ensconced in his favourite armchair

"I suppose you hung out with the police down there."

"Carabineros. Isla de Pascua Carabineros. I met a guy called Te Ave Teao, trained in Chile but born and raised on the island. There's no crime in Rapa Nui — nothing serious. Mostly, I kept to myself. What's happening with our major case? I'm assuming it's still our major case."

"Can't tie the victims to each other or connect either of them to the house. A lot of dead ends, so to speak. I think we're dealing with murder for amusement — the arbitrary indulgence of an inspired psychopath."

She was aware she was echoing a conversation she had had with Rachel. This made her wonder how much her intimacy with the young woman had been to compensate for Morgan's absence. *Perhaps that explains why we never became lovers,* she thought.

"There's no use looking for motive, then," Morgan was saying. "Method we know. Opportunity was at the killer's convenience. So we focus on what?"

"The entertainment factor. I know it's grotesque, but maybe our only hope is to interpret the crime as a creative event. Morgan, we have to shift from motive to intent. The ring and the cross are no longer clues to what happened; the hidden crypt is no longer evidentiary; the colonial clothes, the mummification, the eternal embrace, these aren't factors that will help us to explain the murder itself. Everything is turned around. Don't you see?"

"Not yet, but I'm trying."

"Clues and evidence won't lead to the killer directly, since they were arranged with pathological intention to achieve an aesthetic effect."

"All art is pathological."

"Now that is profound."

"But true. The artist plays life against death without a twinge of conscience. Suffering, brutality, sadness — they're just the raw materials."

"Joy, triumph, ecstasy — they're raw materials, too. 'Inferno' is only one part of the *Divine Comedy*, Morgan. That's why it's divine!"

"What about Freud?"

"What *about* Freud?" she retorted — but she already knew where he was going. It was good to have Morgan back in the game.

"There's a disjunct between the signifiers and the signi-fied —"

"You're switching discourses, Morgan!"

"No, I'm piggybacking Freud on Saussure. We're trying to make a story out of signs that make no sense — we should forget the story and look for the author embedded in the mystery itself."

"Yes," she said. Morgan's back.

"There's a subtle distinction, but incredibly important. We can't explain the psychopath's madness by interpretation, but we can find him there, hidden among symbols and artifice, expressing his madness. It could be Freud: about issues of love and sexuality. It could be Aristotle: about hubris and achieving catharsis. It could be Beckett —"

"That's what I said, Beckett."

"A story about nothing but itself."

"So we all become characters in search of an author. Holy Pirandello, Batman! It's a challenge. When you're inside the play, he gets to be God."

"You said what about Beckett, to who?"

"To whom! To Rachel Naismith, my new best friend."

"You are a fickle woman."

Morgan got up from the sofa and moved around the room. Lack of sleep made him restless but he felt exhilarated to be working again.

"We have a cold-blooded killer with talent," he said. "Do we have a pattern? If this is his masterwork, did he serve an apprenticeship? With whom? More to the point, *on* whom? If this is the first display of his deviant aptitude, I have the distinct and uneasy feeling it will not be his last. "

"That's just what I'm afraid of, Morgan. Success spawning success. There's no precedent — nothing like it at all in the States, or here. Nothing with comparable flair, or the same intellectual self-consciousness."

"You tried the Ontario Provincial Police?"

"Nothing. They ran it through ViCLAS —"

"ViCLAS?"

"Violent Crime Linking Analysis System."

"I knew that."

"The Orillia OPP are cutting edge. Nothing."

"Did you try Interpol?"

"Of course. I was thorough. And imaginative — I was open to variations on the theme. But nothing, nada, rien."

"So we wait. It's grotesque, but that's all we can do. Have you talked to Pope again? Or the anthropologists? How in the hell were they fooled, if Pope saw right off that the scene was a fake?"

"Forewarned is forearmed. He knew after you called what to expect. Poor Birbalsingh and Hubbard — they walked in cold. They had no reason to be skeptical. The condition of the bodies, their dress, the sealed crypt, it all seemed consistent. It was an archeological site"

"Their findings to be entered in the annals of science."

"Does science have annals? Yeah, Morgan, I went back to talk to them both. Professor Birbalsingh was amused more than anything. And intrigued. He said when we catch the killer he'd like to talk to him. It might help in his forensic research with authentic antiquities. Dr. Hubbard was less sanguine. I asked her if she could put a trace on the clothing. She already had, and came up with nothing. It would be virtually impossible to track down unless it had been stolen from a collection, she said. More likely it was bought in one of those strange little shops in London that cater to every imaginable taste. I couldn't argue. I've never been to London."

"Is it worth getting Scotland Yard to check around?"

"I've already asked. The chap on the phone was absolutely charming, asked me to fax the paperwork and they'd get right on it, and wanted to know if I dated."

"If you're dated?"

"No, Morgan. He was flirting. It was quite flattering."

"Desperate measures, given the Atlantic —"

"He said I should look him up if I ever got over. Constable Stenabaugh. He sounded quite handsome."

"You are a desperate and fickle woman."

"Rachel and I went out to see Alexander Pope."

She knew that would surprise him, that they went together.

"He is a lovely man," she continued. "And he has a breathtaking home. Pre-Victorian, I don't know what you'd call it — Georgian Colonial, neo-American Federal. You've got to see it; you'd love the furnishings. Some of the paint must be ten layers thick, some of the pieces he's made himself, right down to faking the paint. We stayed for a sauna. He's a fascinating man. Beautiful body — he must be fifty."

He looked at her quizzically. In his brief absence she had made new friends. He would not have anticipated the relationship with Officer Naismith. Miranda was generally slow in warming to women. Her explanation was a paraphrase from the old comic strip *Pogo*: "we have seen the enemy and it is us." Pope was less unexpected. What Morgan had taken as the man's pleasantly austere asexuality, he now realized, from the tenor of Miranda's voice, was mistaken by women for smouldering passion refined through an aura of eccentric gentility.

Strange, he thought. We can't both be right.

"Did you ask him for a list of people who might have the skills to close in the alcove?"

"Yeah. He laughed. He told me there's nobody, apart from himself. And, he assured me, he was working in Arlington, Texas, through the fall and winter. It checked out. He's got a major reconstruction project down there, where they're anxious to pay for their past — unlike post-colonials who try to obscure it. He was on the job every day, seven days a week, for a full five months."

"And they died during that time?"

"Ellen Ravenscroft wrote the report. She was sure they died in the depths of winter. Fairly sure."

"How could she tell?"

"Micro-organisms; decomposition tables; schedules and charts of this and that. They have their methods. Once she knew what she was looking for, it was easy."

"Ain't that always the way!"

"We ran chemical analyses on the plaster ingredients and paint. It was like an alchemical inversion, Morgan: old ingredients newly mixed to look old."

"What about sexual assault?"

"Tissues were too far gone —"

"This isn't about sex, anyway. Not this one."

"Wrong, Morgan. I think it is. Not the act of, maybe, but it has to be about sex. You wait and see. You don't mount cadavers in a headless embrace without Freud in attendance."

He smiled enigmatically.

"I thought you were in the Cayman Islands."

"No," he said. "No, I wasn't."

Miranda left for headquarters. Morgan planned to walk over to the university and talk with Hubbard and Birbalsingh. He took possession of his wingback again, settled down, and stared into the middle distance.

We wait, he thought. There are cold cases to deal with, and investigative legwork to be done for other teams, but we wait. There is no way to anticipate the killer's next move. Will we even recognize it?

Of course, or he's failed!

It's bound to be different. Perhaps not a theatrical tableau, but if it doesn't evoke the original, his genius is wasted.

To have his bodies remain undiscovered, that would have been failure. So, the sick diorama must have been set up after demolition was approved by the city. But if we're right, spurred on by his success the killer will reach for a cumulative effect. Then he'll have, and we'll have, a pattern.

That's small consolation for the deaths in the offing.

Outside, Morgan surveyed the street. He lived in the heart of the Annex, surrounded by looming Victorian houses and well-kept between-the-wars homes with verandahs. It was well past the middle of April, buds were forming on the huge silver maples along the street, and the occasional willow showed the beginnings of green. Tiny lawns had been raked of winter debris and the pavement was swept clean of the gritty detritus that had accumulated through winter in ridges by the curb. A few crocuses and hyacinths poked upwards in flower-beds, above tulips and daffodils that were secretly breaking out of their chrysalises in the cold earth below. Cars gleamed; in the winter there was no point in keeping them washed. Windows on houses were sparkling clean. Robins squabbled in the air and squirrels raced under cars, over lawns, leapt among branches in desperate games of hide-and-go-seek.

As he walked down to Harbord Street, he conjured with images of Rapa Nui, playing them through his mind against the backdrop of his neighbourhood in the Annex. Cabbagetown had changed. Suburbia was foreign territory. High-rise condos sapped the soul. But in the Annex, Morgan felt comfortable. The smell of barbeques in summer, the grating of snow shovels in winter, the excitement of spring, the slow apprehension of autumn, cars in all seasons parked bumper to bumper — these defined the dimensions of home. At any one point in the year, he was aware of it all.

Sometimes, among the most striking moai buried to the shoulder in ravines below the quarry, great statues leaning forward, gazing over the grasslands of the island toward the Pacific, he felt a vague longing for the more familiar world against which his experience on Rapa Nui was shaped and measured. It was this merging of worlds within that made his adventure exciting and poignant. Travel is about being someplace and being away from someplace at the same time.

The moai that reached the coast were set on platforms called *ahu*, and they would have been given eyes of obsidian on polished coral and faced with their backs to the sea.

In his mind he could still see stone and wood tablets in the marketplace, meticulously etched with the island's Rongorongo script by carvers who could not understand the writings of their ancestors, yet honoured the indecipherable glyphs by their scrupulous reproductions. He could see rich Polynesian complexions and luxuriant long hair, and a few mirroring variations of himself, slathered in sunscreen, shielded under the wonderfully familiar floppiness of an old Tilley hat. He could see the clean streets of Hanga Roa, the bustling village on the southwestern shore where virtually all of the island's population live, and on the streets the occasional car and the horses and dogs and people vying for casual pre-eminence. All this mixed in a mental mélange with his perceptions of Toronto in the promising spring.

He had gone scuba diving while he was there. The young men at their shop in the small harbour had coached him in Spanish, which he did not understand very well, and in Rapa Nui, which he understood not at all. Still, he thought he had learned the basic skills on dry land, and when they took out a couple of New Zealand women who were experienced divers, he went along and the women explained details about clearing his mask and sharing the emergency mouthpiece, so that by the time they all toppled over backward from the boat into the pellucid blue waters within sight of the town, he felt giddy but confident.

The pain in his ears as he descended surprised him. He held his nose and blew, popping the pressure as he had been told, and managed to arrive at the bottom, twenty metres down, with only modest qualms of incipient panic. He had come to rest on a patch of sand. He looked around and the others were hovering a few feet above rocky outcroppings, surrounded by curious fish. He fiddled with his buoyancy vest, shooting up, then dropping, eventually adjusting to zero, then he fluttered gently up and over the coral, forgetting his apprehension, in harmony with the exquisite undersea beauty surrounding him.

He knew nothing of nitrogen narcosis or the bends until he bought a PADI manual in English on the way home, and discovered how perilous such beauties can be. He felt a bit sheepish about being so foolhardy. He would tell Miranda, but later. He suspected he would be low-key about the entire trip. People resent the extravagant experience of people they know, admiring in strangers what they resent in their friends.

Crossing St. George, he entered the university campus proper. The Robarts Library behind him loomed as a warning to anyone seeking refuge among the more intimate quadrangles and passageways that connect the colleges that this was a formidable place. From the air, he had been told, the library had the shape of a phoenix rising. From the ground it was a slumbering leviathan, a hunkering mass of raw concrete and forbidding angles. Inside, it was a marvel of spaces and planes, with form following function like a medieval cathedral, both hiding and yielding its treasures with awesome disregard for human proportion. He was more comfortable on the meandering walkways that led past University Circle to the anthropology labs.

Joleen Chau met him at the door of the building. She recognized him immediately and commented on his tan.

"You are kind," he said, "but it's a layered sunburn."

"Cuba?"

"No." He paused, a little self-conscious. He wondered if he had chosen Rapa Nui for bragging rights. I can't be that superficial, he thought, and responded aggressively, "Easter Island."

"Wonderful," she said. "Wow, are you lucky. I've actually applied for a postdoctoral fellowship to study the moai culture. How does a tiny isolated island mirror historical procedures in the rest of the world where social evolution was virtually contagious? Neat, eh? I need to get out of the library; I want to go and commune with the stone. Try writing that up as a research proposal."

Morgan beamed.

"Of course, I could be wrong," she continued. "The historical parallels might be imposed by outsiders like me. In which case, I publish something on the limits of anthropology, about cultural imperialism and stuff like that."

"We'll compare notes when you get back," said Morgan, realizing immediately how pretentious that must sound, given that he had travelled as a tourist and she was armed with years of research and the analytic instruments of her discipline. "You'll love it there," he said. "It's magic." He could not help himself and went on. "The people are descendents of the moai; the statues and the petroglyphs and the Rongorongo are ancestral."

She grinned. She knew what the word *Rongorongo* meant. "You've been reacting to Thor Heyderdahl," she said.

"Yeah, and a few others."

"We'll talk when I get back. If I go. I really know nothing about the place except as a heritage site. How long were you there?"

"Ten days, plus two each way. Two weeks, altogether. You want to go soon."

"How do you mean?"

"I've met Inuit from Baffin Island who say that every family up there consists of a mother, a father, two kids, and an anthropologist. Right now kids ride horses through the streets of Hanga Roa —"

"Streets?"

"Paved with brick. It's a town. There are even a few taxis. Get there before the invasion, Joleen. Tourists arriving on luxury cruises are bussed around for a few hours of sightseeing; a couple of planeloads of visitors, mostly in transit from Chile to French Polynesia, stop over every couple of days; a handful of backpackers hang out, fired with imagination and a shortage of funds. The rest of the outsiders are academics! They're there, studying the people, the language, the environment, the profusion of artifacts, the impact of tourism, you name it. It won't be innocent for long. The Americans put in a high-grade landing strip a generation ago, in case they needed a rescue base for space shuttles in the empty Pacific. I understand Hawaii offers a summer course there for university credit. Go soon."

"Thank you, Detective Morgan. God and the granting agencies willing, I shall. If you're looking for Professor Birbalsingh, he's working at home. It's exam time and there's a lot of marking to do. I think you might catch Dr. Hubbard in her office at the ROM. She's heading out for her cottage later today. Marking. April is the cruellest month."

"Breeding scholars out of discontent. What about you?"

"I have a teaching fellowship. Lots of marking. And I'm defending my dissertation next week. I've gotta go, but I'll get in touch."

"For sure," he said, and he watched her stride off with daunting determination. As her slim figure disappeared around the corner of a building, he smiled to himself and felt oddly wistful.

Shelagh Hubbard's door was open when he found her office after ambling among the Byzantine pleasures of the museum, each corridor leading to further treasures and delights, from explications of the ordinary to expositions of the wondrously arcane. Past the articulated bones of huge dinosaurs, dioramas of indigenous peoples, displays of early Canadian furniture, gemstones, and core samples, dead creatures in animated poses, the gleanings of empire from China and the Near East, he wandered, gradually closing in on the offices of resident scholars.

She was standing beside her desk, arranging piles of examination booklets and essays in a box.

"From this, you will determine their futures," he said.

"Oh, hello," she responded, turning with a radiant expression as if she had been expecting him. "How are you, Detective? I gather you've been away."

"I'm back on the case."

"That would be the case of the enduring embrace," she declared, as if to establish that there was not another murder that might draw them together. "How are we doing?"

"Well enough, thank you."

The blue of her eyes was intense and her hair was pulled back in a relaxed way so that her high cheekbones seemed softly beguiling. The fluorescent light of her office made her pale blond hair look ethereal. Far from the death's head Miranda had seen in her visage, he found her alluring. She was wearing slacks and a modest sweater set that conflicted playfully with her extravagant figure. She seemed brazen and yet almost demure, an anomaly that Morgan found disconcerting.

"Is there anything you want in particular, Detective Morgan?"

"I've been wondering," he paused. What had he been wondering? "If you've had second thoughts about how easily you and your colleagues were taken in."

"And you, Detective, have you been wondering how you were taken in as well? It was brilliant, wasn't it? They had us completely fooled."

"They?"

"Do we know it was only one person?"

"No, we don't, but it seems likely. Psychopathic depravity isn't a group sport."

"Not when the act is so well accomplished, I suppose. I find it all quite intriguing. Disturbing, of course, but very good drama."

"You've worked with old bodies before."

"Of various vintages, yes. With mummies from ancient Egypt, and mummified bodies in Mexico, and corpses drawn from Scandinavian bogs, and the preserved bodies of saints in sacred crypts. And they all look the same — very dead — and each one is different. Each negotiates the passage of time in its own grisly way. There was no reason to think our lovers were otherwise; they were simply themselves, the story of their deaths determined by their place of discovery. It was our job, in the circumstances, to determine *how* they had come to be as we found them, not *why*. That would be your job, I should think."

"Now. Yes."

"I understand your expert, the tall poet fellow, confirmed the mode of concealment was worthy of his own talents."

"Do you know him?"

"Alexander Pope? By reputation. You must admit, the crime scene was a wondrous creation. Quite omnificent. An expression of extravagant vanity."

Omnificent! he thought, repeating the word to himself. Such a lovely word.

"Vanity, for sure," he said. "It was done for our appreciation."

"You're very solipsistic, Detective. Maybe it was done for private reasons and you, we, are accidental witnesses, incidental to a flawless performance."

"People died."

"Yes, they did. Life, or should we say death, imitates art. But art imitates nature. And nature, Detective, what does it imitate? God's daydreams, I suppose."

Morgan did not want to like her, but she had an interesting mind, and seemed unconcerned about the risks of thinking out loud.

"I appreciate your cooperation," he said.

"Have I been cooperating?"

"I'll keep you posted. We'll crack this."

"You and your partner, Detective Sergeant Quin. Why aren't you a detective sergeant, Detective?"

"I am. If pressed, I can show my credentials."

She was perched against the side of her desk. He was leaning against the wall inside her door. They could have been academic colleagues or old friends.

"I have to go," she said apologetically. "I'm heading up to Georgian Bay for two weeks of wretched solitude."

"Marking?"

"Essays and exams."

"You have a cottage?"

"I have a perfect fieldstone farmhouse in the middle of a rolling field near Owen Sound. Trees along the drive, a classic four-storey barn, a drive shed, and the fresh smell of spring. Otherwise, there's nothing to distract me for miles."

"D'you own the farm, the whole thing?"

"I lease my fields to neighbours, mostly for grazing. When I bought the house, it was a shell. I've restored it over the last few years, from floor joists to roof. It's a project, David, a labour of love. You must come and visit. Please do. Come up on the weekend. Tell me about your vacation. Give me a break from the drudgery. I'll take you to dinner in Collingwood, the Elvis-impersonation capital of Canada, with some of the best restaurants north of Toronto."

As she offered the invitation, she arched slightly, making her breasts rise against her pale blue sweater, and her legs stiffened, accentuating the firmness of her thighs through her slacks. She can't help herself, he thought. Her eyes glistened disingenuously. A cheerfully blatant sexual predator — he had no intention of accepting her invitation.

"I just might," he said.

"Here's my number. I'm easy to find. Do come up, David. Live dangerously."

## chapter seven

# The Georgian Bay

It was late Saturday afternoon when Morgan got away. As Miranda's vintage Jaguar coursed through the Caledon Hills, the long descents forced him to gear down and the car lagged with a gratifying rumble, then roared as he raced up the far sides of the valleys and broke into the clear evening light. It was easy to imagine the city left in darkness behind him. He rushed through the landscape like the sole spectator in a wraparound movie, with the machine an extension of will; an astonishing experience — he almost liked driving. By the time he reached the alluvial terrain sloping down to Georgian Bay, it was night.

Shelagh Hubbard had given him explicit instructions but he pulled over several times onto the shoulder to read the map in the violet glow of the dashboard instruments, not having fathomed the secret of the maplight. He anticipated confusion, even though there were only a few intersections to negotiate along the way and the turnoff from Highway 41 was clearly marked.

Miranda had been wary about lending him the car.

"You know," she had told him, "while you were checking out the voluptuous Dr. Hubbard at the museum, I dug up an ominous bit in her academic files. It seems she once took a course sponsored by the University of London and the British Museum. Morgan, it was on adaptation of old-world building methods to conditions in the settler colonies, namely Canada, Australia, and New Zealand. So guess who taught the hands-on part of the course."

"Alexander Pope."

"The same. He laughed when I called him and said he'd taught dozens of courses over the years, with hundreds of students. We had a nice chat. He asked me to come out again sometime, said to bring you. He's a wonderful source if you want to find more about Canadiana —"

"What a dreadful word, Miranda."

"You use it all the time. So what do you think about your Dr. Hubbard, now?"

"She invited me up to her farm."

"You're kidding! Whereabouts?"

"Near Georgian Bay. She's going for a couple of weeks. We can't just have the OPP pick her up on spec."

"It's their jurisdiction."

"You can hardly arrest someone for taking a course."

"Did she take it as a scholar, do you think, or a necromantic apprentice? Has she finally put her learning to practical use?"

"'A little learning ...' That's Alexander Pope, I believe; the real one."

"Wait until Monday. We'll drive up together."

"Monday?"

"Rachel is taking Jill and me to the Metro Zoo tomorrow."

"Then you won't be needing the Jag."

"You can't resist a dangerous woman."

"If you lend me your car, you'll reap heaven's reward: seventy-seven virginal youths."

"How thoroughly repugnant. Men who dream of virgins make lousy lovers; virginal men are by definition lacking experience, inept."

"So much for that."

"You go, big boy. Don't say I didn't warn you. Just keep your head. On your shoulders. And stay out of closets. And don't sleep with her, Morgan, for God's sake. If she's the killer, you'll feel like an ass — if you survive the experience. And if she's not, you'll feel like an ass, anyway."

"Anything else?"

"Call me if you get scared."

The darkness had turned into a dismal gloom on the back roads, defined only by the merging cones of the Jag's headlights penetrating the mist-laden air. Morgan was relieved when an old-fashioned mailbox appeared with the name *Hubbard* stencilled on the side. The metal flag was raised, which he knew intuitively meant there was mail, so he stopped and picked up an accumulation of letters and fliers, jockeying the car so he did not have to get out. Driving slowly down the long driveway flanked by the shadows of soaring spruce trees, he cringed as sodden clumps of grass scraped against the bottom of the Jag. He pulled up to the front of the house, parking on an angle so the high beams illuminated what turned out to be a splendid stone cottage, not built in the vernacular style of the Georgian Bay area, which tended to be multi-hued granite blocks set with geometric precision. Nor was it like the stone houses of eastern Ontario, he thought, masterfully built by freelancing Scottish masons after they finished work on the Rideau Canal, nor was it fieldstones artfully placed as were the houses of Mennonite farmers that Miranda had shown him in the country around Waterloo County. Much more cement showed. It was almost a rubble construction, and the effect was ominously seductive.

"Welcome to The Georgian Bay," Shelagh Hubbard called from the door. "Park around the side. I'll meet you."

When he stepped into the summer kitchen that stretched across the back of the house, connecting it to a drive shed, she was just coming out, having, he noticed, tightened her hair in the interim. The bare overhead bulb illuminated her features, casting a pallor over her skin and accentuating her cheekbones and the sharply defined line of her jaw. She was dressed casually in slacks and a sweater, wearing makeup.

"My goodness," said Morgan, "you have a beautiful place."

"Thank you."

"Do I get the tour?"

"But of course. We're in the summer kitchen. The ceiling is sagging, but in no danger of immediate collapse. To your left are two doors. The choice is yours: the lady or the tiger. One leads to the shed and the other, the sauna, which is fired up in case we want to relax later on."

There was no mistaking which door led to the sauna. It was made of double layers of heavy tongue-and-groove cedar, reinforced with iron flanges extending from the hinges across it entire breadth, and with a heavy bolt, securely padlocked.

She interpreted his gaze with an explanation. "I'm wary of kids getting in there; you've got to think about things like that when your house is empty a good part of the year. Imagine: if you were racing around back-country trails on a snowmobile in sub-zero weather, the sauna might be an irresistible temptation. They could burn the place down."

"Why not just turn off the power?"

"A lovely idea, David, but it's an old-fashioned wood-burning affair. The stove is underneath, stoked up from outside."

As an inveterate urbanite, such things were beyond his experience. Saunas were something he avoided in gyms. He couldn't imagine going outside in mid-winter to build up a fire so that you could roast yourself in an airless room, then go back out and roll in the snow.

"It would be too dangerous with the fire inside," she explained. "You could turn the room into a raging inferno; or it would suck the air out of your lungs; or create a bone-shattering draft from under the door. Or you'd scald yourself trying to cool the flames."

She seemed to be mocking herself, reciting her litany of possible disasters as if the full range had never before crossed her mind.

"Burn, bake, or broil," she went on. "Steam cook, dry pre-serve, or boil — everything but fricassee or southern fried! It gets hot as Hell in there; it's an oven, after all."

He glanced at the bottom edge of the door. It looked to be a pretty tight seal.

Morgan sniffed the air like a cat trying to determine whether it is the predator or the prey. Shelagh Hubbard leaned against a workbench and watched him, apparently fascinated by his ambivalence.

His mind shifted and, leaning against the bench beside her, he relaxed. He was not used to the sensuous impress of a country place. He could separate the sweet odour of a smoky fire from the dry smells of ancient boards and musty walls that were stuffed with horsehair and dust, and the organic smells of linoleum ground through with dirt from the fields and the barn, smells of leather cracked with age, of horse collars and harnesses hanging from pegs against the stone wall. The visual scene was as rich. A couple of bicycles leaned at the end of the bench in casual clutter, an older one supporting the weight of a sporty all-terrain model. By the outer wall, between the shed door and the sauna, a derelict sideboard — with layers of original paint showing through in a medley of blues and greens — held a motley array of old bottles, canisters, and arcane culinary instruments, including a potato peeler and a small glass butter churn. Dusted off and placed on display in a shop on Avenue Road, all this would be worth a small fortune. On the floor was a hooked rug in such disrepair as to be of indeterminate design, yet strangely enough it was clean. There were several pairs of rubber boots and workboots in various stages of decomposition beside a new pair of cross-country Solomon ski boots. In the corner, by the door he had come in, a twenty-two calibre single-shot rifle leaned casually against the wall.

"There's no bolt in it," she said.

"What?"

"The gun. I keep the bolt with the cutlery and the bullets by my bed."

"Why?"

"Strategic disarray — it's a psychological prop. I would not enjoy shooting someone."

"Really?"

"Too abrupt. With a bang, everything changes. There's no time to consider the consequences. Guns are for stupid people, present company excepted. Are you carrying a gun?"

"No."

"Good."

"Do you hunt?"

"It's only a twenty-two. For varmints, really."

"Varmints?"

"Rats, I suppose, but I've never even seen a rat — the barn's been abandoned for years. Come on, let's get something warm into you. We may be in for some weather tonight so I've cooked dinner. I figured we'd eat here."

Morgan was astonished by the work in progress. The kitchen had been completely done over to create an ambiance that honoured the past while acknowledging the present. Major appliances were new, sheathed in stainless steel, and a pantry wall was staffed with all sorts of food processors and culinary paraphernalia. But the walls were antiqued plaster and the woodwork had been lovingly restored. Wood and plaster were painted in deep colours of the early Victorian era, before garish hues and wallpaper came into vogue. Beyond the kitchen, the central front hall was in a state of suspended endeavour, with a stepladder still in place and tools on the floor.

"Now you see why I admired the handiwork at your Hogg's Hollow crime scene," she said, gesturing with a sweep of her arm. "I'm doing this myself. It's slow-going, but it's coming along. Looks pretty good, eh?"

He felt a chill as he surveyed her work. Was she taunting him? Why would a person capable of devising horrors with pathological precision now run the risk of exposure, simply to show off her talent in a far more conventional context? Unless that was the point; unless she felt certain she would not be caught, and got a thrill from being under suspicion. A dangerous game, he thought.

Despite her protestations that dinner would be made up from a few odd things lying around, as she hadn't had the opportunity to get into Meaford to shop, the meal was sumptuous. She had fresh romaine in the fridge and made up a delicate dressing of olive oil, mint, garlic vinegar, a dash of maple syrup, salt, and a grinding of pepper. While she fired up the electric grill and got the vegetables on, she sent Morgan out to retrieve a bottle of Brunello di Montalcino from the sideboard in the summer kitchen, which, while she was in residence, remained above freezing but a little too cold for

Brunello, he thought. She asked him to bring in a package of lamb chops from the large chest-freezer in the drive shed. The freezer, Morgan observed, had been recently defrosted and immaculately cleaned. It was almost empty.

During dinner they chatted amiably. He told her about Easter Island and she talked about her project in the nearby Midland area, where she intended to dig in the coming summer if her grant came through. Digging up saints, she explained.

"Seriously, I'm on the trail of the bones of the Jesuit martyrs."

"I thought they were burned at the stake."

"Cooked; then the flesh was stripped from their bones. But their bones, Morgan, their bones were strong medicine. The Black Robes died with extreme valour, and so their bones were venerable artifacts for the Hurons who killed them — my theory is that they were treated like holy relics in the Middle Ages. At first I thought bits and pieces might be found among medicine bundles. Now I suspect their bones were gathered together at some point and buried in a sacred place."

"What an astonishing irony," said Morgan. "Like King Henry sanctioning Becket's sainthood after commanding his execution."

His allusion seemed of no interest. He shrugged as they got up and moved closer to the fire. He had grave doubts about this strange woman, which she seemed to cultivate, and her project sounded far-fetched. Research proposals were peer reviewed, of course, although perhaps her peers were equally delusional.

"So, how do you get permission to dig up a sacred aboriginal site and/or the grave of a saint?"

"You have the good fortune of being able to trace the bones to unsanctified ground on the edge of a farmer's field."

"You've done that?" he asked, a little incredulous.

"No," she said, as she tilted a decanter of port and poured them each a good portion. "Not exactly. I have been shown a place where there is a stone cairn and what might be a burial mound, on land that may once have been a Huron settlement. The native residents have long since disappeared, pushed out by successive waves of Iroquois, French, and then settler invaders, none of whom were interested in a hallowed sight of the vanquished. I'm playing on more than a hunch, though. By reading Jesuit texts, reading the lay of the land — it would have been a perfect setting for one of the Huron people's moveable villages, a pocket of good earth for agriculture, the stonework appears to be Huron — everything led me to think the farmer who owned it, who called me out of the blue, was on to something. He knew about the mound all his life but waited until he got old before risking anything that might interfere with working the land. Unfortunately for him, he waited too long. He died. But the new absentee owners from Toronto don't mind me prowling about. In fact, they're quite pleased, and they don't even know what I suspect is interred in the mound, only that they are, as we say, stewards of our archaeological heritage."

Shelagh Hubbard was an odd anomaly. As she leaned toward him over the table, gesticulating with her wine glass, the candle flames caught in her eyes and flickered. Morgan was drawn to her and repelled, and she seemed amused by his ambivalence.

"This is my sanctuary, Morgan. My sanctum sanctorum, where anything seems possible and all is forgiven."

Planes of firelight gleamed on the walls, the fire burned bright and clean, the air shimmered with a timeless warmth. It had never before occurred to him how different light must have been as a medium before electricity. The air had dimension, the eyes were not passive receptacles but reached out to connect. He felt comfortably removed from the familiar world.

"It's hard not to like it here," she observed. "I'm glad you came, whatever your reasons."

He glanced at her and away, looking into the heart of the fire.

"It's always interesting," she said. "The Georgian Bay is filled with enticements. And secrets, as well."

She was taunting him.

"Why do you call it 'The'?"

"Playful pretension. The nouveau riche who buy up those rambling old cottages in Muskoka say 'The Muskokas.' It's parody — just a bit of fun."

Either this was a profound revelation of character or as trivial an affectation as the one she was mocking.

"Tell me about your wife," she asked, reaching across to replenish the blood-red port in his glass.

He could hear Miranda warning him. When they start offering consolation for your love life, Morgan, you know you're in trouble. He gazed into the flickering fire in her eyes and sat back in his chair.

"You've been wounded, David. Invisible wounds leave invisible scars, but they're there to the touch."

She tilted her head slightly. She was so obvious, and yet emotional need overrode sense and he felt himself opening to her. Perhaps because he suspected her guilty of unspeakable crimes, he was drawn to self-revelation. Embraced by the profound amorality of a psychopath — the perfect conditions to exorcise demons. An absolute absence of judgment seemed dangerously seductive.

"We were deeply in love," he said, "but not with each other. We loved an idea of what the other could be. It didn't last long."

Shelagh Hubbard swirled her port and raised it high to observe his image distorted through the crimson depths of her glass.

"Six weeks after we were married ...," he paused. This was something he had talked about to no one. "Six weeks, and she went back to her former boyfriend. Just for a weekend. She came home, told me where she had been, said she loved me, said she had to be sure. The absurd thing is, I knew all weekend where she was, what she was doing. We were supposed to meet for dinner on Friday at the corner of Yonge and Queen. Six o'clock. I waited for her in the drenching rain. I waited until ten o'clock. I was twenty-four years old. I knew where she was. I went home.

"She thought I could be a better version of him; he was a bit stupid and psychologically abusive and struck me as sleazy, the one time we met. But he understood her in ways I couldn't. He played on her weaknesses and I played to her strengths. Inevitably the game went to him."

"Was it a game?"

"Yeah, for her it was. Not a party game, more like medieval jousting. Tears of anguish, histrionic emotions, malevolent acts, and melodramatic confessions. And of course I wasn't him. It sunk in, eventually. I wasn't even a very good version of myself."

"And what about her? What did you want her to be?"

She got up and put a hand on his arm, giving it a lingering squeeze, then stirred the embers and added a couple of split maple logs, returned to her chair, and leaned forward into the candlelight.

She was drawing him out, like a succubus ingesting his soul. There was something sexually charged about her silence that made him afraid not of her but himself.

"At that point in my life, I wasn't after a mirror opposite, but the mirror itself. No matter how I held it, I wanted to see me. I hadn't learned yet to be alone."

"And have you now?"

"Yes, I have."

"You and Detective Quin are very close."

"Yes."

"But she's not like you at all."

"No."

"And you like that — you both do."

"We're good to each other. My marriage, brief as it was, was brutal and bitter. I learned that being alone is a primal condition of being. I'm okay with that."

"How sad."

"Not really."

"You retreat into esoteric allusions and arcane pursuits, with a friend too close to be a lover."

"Hardly makes me a figure of pathos."

"But rather restricting. A good relationship can change your life without changing who you are." She paused, as if trying to determine the truth of her own statement. "Do we have a good relationship, David?"

He did not answer. A woman quite possibly guilty of the most grisly of murders, of being a psychopath, was giving him advice. And he was listening.

"Let's have that sauna," she said. "You'll find towels in your room, top of the stairs to the right. It's the only room upstairs that's finished."

He wondered if it had a lock on the door. It did not.

When he came down, she was already in the kitchen cleaning up, wrapped in a large towel. He remembered when women wore slips, when Lucy used to walk around with a half-slip pulled up over her breasts, like a micro-mini just skimming her bottom. He felt a familiar surge and tugged at the towel draped over his shoulders and adjusted the other one wrapped tightly around his waist.

The room was warm from the fire and they did the dishes together without talking, except to get the job done.

When they went out into the damp chill of the summer kitchen, Shelagh excused herself for a moment and disappeared in the darkness to stoke up the fire, which must have been started in the afternoon, then returned and unbolted the sauna door. It was a larger room than Morgan had expected, with two benches banked along one side long enough to stretch out on and a single bench along the back wall holding a wooden bucket, half-filled with water, and a bundle of birch switches. There was an iron grate in the floor where water could be thrown directly onto the stove-top below. The sweet meaty smell of smoke-dried cedar was intense. As they entered, it was like passing through a wall of heat into another dimension.

Shelagh scooped water out of the bucket and drizzled it through the grate. Clouds of steam surged upward and transformed into waves of dry heat. She climbed onto the upper bench and Morgan joined her. She undid her towel and let it fall away, being careful to keep it under her to avoid scalding against the wood. He dropped the towel around his shoulders onto the bench and loosened the one around his waist. For a short time, his skin felt radiant and dry, then his pores opened and quite suddenly he was covered with beads of sweat that gathered and descended in random streamlets, tickling as they chose the courses of least resistance down his sides and over his stomach, some of them pooling in the depression between his thighs, which were clenched in an autonomic gesture of modesty, his penis tucked between in shy denial of the tumescence that threatened when he had first seen Shelagh towel-wrapped in the kitchen.

Following what he assumed was sauna protocol, Morgan avoided looking sideways in Shelagh's direction, but as perspiration began to gather between her legs she relaxed her own posture, her towel settled to the side, and he could not avoid observing the shadowy promise as she spread her legs comfortably apart, the soft voluptuous contours of her vulva enhanced by a thin tangle of damp curly hair. He glanced down at himself; shrivelled in the heat to a mushroom, embedded in a wiry cluster of wet moss.

Unused to the extremes of a sauna, Morgan was disconcerted by the contradictory responses of his body. He felt intensely aroused, almost to the point of climax, and yet the instrument by which he normally measured such things had been rendered inoperative. For an instant, the memory flashed through his mind of his first and most troubling orgasm, when he was about seven years old and had had to pee desperately, but lay back under the covers because the sensation of holding back sent exquisite shivers coursing through his entire body, until finally he squeezed his penis between his fingers to restrain from wetting the bed, and suddenly his body and mind convulsed, and almost immediately he had to run to the bathroom, still pinching the end of his penis to stop the pee from flooding out. He had been so frightened by the experience, for the next year he would stand beside the toilet and practice peeing without touching himself. By the time he was nine, he discovered the delirious thrill was a separable experience from urination. Thus began an odyssey of self-gratification that carried him through adolescence in seemingly infinite expressions of self-loathing ecstasy.

He shifted away from her and she immediately responded by swinging gently around to face him, raising her legs and pushing against him to wriggle and slide across the towel until she could lean with her back against the wall, which she did after placing his second towel between her flesh and the searing wood.

The light was muted red from a coloured bulb recessed in the ceiling and, while much of the illumination was absorbed in the rough-cut cedar surrounding them, a residue gleamed radiantly on their sweat-drenched skin.

Morgan was not normally shy — he was comfortable with his own body, but Shelagh Hubbard was a different experience. As he turned slightly toward her, he recognized the strange feeling within as a blend of sexual and intellectual excitement tinged with unmistakable fear. For the first time since entering the sauna he looked at her eyes. Her lids were draped down as if she were snoozing. He surveyed her body, touching her breasts with his gaze. They were large and voluptuous rather than pendulous, with high-set nipples. Her stomach was tight with a slight ridge of muscle. He looked up at her eyes again, still closed, then down between her legs, into the folds of glistening and textured shadow. Despite his experience with women, he was perusing unfamiliar terrain. He swallowed, aware of the moisture pooling inside his mouth, felt himself falling inside his own body, motionless but yearning immersion, the breath coming hard through his nostrils. He glanced up and saw that she was staring at him, her eyes wide open, watching his secrets revealed.

She smiled.

He looked down at himself. She lowered her gaze, continuing to smile. Yet, strangely, she seemed more amused than wary or beguiled. For an instant, he felt like the little boy, caught in his precocious act of pre-sexuality, uncertain what response was required.

"You have a tattoo, Morgan. I'm surprised."

Her apparent intention was to deflect from the sexual, yet in acknowledging his body as an object of observation she heightened his awareness of their both being naked. She seemed absolutely relaxed in the red glow, sweat defining the shape and texture of her flesh, her legs casually apart, arms resting at her sides.

"I wouldn't have thought you would. Anthropologically speaking, you don't fit the profile."

"That's probably why I got it," he said, for the briefest moment bemused by the reference to profiling. "It's a Rapa Nui design."

"Really? Let me see." In a dark swooping motion she stood and settled close beside him. She clutched his shoulder and twisted him toward the light. Her breasts pressed against him as she drew him forward. He shuddered involuntarily. She seemed comfortable, resting against him so solidly they seemed in the heat to merge where they touched.

"It's a bird-man," she said.

"*Tangata manu*," he clarified. Then he added, "It's not cultural appropriation, it's a tribute."

"To whom? Ah, Morgan, you're such a sweet rebel."

She leaned into him, letting her hand slide over his body and fall onto his lap. Her fingers curled around his penis, briefly holding it like a fallen bird cupped in her hand.

"The little fellow is confused," she said, giving a gentle squeeze and pulling it longer, then tucking it back.

Then, as quickly as she had descended on him, she withdrew.

Standing up, she reached for the ladle in the bucket and poured another splash of water on the stove through the grate.

"Are you okay?" she asked. "I'm just running in for a pee. You don't want to stay in too long. You might shrivel up and never recover."

She was out the door with it shut tightly behind her before Morgan had recovered from their close encounter, which had left him short of breath and oddly deflated.

Had she bolted the door? he wondered, trying to summon the sounds of the heavy door closing. He did not move,
transfixed by the possibility.

He listened, immobilized by his astonishment at the
absurdity of his predicament. He could hear the crackle of
the fire underneath the floor. He felt parched. His throat constricted and his eyes clouded painfully. If the door was locked,
the process of his mummification had already begun.

Morgan realized he was light-headed — he had been
in for too long. He rose to his feet but his balance was off
and he lurched back onto the lower bench, feeling the wood
sear against his buttocks. The second time, he stood up more
slowly, wiping the sweat from his eyes, and reached for the
wood handle of the door. He pulled on the handle but it
resisted. He heard a gut-wrenching slash of sound as iron bars
slid against iron.

Suddenly, the door came alive against his hand and for
a moment there was a tug of opposing forces. Then it swung
outwards into the summer kitchen and there stood Shelagh
Hubbard, wrapped demurely in her towel, which was tucked
neatly in a fold over her breasts.

"It's about time you came out of there," she said. "For a
man with a medium-rare complexion, I'd say you look overly
cooked."

"Shall we roll in the snow?" The bravado in Morgan's proposal betrayed his relief at evading death and, equally, avoiding making an utter fool of himself.

"There isn't any," she said. "Let's run naked under the stars."

## chapter eight

## Countryside

"You didn't!" Miranda exclaimed. "I thought you could take care of yourself! What if ... What would have happened to my car? Mired at the bottom of a pond beside Norman Bates's motel. With your head in the boot. My God, Morgan, how could you?"

"We say 'trunk' in these parts — those of us who don't own vintage Jaguars."

"Trunk is what would be left of your body after your paramour finished with it. The defective detective. What were you thinking? It's obvious what you were thinking *with*!"

He grinned across the table at her. They were meeting for a coffee and Danish at Starbucks expressly so Morgan could fill her in on what he'd discovered during his unorthodox investigation of their principal suspect. He felt sheepish about admitting he had momentarily panicked in the sauna, yet it was a necessary prelude to confessing his ultimate innocence. First, he would allow himself to appear compromised, then admit to having further avoided her charms.

"So, you're trying to tell me you didn't sleep with her. What do I care, Morgan? You probably missed a golden opportunity, if you were up for it." He exuded a boyish good cheer that irritated her immensely. "If you did sleep with her, I would imagine the conquest was hers, and if you did not, that was probably her doing as well. So tell me, were you good together? Either way, who cares?"

The odd thing to Morgan was that it had never come up as an issue, whether or not he and Shelagh Hubbard would be lovers. After running around like adolescents on the soggy lawn, leaving dreadful footprints to be rolled out later in the season, they had briefly returned to the sauna to warm up, then separately showered in the bathroom off the kitchen where they returned to dry un-self-consciously and make hot drinks of cocoa that they sipped in front of the dying fire. She rose first, leaned down, kissed him on the forehead, and retired to her ground-floor bedroom. After a few minutes, lingering to watch the embers fade and fall, glowing gold and vermillion, he had gone upstairs and crawled under the duvet where he slept soundly and wakened in the early light, feeling completely relaxed. He had not bothered to lock the bedroom door.

Miranda didn't know whether to believe him or not. "You're a bit of a whore, you know. Was it worth the effort?"

"Is it ever, Miranda?"

"It all sounds quite adolescent," she said, and could not stop from reinforcing her previous disclaimer, "I don't care what you did."

"Good," he said. "Then it's settled."

"Yes it is."

"And what about you? Did you have a good weekend?"

"Yes."

"At the zoo?"

"And otherwise."

"Now, what does that mean?"

"It means I might have been whoring, myself."

"Not likely."

"You're sweet, Morgan."

"But foolish?"

"Yes."

"Well, I don't think she did it — that's my judgment after two days of foolishness." They ordered more coffee and proceeded to sort through the facts and hypotheses. "There's no pattern," he said

"Not yet. The pattern will become clear when she does it again."

"Don't hold your breath. One funny thing she said —"

"Only one?"

"She made a point of telling me she had never been abused as a child."

"What an odd thing to confess."

"Yeah, over breakfast, she asked about my growing up, but it felt like an excuse to talk about herself, then she explained she'd never been abused, assaulted, molested, or in any way damaged, that she had had a thoroughly ordinary upbringing, absolutely average, absurdly normal."

"Now, why would she want you to know all that?"

"Establishing her credentials as a psychopath manqué."

"What the hell does that mean, Morgan?"

"A failure."

"As a psychopath?"

"Perhaps a declaration that there is nothing in her background that would drive her to murder." He paused for effect. "Or possibly the dead opposite — something more sinister: a declaration that she takes full responsibility for what she's been doing."

"You'd rather it wasn't her."

"I'd rather it wasn't her."

"She's not a nice person, Morgan. Sometimes I worry about you. Do you really think she's innocent?"

"*An* innocent, no. Innocent? Possibly."

"I have my doubts."

"Yeah, me too."

"Grave doubts, Morgan."

"You're on shaky ground, you know. Guilt isn't generally determined by personal animosity."

"Nor innocence by affection. It seems to me you were the one on shaky ground."

"You cannot convict someone for having a sauna," he said.

"Not at all. I've had a few myself."

"No, no, I mean *owning* a sauna. This is not about you."

"But it is, perhaps, about you, since you managed to insinuate yourself into the middle of things, so to speak."

"I mean, she has a sauna, so does Alexander Pope. That doesn't make them killers."

"Morgan, I survived my sauna at Pope's with virtue intact. Rachel and Alexander and I did not compromise anything beyond the limits of modesty. Your friend's sauna could easily be an oven for the mummification of human remains, even a chamber of execution. And she does own a coffin-sized freezer and she does live in an isolated farmhouse and she does have the requisite talents and arcane knowledge."

"Circumstantial. Half her neighbours could be accused of the same. All those Torontonians with country retreats."

"But not the professional training, nor the warped personality. There's no such thing as a normal, average, ordinary childhood, Morgan."

No, he agreed, there is not. He said nothing.

"Look," she said. "We could send in forensics, but I doubt we'd find much at the abattoir. She'll have cleaned up perfectly. It's a matter of aesthetics."

"Maybe she's just a normal forensic anthropologist. You know, an intellectual more at ease with the dead than the living."

"A vampire with very big breasts."

"I found her charming. Gracious, intelligent, sensitive, good-humoured. Any of those sound familiar?"

"Morgan, she's fucked with your mind."

"What a nasty expression. She charmed my mind. I would much rather think she is innocent."

"The last thing that woman is, is innocent."

Miranda spent the rest of Monday and most of Tuesday going over the accumulated file, looking for missed connections and anomalies. She had been dividing her time over the past couple of weeks, working on other cases that were not in her portfolio, doing background for detectives more directly involved. She responded to inquiries from outside their jurisdiction — one from the FBI and a couple from Scotland Yard. She spent time off duty looking into private schools for girls. The housekeeper who looked after Jill was returning to be with her children in Barbados before they completely grew up. She had dinner with Rachel a couple of times and neither of them mentioned their intimate encounter, although they were comfortably affectionate in each other's company. She called Alexander Pope from police headquarters to ask him esoteric questions about plaster and paint and the conceal-ment of bodies, and stayed on the phone for over an hour, chatting about his latest reclamation project — the restora-tion of an infamous abandoned church north of Toronto as a museum of some sort, or a gallery. She dropped in on Ellen Ravenscroft at the morgue and they chatted amiably, but she found little had been revealed in the tissue tests they had run; the causes of death were still deemed extreme dehydration and asphyxia, but whether from a singular cause or a sustained condition was indeterminate.

She was annoyed with her partner. He knew it and stayed out of her way. After they'd left Starbucks on Monday, he had walked with her over to headquarters, but remained outside. She disappeared into the planes of glass and pink granite, while he stood on the sidewalk, admiring the postmodern architecture of the massive edifice, acknowledging to himself the possibility that the austere obscenities of modernism were at last giving way. A police building with a stream flowing from its centre was a blow for imagination and form over function. He spent the rest of the day walking.

Tuesday he got up early, had breakfast out, and walked some more. He was looking for something and it was locked inside. Wednesday morning he called Miranda. She was already at her desk.

"You busy?" he asked.

"No. Are you coming in?"

"Meet me for lunch?"

"Sure. You name the spot. Rufalo was asking what we were up to. He didn't come right out and say, 'Where's Morgan?' but he wanted to know."

"He's trying to get his mind off personal problems."

"His or yours, Morgan?"

"Must be his. Did you tell him I'm out here doggin' some leads?"

"Something like that. I told him you were hard at work, that something would break pretty soon."

"I hope not another murder tableau."

"Have you heard from your friend?"

The silence on the other end of the line declared his

unease. She was not sure if it was with her or with himself. He had obviously moved on from infatuation. She would find out soon enough which way. They agreed to meet at the nondescript little Italian restaurant where she and Rachel had dined two weeks before.

Morgan found himself standing on the corner of Queen and Yonge. He leaned against an opaque glass wall. This was exactly where he had waited for his wife, nearly two decades ago, sheltering from the rain in the lee of the building, waiting motionless, four hours, knowing where she was, not knowing why she wouldn't come, raindrops sliding down his cheeks into the corners of his mouth, salty, like tears.

Shelagh Hubbard was Lucy. In the middle of the night, last night, Morgan was startled from sleep by the shock of a recognition that had eluded him while awake. They looked nothing alike, but they were one and the same. The forensic anthropologist and his former wife. If Lucy had aged at half the rate he did, a preternatural possibility given her facile personality, she and Shelagh could be twins under the skin. One was full-figured with a head like death as a temptress; the other had the slender and sinuous body of a classical ballerina destined by demeanour always to play roles of betrayal and loss. Both could be ravishingly attractive and, with a shift in the light, a change of attitude, beautifully grotesque. They both embodied ambivalence, playing affection against anger, emotional austerity against blatant sexuality, sympathy against strength. Each was a siren to Morgan's unfettered Ulysses.

All morning he wondered about the siren's call. Was it the sound of his own weakness tolling in the chambers of his heart, or was it truly seduction, the melodic ululation of his heart's desire? By the time he reached the restaurant, walking up Yonge Street, he was convinced that regret was a waste, that he had not stuffed up his ears but had listened, first to one, then the other. Their songs were the same. Surely, he thought, it's better to wrestle with demons and sleep with the devil than not.

His line of reasoning, such as it was, collapsed when he saw Miranda sitting at a back table, patiently waiting. She smiled receptively. As he leaned down to her, she reached forward and with the back of her hand brushed gently against his cheek. He was startled for a moment, until she blew him a pouting kiss, and he decided he was forgiven. He would not tell her about the connection, the siren. He suspected she would understand. Instead, they would have lunch, talk about antiques and things. Maybe he would tell her about his tattoo, although it was unlikely.

Thursday; they met in front of Professor Birbalsingh's office. The professor had pretty much lost interest when the bodies were declared modern. Postmodern, in fact, he had quipped. "It is not a question of contemporaneity," he explained to Miranda when she had dropped in to interview him on her own while Morgan was away. "They are, of course, recently deceased. I am saying we would have discovered that, although perhaps not for a few more hours. A science like ours works incrementally, you know, building one small observation upon another and another, until sometimes we have constructed a dinosaur, Miss Quin, from an elephant's remains. But eventually, the elephant will out, so to speak, declaring its trunk not a tail, despite our scientific efforts to the contrary."

"Postmodern?" she had said.

"Indeed, Miss Quin."

"Detective."

"Detective Quin. I am sorry. Titles are so very important in my line of work and I am assuming in yours also."

"They can be, yes."

"Well, I am saying 'postmodern' because it strikes me as a crime that breaks all the rules. You know it is a nasty murder but you feel it is an estimable achievement, nonetheless. In spite of your capacity for empathy with the victims you admire the artistry of their rather hideous demise. You know, it was a scene of undoubted melodrama and of comic absurdity, but certainly presaged by tragedy, devised for ironic effect. All very academic, in fact. Four modes in one. My late esteemed colleague, Professor Northrop Frye, would have been very much pleased. Perhaps 'pleased' is not the most appropriate word."

"So," Miranda had said, fascinated by his convoluted assessment. "Our killer is an academic?"

"Dear me," he responded, "I should say so, but that would perhaps be presumptuous. Not a university person, in the strictest sense, perhaps. No, quite unlikely. The university life does not leave room for such a flourish of imagination, I am afraid. Too many committees and subcommittees and granting agencies with juries. A project like this would die in the seminal stages." He paused, raised his stentorian eyebrows, and added, "As, of course, it should."

It had occurred to Miranda as he had been talking that Dr. Shelagh Hubbard fit the description. She had the academic credentials to be an adjunct professor, but she was employed outside the university, doing most of her work through the ROM. It was following this conversation that Miranda ran a close check on Birbalsingh's associate and came up with her connection to Alexander Pope, studying methods of domestic construction in British colonial times. Otherwise, the woman's curriculum vitae read like an academic prototype, and her personal dossier suggested life was a subsidiary activity to scholarly pursuits.

She liked Professor Birbalsingh and was happy to come along when Morgan suggested they interview him again, even though Morgan did not seem to have particular questions in mind.

When the professor opened his door, he seemed relieved at their presence.

"I was going to call you," he said. "Come in, come in. Be seated." He had a pair of comfortable leather chairs in his cramped office, both of them piled with books that he distributed among a clutter of papers and other books on the floor. "Now then," he said, sitting down behind his desk in a chair strategically placed in front of a narrow window to cast a luminous glow around him while obscuring his features in shadow. "I am happy to have you here. I was wondering if you might be hearing from Dr. Hubbard."

Good grief, thought Miranda, was word already out about the sauna? Has Morgan offended academic protocol? Are the university authorities holding him responsible for her whereabouts?

Morgan responded, "No, I dropped in to see her last weekend at her farm. She was marking papers and exams. Is there a problem?"

"There is. She was expected back yesterday noon."

"And she's late by a day," said Miranda. "Did you call her?"

"Oh, yes, I did, but there was no answer."

"And is that a grave problem?" she said.

"Yes, very grave."

"How so?" asked Morgan.

"Well, you see, she was expected to speak to the tenure committee yesterday at four o'clock."

"And it was a bad thing to miss her appointment?" Miranda posed this as a question but the answer was obvious.

"Yes, very bad. She was being considered for tenure and there were questions to be asked about her publication record."

"Is that standard procedure?" asked Morgan.

Professor Birbalsingh leaned forward over his desk so that his facial features emerged into the light of the room. "It can be," he said. "Especially if there are ambiguities."

"Such as?"

"Just ambiguities. The committee wanted clarification."

"About what?" said Miranda. "I've read her CV. It's impressive."

"Perhaps that is the problem, Miss Quin — Detective."

"I know she was waiting to hear about a grant proposal," said Morgan. "She told me about a Shirk application —"

"Shirk," said Miranda. "SSHRC. Social Sciences and Humanities Research Council." She was quite pleased with herself. Usually it was Morgan who had access to the obscure meanings of acronyms and abbreviations.

"I was not aware of such an application," said Professor Birbalsingh. "Even if she applied through the ROM, it would have gone by me. No, I do not think she applied this year for funding of any sort."

Morgan was perplexed. He described her research project. Professor Birbalsingh reacted with mounting astonishment.

"I do not think it likely, Mr. Morgan — I am sorry, *Detective* Morgan. Perhaps you would prefer to call me Iqbal. But no, we will let such an opportunity pass. What Dr. Hubbard told you seems a rather quixotic venture. I doubt very much there would be money or interest to sustain such a project. There is not much of a market for saints in Ontario. Perhaps in Quebec, though I doubt it. And it all seems very conjectural. I suspect she was spinning a fantasy. Such are the ruminations of the forensic anthropologist."

"But she has, perhaps, spun a few others in her pursuit of tenure?" Miranda found Shelagh Hubbard's predicament mildly amusing.

"No, not exactly. But as I am her sponsor, so to speak, having encouraged her cross-appointment with the museum, I am dismayed by her failure to appear before the committee."

"Did you call the police?" asked Morgan.

"I was about to when you arrived, unsummoned."

"You'd have to call the OPP. It's provincial jurisdiction."

"Morgan, it's only been a day. She could have been out for a walk when Professor Birbalsingh called, or in the bath, or simply not answering the phone. Try again, Professor. Let's give it another day. You call us tomorrow, if she hasn't turned up. We'll look into it. I wouldn't worry. I'm sure Dr. Hubbard is in her own capable hands. She'll look after herself."

"Was there something else that brought you all this way to my office, or was it a social call?"

If there had been a purpose, Morgan seemed to have forgotten. He turned to Miranda. She shrugged amiably.

Professor Birbalsingh nodded gravely and rose to his feet, indicating their interview was over. "Then I am sorry for your wasted time. I am afraid I must say goodbye," he said, shaking both their hands.

In the corridor, after they heard the lock click, Morgan and Miranda exchanged knowing glances. There was something endearing about a man so much the caricature of an academic. They walked out into the sunlight of University Circle and, immediately, each was taken up with a medley of personal memories from when this had been the centre of their separate worlds.

When Professor Birbalsingh's call was relayed to Miranda early Friday morning, she told him they would look after it and she called Morgan.

"You know, I think we should take a run up there," Morgan said.

"It's OPP jurisdiction."

"Exactly my point. I'd like to get there first, have you look over the place before they get involved."

"We're not breaking in, Morgan. If we get there and no one's around, we call the Provincials."

"Oh, for sure," he said. "Want to meet for breakfast?"

"I've got to go into the office. I'll pick up a car and be over in an hour."

Morgan showered and got dressed, then decided he might as well cook up breakfast for both of them. He put a frying pan on to heat and broke eggs into a bowl, ready to scramble as soon as she pulled up in front; put the coffee on; took six pieces of back bacon out of the freezer which he carefully pried apart with a bread knife and put on to fry — this was double his weekly allotment; he was feeling magnanimous. By the time Miranda came in, toast and juice were on the table, coffee aroma filled the air, the eggs were cooking, and there were four pieces of cooked bacon left, to be split between them.

"You have something on your lip," she said when she sat down. "Bit of bacon? Are these four mine, then?"

"I was just testing."

"The point of hoarding a commodity is not to enhance consumption but to control distribution."

"Sounds like Economics 101."

"Not the bacon, dear, I was thinking about murder. Did she deep-freeze her victim while she figured out what to do with him? Or did she know from the beginning and was just using the freezer for storage until the right woman came along to complete the coupling she had always intended?"

"All that because I snuck a bite of my own bacon? You can't say 'she,' for sure. We're a long way from having a case."

"Ring ring," she said.

"Did you say 'ring ring'?"

"I did. It's my vibrator," she said, reaching for the cell-phone on her belt.

"That's an odd place to keep a vibrator."

She gave him a mock smile and he mumbled to himself, "ring ring."

"Hello, Quin here."

"Detective Quin," said the voice in the phone. "Singh, here — Owen Sound Police. I have had insistent calls from a Professor Birbalsingh — several calls. He gave me your name. They've patched me through from your office."

"Yes?"

"Do you know Professor Birbalsingh?"

"Yes, Officer Singh, I do. I assume this is about Shelagh Hubbard."

"He apparently called the OPP to report her missing."

"I gave him their detachment number."

"I gather they explained that since she's a part-time resident, it would not be unusual for her to be away. It struck them as most likely Miss Hubbard had simply left for Toronto or elsewhere. He was most upset. He called us, as the nearest municipal police. I called the OPP myself and they sent a car out at my request."

"And what did they find?"

"Nothing. Everything appeared normal. No evidence of forced entry. They felt they had neither just cause nor author-ity to pursue the matter."

"I appreciate you letting me know, Officer, but where are we going with this?"

"Professor Birbalsingh was insistent. He said you would confirm that a most serious problem was happening."

"My partner and I are involved in a murder investigation. We would like to question Dr. Hubbard —"

"She is a doctor? I did not know that. We need more

doctors up here. Shall I drive out and look around? Unofficially, of course."

"That is very kind, Officer Singh. But no, my partner and I will drop in and check things out. If there's anything irregular, we'll let you know."

"Thank you, Detective. Is Dr. Hubbard a murder suspect? Is she a specialist?"

"She's a Ph.D. in forensic anthropology, and no, she is not a suspect, as far as Professor Birbalsingh is concerned."

"I take your meaning, Detective Quin. If he calls back, I will be most discreet."

"Thank you, Officer. I'll keep you informed." She snapped the cellphone shut.

"So, it's on vibrator mode, is it?"

"Resist the double entendres, Morgan. The word 'vibrator' is not inherently comical."

"I take it my friend is still missing. Do you want that piece of bacon?"

"I do," she said, snatching it out from under his swooping hand and popping it whole into her mouth. "Arghixtphtuftisdngtoo."

"Is that anything like 'ring ring'? Mustn't talk with your mouth full."

"Fktfu."

"You too."

When they turned in at the mailbox that starkly proclaimed Hubbard the resident, Miranda was surprised by the austere beauty of the scene. The landscape was rougher than the rolling hills of Waterloo County. The fields surrounding the house sloped in irregular planes this way and that, drifting downward from the high hills of the meandering escarpment to the southwest, while in front of the house they seemed poised, gathering momentum for an eventual rush to the Georgian Bay shore. Towering black spruce hovered along either side of the drive, making a dramatic statement of proprietorial authority against the drab earth and dry grasses newly released from their cover of snow but not yet aroused into life. As they approached through the tunnel of spruce, the house was revealed to be charming, one-and-a-half storeys, with a front gable, shutters smoky-green against the rubble-stone walls. Miranda was so distracted by the paradoxically harsh and yet pastoral setting that she momentarily forgot why they were there.

At the side of the house they were surprised to find a police cruiser parked facing out with the driver's door open, as if the driver were anticipating a fast getaway, but the driver was nowhere in sight. Miranda chuckled to herself when she saw on the side of the car the insignia of the Owen Sound Police. She gave a congenial beep of the horn as they pulled in beside the cruiser, and as they were stretching from the long drive the figure of a young man appeared in the stable door under the overhung side of the old wooden barn. He was in uniform, wearing a turban. As he walked toward them, trying not to look awkward for being there, Miranda greeted him.

"Officer Singh, I presume."

"Detective Quin," he smiled radiantly, having already forgiven himself for venturing well outside his sphere of authority, knowing the detectives were on equally ambiguous ground. "It is so good to meet you. Welcome to the countryside."

"This is my partner, Detective Morgan. Just call him Morgan. I'm Miranda."

"My name is Peter."

They all shook hands. The young officer could not stop smiling. His smile was infectious, and the three of them stood for some time, motionless, smiling.

"I am happy to be of assistance," he said. "Murder is a rare occurrence in Owen Sound. Mostly domestic violence, and very unpleasant. I have been reading about your case, I believe. The very old bodies in the very old house. And then not so old, after all. It has been intriguing, but it did not stay very long in the papers. I recognized your names. When Professor Birbalsingh told me, I knew who you were."

As he mentioned the call, he indicated with a hand gesture the universal telephone sign, little finger and thumb extended, the other three fingers folded in.

Morgan said, "We are appreciative, Officer Singh." He addressed the young policeman with a conspiratorial wink. "We will work as a team. Did you find anything of interest in the barn?"

"Oh, yes. Barns are of infinite interest. But nothing suspicious."

"Good work," said Morgan.

"Well," said Miranda, noticing the cobwebs on his turban, "I'm sure, then, we can turn our attentions to the house." She realized both she and Morgan were being a trifle patronizing, but, she thought, with good intentions. Peter Singh's ingenuous enthusiasm made him likeably vulnerable and they were instinctively trying to create protective barriers around him, before either lapsed into cynicism. "Have you been here long? You look like you were getting ready to leave," she said, nodding at the open door of the cruiser.

"Oh, no," he said. "I estimated the drive would take you three hours if you left right away." He indicated driving with two hands moving an imaginary steering wheel. "My car is like that to reassure anyone here of my goodwill."

"Is anyone here?" asked Miranda.

"No, I do not believe so. Not alive —"

"Peter," Morgan said, "we're not looking for bodies, we're just trying to find Dr. Hubbard."

"Who is a person wanted for questioning in a homicide investigation."

"Yes. Who appears to be missing."

"A very nasty homicide."

"Yes," said Miranda. She opened the summer-kitchen door. It seemed reasonable to step inside, to knock on the house door. Immediately, she recognized the door to the sauna from Morgan's description of the bolt and flanged hinges.

"There are five doors in this room, Morgan. I was expecting two. One for the lady and the other for the tiger."

Morgan and Peter Singh had followed her in. Morgan grimaced, but Officer Singh asked, "What do you mean? What tiger?"

"It's an old story. A man has a choice: does he choose the door concealing the lady, or the door concealing the tiger?"

"Oh, I see," he said, looking quite perplexed. "A difficult choice."

"Well, what do you think, Morgan. Shall we give the door a try?"

"How about knocking first?"

"Officer Singh already has. I'll just try the handle. You never know."

Miranda depressed the handle and pushed and the door swung open into the kitchen. She leaned in and called a piercing "Hello-o-o."

There was no answer. She stepped inside.

"Morgan, come in. We have a problem."

Morgan entered and walked by her into the centre of the room. Peter Singh crowded in behind.

"Familiar territory, Morgan?"

He glowered. Peter Singh offered the opinion that it was a beautiful house. The renovations were clearly of the highest calibre, he noted as he made a rapid hammering gesture with one hand over the other, and it was very neat.

"Notice anything?" Miranda asked.

"The door wasn't locked. It's unlikely she'd leave it unlocked."

"Yes," Miranda said. "But even more telling. Feel the temperature. It's warm in here. The furnace is on. No one, not even on a professor's salary, would neglect to turn the heat down if they were planning to be away. She's been gone, I'd say, three days."

"How do you know that?" said Peter Singh.

"There's a sweet, yeasty smell; the garbage under the sink is a few days old, not long enough to be rank, too long to live with."

"Very interesting."

Morgan looked at her with particular affection. She was good at this.

"Does your nose tell us if she's still on the premises?"

"She isn't here. We'll check all the rooms, but the air is unsullied by human remains. I would think she left in a hurry and under duress, probably in the evening."

"How so?"

"The dishes are washed; after breakfast or lunch there'd still be a few cups around, a few crumbs, but everything's been carefully put away, the counter and table are wiped down. I'd say it was the final cleanup of the day. And look on the table: three pieces of paper, with holes for a three-ringed binder. And a pen. She was settling down to write journal entries. And a wine glass. Clean. Empty. She was going to pour herself a glass — did you say she drank port? — a glass of port. She was about to record her memories of the day, her dreams and her plans. There are no essays in sight — she was probably finished her marking. And there's not a single book off the shelves. Academics invariably write with books spread open around them."

"Invariably? Perhaps you're projecting from stereotype. I think we've got about as much here as we're going to get without a warrant."

"We have reason to believe a crime has been committed. She didn't leave of her own accord, Morgan. I think we should look around."

"I'll check upstairs," Officer Singh volunteered.

Morgan sat down at the table and stared into the cold ashes in the fireplace. He got up and closed the damper. Heat from the furnace would be pouring out the chimney. She wouldn't have left it open. He sat down again, pleased to be alone as Miranda checked out the parlour and downstairs bedroom. He felt something strangely akin to nostalgia. This was absurd, for he and Shelagh had spent only a short time together, and it had been an emotional roller coaster, leaving him both frightened of her possible capacity for evil and irredeemably enthralled.

"Morgan," Miranda's voice echoed from Shelagh Hubbard's bedroom. "I think you should see this."

As he walked through, Peter Singh came clattering down the stairs, eager to miss nothing. The three of them crowded into the small room, along with a pressed-wood chair, a deal dresser, a three-quarters size bed — neatly made — bedside shelves stuffed with books and a braided rug. Miranda was sitting on the edge of the bed. On her lap was an open three-ring binder with a blue plastic cover. Two others were lying on top of a bookshelf. She turned the binder for Morgan to see in the glare of an overhead bulb suspended from the ceiling. This room had not yet been refinished.

He could not read without projecting his shadow across the open pages, so he took the book from her and turned into the light, only to have it blocked by the young officer who was simultaneously trying to read over his shoulder and stay out of his way. Morgan turned to Peter Singh and, making the universal gesture of two fingers walking, said, "I'll just walk out to the kitchen with this. There's better light."

He sat down at the harvest table with the book open in front of him. Slowly, he thumbed through, opening the pages at random, moving backward and forward, taking in brief descriptive passages, drawings, recipes for plaster and paint, details of antique clothing, outlines of plot, lists that included a crucifix and a Masonic ring, a clinical accounting of the extermination of lives and the preparation of corpses to fulfill their grisly roles in a ghastly embrace. A sketch showed severed heads resting face to face, lips touching lips. They had missed that, when they had lifted the heads from the chute — that they were meant to be kissing. Miranda stood in the small archway leading into the central hall with Officer Singh beside her.

Morgan for a moment envisioned his former wife as the author. He imagined Lucy making notes about buying a freezer big enough for a body, adapting a sauna for murder and mummification. He could picture her planning out a tableau for her own amusement, arranging desiccated corpses like dolls in a depraved parody of affection. Separating bodies from heads — passion is in the mind, she would say. The body is merely the medium, the message is always obscure. He could read his former wife's personality in the disinterested precision of Shelagh Hubbard's records.

"Morgan, I think you'd better take a look at this one, too." Miranda set another blue binder down on the table and turned it open to the final page. Below the text was a very accomplished sketch of a Huron burial mound, as it was labelled, and a list of necessary artifacts to create an illusion of authenticity. On the bottom of the page there was a brief note: "Needed, one saint — a sinner will do." Morgan turned over the page. Taped neatly to the obverse side was a newspaper clipping, carefully scissored to eliminate extraneous detail. Cut from the caption and taped as a label beneath the picture were the words, "Detective David Morgan, Homicide."

Miranda placed her hand on his shoulder. He showed no external emotion but sat very still. She could feel a slight quivering as he gently leaned into the reassuring pressure of her hand. Sensing a mystery beyond comprehension, Officer Singh made a slight walking gesture with his fingers and slipped out the door. He was perturbed by how personally engaged the city detectives appeared to be with their work.

# chapter nine
## Owen Sound

"It's pronounced 'Bo-slee,'" Miranda explained over dinner in a Collingwood steak-house. "It's spelled 'Beausoleil,' but it's pronounced 'Bo-slee,' like the nerdy factotum in *Charlie's Angels*."

"He was Bawz-lee. There was a street where I lived in London called 'Beechum' Place, spelled 'Beauchamp.' But of course, Londoners declared the spelling aberrant, not the pronunciation."

She sat back and sighed. "It's been quite a day," she said. "Thank God we're not driving back tonight. Rufalo said the budget's good for a couple of rooms and dinner."

"No breakfast?"

"And breakfast."

"We could find a motel with breakfast included."

"A doughnut and coffee. They call it 'Continental.' Anyway, Beausoleil is a crossroads hamlet near Penetang. Alexander Pope has a restoration project there. Artwork of some sort in an old church."

"The only thing I know about Penetanguishene is there's a prison for the criminally insane."

"That's where your new best friend will go, if we ever find her," said Miranda.

"Well, if we can get your own new best friend on the case, we'll find her in no time."

"She's following the case from afar."

"Who?"

"My new best friend."

"I meant Officer Singh of Owen Sound Police Services."

"I thought you meant Rachel."

"You're very fickle. What about me?"

"Why don't we compromise? Officer Singh is our new best friend, together."

"He's a nice kid," said Morgan. "He'll make a good cop some day."

"Oh, go on. He's a good cop now. You all right?"

"Yeah. A little shaken, a little humbled, a lot embarrassed, and very relieved. I wonder why she didn't do me in when she had the chance."

"I think she was pretty confident she could get to you later. And she knew that I knew where you were. Her notes make it clear your little episode in the sauna was just a dry run, so to speak. Maybe that's why she didn't climb into your bed — assuming she didn't. Extended foreplay. Prolonging the game. If you and the lady had been intimate, Morgan, I'm sure you would have been graded."

"How did you convince the OPP to let us have the binders? All we're dealing with at this point is unlawful disposal of human remains."

"Until there's proof the murders happened on the farm, it's our case. That's what Rufalo says. Anyway, the binders just happened to be in the back of our car when the Provincials arrived." She smiled. "I told them about them, of course. I might have implied they were already on the way to Toronto."

"And meanwhile, where was I?"

"You were a bit discombobulated. You went for a walk."

"I just went out to the barn. I was looking for her car. It wasn't in the drive shed. I don't think I've ever actually been in a barn before — not one that hasn't been converted into an antiques emporium. There's something comforting about a four-storey haymow with light beams poking through, aslant from the sun —"

"Is that a quotation?"

"I think so, I'm not sure. Anyway, when I came out, the place was swarming with cops."

"They're a committed bunch, the Provincials. They pulled out all the stops. If there's DNA anywhere, in the freezer, the sauna, wherever, they'll find it. They'll find yours, of course."

"Oh, for goodness sake!"

"Are you on file?"

"Yeah, I imagine."

"I'd say you're an indelible part of the story, sauna or not. You were being set up as her next victim. Maybe you should recuse yourself from the plot."

"*Au contraire*. It makes me an invaluable asset to the investigation. Fifth business, at least."

"Fifth business, yes. You'd have to be dead to be the villain or the hero in this story. That's how her stories work."

"They're brilliant, actually, narratives frozen in time, like eighteenth-century court tableaux; everything is posed. The absolute stillness excuses all excess — there is no obscenity, nothing is admitted as vile, even death is held in suspension."

"Well, it's better your death is held in suspension, for the time being, at least."

They skipped dessert and lingered over coffee. Morgan added double-double and Miranda pretended not to notice.

"What's in the third binder?"

"I don't know yet. It appears to be set in England."

"You think it was a similar crime?"

"Comparable, not similar. The Hogg's Hollow case and the project she was developing for you are entirely different —"

"But equally depraved. Equally ingenious."

"You can't help yourself, can you? You admire her."

"She was intending to kill me."

"I've had relationships like that."

"Something about her — my response to her — reminded me of Lucy."

"Oh, Morgan, how sad."

Although he had been divorced before he teamed up with Miranda over a decade ago, and despite the fact that he seldom talked about his marriage, he occasionally mentioned his former wife on a first-name basis, as if Lucy and Miranda had once been friends. Miranda had very ambivalent feelings about Lucy. She knew Morgan had been through an abusive relationship and that his former wife was a manipulative bully, and yet Miranda felt empathetic, knowing Morgan could be intellectually overbearing and emotionally elusive.

"So, what about Alexander Pope?" said Morgan. "He's your new friend, too."

"He's interesting. Maybe we should drop in and see him tomorrow. Beausoleil isn't far from here, really."

"Would he be working on Saturday?"

"Oh, for sure. I'd think when he's on a project he must work through weekends and holidays. He's a man driven by God knows what."

"Possibly. He's working in a church."

"An abandoned Roman Catholic church."

"I didn't think Catholics did that."

"It's been deconsecrated, or whatever they do. It's decommissioned. Secular territory. It's just a building, now."

"There's gotta be a story in that."

"So, let's check him out on our way home."

"It's north of here. Home's south."

"Not very far north."

"Sounds good. Where do you think Shelagh Hubbard has got to?"

"The abductor abducted! I don't have a clue," said Miranda. "Maybe there was someone else involved in her godawful plots."

"I don't think so. That's not the impression I got from her notes. A monomaniacal psychopath couldn't abide sharing credit."

"Monomaniacal?"

"To do the crimes is psychopathic; to plan them, monomaniacal. To conceive of their elaborate contexts, to play author with other people's mortality ... there's only one reality for such a mind."

"Her own."

"No one else matters, except to flesh out the context of her own existence."

"So, whodunit? Who took her away? She didn't drive off, leaving things the way we found them."

"Maybe it's coincidence. Her disappearance might have nothing to do with the case."

"Morgan, what if she's setting us up again? What if she wanted us to find her notebooks? She is a woman with powerful needs; maybe she couldn't wait any longer."

"Go on."

"So everything was arranged. By missing the tenure committee summons, she knew she could count on Birbalsingh to get excited, and she could count on us to get involved. She left the heat on in the house, did everything just so, to fake her abduction. It was a set-up, Morgan."

"Could be."

"Maybe it was time to move on. She connected with you. Maybe that threw a wrench in the works. Psychopaths aren't supposed to feel — there's no room for empathy."

"Miranda, we didn't really connect all that much. It would seem from her notes even less than I thought."

"Maybe more than you know. She is a woman of infinite complexity. Maybe you touched something human."

"We've agreed: interring my bones in the Huron burial mound was only in the planning stage — written up as if she were preparing an application for a scholarly grant."

"Let's say she lost her confidence in the project, whatever the reason. It was time to move on. We were meant to be her witnesses. Megalomaniacs need affirmation even if psychopaths don't. Who better to witness a criminal achievement than professionals in the business of crime? We're the equivalent of critics in the audience on opening night. Maybe the third volume is actually the first in a series. From another, earlier version of her life. Maybe she was successful with whatever diabolical tableau it records, but she felt it didn't get the attention it deserved. Maybe it was never discovered. So she moved on. I'm betting it's set in England — she studied over there. And not a hint of an English accent, did you notice that?"

"There is, actually. A bit of an Oxford lisp. I'd guess she grew up in Victoria."

"Almost right. Vancouver. Shall we go? I paid the bill when I went to the washroom."

"I'm ready."

"There's a good motel on the edge of town," she said. She leaned back in her chair, stretched sinuously, and declared in a throaty voice, "It's past my bedtime, darling!"

Morgan looked around. Diners at the tables on either side of them had overheard in that selective way people have of filtering anything salacious from the general hubbub of public conversation. The man to his right gazed openly at Miranda, assessing her attributes. Morgan shifted in his chair. The man looked away. The woman with him, however, caught Morgan's eye and almost winked. On the other side, an older couple stared glassily at each other, chewing voraciously, ostentatiously pretending they had not heard Miranda's proposition.

"Yes," he said. "Enough foreplay. Let's go!"

Arm in arm they sauntered to the door.

When they pulled up at the motel, Miranda turned to him and said, "Morgan, can I sleep with you tonight?"

"Miranda!"

"In the same room, *darling*. We'll get separate receipts."

They were inside the room with their coats off before Miranda noticed the bed. "I thought you asked for twins?"

"I did."

"Well, that looks like a double to me."

"King size, Miranda. We'll put pillows down the middle like a bundling board."

"At least you won't get slivers."

"Nor you."

"Maybe I should get another room," she offered.

"No, stay here. I need the company. Why don't you relax and watch TV? I'm going back to the variety store to pick up some toothpaste and a razor. You want anything?"

"Toothbrushes. Baby-powder-scented deodorant. Condoms. Pantyhose. Tampons."

"I don't do tampons. Pantyhose, maybe."

"Just testing, Morgan. Actually, I'd like some pantyhose if they have any. And some antacid pills. Hurry back."

"Do you really want tampons? I don't mind."

"No, Morgan. Hurry back."

"Condoms?"

"Forget it."

Miranda showered and washed out her underclothes, wringing them almost dry inside a rolled bath towel. She climbed into bed naked, pulling the covers up to her chin, then folded them modestly down so that her arms were free to hold the third blue binder, which she propped up on the blanket over her breasts and proceeded to read. The text was so horrifically absorbing, when Morgan returned she hardly looked up.

He set down their bag of supplies and took off his coat. She looked radiant in bed, with the reading light casting a warm aura around her head and bare shoulders. He opened a closet and retrieved from the top shelf two extra pillows and a thick blanket. The blanket he rolled into a cylindrical shape and placed down the middle of the bed. Without speaking he walked around to her side of the bed, and she leaned forward while he tucked another pillow under her head.

He took the variety-store bag into the bathroom. Before closing the door, he tossed a new T-shirt out across the bed. "Present for you," he said. "Hope it fits." She held the T-shirt up in front of her. It was extra-large, white, with a generic Group of Seven windswept-pine-on-rocky-coast design, underneath which were emblazoned in neon colours, "Owen Sound: A Nice Place to Visit." She chuckled, completing the familiar aphorism in her mind. She assumed the "wouldn't want to live there" part was beyond the Taiwanese manufacturer's cultural grasp, and wondered if the merchandiser, probably Toronto-based, was being intentionally subversive.

She shook the newness out of it and put it on. It was big enough to be a nightgown. "Thanks, Morgan," she shouted, but he obviously couldn't hear her over the sound of water beating like a monsoon against the shower curtain.

After the shower stopped running, he poked his head through the door. "Did you yell?" he asked.

"I said 'thank you.' Thank you for the wearing apparel."

"You're welcome," he responded, waving his right arm in a discreet salute.

"Morgan!"

"Yes!"

"What's that on your shoulder?"

"*Tangata manu.*"

"Who?"

"He's the bird-man. He's everywhere on Rapa Nui. The moai — or giant statues — the bird-man, and *komari*. Everywhere you turn, there are images — and Maki Maki, he's the main god. Komari are vulva. There are hundreds and hundreds carved into the lava rock."

"You do know how to deflect questions, don't you! Hundreds of vulva?"

"Hundreds and hundreds."

"Morgan, you have a tattoo."

"A little one."

"Don't you feel guilty?"

"For cultural appropriation?"

"Bad taste."

He snarled fake anger and retreated behind the closed bathroom door.

She listened to him moving about, mumbling to himself, but when he emerged in his boxer shorts with a towel draped modestly over his shoulders, she didn't look up. In a quiet voice, she asked, "Can I touch it?"

"Sure! What?"

"You know."

"What?"

"Your tattoo."

"No."

He walked to his side of the bed and carefully lifted the covers to slip the bundling blanket between them as he climbed in. In the ruffling shadows he caught a momentary glimpse of her naked legs and he lay back, deciding not to read. He was almost asleep when she turned off the reading light, slipped out of the bed, and went into the bathroom to brush her teeth. Inside the bag of toiletries were a package of super absorbency tampons and a packet of grotesque cherry-flavoured condoms. She looked at herself in the wall mirror over the sinks. She was grinning and shaking her head, and seeing herself grinning, she chuckled audibly and blew herself a kiss. Then she turned and, dowsing the light, edged her way through the darkness to the bedside where she slid quietly under the covers and lay on her back, staring thoughtfully into the darkness.

After a while, she said, "You asleep?"

"Yes," he said.

"Good," she said, "Sleep well, Morgan. Thanks for letting me stay."

"G'night."

Miranda had been reading Shelagh Hubbard's sordid narrative and she knew Morgan might easily have been the next victim, but she felt strangely at peace with the world as she listened to the sounds of her partner sleeping beside her, felt the almost imperceptible surge of the bed in the rhythm of his breathing, and inhaled the fresh scents of their bodies, enfolding them both.

Suddenly, she opened her eyes and realized it was morning. Morgan was up and dressed, sitting in a chair, reading a blue binder. She had slept beautifully.

Morgan seemed absorbed.

"Good morning," Miranda said.

"Mmmnnn," he responded.

"You're sitting on my clothes."

"They're on the bed."

He glanced up. "She writes like Graham Greene," he said. "All moral complexity and no resolution. So completely matter-of-fact you forget how squalid and corrupt her vision of life really is." He was already back into the text before he had finished speaking.

Miranda gathered her clothes with a sweep of her arm that was impeded by the bulge of the bundling blanket still in place beneath the covers. She rose awkwardly, holding clothes and a pillow in front of her as she backed toward the bathroom. Morgan wasn't even looking. She wheeled around — scorning his indifference — stepped through the door, and shut it behind her. At the same time, attracted by her pirouette, he glanced up, smiled appreciatively at the flash of her nakedness, and returned to his reading.

Her panties were dry but she had to apply the hair drier to her bra before putting it on. It felt warm to the touch as she leaned over and adjusted her shape to its contour. I'm too sexy for my bra, she hummed, too sexy for my bra. As she stood upright, drawing each breast into place with a peremptory tug, she caught an image in the mirror of a woman of no particular age. She loved that. That's how it should be, she thought. And I hope to goodness when I'm seventy, God willing, I'll sometimes look in the mirror and see a woman like me, of no particular age.

When she emerged from the bathroom, Morgan stood up and looked her over. "Good," he said, in a burlesque of the dutiful spouse. "You look lovely today."

"It's a new outfit. An exact replica of the one I wore yesterday. Once you find your style, you stick with it."

"Really," he said. "You look fine."

"I like you better sarcastic. What do you think of your friend's English exploits?"

"We'll talk on the road. Let's grab our coffee and dough-nut and get out of here."

He drove, following the signs to Penetanguishene. She explained he needed the practice. They discussed the third binder, which was first in the deadly trilogy.

"Maybe it's just fantasy," he said. "A prelude to murder. If you read it as fiction, it's brilliantly conceived. I know Madam Renaud's in London. The Chamber of Horrors. I actually have bittersweet memories of being there, twenty years ago. It was a girlfriend thing. A sad parting. I've never told you about Susan."

"There's lot you haven't told me, Morgan. I don't need all the details. Was she nice? If it was sad, she must have been nice."

"Too nice. The problem was she was too nice."

"I can relate to that." She paused, not sure if she could. "Why the Chamber of Horrors?"

"Just a place we knew," he responded, trying to remember which of them had proposed meeting there. He had been on the Continent for months; they had already broken up after sharing a pair of adjoining bedsitters in Knightsbridge for the better part of a year. She had a child before she got married. She had flown over from London to Toronto for dinner, just before Morgan's own wedding. Was that her idea or his? Was she married then or not?

Miranda's voice penetrated his gnawing reverie.

"For Shelagh Hubbard, Madame Renaud's was almost inevitable. I ran across a reference when I was checking her out. She actually worked there after she finished a postdoc-toral fellowship at the University of London — it was an offshoot from studies in forensic reconstruction, working with wax to recreate faces. It didn't seem relevant. It certainly does now. But it sounds like a B movie — Vincent Price on the late show."

"That's the point, isn't it? Turning cliché into reality." Morgan stared at the landscape ahead as the highway rolled under them, periodically reminding himself he was at the wheel. He felt distracted but amused. "Wax figures look dead, even when they're not meant to. If she really did use cadavers waxed-over to create realistic corpses, and then systematically insinuated her macabre creations into the displays in an actual Chamber of Horrors, like she claims, well, it's diabolical, isn't it? Using the dead to simulate death!"

"She'd have to be very good. Not morally speaking, of course."

"If she really did it, and if no one noticed, she must have been very, very good. She would have treated the bodies to resist decomposition, then sealed and moulded them to the precise shape of the murder victims they were meant to displace on display. It's all like a gruesome parody of something. Of death itself?"

"Murder victims disguised as murder victims — it's unspeakably grotesque." In spite of herself, Miranda could see the black humour. "Can you imagine her hanging out at The Nag's Head or The Bunch of Grapes? She'd be eyeballing the clientele for who would make the best corpse."

"Picking up Shelagh would have been a deadly affair."

"She picked up women, too, you know. By my count she did five, altogether: two men and three women."

"If you can trust her notes," said Morgan, who would have preferred not to. "She even enjoyed the existential implications of dealing with the discards. Stripped of their bloodied costumes and rouged to make them appear less dead, they became anonymous in the storage rooms among fallen rock stars, disgraced royalty, and yesterday's politicians."

"Surely disgraced royals were kept on view."

"The hard part was getting the bodies there, I would think."

"You were reading too quickly, Morgan. Her victims came of their own accord, after hours. She did a Ph.D. at Oxford, postdoc at London; she knew how to turn on the charm, English-wise. She would lead them on an esoteric adventure, their visits shrouded in secrecy. Who could resist the chance for a clandestine tour of the Chamber of Horrors? That was her lure: not sex — morbid curiosity. Death on display."

"That seems familiar! What I find upsetting is how easily I entered into the story."

After a contemplative period of silence, Miranda spoke. "Did you ever think about how the way death is experienced was changed by twentieth-century technology?"

"I'll assume you're not talking about embalming and the art of the mortuary."

"No. Being dead."

"So, we're not talking about the collapse of religion and the downgrading of heaven and hell to moral analogies?"

"No. From the point of view of the living, death has lost its absolute edge."

"You are about to launch into a discourse on war as enter-tainment, the ultimate opiate of the masses?"

"Yeah, partly. World War I, grainy black-and-white photographs. World War II, photo essays by Frank Capra and Margaret Bourke-White. Vietnam, television. A genera-tion later, we watch the wretchedness of Afghanistan as vir-tual reality. *Buffy the Vampire Slayer* elicits a more visceral response. No, that's not what I mean. I was thinking about how different death is since we've been able to record our live presence electrically and electronically. The dead aren't dead in the same way. Death is no longer an absolute."

"It is for the dead," said Morgan.

"But not for the living. I have tapes of my mother's voice, photographs of my father. I can turn on television and see Marilyn Monroe and James Dean. I can watch old Bette Davis in a horror flick, and then watch young Bette Davis devouring long-gone leading men with her inimitable eyes, and so on, flipping back and forth through her life by the press of a button on my remote control."

"Not through her actual life, Miranda. Don't confuse the person with the roles she plays."

"Yes! Her life. I know she was an actress — but it's the actress who ages, rejuvenates, plays many parts. Of course, my mother's voice on tape is not my mother, my father's pictures are not my father. But they connect me to them — the ways she sounded, the ways he looked."

"It's still the living who provide narrative context for the dead to endure. I would see and hear the same images very differently. Technology doesn't change death, it only allows for different illusions than the ones offered by the past."

"It always comes down to the story, doesn't it?" said Miranda.

"Renaud's Chamber of Horrors re-enacts crimes. Stories. The display of mutilated bodies and faces distended with horror wouldn't mean much without a narrative context. It would be gratuitous, and in very bad taste."

"That's why her waxworks project was a failure, not because she had no witnesses to celebrate her prowess. That may have been part of it, but, really, it's because the stories were already determined. Jack the Ripper, Dr. Crippen ... They weren't hers. She had to animate *her own* story. Or stories; the ghoulish complexity of her Hogg's Hollow project was only a prelude to what she had in store for you, Morgan. Or, at least, for your charred remains. I wonder if she'd have been clever enough to leave a few bones missing. For authenticity. I wonder what she'd leave out."

They drove without talking for a while, enjoying the quiet, which was broken only by the hum of the tires and the low rumble of the engine. Trees and fields swept by, hills carried them high and dropped away. Occasionally one would speak, and the other would nod.

Before they reached Penetanguishene, Miranda directed Morgan to turn off onto a sideroad. After several more turns and a sharp descent into a valley that broke the grid pattern of the concession roads, they rose high onto a limestone plateau where they could see in the distance a stone church and rectory rising imperiously above the landscape. There was not a barn or a farmhouse in sight. They pulled up between the two buildings, beside a midnight blue van with the name Alexander Pope in cursive script on the driver's door. Morgan leaned forward to peer up at the steeple.

"This is eerie," he said as he got out of the car. "A deserted church, an empty manse, in the middle of nowhere. So much for a hamlet called 'Beausoleil.' No cross on the steeple, no sign of a cross or crucifix except in the graveyard." He nodded in the direction of the derelict cemetery on the far side of the church, surrounded by a tumbledown stone wall. "Do Catholics call it a manse?"

Morgan walked over to the low wall. It struck him as strange, when the church building itself appeared to be in good repair, that graves should be left unattended, with brambles and weeds running riot among toppled monuments, the occasional spire still thrusting toward heaven, although most were on precarious angles. The rectory, on the other side of the church, was a standing ruin.

"I don't get it," he said as he returned to where Miranda was standing in front of the church.

"What don't you get?"

He did not respond. The parts didn't fit; it was like they had entered a world gone slightly askew.

"Alexander told me it was deconsecrated in the late 1800s," Miranda explained. "Maybe the graves were emptied, the bodies dug up and reburied."

"Looks to me more like selective neglect. The church itself is okay."

Miranda spread her arms wide to take in the empty horizon. "Not much call for bingo or euchre in Beausoleil."

"The windows are intact. There's no sign of vandalism. The grass is cut, the shrubs are trimmed." He gazed up and down the concession road. "There's no reason for a church to be here. It's not an intersection, there's no river for a village to grow on. No railway. There're just miles and miles of miles and miles." From close to the building he looked upwards, his eyes following the rough stone to the sky. "It's imposing. I guess that was the idea, but who in God's name would want to restore it?"

"I don't think God had much to do with it," Miranda quipped.

"Well, let's take a look inside."

## *chapter ten*

# Beausoleil

The interior of the church had been gutted, but it was immaculate, and still irredeemably a sacred place by virtue of the Gothic windows, soaring roof, and stone-slab floor. At first they did not see Alexander Pope working on a scaffold raised between two windows. They heard small sounds and, walking in that direction, they discovered him partially hidden by pillars. His back was to them and he seemed almost motionless. There was a large floodlight aslant to the ceiling, illuminating the wall in such a way as to cast no shadows. As they approached closer, they saw he was working with a scalpel, scraping away bits of plaster in small, delicate movements.

Above him the plaster had been stripped away, leaving a colourful mural with the bottom edge ragged, promising a revelation in the ecstatic gleam from the central figure's eyes. There were smaller figures around her, their reduced size indicating lesser importance, not diminutive stature. She was a young woman, not much more than a girl, with flowers woven through her long hair like a Pre-Raphaelite siren. Around her head was a diffuse halo of radiant light. Her hands, which were just emerging from their plaster shroud, were turned palms outward, with blood-red signs of stigmata at their centres.

"Take a look at the others," said Alexander Pope without looking around. "I'll be with you in a minute."

To his left there were three murals that had already been revealed to the light. Whether they had been restored or the original colours had been preserved by their plaster shrouds, they were startling in their vivid portrayal of the same young woman. Both Morgan and Miranda gazed with astonishment at their exquisite beauty, an appreciation for the merging of aesthetics and the spiritual not at all tempered by their differing degrees of agnostic resistance.

The first panel showed her in a posture of acquiescence, dressed in the clothes of a Victorian farm girl. She was sweeping up, in what appeared to be the opulent austerity of a rectory kitchen, witnessed by a disturbingly animate crucifix looming from the wall. Two cassocks could be seen hanging from a peg rail on the adjoining wall. The slight smile on her face was curiously distracted; she seemed detached, as if her mind was on less worldly things than her domestic labours.

In the second panel, her features had softened. She was kneeling at prayer in landscape much like that surrounding the church on the limestone plateau. In front of her was a makeshift shrine of small boulders. The crucifix around her neck gleamed against the rough cloth of her sombre dress. Her eyes were raised to heaven, which seemed in the arrangement of shadows and light to be hidden by clouds that were about to spread open in divine revelation.

The third panel showed the young woman prostrate on the left side of the Virgin and the same young woman kneeling in adoration to her right. Mary, in the centre, stood apart from the landscape, not hovering in the air, but fore-grounded and free of earth's gravity, casting no shadow. Her right hand was raised, revealing a stigmata impressed on the palm. Her pale-blue robe draped sensuously over her body, portraying her as a worldly woman, and yet her face showed the innocence and sorrow of a suffering child. She was the maiden of Bethlehem and the grieving mother at Golgotha, the Queen of the World and Eve restored to the Garden. The young farm woman on her right gazed with rapturous won-der and seemed to be listening, as if she were hearing Mary's voice inside her own head. She had become quite beautiful, her hair had fallen untangled across her shoulders, her eyes glistened, her lips parted softly, her skin glowed in a light emanating from within.

Miranda and Morgan were so enthralled with the nar-rative unfolding in such rich detail, neither of them heard Alexander Pope approach them until he spoke.

"Hello Miranda Quin, hello Detective Morgan. I didn't realize it was you. Welcome to Beausoleil." He pronounced the name in a mid-channel accommodation of both French and English: "Bo-slay." "This is the Church of the Immaculate Conception — or was. I do try to keep it immaculate." He chortled briefly at his own contrived wit. "It fell on hard times, you know. Welcome, welcome. I hadn't been expecting you."

"You invited me to pop in," said Miranda, a little defen-sively. "So, here we are."

"Of course. And you've brought your partner. Your other friend, Miss Naismith, she's not with you? No, never mind. I've had a stream of visitors, more every week. It seems there's some interest astir in the old place. How are you, Detective Morgan?"

"I'm fine, Mr. Pope. And you?"

"Enough of the formalities," he said abruptly, unfolding his long arms and shaking Morgan's hand vigorously. Then, leaning down and, with his hands clasping her shoulders, he kissed Miranda on both cheeks. "I really would like a bit of a break. May I show you around?" He loomed over them both, a gaunt figure in the unusually bright but indirect illumination, his frame almost skeletal under work clothes caked in plaster dust. His cheekbones pushed against his sallow skin and his eye sockets were starkly circumscribed by the marks left from his safety goggles. His face showed a stubble of three or four days neglect. Miranda judged that he had been working obsessively on his newest project and she felt a strong nurturing urge, wishing she could protect him from his own excesses.

"Please," she said, "if we're not interfering."

"Tell us about the paintings," asked Morgan, genuinely interested.

"Well, I have to proceed slowly. They are frescoes done by an anonymous master, one of those itinerant artists from the old country — I'd suspect in this case from Tuscany — making his way through the new world until domesticity took hold in one form or another and he became a common immigrant, like the rest of us, one generation or another in our past. His offspring probably became bakers or farmhands or lawyers. He was inspired, yes, and you'll notice he was also very accomplished — trained in the best schools of Florence. And, fortunately for us, his work was covered over in haste. Relatively little damage was done. If anything, the work has been preserved. The plaster covering was smeared on, in some places it barely adheres, nothing more holding it in place than inertia and the will of the Lord."

"Are you Roman Catholic?" asked Morgan, surprised by Pope's turn of phrase.

"In spite of the papal surname, I am not. In fact, I am rather opposed to religion. I was speaking of the Lord ironically, Detective. I am sure whatever God might have dwelled in this building has long since taken refuge in Rome."

"Yet," observed Morgan, "there is something of the sacred remaining."

"Perhaps the residue of God, Detective. The deity has fled but his influence remains. Gods do not die easily in the Western world."

Miranda found his condescension irritating, although it didn't seem to bother Morgan, perhaps because she wanted to like the man and Morgan was indifferent. She was fascinated by the quality of the frescoes, but Morgan's interest had shifted to the story they revealed and it would take more than an overbearing interlocutor to keep him from finding how it unravelled.

"Are you doing the restoration for the Church?" Miranda asked.

"Absolutely not. This building no longer exists as far as the Church is concerned. A private enterprise — my mentors."

"Art lovers, no doubt," she said.

"It is a labour of love, yes it is."

"So tell us, Alexander. What happened here?" Morgan asked.

They were walking about slowly, absorbing the atmosphere of what seemed, away from the murals, a vast, grey sepulchre robbed of its resident bones. Alexander Pope apologized for being abrupt with them, which struck them as odd, since he seemed quite relaxed. He explained that he had had interruptions not so welcome as theirs and his work was impeded by what he described as his natural inclination to be hospitable. All three laughed at that and they were friends.

"Beneath this floor," he said, "lies the body of a saint. Her story is inscribed on the walls. She was never sanctified, canonized, or beatified and she died in disgrace. But for many she was a folk saint, the people's saint, and to this day there are believers who come here in defiance of their Church and pray for her intervention with God. They have kept the place up for over a hundred years, carefully leaving no sign of their presence. That in itself is a miracle. If the Vatican requires three miracles as the prerequisites for sainthood, their quiet devotion is a good place to start.

"Imagine, people coming here to pray and pay homage. They are not supplicants, they are pilgrims. They ask for nothing. They come singly, sometimes in twos and threes. They come at all hours. Sometimes in the dead of night, when I'm working late, I'll turn around and find someone just behind me, staring at the revelation of their venerable saint. Often, when I return in the mornings, I'll find my instruments have been carefully cleaned, the floor underneath my scaffold meticulously dusted. In the daytime, they tend to stay clear of me, labouring quietly, especially the women, sweeping and scrubbing and dusting and polishing. The men sometimes pick up bits of debris. They seem more distant — they follow the women as helpers or stand by, passively observing. When I try to engage any of them in conversation, they are shy. They listen, but they do not ask questions. When I tell them something from my research about the church building itself or about Sister Marie Celeste, they nod knowingly. I'm not sure whether I offer nothing new, or merely nothing surprising.

"These pilgrims converge on this place from other worlds and treat it as home. I look forward to them, although at times I do find them intrusive. They are not a community, a secret society — as far as I can tell, they are absolutely independent of each other, some of them meeting here openly for the first time ever. It is impossible to say how many there are. If they gathered, would there be multitudes or only a handful in each generation? These are not zealots, yearning for the End of Days and the Divine Rapture. They are modest followers of a compromised saint.

"No one has objected to my restoration project. The Church has no interest, claiming they no longer hold title. Yet there's no record of sale, and the property remains tax-exempt. Curious, isn't it? Almost like it doesn't exist. The people who look after the place, I think they're pleased with what I'm doing. Turning up the light on their darkened world."

"How very strange," said Miranda. "What a wonderful notion, that such things go on in our midst and we don't even know."

"It would not be so wonderful if we did."

"What about the manse, the parsonage, the rectory ... whatever they call it? And what about the cemetery?"

"The rectory, Morgan. It is derelict, of no interest. The cemetery, no interest."

"How so?"

"It is all in how the story unfolds," said Pope, somewhat cryptically. Then, in a sudden shift, he inquired, "What time is it?"

"Half-past nine," said Miranda, glancing at her watch.

"Saturday?" he inquired.

"Yes, Saturday, 9:30 a.m."

"Then you two are here for some other reason."

"How do you mean?" she responded.

"You would not be here this early for a casual visit. It's close to a four-hour drive."

"It's about Shelagh Hubbard."

"The anthropologist from the museum. You say she took a course from me in London."

"Yes," said Miranda. "Apparently she's missing."

"Pardon me," he said, "but you're looking for her a long way from home."

Morgan, who had been gazing about, absorbed in the atmosphere of the abandoned church that struck him as at once very sad and somehow still sacred, returned to their conversation. "She has a farm near Owen Sound. She appears to have been abducted, although there is a strong possibility it's a set-up."

"A set-up?"

"A con. She may have arranged her own disappearance."

"And why is that of concern to the Toronto Police, Detective Morgan? You two are a long way from home."

"The Owen Sound constabulary called us in as reinforcements," Miranda quipped.

"The OPP, actually," Morgan said. "It turns out Dr. Hubbard may be important to our investigation of the Hogg's Hollow murders."

"She's a suspect!" said Pope, apparently delighted. "How very droll. She was one of your forensic experts, wasn't she?"

Morgan flinched imperceptibly. "She was. As were you."

"My dear Morgan, you must find such a convoluted case intriguing. What happens when you find her?"

"At this point she is wanted to assist in an ongoing investigation," said Miranda. "That's how we say it to protect ourselves from libel and the public from hysteria."

"But you are in fact quite sure she's your murderess." The word seemed to hiss from his lips. "I do wish I could remember the woman."

Miranda and Morgan exchanged brief knowing looks. *Murderess* is a term of diminution, suggesting something less on a semantic scale than *murderer*. It exoticizes the crime, lending an air of titillation. They had discussed this before, noting that it was a word frequently used in the tabloids. They were surprised to hear it issue from the rather fastidious mind of Alexander Pope.

"We may eventually need your testimony," said Morgan. "If she acquired skills from the master, then perhaps the master will confirm his influence on her work. I'm surprised you didn't see it at the scene."

"In retrospect only. At the time I was not looking for signs of my own inadvertent complicity. Of course, I will testify —"

"We have to find her, first," said Miranda. "At this point, we can't even issue a warrant. She's still in the category of 'missing.'"

"One mystery at a time," said Morgan, trying to swing the conversation around. "Tell us more about your secular saint."

"Not secular, Morgan. Merely not sanctioned nor sanctified by Mother Church."

"She had a vision, I assume. An encounter with the Virgin Mary?"

"She did. In 1891. The church building was completed in 1867. There were plans to bring the railway through to a Georgian Bay terminus at either Midland or Penetang. This was the median point between. The whole province was swarming with promise. Rail beds were being laid every which way. Confederation promised prosperity. This seemed a likely place for a church, in anticipation of settlers and commerce. Mills no longer determined townsites. The church would provide the locus. At one time there was a school beside the rectory and a Presbyterian church across the road. They burned down years ago."

"1891? Her vision?" Miranda was anxious to hear the story, more than the history, although to Alexander Pope, as to Morgan, the two were inseparable.

They walked at an ambling pace about the empty building as Pope continued.

"There were two resident priests. The school had been built, but students were not forthcoming. The nuns who had been sent here to teach were recalled to Toronto until the population of the area grew sufficient to the enterprise. The priests had a series of housekeepers — usually elderly widows who needed their beneficence. In 1890, a young woman named Lorraine Eliott from a farm several concessions over appeared at their door. She was quite simple, apparently, and could not find work as a domestic until such time as she got married, as girls then often did. Her family, she confessed, were lapsed Catholics. She would work for the priests in exchange for upkeep and religious instruction. By all accounts it was a satisfactory arrangement. Lorraine's family started coming regularly to church and she, herself, learned her catechism slowly but well."

"Where did you find an account of such things?" Morgan asked.

"I have spent large portions of my life in local archives, Detective, pouring through bundles of fading correspondence, diaries, unpublished manuscripts, records. It is surprising how much of our past awaits us, if we take the time to explore."

"And she became devout and had a vision," said Miranda.

"Exceedingly devout. One day, Lorraine was praying at a small grotto she had constructed from boulders against the cemetery wall. The Virgin appeared to her. In radiant glory, as they say. The girl took holy instruction from Mary, her divine mentor, in a vision of sustained ecstasy. She returned late to the rectory. The priests had company — three nuns from Toronto who were negotiating to reopen the school. All five were annoyed that supper was not yet on the table, but the girl appeared before them and spread her arms open with her palms exposed. They were bleeding at the centre, as if nails had just been withdrawn. She spoke, and the nuns reported she was cast in a splendid light and an odour of violets filled the room.

"'I am Sister Marie Celeste,' she said in a soft voice. And then, she was struck dumb, and never spoke again. She collapsed on the floor.

"The nuns took her into their bedroom and dressed her wounds. When they changed her clothes into the best habit they could spare, they brought her again to the parlour. The priests seemed distressed by the intrusion on their ordered lives. They did not understand, but the nuns knew what had happened and were deeply moved.

"One nun, the most profoundly affected, kneeled beside the young woman and took her hands, palms upward. She began to speak, and it was in a voice altogether more resonant than her own. She spoke in the first person, but the words were those of Sister Marie Celeste: 'The Virgin Mother appeared to me, and told me of many things so wonderful I cannot express them. She asked me to share with her the sorrowful burden of our Lord's crucifixion and the glory of His resurrection, our Son's blessing for all the world.' One of the priests was incensed. 'This is blasphemy,' he said. And Sister Marie Celeste smiled, and through the nun holding her hands, she said, 'Our Heavenly Mother forgives her priest his innocence.'

"The priest who had not spoken was so taken aback by the inspired authority of the voice that he dropped to his knees in submission, and was joined almost immediately by the other. The remaining two nuns, not to be outdone, prostrated themselves fully on the Persian carpet. Only the young nun holding the hands of Sister Mary Celeste with the stigmata exposed remained still. Again, the voice spoke: 'It is not by my words or my deeds but my very life that you shall be redeemed.'"

Morgan was uncertain about how much of Pope's story was artistic licence. The question of authenticity never crossed Miranda's mind, although, like her partner, she did not consider herself a person of faith, and certainly not a believer in visions — at least, not those of the Virgin Mary.

Pope had stopped speaking, gathering his resources. They continued in their meandering journey inside the church. The vast interior space seemed smaller, more intimate.

"Someone wrote this down, then?" Morgan inquired.

"The youngest nun did. She lived until the 1950s. She insisted in later years that when she was the voice of Sister Marie Celeste, who in turn proclaimed herself the voice of the Virgin, she was possessed —"

"By the Devil?" exclaimed Miranda.

"By God. She went to the grave a believer, despite excommunication."

"She was excommunicated?" exclaimed Morgan. "For what?"

"For believing. The word spread of Mary's appearance. It happened in April. By September there were crowds each Sunday, and even during the week, if the weather was bad, when the farmers could get away from their fields and their herds. The bishop, the archbishop, the cardinal, all sent investigators. Even the Vatican was aware of Sister Marie Celeste. Naturally, the clergy was cynical. Miracles are much better received out of history than as immanent experience. They demanded further miracles. The vision was not enough.

"All that summer Sister Marie Celeste was a holy terror. Through the youngest nun she made pronouncements on spiritual matters, urged reform in the Church, commented on local politics, on matters of weather for the benefit of farmers, offered advice on affairs of the heart and marital discord, and in direct contravention to dogma and doctrine she declared female submission anathema to the Mother of God."

Miranda, who had grown up in the Anglican branch of the wholly Catholic church, gasped in delight. Morgan, whose parents were lapsed Presbyterian before him — which, he felt, placed him on a theological spectrum closer to atheist than agnostic — thought the sister's radical feminism eminently sensible.

"The two priests were very well pleased to see their collection plates brimming," Alexander Pope continued, "but they resented their servant's success. They had to get a new housekeeper, for one thing. The nun and Sister Marie Celeste took over a wing of the rectory as their own quarters. Sister Marie Celeste's stigmata healed over. Her companion spoke for her in a normal voice, in arranging quotidian details of their lives, but still, occasionally, the voice of Mary spoke through her when Sister Marie Celeste was inspired or provoked."

"Why have we heard nothing of this?" asked Miranda.

"Why would you? There are small miracles all over the world every day, and cults of one sort or another are constantly forming and reforming. The Church is a cult of epidemic proportions that subsumes lesser cults for replenishment. Others fade, some virtually explode, some are erased."

"And this cult of Sister Marie Celeste," said Morgan, "was erased."

"Indirectly."

"You said she died in disgrace, Alexander. What happened?"

"Patience, Miranda. She died. It is as simple as that. In November she died. There was no warning. The doctor could not determine the cause. She expired one night, just over here." They moved up onto the chancel, a stone platform hardly a step above the rest of the floor.

Miranda felt a tremor run down her spine. "Where?"

"Under these slabs, right here. The priests were afraid to disturb her body any more than necessary. She lay in state in an open casket for three days on a catafalque erected over the spot where she died. Here. People came from miles around to grieve, to pray for her, and many, to pray through her to God. When it was time, her casket was sealed. The floor was laid open, and a crypt was prepared in the solid rock underneath. When the crypt was ready, some weeks later, a solemn cere- mony was held, during which her casket was reopened and a strong odour of violets rose from its recesses and washed through this entire building, and her flesh was not corrupt but gleamed in the candlelight and her hands lay in the shallow casket at her sides, the palms turned upwards, and small pools of fresh blood glistened at their centres. The nun who had been her acolyte and companion stood beside her and placed a hand on Sister Marie Celeste's breast, which appeared to rise and fall from the beating of the nun's own heart as she spoke for the final time the words of Mary in her own voice, which resounded through the hearts of all who were crowded in this building to listen."

"What did she say?" asked Miranda, totally enthralled.

"No one knows. Perhaps she was speaking in tongues — each heard in the voice a clear message, but for each it was different. It was not glossalalia, since for everyone present it made sense, yet none could agree on what had been said."

"Not unlike most conversations," said Morgan. "The more engaging the utterance, the more likely we hear what- ever we want, or need, to hear."

"Morgan, you're a cynic," said Miranda.

"Not at all. I'm on the verge of conversion."

"What happened next?" asked Miranda, more interested in Pope's story than her partner's errant soul. She relished the way Pope's words seemed to express something deep within that had little to do with faith, and a lot to do with how humans believe.

"The entire church became her shrine," declared Alexander Pope, turning and facing the gloomy interior of the building, his arms raised — whether in supplication or as a rhetorical gesture, Miranda couldn't be sure. "In death, her fame took flight. The walls on one side were painted with her story, and on the other were images from the Virgin's life. And people came — a makeshift town spread like contagion over the surrounding fields. It was like a gold-rush bonanza. Houses made of canvas and boards sprang up helter-skelter along the road allowance. The schoolhouse was turned into a hospital to care for the sick and the dying who came seeking Marie Celeste's intervention. Some claimed to be cured or relieved, just by pressing the robe of the nun who had been Mary's voice."

"Why doesn't the nun have a name?"

"Oh, she does, but somehow the story seems more authentic if her name is generic. Her name was Sister Mary Joseph. When Sister Marie Celeste died, Sister Mary took to wearing a pale-blue habit, quite unlike the black prescribed by her order. Even after she left the church, she called herself Mary Joseph, and continued to wear a modified blue habit. Her original name was Katherine Morrison, if memory serves. She became known as the Blue Nun."

"You said she was excommunicated. It all ends in disgrace?" Miranda was anxious for more, torn between wanting every possible detail and wanting to get on with the plot.

"The Church was not amused. There was too much about this folk saint that made them uneasy. On the one hand, they like adding saints to the canon; on the other, a saint too familiar — who speaks directly to the people with the voice of the Holy Mother, and directly to God — was, as you can imagine, unsettling.

"The priests for whom she had been housekeeper became her most dogged believers, second only to the Blue Nun in their devotion. When they altered the celebration of Mass to admit the adoration of Marie Celeste into prescribed ritual, however, the Church was incensed. This entire edifice, as I've said, was transformed into a shrine with a hierarchy of its own, featuring Marie Celeste as the principal object of veneration, even before Mary, and certainly before the Holy Male Trinity. Echoes of the voice rang through the revised liturgy, and women were celebrated and sexuality was removed from its burden of wickedness, set free from the pseudo-castrato divinations of a celibate priesthood."

"Excellent," observed Morgan, although it as unclear whether he was referring to Church reform or the speaker's charismatic eloquence.

"Thank you," said Alexander Pope, in no doubt about where the credit belonged. "Nothing inspires like righteousness. But then, in my story, things change. The two priests in the confessional, confessing their sins to the nun, itself a heresy the Church authorities had missed, admitted sickness of the soul so profound it could no longer be contained. Their obsessive adoration of Saint Marie Celeste was impeded, it seemed, by keeping secret a terrible crime.

"Their confessor in turn kept their secret, but demanded such awesome penance that others were appalled. The two priests, side by side, worked polishing the stone floors to a deep lustre, scrubbing the woodwork night and day, cleaning night soil from the latrines that had been erected to accommodate pilgrims, and when they were not engaged in menial and sordid activities such as these, they were to be found in postures of abject obeisance before a statuary image of Sister Marie Celeste."

"The priests confessed to sexual abuse," Morgan concluded.

"Of Sister Marie!" said Miranda, annoyed at the interruption, appalled at the suggestion.

"Think about it," Morgan continued, not in the least nonplussed to be commandeering Pope's narrative. "Beneath all the religious trappings, it is a fairly straightforward story."

He's right, she thought. Everything fits. She turned to Alexander Pope, addressing him almost formally, as if he might assist their investigation in progress. "The nun would never have relinquished her power," she said. "The secrets of the confessional were safe enough. It must have been the priests, themselves, who broke. It is one thing to molest an unschooled farm girl, another to have abused a saint."

"No, they did not break," said Alexander. "They were broken. Rumours and gossip did them in. The more voraciously the two priests atoned for their sins through public humiliation, the more lurid their crimes became in the imagination of pilgrims and the Church alike. Civil authorities seemed indifferent."

It was Miranda, not Morgan, who interjected to suggest perhaps Pope was straying from his documentary sources.

"Not at all," he declared. "I would place more faith in a zealot's diary, the correspondence of spinsters, an old nun's memory, than in the so-called objectivity of, say, a police report. Objectivity obscures the truth, based on the illusion that reason is a suitable criterion for assessing experience, and it is not. The Church, demanding three miracles for sainthood: that is the reduction of wonder to empirical evidence, as if proof were an adequate measure of anything beyond science."

"And science, as we all know," said Morgan, "deals in chimerical absolutes."

"Well said," said Pope.

"I'm only agreeing," said Morgan.

"As I said," said Pope. "Well said."

"What happened?" Miranda demanded. "It was a dark and stormy night ... Then what?"

"On the evening of April 23rd, 1893, the two priests expired before a hundred witnesses, yet no one could say for sure how they died. Some said it was seizures, and some said they had consumed poison in the Eucharist wine — a nasty twist on the sacrament of transubstantiation. Some said their breath was sucked out of them by winds blowing from the sacristy as they emerged with the Host, and some said they were strangled."

"By whom?" Miranda asked with urgency, as if some revelation were at hand.

"No one seemed to know — no one saw what happened," he said, deflating her excitement. "Perhaps in their collective hysteria the witnesses were blinded."

"I think it was the Blue Nun," said Miranda. "She poisoned the wine. She had access, motive, and an obvious capacity for the most bizarre of ironies."

"Motive?" Morgan asked.

"She alone knew what the priests had done."

"The priests themselves granted her the authority of the confessional," said Pope.

"To gather their sins, perhaps, but not the ability to absolve them. And even if they didn't fess up," said Miranda, "the Blue Nun would have known. I mean, what else would have led a young woman like Lorraine to madness, however inspired?"

"Madness!" Pope exclaimed, surprised at the turn his story was taking.

"Madness," she reiterated.

"You are cynical, Detective."

"And you?" said Morgan. "Surely you're not a believer."

"Of course I am," said Alexander Pope. "In the story, not necessarily in manifestations of the divine. But if you can't believe in stories, how will you ever get to the truth?"

Miranda briefly contemplated the difference between what is true and the truth, then took possession of the narrative as if she were a textual critic. "Here was a young woman, somewhat simple-minded, you said, uneducated, for sure, and quite pretty. Living alone with two men, two celibates representing an institution darkly obsessed with sex — men sick with sex because sex is deemed by their faith a sickness and they were men. Do you think they could have resisted? Thousands in the history of the priesthood have not." She looked into the eyes of the other two in rapid succession, then down at the stone floor. "What disgusts me is that they not only shared the girl's body, but they must have absolved each other of guilt, rationalizing to God their shameless brutality with the same facile religiosity they would have used to seduce their victim.

"People remarked on her changed condition," Miranda continued. The story was now hers. "She became increasingly morose; her only relief from her sorrows was prayer. And she prayed to the same God who in her own simple cosmology sanctioned her abuse in the beds of his profligate priests.

"Little wonder she broke. Like a rag doll in a wringer. Of course she saw Mary. Mary was the only one in that heavenly host who wasn't abusing her. And of course she fell mute. She had no words to describe her spiritual fusion with the Virgin Mother. Psychologists today might describe her behaviour as a hysterical response. I think it was the most natural response in the world, given her circumstances."

"And the nun," said Morgan. "What about her? The nun and the voice. Was that exploitation?"

"I would say the Blue Nun recognized rape in the girl's eyes from the first moment she appeared. A survivor of sexual assault will usually know when it has happened to another." She glanced at Morgan for reassurance. "I would say she recognized herself in the young woman's pain and salvation. The two are inseparable — sorrow and salvation — as the Virgin bore witness. Sister Mary Joseph merged her own story, the abuses that led to her own retreat from the world, with Lorraine Eliott's. Together they became Sister Marie Celeste and the voice came to life."

"Why would Mary Joseph do that? Eliminate the priests?" asked Pope. "I would think she had everything to lose."

"Because she could," said Miranda. "It's as simple as that. It was within her power. The three Marys — Mary Joseph, Marie Celeste, and the Virgin Mary — had seized control of the Church, at least in this small outpost of St. Peter's ponderous empire."

"The provincial coroner's report described their passing as 'Death by Misadventure.' That struck me as an understatement," said Alexander Pope.

"It simply means no one was prepared to lay charges," said Morgan.

Alexander continued his story. "The priests were posthumously reviled, and the rumour was officially sanctioned that they had taken their own lives under the influence of Satan. Church authorities lost no time in seizing control of the renegade outpost. They plastered over the walls, cleaned out anything smacking of idolatry, and declared the people's saint a fraud, a disgrace, a blasphemy to contemplate."

"But people went on believing, didn't they, even to the present day?" said Miranda. "Sister Mary Joseph was cast out, and when nothing else quelled the devotion of Marie Celeste's followers, the Church of the Immaculate Conception was declared never to have existed, and its bond with its congregants was annulled like a bad marriage."

"Exactly. The Blue Nun disappeared, but eventually she was found in Toronto, doing good works in a small mission off Jarvis Street for the benefit of prostitutes and battered women."

"You two tell a good story," said Morgan. "I wonder how much came from the tellers and how much from the tale."

"Observe," responded Alexander Pope with a sweep of his arm to take in the lustrous frescoes revealing the life of Saint Marie Celeste.

"Yes," said Miranda. "Nothing is in doubt but ourselves!"

# *chapter eleven*

## Wychwood Park

"I've heard of her," said Rachel Naismith as they drove west on Dupont, then turned up Spadina. "There's Catherine Tekakwitha in Quebec and Marie Celeste in Ontario. I didn't grow up Catholic, but almost everybody who wasn't black in our neighbourhood did. Black people were Baptist, white people were Catholic. That was the order of the world, neatly divided. You'd hear stories about the Huron saint and that girl from Georgian Bay — the Beausoleil Virgin. I don't think, from what I heard, either were virgins, except in the spiritual sense. Inviolate innocents. That's plural for 'innocent,' with a 't.' Not innocence with a 'c.' Innocence is a renewable commodity for Catholics. I think I always envied them that."

"Inviolate innocence. Sounds very floral and colourful. And instead you became a cop," said Miranda.

"I did," she responded with a gleeful lilt in her voice. "I lost interest in innocence 'bout the same time I discovered boys."

"Boys?" Miranda queried, trying not to sound overly inquisitive.

"I like boys, girl! I always have."

Miranda had no idea whether Rachel also liked girls. Since they had spent the night together, they accepted the affection between them as a feature of their relationship, which neither was prepared to risk losing. Their intimacy was open, and perhaps it was the openness that kept it from seeming overtly sexual. They were comfortable with each other. Ironically, Miranda thought, in the same way she was comfortable with Morgan. Except Morgan was more complex. Or she was more complex with Morgan. And sometimes she and Morgan were uncomfortable.

"I certainly do like Alexander Pope; don't we both?" said Rachel. "Now, *he* is a boy you could play with."

Miranda gave a throaty laugh. "I cannot think of another man who has so completely left the boy in his wake. He's one of those people who seems to have been born an adult. He speaks to the world from a position of imperious knowledge."

"He does not. He's warm and kind and ... and lots of other good things."

"Agreed, he's a virtual saint, but he's not snips and snails and puppy-dog tails."

"You can't knock him for confidence, Miranda. He's one of the best in the world at the things he does."

"I'm not knocking him. I like him as much as you do. More — I know him better. I'm just saying I can't picture him as a child."

"He would have been shorter."

"And a poet?"

"A precocious poet, writing in couplets."

"And a garden designer. A tiny, perfect little person penning *The Rape of the Lock* when others his age were keeping their prurience stealthy."

"Did you ever read that?" Rachel asked. "*The Rape of the Lock*?"

"I did."

"Much ado about nothing. I skipped most of the classes."

"That's the point, Rachel. It was supposed to be much ado about nothing."

"Exposing a lost saint to the world. Come on, it's a little more exciting than squawking rape over a locket of hair."

"Rape is a measure of loss. Belinda's innocence is violated."

"Well, I'd appreciate our Alexander no better. He's a poet, but with real things, not words."

"Nothing's more real than words," said Miranda. She suspected she actually believed that was true.

"He has a poetic sensibility," said Rachel, confidently.

"He has," Miranda agreed. "It's like apostolic succession. His great-sire's genes confer upon our present Pope the poetic authority whereby he imbues moribund ruins with life."

"Did you say 'whereby'? I don't think I've ever heard anyone say 'whereby' in a conversation. What about 'notwithstanding'?"

"I've been hanging around Morgan."

"He does talk like that, doesn't he?"

"Sometimes," said Miranda, immediately feeling as if she had betrayed him. "He reads a lot. He has an eccentric memory. Sometimes he remembers whole paragraphs from some esoteric journal or website, and sometimes he can't remember what day it is. That makes him interesting. He's infinitely unpredictable."

"So, why aren't you two together?"

"Don't be ridiculous."

"What about you and me and Alexander Pope. We'd make a good threesome."

"Don't be ridiculous."

"You have a raunchy mind, Miranda. I was talking about friendship. We make good company, just the three of us."

Miranda suspected Rachel's statement was somehow a judgment of Morgan. She felt uneasy talking about Morgan to Rachel. But she was also wary talking about her to him. Friends could be like that, she thought; your friendships could be mutually exclusive. That was the nice thing about their relationship with Alexander: the three of them created a nice ambiance. Nothing intense, just an aura of comfort. Nothing enduring.

As they drove under the lee of Casa Loma, that extravagant anachronism dedicated to a wealthy dreamer's long-suffering wife, Miranda glanced over at her friend. There was something wonderfully direct about Rachel, she thought. Driving through the gates of Wychwood Park, a ravine enclave of cultural entrepreneurs and tasteful Edwardian houses, she revised her judgment. By the time the car pulled up in front of the house where her ward, Jill Bray, lived with the housekeeper, who had virtually raised her from an infant, Miranda decided the secret to Rachel lay in her taking life as it comes. Rachel did not simplify the complexity of the world; she simply refused to resolve the ambiguities.

Jill was sitting on the verandah steps with a friend. "Hi, Rachel," she called. "Hi, Mandy."

"My name is Miranda. I don't have nicknames, I'm not the type." She leaned over and kissed Jill on the cheek. "Hello, Justine."

"Hi, Mandy."

"You can't call her that," said Jill to her friend. "I don't call your mother 'Mom.'"

"Hello Detective Quin," said Justine. "And you must be Rachel."

"How could you tell?" said Rachel.

"Easy," said Jill. "You're the one with short hair. Rachel, this is Justine. Justine, this is Rachel. She is a twelfth-generation Canadian"

"Not quite," said Rachel.

"And Justine is a Canadian *ad infinitum*," said Jill.

"Meaning what?" Rachel asked, and immediately answered, "First Nations, of course. You don't look native to me.... Oh, my God, did I say that? Child, forgive me. You are of course aboriginal, looks are deceiving. Welcome to my world."

"Actually, I'm a mixture of Swedish and Portuguese."

"She refuses to be categorized with hyphenated citizenship."

"My ancestry is the earth itself," Justine pronounced. "My grandparents are buried in Mount Pleasant Cemetery. Ergo, I am of the earth: a native Canadian."

"Well, Justine," said Miranda, "you might find a few authentic First Nations people who would be inclined to find your position presumptuous."

"Mandy," said Jill, with a tone of scorn in her voice that only a fifteen-year-old girl can manifest from the depths of her illimitable experience. "Please. Don't be condescending."

Rachel looked the two girls over with a mixture of righteousness and envy. They somehow managed to make low-slung jeans and tight, abbreviated tank tops obscenely provocative. "You two aren't going anywhere dressed like that."

"No, Rachel. We're just hanging out. But we might go trolling a bit, after Mandy goes. Wanna give it a try?"

"You're not going anywhere until you pull up your pants, girl, and change your little sister's top for something that fits. You don't want to go around showing your titties like they were raspberries on over-whipped cream."

"I don't have a little sister and neither does Justine. We're both orphans."

"My parents aren't dead."

"But they will be, eventually," said Jill, cheerfully. "Mandy's an orphan. What about you, Rachel?"

"Not yet! Only halfway. My father's alive."

Miranda leaned against a verandah column, enjoying the absurd repartee. Rachel was scolding them as if she had known them for years. The girls were responding with good-humoured cheek. Jill's morbidity suggested she was coming to terms with the deaths of her erstwhile parents. She envied the girls their friendship, based on mutual admiration, not convenience, as her friendships had been when she was their age. She acknowledged to herself that Rachel was as close to their age as her own. She looked at all three of them with a surge of parental passion — something new to her and awesomely satisfying.

"Have you thought any more about what I proposed?" she asked Jill.

"Yeah, I talked it over with Victoria. Justine says I can't go."

"And why not?"

"Because she's my friend."

"Then wouldn't she want her friend to have the advantages —"

"Of a private school!" exclaimed Jill. "I don't understand why."

"Victoria wants to go back to Barbados, Jill. She has kids of her own."

"I'm her kid; she can't leave me. She wouldn't want to."

"What did she say?"

"She said she'll stay with me always."

"And me too," said Justine. "Victoria and me. We're her support group."

"Get lost," said Jill.

"I don't want you to go away."

"Branksome's in Toronto," said Miranda.

"Mandy, it's the wrong side of Yonge Street. And you want me to live there!"

"And enjoy it!"

"It's called Branksome Hall. That sounds like a jail."

"Sounds ritzy to me," said Rachel.

"What did Victoria say?" asked Miranda.

"Ask her yourself. Victoria!" Jill called, leaning back on her elbows and casting her voice through the screen door behind her.

There was silence until Victoria appeared in the doorway. "Was I bein' summoned, Miss Jill?" She rolled her eyes. "I ain't birfin' no baby, Miss Scarlet." Then she saw Rachel. She opened the door and came out, extending her hand. "I'm Victoria," she announced, as if it were in doubt. "I am this rude child's significant other — not her mother and I'm not her guardian, and I'm Miranda's housekeeper, not the young lady's housekeeper, in spite of what she thinks, and I'm not her friend since Justine's enough friend for anybody."

"'Significant other' has sexual implications," said Jill.

"For heaven's sake, Jill!" Victoria snapped.

To Rachel's surprise, the girl looked admonished. "Sorry, Victoria. This is Rachel Naismith. She's Mandy's friend."

"And she's twelfth-generation Canadian," Justine chimed in.

"It can happen," said Victoria. "Even 'mong us black folks."

"Pleased to meet you," said Rachel, shaking Victoria's hand.

"How are you? And how are you, Detective Quin? Your girl here is getting quite a handful. Off to boarding school for her — it's the only way."

"Victoria! You told me I could live with you always."

"Or until you got too big to handle, whichever came first."

Jill looked devastated, then burst into laughter. "You don't want to go home, do you, Victoria?"

It was Victoria's turn to look distraught. Miranda interjected. "That's not really fair, Jill. You can't make her choose between you and her own children."

"But she's always been here — ever since I was born."

"But child, I do have my own children runnin' around in Barbados, and they need their mommy. I wanna take you with me, if I could."

Justine interjected. "Can we come and see you for visits and things, like on holidays? Can I come too?"

"Of course," Victoria responded, touched by the naïveté of their love. "You stand up, the both of you." They did, and she drew each of them to her bosom, hugging them with a sweet rocking motion. "You'll both come and stay with me any time you want. That's okay with Miranda, isn't it, Miranda?"

"For sure," said Miranda. She exchanged a knowing glance with Rachel. They had talked about Jill and her need for stability. Boarding school, Rachel agreed, was the answer.

Miranda wasn't prepared to move to Wychwood Park. Her work demanded a central location (she knew that argument was absurd, since her condo on Isabella was little closer to police headquarters). Her work did demand odd hours and a disruptive domestic life. Jill had only two more years in school after this one.

"I'm not going to leave here. I love this house and I love Justine and I'm not going to leave either one. I'll stay here without you, Victoria. Justine and I will live here alone. It's my house."

"More or less," said Miranda. "'Less' would be the operative word, since I'm in charge of your estate."

"Then I'll move in with you."

"Highly unlikely!"

"Then I'll move in with Justine."

"Jill, you can't," said Justine. "I'm too poor. You know there's no room. My dad and my mom, they think you're my twin sister, but there's no way. You're the daughter they had to give up. I sleep on the couch."

"You do?" exclaimed Rachel.

"Only since my little brother was born."

"How old is he?"

"Twelve."

Jill turned to address them all solemnly. "You know about the working poor. Well, Justine's parents, they work and they're poor. They don't live in Wychwood Park. So, we're at an impasse."

"No," said Rachel. "I think we can work it out. Let me have a brief whispering session with the boss lady here." She took Miranda by the arm and walked her to the corner of the verandah.

"Now, it's none of my business, but I'm going to tell you all the same. Jill's expenses are covered by the estate of the old bastard who owned the Jag, right? You take some of the old bastard's money. You set up a fund. You already administer two other funds from his millions. So you set up an education scholarship in her dead mother's name. For girls. First recipient, Justine. Is that her real name?"

"She and Jill both read Lawrence Durrell when they were twelve. It's from there, she's been Justine ever since, except for a brief period when she was Balthazar."

"Neat."

Over dinner, conversation between Miranda and Rachel ran the gamut from boarding schools to Catholic saints, but kept returning to murder. They were in the nondescript Italian restaurant on Yonge Street that had become their special haunt, despite the lacklustre food and indifferent service. Rachel described her year at Alma College near London. That was all her parents could afford. She worked her way through Western, but she had been going through a brief Rastafarian phase and they figured a stint at a school for young ladies would straighten her out. It did, she observed enigmatically, in ways they could never have imagined. Miranda confessed to her own freshman admiration for private-school girls, who seemed, wherever they were, to behave like they had a perfect right to be there. They were worldly — even the ones who had never been to Europe — and they had ways of dressing down with casual authority. She and Rachel agreed: it would be good for Jill to spend her last two years of high school at Branksome Hall.

Sainthood was more problematic. Neither of them came from a tradition where becoming a saint was an option. True, they had both encountered Mormons, with their self-proclaimed status as latter-day saints, but Rachel found them racist and too cheerfully morbid, and Miranda found them absurd. It's not Jesus coming to North America, she explained. He could go anywhere he wanted. It wasn't the ancient story that got to her. It was Joseph Smith, a convicted felon, translating the sacred tablets into pseudo King James English, in spite of finding them in New York State in the nineteenth century. The assumption that God spoke to humankind in a seventeenth-century dialect was, to her, both offensive and silly. Still, she admitted, the few Mormons she had known appeared blessed.

"What does that mean?" asked Rachel.

"Like 'radiant': touched by the light."

"You mean, smug and sanctimonious."

"Don't you envy people who know the answers?"

"Miranda, I haven't even figured out all the questions."

"Exactly."

"So, you like televangelists, exuding righteousness, ooz-ing self-unction, offering deliverance on the wings of a buck and a grin. Yechh."

"No-o-o," said Miranda. "But look at the other extreme — the spiritually humble."

"Where do you find them? Not saints, surely not in Sunday church."

"We see people doing good works all the time. What about them?"

"Exactly. They're the true saints. There is no correlation between religion and goodness."

They conceded there are good people in the world, and they also conceded that they were both being tremendously arrogant, pronouncing on other people's states of grace and salvation. Neither could fully comprehend sainthood in the Church calendar, although many canonized saints extended their presence far beyond the boundaries of Catholicism or even of organized religion: St. Nicholas and St. Valentine, most commonly, but others as well, like St. George and his dragon, St. Patrick and Ireland.

"It's nice to know she's making a comeback," said Rachel.

"Who?"

"The Virgin Mary."

"What are you talking about?"

"Don't you read the tabloids, Miranda? The image of Mary has appeared on the wall of a derelict church. I was reading in the lineup at the supermarket last night. Turns out, it could be the church in Beausoleil. They're vague on the details. And they quote an unidentified authority as saying the image may only be a water stain bleeding though the plaster."

"You're assuming Alexander's the authority. There's no water damage in his church."

"Well, the paper said that the authority admitted it might be a wall painting under the plaster showing through, in which case it wasn't the Virgin but a local folk saint."

"Sister Marie Celeste! Amazing. Why didn't you tell me?"

"I assumed you keep tabs on the tabloids."

Miranda could imagine Alexander Pope's annoyance at this turn of events. Rachel thought it an amusing bit of trivia, but Miranda knew he would be swarmed with fanatics, desperate for a sign — the same people who yearn to see Christ's face in a tortilla, his Holy Mother in cracks on a ceiling. It was diverting enough when the followers of Sister Marie Celeste hovered silently in the background or solemnly cleaned, but tabloid salvation is a raucous affair. His work would become unbearable. And how could he protect the revealed frescoes from vandalism when zealous visitors pried bits from the wall as holy relics? She hoped whoever Alexander's angels were, underwriting his project, they would have the power to restrict access to the building until the inevitable frenzy dissipated. As it would, once Alexander revealed the source of the image in the fresco beneath.

"What I don't get is why Sister Marie would not be the perfect saint, from the Church's perspective."

"Because," said Miranda, "she was beyond their control."

"She was dead."

"Exactly. It's harder to control the dead."

"I would have thought it was easier," said Rachel. "They can't argue back."

"But they can. The dead can speak eloquently. It's the living who can't argue back. The dead have the authority of having crossed over, and even the pope can't pretend to do that."

"But sainthood is all about what the living can make of the dead."

"What the living can make of the dead? That's what the Church is all about. And Shelagh Hubbard. Think about what she made of the dead. We'll have to ask her if she was divinely inspired."

"If you ever find her."

"We'll find her," said Miranda. "You can count on it. There's no way someone like her can stay hidden for long."

"Not if she's competing with Rome."

Miranda was uneasy. In spite of being an agnostic, she was not as far off the scale as Rachel or Morgan, she was sensitive to what a believer would consider blasphemy. Her conditioning in a Christian world and her affection for the rituals, her respect for the fundamental values, made her uneasily defensive about organized religion. At a visceral level, she thrilled to the idea that there was something inaccessible in her life that was holy. Yet she knew with certainty that she would never turn, in either peace or in sorrow, to what her world had constructed as God. That, she thought, would violate her sense of the truly spiritual in human experience.

She revised their postulation. "I think what Shelagh Hubbard has done is antithetical to religious practice."

"You sound like my religion professor."

"The woman discards the souls of her victims as refuse. She uses their physical remains like so much clay. She sculpts and positions them into shapes that amuse her. I'd say that's the polar opposite to what religions try to do. Virtually all religions celebrate the spirit within, whether to set it free or contain it with meaning. The end result may be not that much different — posing the dead for the living — but the intent surely is."

"So, she's kind of an Antichrist."

"No, I'd say she's the antithesis of the Mary triumvirate. At least Sister Marie Celeste and Sister Mary Joseph and Mary, the Mother of God, co-opted each other in good conscience. They brought something profound to the lives of their witnesses, even if you and I don't have access to such things ourselves. If they offer female salvation of sorts, Hubbard exemplifies its absolute absence."

"So, she's the anti-Marialogical principle at work."

Miranda stared at her friend, amused and yet dismayed at the cheerful cynicism that she wrapped around herself like invisible armour. She reached across the table and touched her hand. Miranda's own hand was pale and lightly corded with blue-green veins — a beautiful, mature hand. And Rachel's was dark and smooth, with flecks of childhood scar tissue — the hand of youth and promise.

Rachel rolled her hand over and gave Miranda's a squeeze, then they both sat back and for a few minutes said nothing.

It was Rachel who brought the conversation back to murder. She wanted to work homicide eventually. The bodies at Hogg's Hollow were her first murder victims.

"It's been two weeks since Hubbard disappeared," Rachel said. "You've read her journals cover to cover. The forensic evidence is in: they were killed in the farmhouse. The provincial coroner's office concurs: they died separately in the sauna — him first, and he was stored in the freezer. So, what don't you know? What will she be able to add? You've got an airtight case, right?"

"Well, she could add herself, for a start. It's hard to prosecute without her. But at least we won't have another deadly scenario."

"How so? How can you be sure?" The younger woman clearly regarded Miranda as her mentor in criminal matters, although Miranda suspected they were equally experienced in life.

"She doesn't have access to the tools of her trade, so to speak. Think about reducing Morgan to a bunch of old bones and secreting them in an Indian burial tomb. That would have been a very complex affair."

"Morgan was lucky."

"Yes, he was. Of course, it was probably his one shot at sainthood."

"Pity."

"He'll live with it."

"A lot of what you do is wait."

"For comics and cops, timing is everything."

"You don't really think she was abducted, do you?"

"No, I think she staged her own disappearance. Which means she'll stage her reappearance as well. I suspect it'll be spectacular. I'd say she set it up just so. Even leaving her journals behind. She wanted us to know what she's done. She's building anticipation like an impresario. By flaunting perfidy, she stays in control."

As Miranda walked home from the restaurant, Rachel's questions about Shelagh Hubbard troubled her. She had read the journals with the meticulous care of a textual scholar, but what resonated in her mind was the embedded personality, so blatant and yet obscure, taunting with its inaccessibility. It was as if from the beginning Hubbard wrote her journals for the eventual appreciation of witnesses. Were she and Morgan the only readers, so far? Presumably, yes. Morgan still had the binders at home. They had not compared notes, but she was sure their readings would differ.

Scotland Yard had responded to her queries about Madame Renaud's and the Chamber of Horrors with surprising delicacy. They would look into the matter, they said. But

Renaud's is a venerable institution, housing effigies of great personages from throughout British history. It was not as if the police could simply march in and start peeling wax from faces that had accrued sanctity in their own right by virtue of their celebrity as fakes. They would get back to her.

It was a warm evening. The two men approaching through the dappled shadows on Isabella Street were in shirt sleeves. They had been drinking. Miranda tensed, and felt the reassuring bulge of her semi-automatic against her back. Their reeling became more exaggerated as they got closer, and on the excuse of intoxication, one of the men lurched against her. She pushed him out of the way, but the other man, on the pretence of assisting her, grasped her shoulders. She shrugged him off. Somehow, she was between them and she tried to sidestep off the curb.

Seeming to steady himself, the first man threw his arm over her shoulders. As she slipped out, the second man took hold of her waist from behind and lifted her. She kicked out and, breaking free, she reached for her gun. As she swung it around from the holster, both men froze.

"Hey, lady, we were —"

"Shut up," she said, heaving to catch her breath.

They looked terrified. They were young, probably university students. She motioned with her Glock for them to prostrate themselves on the sidewalk. Shocked sober, they fell to their knees and tumbled forward. One of them started to cry, sobbing softly into the pavement. A pool of urine spread between his legs. Both were shaking.

"Now, stay there," said Miranda. "Don't move. Don't move a muscle."

As she walked down the street, she could hear whispering. She stepped into shadows and looked back. They had lost sight of her. In a sudden scramble, they were both on their feet, stalk still, then running madly toward the lights of Yonge

Street. Miranda put her gun away. She knew enough not to draw a firearm in a situation like that. She could have talked her way out of it — she only had to say she was a cop. On the other hand, she thought, they'll think twice before hassling another woman. She might be packing a gun.

Her recovery rate was a testament to experience and by the time she got to her condo she had dismissed her muggers as nothing more than a nuisance. She whimsically rang her own buzzer, as she always did, in a ritual meant to scare burglars out of her apartment, avoiding the confrontation if she walked in on them unannounced.

She went straight to bed, but she tossed restlessly. The words in the binders echoed through her head in Shelagh Hubbard's voice. Miranda felt she had been given an extensive tour of the innermost recesses of a psychopath's mind and could not find her way out again. She had been enthralled as she read and disturbed to find herself understanding Morgan's nearly lethal fascination.

Shelagh Hubbard's prose was detached and precise. She described selecting her victims for their resemblance to the mutilated prey of murderers already on display. She described stalking her victims, befriending them, luring them to the chamber, poisoning them, bleeding and embalming the bodies, waxing, reconstructing their features, all as if she were recording daily activities in a diary. She wrote very well, with a curious blend of passion and restraint. Morgan had suggested all three binders read with the contrived disengagement of applications for scholarly grants, but he had missed the strong personality, evident by its absence. Staring into the darkness, Miranda could feel Shelagh Hubbard somewhere in the room. She did not believe in ghosts, but she recognized how inseparable in her mind the woman was from death itself.

# *chapter twelve*

## Fire Road #37

---

$\mathbf{M}$iranda woke up confused by images of the undead that flickered on the borders of consciousness. The undead. In the real world people were either dead or they were not. Life and death were mutually exclusive. There was being and non-being, with nothing between, except zombies and vampires. Nonsense, she thought. A stick of celery in the refrigerator was dead, but it had being — it existed. A body existed, no less in the world as a corpse than when it was alive. The Jewish man from the States and the young lesbian student who were posed in Shelagh Hubbard's grotesque parody of the eternal embrace were more real from certain perspectives after they had died than before.

That is the problem with working homicide: the bodies have more significance than the lives they led. Miranda shuddered. We have that in common, she thought. Shelagh Hubbard and I, we both see life through the eyes of the dead.

The telephone rang.

"Morgan? Thank God it's you. I've been thinking —"

"What a destructive thing to do, this hour of the morning."

"It really is. Is there such a thing as philosophical morbidity?"

"Philosophy is morbid by definition. Any concern with the meaning of life is inseparable from knowing how it all turns out."

"That's pretty profound for seven a.m."

"What's the problem?"

"What? Oh, I was lying here ruminating. I think I'm like Shelagh Hubbard in some ways. It's very distressing."

"I told you, she's like my ex-wife. More so, the more we know of her. And you are nothing like Lucy at all. Ergo, you and the genius of depravity are nothing alike. You have nothing in common with Shelagh Hubbard except you both find me quite attractive."

"She found you resistible, Morgan. I've read her account of your night at the farm."

"And you?"

"You've got good bones." She shuddered. "But I find you more useful alive. What's up?"

"Up?"

"You called me."

"Did I?"

"Yes."

"I got a wake-up call from the superintendent. London's in an uproar. It appears certain effigies in Madame Renaud's Chamber of Horrors are human cadavers with a wax veneer. The museum has been closed down while every figure in the place is punctured with needles in a search for human tissue. It seems the tabloids are having a field day. They'll even have to test out the queen in her various ages and stages. The British love cheeky scandals."

"It's only figures of murder victims who were replaced with corpses. I made that clear to Scotland Yard. Why bother with the rest? Shelagh Hubbard's only interest was to replicate the obviously dead."

"Also —"

"There's an also?"

"This morning's *Globe* has a story buried —"

"No," said Miranda. "They've picked up on Alexander's Virgin, haven't they?"

"They have. How did you know?"

"Don't you read waiting at the supermarket checkout? That's how I keep up with current events."

"Yeah, well the *Globe* names Pope as an authority on apparitions. As I read it, the Virgin Mary has appeared on a plaster wall of his church. Why, I cannot imagine. If she wanted to communicate with believers, why such an inept mode of expression? You'd think between Mary and God they could come up with something a little more substantial than blobs on a wall."

"They work in mysterious ways, the celestials."

"They do. But Alexander Pope seems unmystified. He's declared the manifestation nothing more than a seepage stain from a fresco underneath the plaster. Sounds to me like he's getting a bit of publicity for his reclamation project."

"Which I cannot imagine he wants."

"It depends, doesn't it, on his motivation for restoring the paintings? It may be a labour of love, but love for what?"

"For a job well done? For giving us back a bit of our past?"

"You can't give back the past. By definition."

"Morgan, it's too early for pedantry. What's past is pro-logue, et cetera. Can I go now?"

"No. I called to tell you three things. Ready for number three?"

"Shelagh Hubbard's been arrested?"

"No, but close."

"Sighted?"

"Almost. They've found her car."

"Where?"

"In the bush. Someone phoned Officer Singh —"

"*Our* Officer Singh? Peter the Pointer?"

"The same."

"Why him? Was the car found in Owen Sound?"

"No, in scrub bush near Penetanguishene. It was an anonymous call — probably a local hiker. The boss asked us to drive up and take a look."

"There was blood, of course."

"Apparently."

"Morgan, do you trust anything about this woman? It's a set-up. What's a little blood? She's a master of special effects made from authentic materials. She's still writing the story. She's leading us on a wild goose chase. This is more fun for her than playing with corpses; she gets to manipulate real cops. Maybe you were her inspiration."

There was silence on the other end of the line.

"Morgan?"

"I'm thinking."

"About?"

"I think she's been abducted; she could be dead."

"When you play with life and death, you don't easily give up control."

"Are you thinking like yourself or like her right now?"

"As I said, I'm not sure there's a difference, Morgan."

"That's scary."

When they arrived at the scene, Morgan walked around the abandoned car in concentric circles, starting from a point where the car could barely be seen and slowly closing in. Miranda circumscribed the scene in an expanding spiral, beginning at the car and moving gradually outwards. The OPP had done the forensics, photographed the scene minutely, and as a courtesy had waited for them to appear before towing the car away.

Peter Singh, who turned up immediately after they arrived, explained in a low voice to the officer in charge that this is what made them such a formidable team. He made swirling motions with the index finger of one hand on the palm of the other, trying to replicate their complementary circuits.

"As fine an example of the difference between inductive and deductive investigation techniques as you're likely to find," he offered, going on to declare their legendary status. The OPP sergeant listened politely. She had never heard of them. But she was experienced enough not to expect a great revelation when they completed their perambulations and approached. Singh, however, anticipated a major pronouncement, and was briefly disappointed when neither had much to say.

"Is there anything else?" asked the sergeant. "Do you want to catch up over at detachment headquarters? I don't think there's anything we haven't already sent on."

Miranda bent down and peered in through the open door on the passenger side of the car. Morgan followed with his eyes on the trail that led through spindly hardwoods and gnarled cedars to the fire road they came in on that ran alongside a dense and orderly array of pines in a reforestation project. He shook his head.

"No," he said. "That's about it. I think we'll head back."

Miranda looked up and concurred. "Thanks for waiting," she said. "Let us know if anything turns up. She's long gone, wherever she is."

"Okay," said the OPP sergeant. "Sorry it wasn't more productive. It's a long drive." She turned to the truck operator. "Let's haul her away."

Miranda and Morgan and Peter Singh stood in a small group to the side, watching the tow truck jockey into position, crushing scrub foliage in the process. Once it got a good purchase on Shelagh Hubbard's car, the sergeant signalled goodbye and hopped in beside the driver, hitching a ride out to the highway where her cruiser was parked.

"Did you see that?" said Morgan, focusing for the first time on their friend from Owen Sound Police Services.

"What?" asked Peter Singh, pleased to be included.

Morgan looked at the young officer's turban and smiled, wondering how he managed to get enough headroom in a car. He held himself tall, and the turban added several inches to his height.

"My turban," said Singh. "Is it not clean?"

"Oh, yes," Morgan answered. "Good to see you." He reached out his hand and gave Peter Singh a hearty handshake, much to the latter's bewilderment, since he had been on the scene for a half an hour or more.

"What is it I saw?" asked Singh.

"You can see this spot from the gravel road, there."

"Yes, the fire road, number 37, for fighting forest fires."

"But you can't see it from the highway."

"No," said Singh. "The fire road has not been graded since last year. That is why we both parked at the side of the highway."

"And?" Miranda wanted Morgan to finish his thought.

"And, it means I agree with you."

"That's nice. About what?"

"That Shelagh Hubbard set up this whole thing. She wanted the car to be discovered, just not too soon. She could be pretty sure no one would travel the fire road until the weather turned. Spring brings out hikers. Is it fishing season yet?"

"Walleye, last weekend, I think, said Peter Singh.

"I'll bet there's good water back there beyond the pine grove. She knew someone would come through. She could have driven another thirty feet and it might have been years before anyone found her car."

"Glad to have you on side," said Miranda. She paused, smiled at Peter Singh, and asked him, "Did you notice anything peculiar about the bloodstains in the car?"

"They weren't hers?"

"Oh, yes, they were. You can count on it."

"They were on the back seat?"

"Yes, but that's where you'd expect them to be if she'd been abducted. There or the trunk."

"And?" said Morgan. The two men looked at her expectantly, and for a brief moment she enjoyed the suspense.

"You didn't look inside the car, Morgan."

"I knew you would. So ...?"

"The blood was spattered, not smeared."

"Yeah?"

"Neat drops of blood distributed in a strategic design. Too neat, too strategic."

"Then if she did it herself," said Peter Singh, "how did she get out of here?"

"There had to be another vehicle," Morgan suggested.

"That's what we're to assume. But Morgan, did you see any evidence in your meandering of a place where a car turned around?"

"Maybe he backed out," said Morgan.

"Who?" Miranda asked.

"The person who abducted her," said Peter Singh.

"Or he left his car parked at the road," Morgan offered.

"Too suspicious."

"He could have backed out," said Morgan.

"Who?" said Miranda. "Listen to you two. I thought I had you convinced she staged this. She walked out. People walk. This isn't a conspiracy."

"Okay, so once she got to the highway, what then?" Morgan asked.

"She could have had a bicycle with her. No one notices someone on a bike. She looked in pretty good shape. She was in very good shape, wasn't she, David?"

"Wherever she's got to, she must have had transportation — maybe another car stashed near here or back at her farm."

"We can check the registration," suggested Peter.

"I don't imagine she'd use her own name," Miranda answered.

"Oh."

"I like the bicycle explanation," said Morgan. "But she'd need the other vehicle. This seems an extravagant device, dumping her car."

"It's ten years old, Morgan. I'll bet she replaced it with a sports car."

"A Jag."

"I doubt it. Maybe a Miata."

"There was a bicycle," said Peter Singh, grasping imaginary handle bars. "I remember a very old CCM beside the back door."

The layout of the summer kitchen came back to Morgan. "There were two bikes," he said.

"No, for sure I know there was one bike only."

"One bike, an old one," said Miranda. "With a dropped crossbar, red with black piping, CCM, wide handlebars."

"Not two?"

"No."

"Well, there you are. She made her getaway on an all-terrain model."

"Unisex, blue, wide tires with whitewalls?"

"Yes."

"It was leaning against the inside back wall of the drive shed."

"Oh, she moved it. There goes my theory."

"Not at all, Morgan. It reinforces it, circumstantially. She had a bike, she rode it somewhere. It just means her other car was back at the farm, not somewhere closer."

"Precisely," said Morgan.

Peter was fascinated and a little annoyed. As soon as the OPP had left, the dynamic duo had swung into action, but not before. He had wanted them to be impressive, verifying his acumen as a judge of their worth, but they had waited until now to display their considerable skills. Still, he was flattered to be there.

"I think before you leave these parts of the country," he said in an eager voice, "you would like to go to the church where the Virgin Mary is appearing. I have been there already and it is very strange. She can be seen by believers and non-believers alike."

"In Beausoleil?" Miranda responded. "We know the man who discovered her."

"The Virgin?"

"The image. He's a friend of ours."

"The man who is restoring the beautiful walls?"

"Reclaiming them, yes. His name is Alexander Pope."

"I saw him there. I introduced myself. There were many, many people. He seemed quite disturbed, and he was relieved to see my uniform. This was today, on my way here. Very indirectly. He thought I would keep the people away, but I explained my jurisdiction is Owen Sound, not Beausoleil. Still, I helped him set up a barricade to keep them back. He was most gracious."

"Okay, Morgan? Let's go and see what Alexander's come up with."

"It could be a scam to raise funds for his project."

"He's got money. He has angels behind him."

"Haven't we all!"

Several concessions before they got to Beausoleil, even before the church spire was in sight, they noticed the traffic. Normally on a back road like this there might be the odd pickup or a tractor rumbling along, hauling farm implements or a hay wagon. But a modest congestion of cars such as this was remarkable. Morgan and Miranda parked a ten-minute walk from the church, but Peter Singh, who had followed them in his clearly marked cruiser, picked them up and drove right to the door, where he double-parked with the unabashed authority of his office.

What Morgan noticed most was the silence. There were crowds milling around in clusters outside, and parallel streams of people shuffling in one side of the double-door archway at the front and out the other, having organized themselves spontaneously to give everyone the opportunity to witness the apparition. But there was virtually no conversation among them. It was eerie how quiet they were. Even the children played noiselessly, either in deference to their parents' solemnity or in imitation of their awestruck behaviour.

With Officer Singh leading, the three of them slipped through and into the building. The crowd was moving in an orderly column down the centre of the nave, so they cut behind the pillars to the side and past the frescoes they had seen before, all of them now beautifully illuminated. The scaffolding was still against the wall beneath the fourth panel that Alexander Pope had been working on a fortnight ago. The plaster had been peeled off entirely. Sister Marie Celeste appeared to be hovering in mid-air, toes pointed like a ballet dancer to display additional stigmata where nails had been thrust through the flesh of her elongated feet. Smaller figures could now be seen toiling at the ordinary tasks of a farming community. She was clearly one of them, yet divinely enhanced, with size and evanescent colour and an ethereal demeanour testifying to her inspired estrangement from the world.

Alexander Pope was standing in front of the window beside the fifth and final panel, which, from the oblique angle of their approach, was nothing more than hand-smoothed white plaster. He seemed an ambiguous presence. He might have been a security guard or Charon at the gates of Hades. He looked haggard, as if he had not rested in a long time, and yet somehow triumphant. Was this, Morgan wondered, what he had secretly been working for all along? The adulation of the masses for the gift of his genius?

Yet no one seemed to be paying him much attention, apart from responding to his solitary posture, facing away from the wall, as a warning not to approach too closely.

When Pope saw them, his wan smile suggested long-suffering forbearance. Miranda gave him an awkward hug, Morgan shook hands, and Peter Singh made incomprehensible gestures meant to indicate he had returned under forces over which he had no control, his pantomime ending with an open-palmed shrug.

"Alexander," said Miranda. "What on earth have you been doing? Your gentle pilgrims have multiplied."

"Exponentially," he responded. "It's all quite unexpected, and ...," lowering his voice, he continued, "quite undesirable."

"What do your sponsors think?" Morgan asked.

"Oh, well, you know, I'm not sure."

"If they wanted a tourist attraction, this could be another Lourdes."

"No, I think not. One is more than enough. The object of this project was not to arouse shallow religiosity, but to bring an aesthetic wonder back into the world. I have not the genius to create such a work, but perhaps I do, to give it new life."

"A not-modest undertaking," said Morgan, mimicking what he heard as mildly condescending locution.

"But humbly undertaken," Miranda countered, a little defensively.

Alexander Pope seemed unaware of or indifferent to the subtleties of their discourse. "These people interfere with my work," he declared. "The quiet and calm is deceptive. I would be torn limb from limb as a heretic should I resume my labours by peeling away their sacred image."

"They seem a gentle crowd," Miranda interceded.

"Hell hath no fury like a zealot denied."

"They do not seem zealous," she responded. "Maybe the zeal is your own, and the fury, your suppressed rage at the intrusion."

He looked down at her and curled his lips in a tight smile. "I am at a standstill, an impasse."

"Celebrity is fickle," Morgan observed, without lack of sympathy. "Fame interferes with what you are famous for doing."

"It is not about me, Detective, I assure you. I am merely a talented enabler. I reveal what already exists. But they see what they wish, not what is there."

Alexander Pope blinked several times and leaned back to his full height, gazing over at what, from their side-view perspective, still looked like a blank plaster wall. Morgan was intrigued by the arrogance of the gaunt man peering down

at him. Miranda felt sorry for him. He was obviously distressed by his reduced role. The apparition was no longer his
to present, but rather his to protect; it was the property of
those who saw in it a miraculous vision. Peter Singh found
the whole situation entertaining; he was bemused to see this
rather austere and pompous man bereft of authority.

"Well," said Miranda. "Let's take a look. Lead on, Peter.
You have the uniform."

Singh walked straight into the double columns of people
who were shuffling up through the nave and circling at the
chancel to pass down in front of the panel before moving
out through the vestibule. The crowd parted and let them
through. From the far side, they looked across and Pope's
three visitors were astonished to see a brilliantly illuminated
portrayal of Mary's Assumption.

"My goodness," said Morgan.

"My God," said Miranda. "It may not be a miracle, but it's
magnificent. Alexander, I had no idea."

"It is very beautiful, isn't it?"

"It is the Virgin Mary on her way to Heaven," Officer
Singh observed.

"Actually," said Alexander Pope, "it is Saint Marie Celeste.
These people," he said, lowering his voice to a discreet whisper, "most of them have never heard of Sister Marie. For them,
it is Mary. They want miracles, but they want them familiar.
Nothing too taxing on the imagination."

"I would think your pilgrims are wonderfully imaginative," said Morgan. "These people invest a beautifully rendered apparition with supernatural powers. Faith outruns
reason; surely that's imagination. Just not yours or mine."

Miranda listened to Morgan with some surprise. He was
the one who'd admonished her for saying she was an agnostic, when clearly, he would say, she's an atheist, the same as

him. And here he was, rising to the defence of the spiritually desperate. Yet she looked at the faces in the stream flowing by and saw no desperation, only a kind of suspended worldliness, a wishful innocence, a haunted yearning to touch with their eyes a vision of God.

"It is beautiful, Alexander," she said. "Did you do it?"

Taken aback, he stammered, "No ... I ... How ... I have not started on that wall. The plaster ... perhaps it is what lies underneath. Somehow the image shows through."

Miranda laughed. "I didn't mean literally. But, like, did you orchestrate the phenomenon? Did you make all this happen?"

"No, absolutely not. I'd rather get back to my work."

"But what do you think?" Morgan asked. "Where did the picture come from? Is it by the same artist who did the others? Maybe the plaster covering peeled away in the night —"

"And was cleaned up by the pilgrims," Miranda added, wanting to be part of the resolving discourse.

"It is possible," said Peter.

The other three looked at him as if he had overstepped an invisible boundary. He brushed an imaginary speck of lint from his chest and repeated, "It is quite possible."

"No," said Alexander Pope. "It is not. The plaster on this one is the same vintage as the shrouds I have removed from the other four panels. It is not the same age as the original frescoes."

"Is it possible for a fresco to bleed through?" Morgan asked.

"Perhaps, but not spontaneously. Perhaps over years the colour might seep, but not like this. It would not be such a clear replication."

"Do we know what lies underneath?" Morgan continued.

"No, although logic suggests it would be the ascension of

Marie Celeste, affirming her rise to the heavenly order. That in itself would have made the picture blasphemy in the eyes of the Church. Only Rome confers sainthood; God merely affirms the decision."

"And this is clearly Sister Marie," said Miranda. "You can follow her progress. In the fourth panel, she is beatific, but still of this earth. Here she has broken free of mortality; she's not just floating, she's soaring. Her stigmata have faded away. Her eyes are no longer raised heavenward — they look straight ahead and are radiant. Her dress is sky blue and her hair is the colour of sunlight. Alexander, she is breathtaking, stunning, a portrait of the truly divine. But it is clearly Marie Celeste."

"Are we assuming this is by the same person?" asked Morgan.

"Oh, it is, Morgan. It has to be."

"I'm inclined to agree," said Alexander.

"And I as well," said Peter.

Abruptly, Pope pulled away from their little enclave and pushed through the crowd, back to the base of the panel. When the others joined him, he said, "Sorry, I thought they were getting too close. They weren't actually. They seem to be self-policing. Still, I worry."

"You look absolutely exhausted," said Miranda. "Why don't you take a break, go out to your van for a nap, take a run into Penetang and have dinner? We'll stand guard for a while."

"I have a better idea," said Morgan. "Close the place down for the night."

"They'll riot," said Officer Singh.

"No they won't. Believers climb mountains on bloodied knees for a glimpse of the shadow of God. Waiting overnight in a car will be welcomed as penance for imagined sins. They'll feel they've earned their revelation if they have to wait."

"How do you propose we go about this?" said Miranda.

"Simple. We close the door. Put up a sign that says 'Visitors Welcome,' followed by a clear indication of hours, say ten a.m. to four p.m. Make them feel welcome, but control their access. Let those in here file out. Close the other door. Alexander then has eighteen hours to do what he wants. Daily."

"Let's do it," said Peter Singh.

"Agreed," said Alexander Pope. "A very good idea, Detective. And with Officer Singh in his uniform, and you two looking like police —"

"We don't," said Miranda.

"A compliment, my dear. You both carry yourselves with unmistakable authority."

Miranda looked at Morgan's habitual rumpled demeanour and laughed.

When the building had been cleared, the four of them stood in front of the revealed apparition. From the centre of the nave it was not quite so distinct as it had been from farther away. The closer they got to it, the more blurred it seemed, until right beneath it the lines were quite vague and the colours, while still somewhat opalescent, were subdued. As Miranda had noticed before, when they moved to the side, the bright illumination virtually washed the colour away and the entire panel glowed in a white sheen.

It is interesting, she thought, that the people filing through, while they could see it more clearly from across the nave, did not really respond until they were closer. Close up, perhaps, it was less an aesthetic experience. In the dramatic blur, when they could almost reach out and touch the holy apparition, there might be satisfaction of a deeper kind, one she did not fully apprehend.

They heard a shuffling noise in the shadows. Miranda wheeled around. Two of the original pilgrims moved quietly into the light and walked by them, brooms in hand. These were true believers in Saint Marie Celeste, who somehow had access to the building through the sacristy. It did not occur to Miranda or Morgan, or Alexander Pope, or even Peter Singh, to interfere.

Stepping up onto the chancel where the altar would have been, they turned and looked down into the empty church, each of them imagining what it must have been like when Marie Celeste was alive. There was something quite moving about the empty building, restored to meaning by a picture on a wall. Three more acolytes appeared from the shadows and busied themselves cleaning and dusting. It was eerie, Miranda thought. And satisfying, somehow. And strangely affirming.

She was the first to notice. "Do you smell something?" she asked.

"What?" said Peter Singh.

"Fleur de Rocaille," said Morgan.

"What?" said Miranda.

"It's a perfume."

"I know it's a perfume. Is that what you smell?"

"Lucy used to wear it."

"Who's Lucy?" asked Peter.

Morgan ignored him. Miranda answered, "His wife."

"What is it?" said Alexander. "I'm not sure I smell anything."

"Oh, you do," Miranda insisted. "A strong odour of violets."

"Yeah," said Morgan. "Violets. Was it here all along or did it just come in with the pilgrims?"

"I think it was here. It was masked by all the people, but it's here."

"The smell of saints," Morgan observed, his voice suggesting he found his own statement at the edge of credulity.

"When they're dead, their bodies exude the odour of violets."

All five pilgrims had gathered at the edge of the chancel and stood watching them, listening.

"Well, what do you think it is?" Morgan said to the one closest.

"I think it is Saint Marie Celeste," he responded in a matter-of-fact tone. "We sometimes smell violets when we work here at night. She is buried beneath where you're standing."

Miranda instinctively took a step to the side, the way she would in a cemetery when she became aware she was standing over a grave. But here there was no marker. Just slabs of limestone, each big enough to cover a body.

Morgan smiled at the man. It was the first time he had heard one of them speak. "Do you think she is still here?" he asked. "Perhaps the Church removed her body."

"No," the man answered. "It was the Church who left."

Morgan nodded.

"They left; but this is a holy place. You cannot change what the Lord has done, though you speak with the words of the Lord."

"Undoubtedly," said Morgan. "So where do you think she is? About here?" he said, indicating a slab at his feet.

"No," said the man, stepping up. "Under this rock, here."

"Shall we look?" said Morgan.

"If you wish," the man responded.

"Morgan!" said Miranda. Turning away from him to address the pilgrim, she asked, "What do you think of the ...," she paused, nodding in the direction of the wall panel, "... the Virgin Mary?"

"It is a picture of Saint Marie Celeste," the man said in a quiet voice. "It is only a picture. Her remains are beneath this stone — of no use to her, now — and she is with Mary in heaven."

Alexander spoke up. "Would you have no objections if we took a look?"

"None at all," said the man. "It is your building. But only what is in it. The unseen ... that is ours. Do as you wish."

Morgan and Alexander exchanged looks. Like boys engaged in a conspiracy, Miranda thought.

"Is it legal?" she said.

"Yes of course," said Morgan. "Alexander has the authority. If he says it's okay, it's okay."

Alexander stepped down and walked over to his scaffold where he reached underneath and retrieved a crowbar and a smaller pry bar. Together, he and Morgan prodded the cracks between the slabs, relieved to find as they pushed accumulated detritus away that there was no mortar between them.

"We might as well start with this one," said Morgan, looking at the pilgrim for confirmation.

Miranda breathed deeply, inhaling the odour of violets into her lungs. She exhaled slowly, trying to prevent herself from hyperventilating. She was very uncomfortable with their ghoulish behaviour, and yet oddly curious.

The two men got their bars under a corner of one slab and lifted. It was five to six inches thick. Peter Singh rushed over to the scaffold and retrieved several four-by-fours, one of which he slipped under the raised corner. They moved around the slab, prying and lifting, until it rested on the beams. The odour of violets had become intense, almost sickening. The pilgrims moved close. Everyone except Miranda leaned down without orders being given and grasped the edge of the limestone and simultaneously lifted, walking it off to the side.

Miranda gasped. As the shadow of the stone slid across the opening and light flooded the cavity in a small stone crypt, she could see a woman's body dressed in sky blue lying on rock, with only a smooth boulder beneath her golden hair to support the head. Her skin was the colour of alabaster and her lips were as bright as blood. Her eyelids curved softly over closed eyes. Her lashes flickered in the bright illumination as if they were going to flash open, and her lips were poised as if she were about to speak. She was full-bodied and lithe in her absolute stillness, sensuous and innocent. All gazed at her in a profound hush, the mystery rendering them silent.

Then Miranda spoke. "It's Shelagh Hubbard," she said.

# *chapter thirteen*

## Yonge Street

---

The old church took on new life, swarming with Provincial Police. Peter Singh watched closely as they poked and prodded into every corner and shadow, assessing infinitesimal details of forensic interest, from dust motes to cobwebs. They had questioned him and Morgan and Miranda separately, hoping to find some anomaly in their description of events that might yield unexpected insights. They questioned Alexander Pope at length, but he seemed bewildered, as if his sacred trust had been violated. They interviewed the five pilgrims, finding them forthright and elusive, and of little value, it seemed, to the investigation. The pilgrims were told to go home, which they did.

Peter Singh observed all the activity in utter amazement. How did he have the great fortune to witness such an astonishing turn of events? Detectives Morgan and Quin had read the scene at the abandoned car like a novel, but they had been wrong, for their villain was here in a cold, stone crypt and very dead. Yet, inexorably, they had been drawn here — he seemed to have forgotten it was at his suggestion — and the body had been revealed. They had been redeemed, and he marvelled that he had been with them. He was inextricably a part of the plot.

"It must be disappointing for them," Miranda observed as they left through the sacristy.

"I don't think so," said Morgan. "As far as they're concerned, Shelagh Hubbard never existed. What they have seen tonight is the body of a saint, and it is exactly what they expected: smelling sweetly of violets and un-decomposed. I'd say the evening has been a singular success from their point of view."

"Do you really think they believe it was her?" said Peter Singh, spreading his hands out to indicate a body lying in state. "We have told them it is not."

"And who would you believe?" said Morgan. "Us or God?"

"God?"

"Their God has given them the corpse they believed would be there. He has confirmed their faith. Anything we say is irrelevant. Faith overrules facts every time."

"It's almost enough to make me a believer," said Alexander Pope. Miranda looked up at him; he was pale as a ghost.

"It's not your fault, Alexander."

"But it is. I created the context. I revealed the frescoes, I set up the scene."

"Alexander, this is not about you," said Morgan, not unsympathetically. He found the man more likable now, when he was standing on unknown ground and his project seemed to be slipping from his grasp. "How could you know this would happen?"

"I've been here most of the time, or sleeping in my van. Sometimes I drive into Midland or Penetanguishene for supplies. Otherwise, I've been here."

"One thing is certain," said Miranda. "Good though she was at her craft, she didn't put herself in there without help."

"She has never looked better," said Morgan, staring over the forensic team clustered at the opening of the small crypt.

"Blue suits her, although I must say the cut of her dress isn't quite *au courant*," Miranda observed. "It's obviously meant to look like the outfit Saint Marie is wearing for her ascension." She stepped down from the chancel and walked along the nave until opposite the fifth panel, in which Mary the Mother and Marie Celeste seemed to merge as one. The other three followed. "Look at that," said Miranda. "Funny, though, I didn't see it before. I thought she looked familiar but I didn't make the connection. That could be an inspired portrait of Shelagh Hubbard!"

"And then there were four," said Morgan. "Saint Marie Celeste and the Virgin Mary and Sister Mary Joseph and Saint Shelagh herself. It's not a coincidence she's laid out in a pale-blue habit."

"Robe."

"Habit. Anyway, the resemblance is uncanny, and it's not a coincidence that Shelagh Hubbard and Lorraine Eliott are dead ringers."

"What an unfortunate choice of words."

"So, where are the bones of Lorraine Eliott?" said Miranda aloud, but more to herself than the others. Then, addressing Morgan, she said, "We'd better caution forensics to check the crypt carefully for residual traces of a much older body." She stepped up onto the chancel to confer with the OPP.

"Where do you think they got to?" Morgan asked Alexander Pope.

"The bones? I have no idea. What would a person do with old bones?"

"Discard them, I suppose, or set up a morbid tableau. But there would have been more than a skeleton in the tomb. It's a stone crypt, cool in summer and frozen in winter, and we saw how well it was sealed. I would imagine there was a mouldering corpse in there, swathed in the remains of a pale-blue robe."

"Unless, of course, she was truly a saint," Alexander observed. "Then she would have been perfectly preserved and smelling of violets. Perhaps the violets we smell are a lingering reminder of her inviolate flesh. How very eerie."

When the county coroner's people lifted Shelagh Hubbard's body out of its tomb, Morgan moved closer. He watched them set her gently on the gurney. He stood beside her, looking down at her face. He felt a strange mixture of emotions. There was no doubt she was a pathological killer. His own fate had rested precariously in her power, and she had clearly articulated plans in her journal for extinguishing his life and using his bones to fabricate the charred remnants of a Jesuit saint. It seemed almost silly now, a quixotic subterfuge doomed to exposure. And he could not help but feel the pathetic irony of her present predicament, having herself been used after death to supplant another saint's earthly remains. And as he scanned her face, her deep-set eyes pressing with suppressed vitality against the membrane of their lids, full lips poised as if about to utter a benediction, cheekbones pushing at their thin veneer of covering flesh, he found her hauntingly beautiful and it made him sad, and he felt sympathy for her powerless state as an exemplar of death.

"Morgan, you all right?" Miranda pressed to his side, holding his arm against her breast in a subtle gesture of affection no one else could see.

"Yeah," he said. "Better than her."

"Come on, let's look around. It's still our case; the abductor abducted is now the murderer murdered."

"Okay."

He kept staring at the dead woman's face. Miranda spoke in a low voice — not a whisper, but a private communication. "Morgan, it's okay, it wasn't evil you were attracted to but the disguise she gave it. And look at her — it was an enticing disguise. Forgive yourself for being her victim, Morgan."

He turned to her; they were standing so close, in other circumstances it might have been an embrace. He spoke in a firm voice. "Think about that."

"No," she said. She was not about to collapse her life story with his.

The two of them looked down at Shelagh Hubbard, who seemed to be listening.

"She's had better days," said Miranda.

"I wonder."

"Death becomes the lady, Morgan. Pallor suits her."

The implied intimacy of how close they were standing suddenly made both of them uncomfortable. Morgan stepped back and nearly trampled Officer Singh, who had just approached from behind. Miranda moved to the side and pushed against the gurney. A coroner's assistant, taking that to be a signal, drew a white cloth over Shelagh Hubbard's face and signalled for another assistant to help wheel her out of the building.

"Does this mean our case is resolved?" said Peter Singh.

"Well, in some sense it does," Morgan answered, swinging around to respond and finding himself awkwardly close, but still able to appreciate the young officer's odd gesture of closure, swiping his hand across his throat in a guillotine motion. Morgan held his own hand up, patting the air. "And in some sense it doesn't."

Miranda chimed in. "Scotland Yard will be pleased she's dead. Our superintendent will be pleased she's way out here and she's dead. Morgan's eventual heirs will be pleased she's dead. But there's a lot to find out before the story is over."

"The important thing, apparently, is that she's dead," said Alexander Pope, who had meandered through the tangle of investigators to join them.

There was an awkward silence.

"This one's definitely out of our jurisdiction," said Morgan.

"Unless," said Miranda, with a devilish gleam in her eye, "she was killed in Toronto and brought back here for burial. Then it's the same deal as with the Provincials, in reverse."

"Could that be possible?" said Officer Singh.

"Anything's possible," Morgan responded.

"We're on this," said Miranda, "until, can I say in oral quotation marks, 'the circumstances of her death have been resolved.' We'd like to understand what led her to do what she did, why she kept such meticulous records, where the predilection for grisly scenarios came from. That's part of our mandate, unofficially, if not on the books."

"Well, I must say," said Alexander, "I will be relieved when this latest development in her story is over. I really would like to get back to my work."

"Of course," said Morgan. "It's good to keep things in perspective."

More sympathetically, Miranda said, "I think the believers have already begun to disperse. Let's check them out." She led the others toward the front of the building and pushed one of the double doors open. The OPP officer outside made way and they stepped into a garish glow. Miranda was startled to realize the night had fled to the west and the grey sky was streaked with pink and orange as the sun pushed upwards against the eastern horizon. The crowd had thinned to a few clusters of diehards who seemed as thrilled to be associated with murder as with the holy apparition that it had displaced.

"It's funny, isn't it?" she said, taking a deep breath of the crisp morning air. "The paintings on the wall haven't changed, but now they're just paintings. For these people out here, Shelagh Hubbard's appearance in the grave of their saint seems to have taken the magic away, if not the mystery."

"Not their saint," said Morgan. "She's the saint of the housekeeping pilgrims. What these other people saw was an image of the Virgin Mary, and it undermines her mani-festation to be associated with a criminal investigation. Logic kicks in. Maybe it's only a picture of the folk saint after all, and suddenly the apparition is reduced to cult status, an awkward archaic curiosity. So, home they go, to wait for another sign, next time on a pizza crust or a washroom wall."

"You are quite cynical, Detective Morgan," said Alexander Pope. "I think the frescoes are the very beautiful works of unheralded genius. As art they are much more significant in the long run than an apparition of the Virgin Mary or, for that matter, the recovery of a saint's untainted corpse, or even the surprise appearance of a dead murderess."

"And you think I'm the cynic," said Morgan.

"'Sailing to Byzantium,'" said Miranda, who bristled at the word *murderess*.

"What?"

"Yeats. 'Sailing to Byzantium.' 'Art above life.'"

"You're speaking cultural shorthand," said Morgan, unsure whether he was complimenting her or censuring her for inappropriate erudition.

"How long was she dead?" said Peter Singh.

"Who, the saint or the sinner?" Miranda responded.

"The woman we have been looking for."

There was a pause. Then Miranda answered. "It's hard to tell. She had been embalmed, she was sealed in, the crypt was icy cold. I'd say she could have been there a week or more."

"And the violets?"

"Injected through her veins, I imagine, with the embalming fluid."

"Oh, dear."

Miranda turned to Morgan, who seemed radiant in the morning sunlight. "Well, partner, it's time to go. Let's check in with the OPP and then check out."

"My goodness," said Peter Singh. "I'm on duty in an hour. Goodbye. We will keep in touch."

"For sure," said Morgan.

"As for me," said Alexander, "if no one wants me for anything further, I'm off to Midland and a good day's sleep in a choice motel."

"Very reasonable," said Miranda. "I'll tell the OPP they can reach you here later on. I imagine they'll want you to keep clear of the crypt, but you can carry on with your project. I'll ask, but I don't see why not. I'm anxious to see how the story turns out."

"The fifth panel? I'll leave it for the time being. It is what it is: a stunning *trompe de l'oeil*. The panels on the other side of the church, I don't anticipate anything special. The apotheosis of Sister Marie Celeste would be hard to top."

"Unless her body turned up," said Morgan, "unravaged by time."

"Morgan," said Miranda, "let's let these guys get on their way." She took him by the arm and turned back through the door. "Come on, we'll go in and say our goodbyes."


Six weeks later, Morgan was walking down Mount Pleasant Boulevard, taking in the green of mid-June despite the traffic roaring by. Ahead, leaning against the abutment of a pedestrian overpass, he saw a half-dozen girls in school uniforms. Their blouses were untucked, draped loosely over their skirt bands, and their knee socks were scrunched around their ankles. These were older students, intent on declaring their personal style by compromising the prescribed apparel of their school, looking as dishevelled as possible. Nothing and no one, thought Morgan, will test the limits of privilege like those born within it. Still, there was something dangerously sexy about their wilful abandon.

Feeling a lascivious twinge of guilt, Morgan looked away as he walked by. A familiar voice shrieked an indecipherable inanity, and he saw out of the corner of his eye that one of the girls was Miranda's ward and another was her friend Justine. He stopped dead in his tracks. The girls went silent, then Jill recognized the slightly unkempt pedestrian who seemed poised on the edge of a decision. She dropped her cigarette to the ground. Justine did the same. The other four girls, unaware of the implications, kept on smoking.

"Jill," Morgan said, awkwardly. "Good to see you. Good to see you, too, Justine."

The two girls rushed him, Jill throwing her arms around his neck and giving him a smoochy kiss on the cheek, Justine hugging them both and blowing kisses into the air.

"Do you know this man?" said the tallest girl.

"No," said Jill. "But isn't he handsome!"

"He's my mother's boyfriend," Justine announced.

"Your mother is married," said the tall girl. "I met her, remember? And your father."

"Well, he would be if he could."

"Actually, he is the favourite boyfriend of my official guardian," said Jill.

"Morgan!" said the tall girl. They, of course had heard of

Miranda and Morgan and some of the sordid details of Jill's past. That is how she chose to maintain control of her own narrative: by being forthright about the publicly known story, and perversely whimsical about the details.

Before Morgan could mumble that he was not Miranda's boyfriend, the other girls gathered around him. Justine maintained a proprietorial grasp on his arm. He was embarrassed by the attention, and several times tried to excuse himself. Finally, he explained that he was on duty and really had to get going.

"Murder," Justine announced. "Murder is Morgan's business."

Morgan took Jill gently by the arm and said, "Walk along with me a bit." The others, even Justine, picked up the hint and fell back.

Once they were out of earshot, Jill said, "I know what you're going to say."

"What?"

"Miranda is death on smoking."

"But she's not as much against it as I am."

"Oh."

"I thought you had more sense."

"I do."

"Then —"

"It's not about sense, Morgan. It's peer pressure."

"Bull!" He couldn't help but smile. "Peer pressure is no match for intelligence and a modicum of imagination."

"Right. Actually, I've been conned by subliminal advertising. Did you notice cops in movies smoke?"

"Only the ones who can't act."

"Yeah. Dumb, eh?"

"Really dumb, Jill."

"So okay, let's make a deal. I'll never have another cigarette if you bribe me. And Justine. You have to bribe her, too.

You see, what happens is, like a girl in my dorm, her parents wrote her a cheque for a thousand dollars when she turned twelve, and postdated it a decade ahead. If she makes it to twenty-two without smoking, it's hers. Neat, eh?"

"And what if she smokes? How would her parents know?"

"She'd tell them."

"Simple as that."

"Simple as that. Being a rebel and a renegade and a maverick doesn't mean you're dishonest, Morgan. So how about it? Wanna bribe me?"

"Sure."

"How much?"

"Twenty."

"Each?"

"Each. But I pay you now. Then it's your problem, not mine."

"Agreed. I agree for Justine, too."

Morgan took out his wallet and handed her two twenties. She took them and tucked them down the front of her blouse just as a police cruiser pulled to the curb. She leaned up and kissed him. "Love ya," she said, and she strolled with an exaggerated swing of her hips back to her friends.

"A little young for you, buddy," said a voice from the cruiser. The driver leaned forward to look up at Morgan through the passenger window. "Detective Morgan! Still, she is a bit young."

"Officer Yossarian." Morgan was amused and a little disconcerted by Yossarian's assumption. "You found me."

"No, sir, I wasn't looking. Just cruising."

"Can I use your radio?"

"Sure. Where's your cellphone."

"At home with my gun." Morgan slid in beside Yossarian. He waved to the girls, who were clustered together in excitement. The cruiser made his credentials more authentic. "Let's drive," he said.

"Groupies?"

"Yeah, well, you know. It goes with the job."

"Me, I like working uniform."

"Yeah. I never did it."

"You started in plainclothes?"

"Yep."

"I'm going back to school."

"Yep, good idea," said Morgan. They were driving up Mount Pleasant and Yossarian wheeled left onto Lawrence Avenue. "So where are you taking me?"

"Dunno. Are you working?"

"Yeah," said Morgan. "I was thinking."

"You got a case I should crack for you."

"If you've got time."

They bantered until they got to the Yonge Street intersection.

"Pull over here," said Morgan. "I'll walk down Yonge for a while. Do me a favour: call my partner, tell her where I am, and tell her I'm working."

"Sure thing, Detective. Keep thinking. You take care, now."

Morgan got out and ambled south down the east side of the street to enjoy the foliage along the cemetery boundaries and the TTC lines where the subway is elevated to ground level and the tracks carve through green ravines. He was deep in thought, but aware of his surroundings. It troubled him that the Shelagh Hubbard murder had not been resolved. They couldn't lower the curtains on the Hogg's Hollow drama until her file had been laid to rest. Initially, there had been a certain relief over Shelagh Hubbard's death. There would be no more horrific tableaux. But as time passed, he and Miranda both struggled with the lack of resolution. She wanted to understand. Morgan wanted closure.

They kept in daily contact with the regional OPP through the woman in charge, who was the sergeant at the scene when they had gone up to check out the abandoned car. They had had several routine cases after that: one in Rosedale — a situation that was euphemistically described as justifiable homicide. Politically sensitive. No charges were laid. There was a shooting in Yorkville, and another on lower Jarvis Street. Both saw the demise of pathetic outsiders — social misfits murdered by friends. Arrests were made without incident. The paperwork for all three cases was staggering.

Morgan had fled the office earlier in the day, before Miranda got in. Sitting hunched over his desk, images kept intruding on words. He was haunted by the memory of Shelagh Hubbard when they saw first her inside the stone crypt. For a fraction of a second he had thought it was the sanctified body of a dead saint! Perhaps he saw Lucy, he wasn't sure. Marie Celeste seemed to obscure the edges of identity, even when she wasn't there. Perhaps that's what a saint does, he thought. He wanted to avoid Miranda until the images sorted themselves out.

Despite the early onset of summer, the case had turned cold. The confusion of saints and sinners refused to unravel. The OPP had focused on Alexander Pope for a while, but as Morgan pointed out, the guy was a harmless eccentric. Sure, his prints and residual bits were everywhere in what was formerly the Church of the Immaculate Conception, but the place was, in effect, his studio. There wasn't so much as a fleck of skin, a fingernail paring, a loose hair on the elevated chancel near the opening in the stone floor — apart from his DNA adhering to the slab where they had lifted it away when they opened the crypt. Morgan's was there as well. There was, indeed, a connection between Pope and the murder victim, but he had been her teacher, not her mentor, and more recently his involvement was at Morgan's request.

Alexander Pope, himself, was apparently undeterred by the macabre turn of events. Miranda talked to him several times on the phone, getting progress reports on his project. Officer Peter Singh dropped in on him periodically and let Morgan and Miranda know how he was doing. Morgan envied Pope — a man consumed by his work to the exclusion of anything else; an artist obsessed.

In London, the Chamber of Horrors affair was already forgotten. Once the tabloids realized the Canadian involvement, they lost interest. Few Britons knew the notorious Dr. Crippen had practised in London, Ontario, where he refined his lethal techniques before dispatching so many English women to their untimely departures. Canada is too culturally bland to inspire much interest, even in murder, thought Morgan, wondering whether it was the fickle British or Canadian diffidence that made it so.

In Toronto, the Hogg's Hollow murders had slipped from the public mind into the irretrievable past. Despite the fact that the bodies were of recent vintage, the whole affair was smothered by a general indifference to the city's colonial heritage: it was as if they really had been long-dead lovers, not unfortunate strangers visiting a modern metropolis.

In Owen Sound, and all the way from Meaford in the east to Southampton in the west, and north to Wiarton, the reputation of Officer Peter Singh had spread like a rumour. Even his parents were now firm supporters in his choice of career, despite his father's earlier disappointment that he had not gone into the military, or at least the RCMP.

In Beausoleil the deconsecrated church was once again a cultural curiosity. The significance of the frescoes had been

greatly enhanced by renewed secular interest in Sister Marie
Celeste. The true pilgrims came only in the dead of night
and eventually stopped coming even then, but museum cur-
ators and art historians were received by appointment during the day.

"Whoa, Morgan! Where are you going?" It was Miranda,
stepping out the door of Starbucks just over from police headquarters on College. "Talk about a man lost in thought."

"No," he said. "I wasn't thinking about anything. My
goodness, I've walked all the way down from Lawrence
Avenue. Holy smokes, that's a walk."

"I knew you'd be coming. Yossarian called. Said you were
determined to walk the length of Yonge Street. Thank God
you turned south. Come in for a coffee — take a break from
your travails and travels. I'll buy you a cappuccino."

"How long have you been waiting?"

"I figured you'd walk the distance, so I didn't come over
'til maybe twenty minutes ago."

After they settled in with their coffees, Morgan asked,
"What's up?"

"Well, I had a call from Sergeant Sheahan."

"Who?"

"OPP. In charge of the investigation at Beausoleil."

"So, what's Sergeant Sheahan got to say?"

"Nothing. That's the point. Nothing, nada. They found
DNA traces at Shelagh Hubbard's. Our Hogg's Hollow bodies
were processed at the farm, for sure. Beyond that, nothing.
They're virtually closing down their investigation. That's what
they mean when they say 'leaving it open, pending further
developments.'"

"Yeah. So where does that leave us?"

"With a mystery of unknowable proportions."

"They're the worst kind."

"Or best. The most mysterious mysteries are best."

"For whom?"

"There's got to be something to connect with," said Miranda. "If it won't deconstruct, it's indecipherable. There has to be a way in."

"My dad used to say, 'If it ain't broken, you can't fix it.'"

"A wise man."

"And Ellen Ravenscroft once said 'The hardest autopsy is when nothing seems wrong.'"

"Except the patient is dead."

"Yeah, the client."

"Is that what they call them? 'Clients'?"

"I dunno," said Morgan. "But 'patient' implies recovery."

"'Client' implies payment for services rendered."

"Dead people. Let's say they call their clients 'dead people.' And they do get paid, just not by the dead people. By taxpayers."

"I do not like to think I pay Ellen Ravenscroft's salary. I prefer knowing she pays mine."

"Miranda?"

"Yes?"

"Why did you waylay me here? I could have been to the harbour by now."

"And then what?"

"I would have turned around and begun to walk north." He sipped his coffee. "Let's go back to our theatrical analogy. Shelagh Hubbard was creating drama, recording the scenes she created; killing was an extension of the authorial imagination."

"Okay," said Miranda. "Then someone else cleverly reduced her to one of the characters in a narrative that swallows up hers. A meta-narrative."

"And disposing of her as an aesthetic diversion, her killer

subsumes her achievement, such as it was, into his or her own."

"We sound more like literary critics than detectives, Morgan."

"Okay, but if we see the whole thing, her grisly machinations in London and Toronto, and her disappearance, her death, and the Gothic disposition of her body, all as part of the same story, one continuous narrative by several authors, where does that lead us?"

"Exactly. Where? A single text; so what?"

"How did she die?"

"Poison."

"Where?"

"At her farmhouse."

"How did the blood get in her car?"

"The killer, her killer, put it there. Drained a bit during embalming, kept it fresh."

"Same story as if she had written it, to this point. The killer wanted her death to be gentle, her car to be found. They wanted us to think she had staged her own abduction. Left the heat on in the house. Moved the bicycle. Arranged all the details, even the blood. Why?"

"To buy time."

"Exactly. To buy time. Why? To merge their stories, to make her an inextricable part of the revised script. To process her corpse, to encrypt it beneath the altar."

"There's no altar. The chancel. But why there? To implicate Alexander?"

"To subsume her in a story larger than her own but under the killer's control, to give it the mythic status of Sister Marie Celeste. Why the odour of violets?"

"To make her seem like a saint."

"Or! To make sure her body was discovered."

"In a saint's grave."

"Exactly," said Morgan. "A diabolical irony: drop a depraved killer into a saint's tomb. With flamboyant finesse."

"Why?"

"Why not? Whoever is devising the plot enjoys the perversity."

"Remember," said Miranda, "the literary thing — the writer getting off on his own creation — it's only an analogy. The killer as a killer is real."

"Whose creation is not yet complete. It's not over, so we wait."

"That could be dangerous," Miranda said, and she smiled.

"Yes," said Morgan. He didn't smile.

# *chapter fourteen*

## Penetanguishene

---

Miranda left police headquarters early to miss the Friday traffic. Morgan was working at home, but when she called him he wasn't answering. This didn't mean he was out — he could have been in the bathroom or he was just being perverse. Sometimes when she left a message, he would pick up midway through, explaining he was screening his calls. From whom? Whoever. But she was used to checking in with him. She felt reassured if he knew where she was. She turned outside the building and looked back up at it, thrilled at how articulate architecture can be, enjoying the fact that she worked within this splendid postmodern extravaganza where glass and multi-hued granite the colour of the Canadian shield create shapes in the eye that celebrate through artifice the natural world. She loved working in a building that spoke so eloquently of great things over small, like a medieval cathedral. Not, she thought, like skyscrapers, which celebrate the tyranny of commerce and trade.

Feeling quite pleased with her train of thought, she wheeled around into Morgan's arms.

"Admiring the scenery?" he asked, steadying her, then standing back. "It's a great building, isn't it? Powerful, psychologically accessible. Just what a cop shop should be."

"I left a message on your machine."

"Okay, so tell me."

"I'm in a rush. You'll hear it when you get home."

"I can listen from here. I'm clever that way."

"Well, I said, 'Hey, Morgan, see you on Tuesday. Alexander's invited Rachel and me up for the weekend. He's nearly finished, he wants to show off. So we're taking the Jag, top down, and going camping. She's got three days, we're going to set up a tent, there's a campground outside Penetang. He invited us to pitch it in his parking lot, but, like, it's not all about him. I haven't camped since I was a student. We're going to have fun. You too. Have a good weekend. Bye-bye.'"

"That's it?"

"That's it."

"Press erase and you're gone."

"I'm gone. Outta here. You take care."

"You taking your cellphone?"

"We're going camping, Morgan. Living in a tent for the weekend."

They chatted for a couple more minutes, then she wheeled away, blew him an ironic kiss, and went striding along the sidewalk toward the subway. He watched her go and for an instant he felt lonely. After she descended underground, he turned and entered the ambiguous embrace of steel and granite.

When she got home, Miranda had a quick shower and called Rachel to see if she was ready. They had both packed up the previous night, conferring by phone about just what to bring in the event of hot weather and cold, rain or shine, mosquitoes and sunbathing. She drove to Rachel's with the ragtop up and together they tucked it away. Miranda tied a kerchief around her head and Rachel pulled a Metro Police ball cap out of her kit that she put on backward at a rakish angle, so the band cut across high on her forehead with a feathering of hair poking beneath it.

They told Alexander they wouldn't be there until Saturday, so they drove straight to the campground and set up their tent on a rocky knoll overlooking Severn Sound. It was a tent Miranda had purchased specially for the occasion — a good quality all-season tent, in case she ever wanted to try winter camping. It was cozy without being cramped, and as long as there was a breeze, it wouldn't be too hot with the zippered doors open and the flaps of the vestibule set to catch the currents of air.

After a picnic supper, they chatted in the waning light of the evening. The mosquitoes came out in force but were easily discouraged by the flapping of hands. Miranda talked about her mother and about her sister in Vancouver who had kids and a career and patronized Miranda for being in police work. At least when she was with the Mounties, she had a certain panache, but with the Toronto Police, according to her sister, well, she could have been a lawyer if she'd set her mind to it. Rachel described her own family life, growing up with three brothers and two sisters. "My parents were influenced by our Catholic neighbours. Everyone around there had big families. It was a form of self-defence. If you can't out-buy the buggers, outnumber them. That's what my father used to say. Never was clear who 'the buggers' were."

Rachel's father was still alive, in his fifties, but her mother was dead. "Just wore out, my dad says. But does he ever miss her. We all do."

"I miss my dad, too. I was just hitting puberty when he died. It was like everything changed, you know, everything. Sometimes I wonder if I really remember him, or if it's a fantasy I've constructed to take his place."

"That's what all memories are," said Rachel. "They're stories we tell ourselves to keep the past alive. I remember my mamma differently every day."

"Wanna go for a swim?" said Miranda.

"Skinny dip?"

"Sure. It's dark enough; and it's cool enough that the mosquitoes are pretty well gone, and the water's gonna feel warmer. Georgian Bay is notoriously cold, you know."

They edged their way down the smooth stone to the rocks by the shore, stood up in the light of the moon, stripped off their shorts and tops, giggled like girls, and slipped out of their underwear. Each lowered herself carefully into the frigid water, quietly so as not to attract attention. They could hear voices and see several campfires glowing against the dark landscape, and the water rippled with dazzling striations of moonlight. They swam away from shore in companionable silence until they couldn't make out what people were saying, then floated on their backs, sculling with fingers at their sides, so that only their faces and breasts and their toes broke the shimmering surface, and the rest of their bodies were swallowed in the impenetrable black of the water beneath them. Sometimes as they arched, their pubic hair caught tangles of moonlight, and in the cold their nipples stood proud. Each looked at the other sideways from time to time, lifting her head so that her body sank into the darkness, admiring the gleam of wet skin. After fifteen minutes or so, without exchanging a word, they began manoeuvring back to the rocky shore.

The air was cold when they stood up, but the smooth stone by the tent still glowed with the residual warmth of the sun. They lay down side by side on towels, shivering from the air, their backs warmed by the stone. Rachel reached over and clasped Miranda's hand and together they stared into the depths of the night. The moon washed the sky clean of all but the most brilliant stars as it shone through a thin veneer of cloud covering. Tomorrow would be rain.

Shortly after midnight, the rain began, waking them both from sound sleep, beating on the tent fly in a sustained fusillade as wind whipped against the flimsy dome structure that had seemed snug and secure when they dowsed their flashlights and settled into their sleeping bags only hours before. They sat up together, surrounded by shuddering darkness and the crackling shriek of the thin yellow membrane that shielded them from the fury of the elements.

"Oh, my God!" Rachel shouted over the din. "We're gonna be blown away."

"Or the tent's gonna tear into ribbons."

"Or we're going to float into the lake. My God, can you feel the water flowing beneath us? No wonder no one else pitched a tent here. Pine needles in a depression on the rock. Great place for a tent, you said. It's a pool — we're practically floating."

"Look on the good side," Miranda shouted. "It's not leaking."

"Not yet. Is it guaranteed?"

"It's a North Face, guaranteed for a lifetime."

"Against acts of God?"

"It's in the fine print."

"That's a relief."

"I've gotta pee, all this water swirling around —"

"Pee in a cup."

"We don't have a cup. Kitchen gear's outside, probably washed away. I'm gonna batten down the tent lines, anyway. Rather drown than be airborne."

The words were swept from her mouth as she crawled across Rachel and unzipped the inner door, then extended her upper body out into the tiny vestibule and slid the zipper on the outer door open. The material flapped violently against her face as she crawled out into the wild night. She stood up, the wind and the rain beating against her, plastering her pyjamas instantly to her skin in a clammy embrace. Diffused moonlight filled the sheeting air with a sublime evanescence and the whitecaps on the sound rolled gloriously against the shore, smashing in waves of thunder. She stood tall, and felt her skin burn in the furious onslaught, and grinned, catching rain-laden wind in her teeth.

She leaned down and shouted into the tent, which Rachel had zipped tight behind her. "You gotta come out here! It's beautiful." The outer zipper lowered a palm's width and fingers appeared in the slit, wiggling it wide enough for a voice to pass through.

"You're nuts. No way."

"Rachel, it's magnificent. Come out here."

Slowly, the zipper edged downwards, then with a sudden movement Rachel leaped from the tent, grabbed Miranda, and hugged her, shivering against the storm, shocked by her own audacity. Then she released her hold and they stood side by side, pyjamas drenched, facing the luminescent lake, addressing the storm with silent grace as it swarmed roaring around them. They looked at each other and grinned, water streaming over their features, disguising them as sea nymphs. Miranda reached for Rachel's hand and clasped it in hers. It was a magical human moment in the midst of natural chaos.

When they began shivering too vigorously to endure, they gathered small boulders and placed them against the sides of the tent and on top of the pegs anchoring the guy lines. Miranda walked shyly to the side and as the wind whipped

strings of rain against her she squatted and peed. Then they
crawled back into the tent, pushed their sleeping bags into
a corner while they stripped off their sopping pyjamas and
dried off with beach towels. The floor of the tent was spongy
from the water pooled underneath, but only damp; there was
no seepage. Next, time, Miranda thought, I'll bring a sleeping
mat like the guy was trying to sell me.

Miranda tossed their wet pyjamas out into the vestibule
and when she zipped up the door, there was a momentary
hush in the storm, then it picked up with renewed fury.
They wriggled into their clammy sleeping bags. Before either
zipped up, Miranda leaned over and kissed Rachel on the lips.
They held the embrace for a long time, then Miranda slipped
back into her own space. Both of them knew this was a turning point — that somehow they were destined never to be
more intimate than at this moment, and that morning would
bring with it an enduring friendship. Miranda smiled to herself, feeling strangely relieved. She turned her head to look
at her friend. The wind howled wildly outside and the rain
rattled against the shuddering walls, and in the diffused light
of the hidden moon she was surprised to see that Rachel had
fallen asleep.

When they pulled up in front of the Beausoleil church,
they were taken aback to find that Alexander's van was not
there. The front doors were locked but they walked around
the side to go in through the sacristy. There was an imposing
padlock on the sacristy door, but Miranda knew that a bit of
a shake would open it. She had watched the pilgrims come in
and out the back way, and clearly Alexander was content to
provide them access, although he had explained on the phone
that none had returned since not long after the discovery of
Shelagh Hubbard in Sister Marie's crypt. He was mildly com-
plaining, since now he had to clean up after himself.

"They will be back," he had assured her. "They're waiting for the publicity to die down. The curiosity seekers and the desperate, false pilgrims, they're gone for good. But the true believers, when they see my pictures again, they'll realize their beloved saint is still here. Her burial niche was desecrated, but the entire building stands as a testament to her enduring presence as a mediator between them and their God. One or two will come, then more and more. The true pilgrims will come back, I'm sure of it."

Miranda had listened, pleased by his confidence although perturbed by his proprietorial description of the frescoes as *his*. She agreed with the implication, in any case, that the pilgrims were the lifeblood of the place — the living manifestation of the story's vitality, if not its veracity.

"Where do you think he is?" Rachel asked, gazing around from their vantage beside the open grave in the floor. "This place is eerie. It gives me the creeps."

Miranda grimaced. This was where the altar would have been, she thought. Instead, there's a hole. She followed Rachel's gaze and saw a vast empty vault of grey stone and white plaster, with light washing through narrow windows, catching myriad dust motes hovering in the air. There was a strong smell of solvents, and a hint of violets emanating from the cavity in the floor at their feet. They could not see Alexander's pictures without stepping off the chancel, although Miranda noted that his scaffolding on the far side of the nave was still in front of the last panel, where the font for holy water might have been. Or did Catholics place the font somewhere else?

"Come on," she said. "I'll show you the frescoes. Let's start at the other end — you'll get them in sequence." She walked over to a switch by the sacristy door and flipped it on. The entire building suddenly flooded with illumination, staunching the flow of natural light seeping through the windows and

bringing the colours of the pictures into striking incandes-
cence. As they moved from panel to panel, Miranda made a
few comments, but Rachel was already familiar with the story.

"My God, they're wonderful," said Rachel. "I had no
idea. I love the changes in her face. It's the same face and
yet it gets more and more radiant. She's almost homely in
the first panel, pretty maybe, and by the last she's Botticelli
at his most inspired, but it's the same face, the same painter,
same technique. Wow. The settings aren't Botticelli — they're
pure Ontario Gothic — but the faces are Italian Renaissance,
especially in the last two panels, and somehow they fit with
the scenes."

"How do you know so much?" exclaimed Miranda.

"I've got eyes. Look at her."

"I see, I agree. But —"

"When I studied art history at Western, I spent two
months in Florence for a double course credit, mostly walking around the Uffizi or drinking Chianti."

"Something obviously sunk in. Botticelli? That's neat,
because she looks late-Victorian to me, sort of Pre-Raphaelite,
but yeah, I can see the face in Botticelli's ... what's it called?"

"The *Primavera*."

"No, the one with Venus poised on the half shell."

"What about you? How do you know such erudite
things?"

"I'm old ... I paid attention ... I don't know. I've never been
to Italy."

"Well, girl, you must go. There's no place in the world
like Florence — *Firenze*! Unless it's Sienna — we spent almost
a week in Sienna. Not so touristy, great buildings, lovely
textures, like you're walking through architectural history.
Italians, they live inside history. Why don't we go sometime?
I'll show the old girl around."

"One thing I like about me is my age. And when I turn forty, I'll like that too."

"And fifty and sixty and seventy?"

"You bet."

"So tell me," said Rachel, almost whispering as she looked around over her shoulder and then leaned in conspiratorially.

"What?"

"Why isn't Alexander Pope a suspect?"

"He checked out."

"And?"

"He's our friend."

"So?"

"No motive."

"Shelagh Hubbard wreaked havoc without a motive."

"She's a psychopath."

"Was."

"Was. Psychopaths don't have motives. That's why they're psychopaths."

"Did you decide she was a psychopath before or after you couldn't come up with a motive?"

"Point taken. But you should read her journals. There's an absolute absence of conscience."

"Clinically detached?"

"Morgan described them as 'self-justifying.' More like an application for a research grant."

"Detailed and aggressively impersonal?"

"Yes. And no. I don't find them impersonal. They're not emotional, but she's there in every word and sketch and turn of phrase. I find them chilling precisely because she is there in her text and yet shows no emotion."

"Sounds psychopathic to me. So, back to our friend Alexander."

"There's no evidence here or at the farm."

"Not of his presence, but not of anyone else, either."

"There's no reason to connect him to her death. As far as the melodramatic disposal of her body, it's unlikely a man so immersed in recovering the story of this place would violate his own project. I mean, why?"

"Why not? He had opportunity on his side, and maybe there's a perverse satisfaction, bringing his saint to life."

"Dead. She was brought here dead."

"Figure of speech, dear. Confusing, isn't it? New bodies passing for old — that was Hubbard's specialty. It's fitting and proper that hers should be used for the same."

"Agreed," said Miranda. "Someone's idea of poetic justice. But not Alexander's — the connection's so obvious it's untenable."

"I'm glad you're on side," said Alexander Pope, stepping out from behind one of the columns separating them from the nave.

"Good God," Rachel shrieked, recovering immediately with a muffled laugh. "How long have you been there?"

"Just arrived, just arrived. Had no time to hear accusations —"

"Suspicions!"

"Suspicions, my darling Rachel, are the poor cousins. Same family. I stand accused. And — thank you Miranda — exonerated."

"Oh, hell," said Rachel. "I guess you didn't do it then. What a relief." She leaned up and kissed him, first on one cheek, then the other. "I'm glad. I could cope with the killing part, but embalming, yuck. Even embalming with violets. Doesn't seem an Alexander Pope thing to do. 'Course, you have an ancestral interest in gardens."

"And in couplets that rhyme. That doesn't mean I go around coupling."

Miranda looked from Alexander's face to Rachel's. He obviously did not feel threatened by her and she was not intimidated by him. In fact, there seemed to be an indefinable current between them, Miranda thought, that despite their radical differences in character and world experience suggested they were, as they say, kindred spirits. Stupidly, she felt excluded.

Alexander Pope turned to her. "Well, Miranda, what do you think? The place is looking good, isn't it? Wouldn't it make a lovely gallery? I'm thinking of moving up here and turning myself into a purveyor of fine art."

"And leaving Port Hope? I don't believe it."

"No, probably not. Maybe for the summers. I could sell antiques here, and spend the winters at home making more. Ha!"

"Ha!" she responded, feeling a lovely bond of intimacy, scolding herself for having felt left out.

"Reproductions!" Rachel challenged.

"I'm getting too old to be rebuilding old buildings," he countered. "I need to fall back on old talents."

"What's with you about *old*? Both of you, in your dotage. Good grief, consider the alternative."

"I have and I do," Pope responded gravely. "All too often."

"What would your patrons think of a gallery?" Miranda asked.

"My patrons? My angel. Oh, well, I can do with this place pretty much what I want, I suppose."

"Does that include burying a saint in the floor?" said Rachel.

"Sinner, my dear. If there ever was a sinner, it was the late Dr. Hubbard."

"No argument here," said Rachel. "Sinning is as sinning does."

John Moss

"Meaning what, Forrest Gump?" Miranda envied the easy repartee. For her, banter always carried an element of self-consciousness, except with Morgan.

"What do you say we go swimming?" Rachel suggested, throwing the non sequitur into the air with dramatic effect. "You guys up to it? Not too old?"

"I swim only underwater," said Alexander Pope casually, as if they had been talking about sporting activities all along.

"Well, good for you. Let's go scuba diving," said Rachel. "We're not that far from Tobermory. Miranda, do you want to go wreck-diving? There's a National Marine Park there; lots of wrecks. How about it?"

They had never talked about diving. Miranda remembered seeing dive gear at Alexander's Port Hope house. Rachel probably saw it, too. And yet, they hadn't discussed the subject with him or each other. It didn't surprise her that Rachel was a diver. It was something else between them. Among them. All three were apparently divers.

"Sounds good," said Miranda. "Tomorrow, if the weather clears."

"It's right as rain right now."

"But it'll take a day for the waves to subside. Georgian Bay builds up really big swells."

"Excellent," said Alexander Pope. "Tomorrow should be perfect. I would enjoy the break. I have never dived in a wreck."

"Me neither," said Miranda.

"Well, let's do it," said Rachel. "We'll rent equipment and a boat in Tobermory. I love it; we'll have an adventure."

Miranda looked at her friend, wondering whether the eagerness was for wreck-diving or the chance to cultivate the great poet's namesake, or for some other obscure reason she could not imagine.

The rest of the day they spent on a charmingly excruciating tour of Alexander's project, getting a detailed explanation for every minute aspect of his work. So great were his enthusiasm and depth of esoteric knowledge about plaster and frescoes, the structure of the building and the arcane stories it held, that in spite of themselves Miranda and Rachel were captivated, and by the late afternoon all three of them were utterly exhausted.

Over a Chinese dinner in Midland, they recapped some of the highlights of the afternoon and made plans for wreck-diving the following day. They agreed to meet at the church and drive over with Alexander. He was clearly excited at the prospects ahead and actually had his complete scuba gear, including a 7 ml wetsuit, in his van.

"You never know," he said. "I thought I might get in a dive or two."

"I've never dived in fresh water before," Miranda announced.

"Actually," said Alexander, "neither have I."

"But you brought your gear?" she queried. Turning to Rachel, she asked, "What about you?"

"What about me?"

"Have you dived in cold water before?"

"Fresh water?"

"Cold fresh water?"

"Only. I've never been to the tropics."

"So, okay, tell us ..."

"As long as you're suited up for it, you're fine."

"I don't like the cold," said Miranda, shivering as she thought about slipping into the depths of Georgian Bay.

They talked about diving for a while, about soaring free of gravity, only bubbles rising to an elliptical plane of light overhead to indicate which way was up. Alexander likened it to the illusions of weightlessness created by dancers in ballet, and Miranda thought of it as walking in space, where direction itself is only an illusion. Rachel chose flying in dreams as her best analogy.

Miranda described Morgan's diving adventure on Easter Island.

"Without proper training?" said Rachel. "He could have died."

"What on earth was he doing on Easter Island?" asked Alexander. "Apart from taunting mortality?"

"Good question," said Rachel. "He probably just wanted to call people 'buddy.'"

"Buddy?" said Alexander. "How very unlikely."

"Divers call each other 'buddy' a lot," said Miranda. "It's like calling your lover 'darling.' Then you don't have to remember his name."

"Why does one go to Easter Island?" Alexander persisted, and then in response to his own query he continued, "I would imagine for the same reason one travels to Egypt to see the pyramids. Some people need to be confronted with things bigger than themselves. It's a form of affirmation: you prove your own existence by witnessing works that have transcended the deaths of their makers, whose past existence is thereby indisputable even if your own is in doubt. Are there people on Easter Island, or is it only populated by giant heads?"

Miranda was slightly appalled by his presumptuous misreading of her partner's existential needs, as well as by his ignorance about Easter Island.

"Morgan," she said, "has no doubt about his existence — the fact of, if not the quality of — and yes, there are over four thousand islanders, called Rapanui. They call the island 'Rapa Nui' — two words — and they have a resounding history of triumph and doom. That's what interested him, more than the statues, which aren't heads, you know, but include torsos — although they're often buried to the neck or decapitated — and they had a written script called Rongorongo, when no one else in all Polynesia had writing, and no other neolithic culture had writing. And now no one knows how to read it. The people faithfully reproduce tablets of Rongorongo for the tourist trade, but they can't read what they're writing."

She realized much of her pedantic oration had been cribbed directly from Morgan, redeeming him, somehow, from the existential limbo assigned him by Alexander Pope.

"Sort of like calligraphy," said Rachel. "The meaning is in doing it, not what it says."

"That," said Alexander, "is the most esoteric of the arts: to write someone else's signature script and make it your own."

Miranda continued, feeling Morgan had been given short shrift. "He loves to immerse himself in the details of a place, and let them swarm around him; he counts on them eventually falling into a comprehensible pattern. He's the same with a case or a culture. Easter Island was an escape to someone else's reality, a way to be himself in disguise."

The other two said nothing, so she added, "He got a tattoo."

"How unlikely," said Alexander Pope. "A tattoo. How very odd for a grown man. Well, it takes all sorts."

Miranda regretted her indiscretion, and seeing this, Rachel came to her aid. "I think it's an adventurous thing to do."

"Going to Easter Island?"

"Getting a tattoo. He doesn't fit the demographic; that's precisely why he would do it. I think it's adventuresome."

"The tattooist's name was Tito," said Miranda.

"There," said Rachel. "Proves my point. Who else would

*John Moss*

know their tattooist's name but rogues like Errol Flynn and David Morgan?"

"Errol Flynn died before you were born," said Alexander. "Before any of us were born, even me."

"He's become his own name," said Miranda. "Like Marilyn Monroe. Like the names of painters. Botticelli, for instance. Rachel thinks the faces in the frescoes look like Botticelli."

"Does she?"

"I do," said Rachel. "Some of them."

"Tell us all about it," said Alexander. Miranda winced, finding his tone condescending, as if he were asking a child to explain why she had coloured the sky orange and green. But Rachel did not seem bothered and, rising to the challenge, she responded with a brief exposition on Renaissance art, the Florentine neo-Platonists, and the achievement of Sandro Botticelli.

"And you think Sister Marie Celeste looks like Simonetta?" Alexander demanded in a quiet but authoritative voice

"Only in the first panel."

Miranda interjected. "Who is Simonetta?"

"The beloved of Giuliano, brother of Lorenzo Medici ... Lorenzo the Magnificent," said Rachel.

"He wasn't modest, was he?" Miranda observed.

"Who?"

"Magnificent Lorenzo. Who was Simonetta in her own right?"

"The model for Botticelli's *Birth of Venus*, somewhat idealized, I would think," said Alexander.

"She's lovely, fragile, and vacuous," said Rachel. "Appropriate for Venus arising, newborn but fully mature, generated from the cast-off testicles of a truculent god."

"Uranus, I believe, at the hands of his son, Cronus the Titan." Alexander spoke as if he were merely providing a reminder for a story he assumed everyone knew.

Miranda was astonished at the level of discourse. She had a general knowledge of art, gleaned mostly from reading Christmas gift-books like Sister Wendy's *The Story of Painting,* but these two seemed comfortable with fifteenth-century aesthetics as a topic of casual conversation. She was especially surprised by Alexander. She knew Rachel had spent a summer studying in Florence, but how had Alexander managed to assimilate such knowledge into his capacious, undisciplined mind? No, she thought, that's Morgan. Alexander's mind is large, but it is quaint and orderly. She had vague recollections of him talking about art school, long before he took up reconstruction, reclamation, renovation, authentic reproduction, and the like.

Restoration. She added that to her list: art restoration. For his project in Beausoleil, Ontario, of course, he would have to know about plaster and painting in Renaissance Italy.

"Are you listening?" Rachel said, nudging Miranda out of her quizzical reverie. "I'm talkin' here."

"Yeah. Botticelli, Venus."

"Right, but I think Sister Marie's other faces come from 'The Allegory of Springtime' — the *Primavera.*"

"Do tell us," said Alexander Pope, like a teacher examining a prodigal student.

"Okay," she said in a voice suggesting she was fully prepared for the occasion. "Panel two, the annunciation imminent. The face is Flora in the *Primavera*, strangely lusty and fearful, gazing upward at the warm wind of spring. Picture the painting in your mind. Picture the frescoes. In the third panel there are two versions of Sister Marie; on one side she's prostrate, her face turned away like the centre of Botticelli's *Three Graces*, and on the other she's enraptured, staring up at the Virgin Mary in wonder. She's the Grace on the left, representing ecstatic desire. The fourth panel shows the face of Venus offering silent benediction. The final panel shows Sister Marie as Flora, again, now fecund with spring, an earth nymph transformed to goddess and the most beautiful, sensual face ever painted. What better way to arise into Heaven than satiated with sex and surrounded by flowers?"

Miranda turned to Alexander. "How'd she do?"

"Excellent," he said. "I couldn't have done better myself."

Miranda looked from one to the other. Despite Rachel's demand for Miranda's attention, possibly Rachel had meant to impress Alexander Pope with her explication and Miranda was merely a witness. Rachel and Alexander sat quietly for a moment, eying each other, perhaps also trying to assess their relative roles in the rhetorical drama.

Alexander smiled, leaned across the table, and squeezed Rachel's hand. She turned it over and responded with a brief squeeze of her own, then withdrew it. Miranda felt excluded again, and yet was impressed with them both. Rachel, for her casual erudition, and Alexander, for his forbearance. He, after all, had been listening to an interpretation of a monumental work of art that was as close to being his own creation as if he had painted the frescoes himself.

## chapter fifteen

## Lakeshore Road

---

**M**organ found himself behind the wheel of a police car in the small hours of early morning, driving east along Highway 401, without being quite certain why. He had awakened from a restless sleep in a cold sweat, at first thinking the telephone had been ringing and it must be Miranda. Out of the darkness the surge of a diffuse premonition that Miranda was in danger had taken hold. He had no idea why he was driving to Port Hope instead of Beausoleil or Penetanguishene, but he knew that somehow, in his sleep, apprehension for his partner's safety had coalesced around Alexander Pope. It was no longer a matter of murders unsolved; there was an urgency to get inside the man's mind. Where better for that than in the man's home, especially when Pope wasn't there?

He knew there was a connection between these feelings of dread and the fax from London that had come through just before he left headquarters for the night. Scotland Yard was reopening their inquiry into the Renaud's murders. Their medical examiners were convinced the cadavers under their wax veneers predated original assumptions by a number of years. Forensic identification of the bodies verified their revised findings. They wanted Morgan to suggest an alternate timeline in Shelagh Hubbard's career. Might she have been in London earlier than previously supposed, perhaps working at Madame Renaud's in some anonymous capacity that would have given her access to the facilities but left no records of her presence?

That seemed something more likely to be determined in London. A quick check through her file, the very same file that had been forwarded to Scotland Yard more than a month previous, suggested she had pursued an academic career on the fast track without a break between doctoral studies at Oxford, a postdoctoral fellowship at the University of London, and her appointment at the wax museum. Renaud's had no record of her employment there before the dates indicated in her journal. Her undergraduate and masters work in Vancouver, at the University of British Columbia, combined with her relative age at each stage of her evolving career, left no time for earlier employment in any capacity whatsoever in the Chamber of Horrors. He had faxed back, suggesting the arcane procedures of post-mortem preparation might have contaminated the normal measures determining time of death.

He also suggested they switch to email and, on a hunch, he requested a scan of Madame Renaud's employment records extending back at least ten years. There might be anomalies Scotland Yard wouldn't see.

Drifting into a troubled sleep, he had been thinking about Shelagh Hubbard, but he woke up with Alexander Pope looming in his mind. Pope would be the key to resolving the anomalies of Shelagh Hubbard's activities among the perpetual dead. His first thought had been to call Miranda. He couldn't call her. She had declared with conviction that she was going to leave her cellphone at home.

"We're going camping, Morgan. No phone —"

"No pool, no pets."

"You get the idea. I haven't been inside a tent since I was a student."

"Yeah, I knew that. I think I did." Sometimes when she told him things, he was not sure whether he'd heard them before, or whether the cadence of her voice was so familiar it only seemed like he had.

A surprising number of trucks were competing for space on the road. A succession of eighteen wheelers roared up behind him and veered into the passing lane at the last moment. He was driving above the speed limit. He was thinking.

He tried to imagine Alexander Pope as a sinister figure — the villain in a strangely elusive drama, perhaps by Shakespeare, perhaps Hitchcock. He didn't fit. In spite of Morgan's apprehension about the danger inherent in Miranda's relationship with Pope, Morgan found the man too much absorbed in his own predilections to be a proactive scoundrel. Shelagh Hubbard, in comparison, fit the bill to a T. She frightened him, even now, after death. It wasn't the crimes; mostly, it was how he had been manipulated in a gruesome entertainment where he didn't know the rules, where he wasn't even sure of the game. He had been played for a fool.

The thought of Marlene Dietrich in *The Blue Angel*, reducing her ridiculous admirer to ruin, and of Mildred in Somerset Maugham's *Of Human Bondage*, how she led her lover into the depths of despair. These images skirted along the edge of his mind, drawing him into their company. Yet, he saw those doomed men as victims in scenarios crafted by misogynous men, while he had been the victim of his own emotional ambivalence.

He loved women. He wanted to be free, he wanted to be loved — but the two seemed incompatible. Mutually exclusive desires. Himself, alone, caught between.

He thought about Lucy as he turned off the 401 on the outskirts of Port Hope. She had drawn him inexorably into an abyss of anguish, and yet, strangely, he missed her in his life. No, what he missed was the intensity of his unhappiness; the way, like the pain of a phantom limb, she had reminded him of what wasn't there.

Morgan clambered out of the car, admired the looming outlines of Alexander Pope's house etched against the pre-dawn sky, and made his way to the side door with its antique lock, which he managed to pick open in seconds. The house was huge inside — larger than he had expected from its outside dimensions — and rambling, despite the severe exterior. There were country antiques everywhere and he could not tell in the dull light of early morning which were original and which were what Alexander Pope described as "authentic reproductions." Running his hands over a sideboard with raised panels, he thought he could feel something in the wood suggesting it was new, despite the layers of chipped and worn paint with oxblood showing through like wounds. It did not have the feel of old wood — it felt cool and dense. If it was a fake, though, it was, to his eye, brilliantly accomplished.

Lying everywhere against the walls and on top of tables and hutches were odds and ends of forged iron and articulated wood that spoke of pioneer life now as remote as the most ancient of times. He realized in a brief thought that he had no more access to his own heritage than the people on Rapa Nui had to theirs. Less, in fact, for although they might not fully understand their cultural legacy, they lived among its monuments, they replicated historical texts they could no longer read, and honoured the past in ways we have forgotten how to do.

He became annoyed with himself for dawdling; nothing would have pleased him more than to linger over each artifact and item of furniture, and to explore the interior spaces of the house itself. But working against that was a diffuse sense of urgency about Miranda's well-being and a more immediate concern with being arrested for break-and-enter.

It was still too dark to see clearly, so Morgan decided to run the risk of turning on lights — which, of course illuminated the diverse colours of the painted furniture and made him yearn to examine each piece more closely. He forced himself to keep moving through what seemed like a vast *wunderkammern*, a live-in cabinet of curiosities. He found two studies, one on the main floor off the central hallway and one upstairs, adjoining the master bedroom. The downstairs study was an office and general workspace, with building plans and business files strewn casually about. The upstairs study was even more cluttered and much more personal. This was obviously Pope's sanctum sanctorum, where only the most intimate of visitors would likely be admitted.

On display were private mementos, including clusters of photographs on a massive corkboard, numerous framed pictures and diplomas, souvenirs of extensive travel. Innumerable books littered the floor, obscuring the patterns of antique Persian carpets. As soon as Morgan entered the room, he felt he was being intrusive. That was what made him sure it was the best place to start his search. Whatever it was he was looking for, it was here.

He slumped down in a leather armchair and gazed around, taking inventory. The carpets overlapped with casual eloquence but the paintings on the walls were Renaissance reproductions. There were two works of Japanese calligraphy, done with the florid discipline of a master. The framed photographs were in pairs, the left ones of log and clapboard houses as crumbling derelicts and the right ones of the same houses rebuilt as showpieces, looking more authentic than they might have appeared to their original owners. He got up and walked about, circling, as he often did, registering everything, waiting for his gathering perceptions to give up a pattern, a revelation, something he could work with. Outside, the sky was taking on colour. The stars had faded with the promise of morning. Turning away from the window, Morgan scanned the constellations of photographs pinned to the corkboard.

Reflections on a familiar face caught his eye. Partially covered by several other pictures was a snapshot of Rachel Naismith in a country setting. He removed the picture from the board, expecting to see Miranda as well. It must have been taken when they were here in the spring. No, he thought, the background was the green of summer. They were here in March or early April. He held the picture into the light. It was a bit worn and faded. Rachel looked younger. Squinting, he recognized in the background a hill town in Tuscany, and the distinctive square towers of San Gimignano.

He scanned the other photographs on the board more carefully and found another of Rachel, this time rubbing the nose of the famous bronze boar in the Straw Market in Florence. Behind it there was a duplicate picture, only someone else was rubbing the bronze. He squinted. It was Shelagh Hubbard. Behind that was another, the same, only this time it showed Alexander Pope with the boar's snout under curled fingers as if he were subduing a wild beast.

Methodically, Morgan began removing the photographs, which at some points were layered in clusters three and four deep. He was no longer concerned about leaving behind signs of his illicit search. He could feel his heart pounding and he had to consciously steady his hands. He lifted a framed photo from the wall and tilted it to the light.

Rachel had mentioned her interest in art as a student at Western. It was a long reach from London on the Ontario Thames to Florence on the Arno. But there she was, in a photograph lost among the pictures of reclaimed Ontario buildings, standing by the wall at riverside, with the Ponte Vecchio in the background looking more like a quaint architectural accident than a bridge. Her dark features were difficult to make out against the dazzling light of the Florentine sky. Beside her was a blond woman, Shelagh Hubbard, whose pale features were equally obscured by the brightness of the sun. It was an odd picture, and yet charming, with the ambiance of the city on full display.

As he expected, Morgan found a photograph with Rachel and Shelagh together. They were standing arm in arm like a couple of honeymooners in the Piazza del Duomo, posing near one of the Baptistery doors by Lorenzo Ghiberti, the "Gates of Paradise." As myriad explanations swarmed through his mind, he could not help but respond to the beauty of the city that had brought this improbable threesome together. It must have been five or six years ago. Morgan had been there fifteen years before that. As personal memories surfaced, he suppressed them. This had to do with Miranda. How did she fit into the picture?

Rifling through the remaining photographs, Morgan found a Polaroid snap by a street photographer taken in front of the Palazzo Vecchio. Alexander Pope's long arms were casually draped over each woman's shoulders, drawing them close to his side. The intimacy of their embrace seemed to Morgan a public celebration that the three of them were lovers. In his mind, however, the images of four people, not three, wheeled in freefall as he struggled to assimilate their possible relationships.

Morgan scanned the room with renewed diligence. He reached out and touched the surface of a painting with his fingertips. What he had taken as reproductions were original copies. Several were in the style of Botticelli. All were of heads only, as if the artist had no interest in the subject matter. Alexander Pope had refined his skills with colour and style in Florence. Had he also perfected the art of the fresco?

As he was leaving the room, Morgan braced for a moment against the door frame to soak in as much as possible of what he was seeing. As he looked about, he ran his fingers along the spines of books at eye level on the shelves nearest the door. His hand stopped over several familiar volumes. He turned to look at them more closely. They were the same blue colour as Shelagh Hubbard's journals, the same size, more like binders than books. Inhaling deeply, he withdrew one and opened it, finding, as he expected, blocks of passages in her handwriting, interspersed with familiar pen sketches, all in black ink, detailing aspects of the Madame Renaud's murders. He quickly opened another volume and discovered what seemed an exact duplicate of her journal describing Morgan's intended fate as a pile of desiccated bones in a Huron burial mound. The final volume inevitably offered a duplicate account of the Hogg's Hollow tableau with the same sketches and horrifically clinical descriptions.

On closer examination, these seemed to be practice copies, as if Shelagh Hubbard had done them in preparation for the final edition that he and Miranda had found at her farm. There was another blue binder lying flat on the same shelf. It was not as large, but much thicker. Morgan opened it and saw immediately that it was a collection of handwriting exercises and practice sketches all in the same black ink as the other three binders. The journals found at the farm were done in various inks, suggesting that they had been written over an extended period of time. He glanced up at the wall on the other side of the door. The framed calligraphy was done in black ink. Written neatly in Roman script on the lower right corner of each was the name *Rachel Naismith* and a date.

Morgan sat down in the big armchair. Had Rachel forged Shelagh Hubbard's journals? Had she written them in the first place? For the final versions did she use a variety of inks to create the illusion of authenticity? Handwriting analysis had not been done on the volumes found at the farm. A cursory comparison with Hubbard's academic notes seemed sufficient verification of authenticity, since their authorship was never in doubt. Now it appeared, in all probability, Rachel Naismith, with the collusion of Alexander Pope, had created both sets. How much of the content were they responsible for? Was there a possibility Shelagh was innocent?

He rose abruptly and picked up the photograph of the three of them together in front of the Palazzo Vecchio. Now what he saw in their eyes was not a play of possession or submission but the sinister glee of conspirators. He looked again. Conspiracy? Lust? It was simply a street photographer's snapshot of three friends — probably, by their demeanour, summer residents not tourists, leaning against each other in a piazza in the heart of the city.

Morgan set the picture down on the countertop with the others and shuffled them into neat, random piles. They would be there when he returned with a warrant, once things fell into place. He snapped off the light and was surprised that the room remained fully illuminated. The sun was well over the horizon; the day had begun.

He wasn't sure whether Miranda and Rachel had planned to connect with Alexander Pope. He knew, now, with a certainty, the three of them would be together. His breath quickened and, after a quick tour of the house to fix it in place in his mind, he slipped out the side door, got into his car, took a deep breath, and drove down the long driveway, turning right on Lakeshore Road and then right again, up to the 401. After a few kilometres, he veered north to Highway 7 and cut across the top of Toronto to avoid the morning gridlock, then turned north. He was on his way to Penetanguishene.

# *chapter sixteen*

## Wiarton

---

**M**iranda crawled from the tent just after dawn. She walked out onto the point of land, feeling the offshore breeze riffle her hair, and looked back along the sound to the east, where, from low on the horizon, the sun skimmed the waves like a red rubber ball. The whimsical images that bobbed in her mind belied her feelings of apprehension. She had not been diving in several years and while she was certified, she was far from confident. She had no experience in wreck-diving, which called for a whole different order of expertise. Being in enclosed spaces underwater ran counter to the freedom of movement that drew her to the sport in the first place.

Still, her friends were anxious to give it a try. The Tobermory wrecks were a world-class site. She didn't want to let them down. It was the kind of dubious adventure that, once into it, would be incredibly exciting, like rock climbing or whitewater kayaking — neither of which she had any desire to do.

It was her father who used to describe the morning sun as shining bright like a red rubber ball. Then he would utter the mantra, "Del Shannon from Rapid City, Michigan," and take strange satisfaction in how the words and the image and the emotional response they evoked were in perfect, private harmony. She had never heard the song; it wasn't something her parents would actually have owned. She could feel the warmth of her father's grin and with it came a terrible emptiness as she wondered what they might have been to each other had he lived.

She sat perched with her knees drawn up and her arms clasped around them, rocking gently against the cool stone. She turned to watch Rachel struggle through the zippered door in the tent vestibule, crawl out onto the pine needles, stand up and stretch, then amble slowly toward her in her oversized teddy-bear pyjamas, rubbing sleep from her eyes and stepping with exaggerated caution over dry grass tufts growing from clefts in the stone. Rachel sat down beside her. Neither of them spoke, and together they rocked in rhythm to the waves lapping against the sheer wall of the granite shore.

As the sun pressed higher in the sky, Miranda rose to her feet.

"You want coffee?" she offered.

"Sure," said Rachel. "I'll help. I hate lighting the stove — I'll measure out the coffee."

"It's in little bags."

"I'll count them. Two, right?"

Miranda smiled broadly at her friend. Apprehension about the events ahead passed from her mind. Diving, done properly, was an exhilarating sport. She was excited by the prospects ahead.

Morgan stopped for a coffee on the outskirts of Newmarket, due north of Toronto. He patched through to Alex Rufalo, asking for a response to his Scotland Yard query the night before requesting a scan of Madame Renaud's employment records extending back ten years.

"It's coming through now," said the superintendent. "Don't go away."

Illogically, Morgan followed the directive literally by sipping his takeout coffee in the restaurant parking lot. It occurred to him he might reach Miranda through Peter Singh in Owen Sound. He did not feel justified in calling the OPP to track her down. At this point there was nothing substantive to suggest she was in danger, although the case was building exponentially in his mind, implicating her companions in multiple murder. He was sure the three of them were together. Officer Singh could unofficially intervene, cut Miranda apart until Morgan could get to the scene.

Rufalo came back on the radio. "Morgan, there's no earlier record that Hubbard worked at Renaud's. Nothing under her own name."

"I knew that," said Morgan.

"But how about this to stifle your disappointment...."

"What? Say on."

"Your good friend, Alexander Pope, did!"

"Did what?"

"He worked at Renaud's — for eighteen months in the early nineties."

"Aha!" Morgan exclaimed.

"'Aha' what?"

"I'll fill you in later. Gotta go. Could you run a background check for me on Officer Rachel Naismith?"

"One of our guys?"

"Yeah."

"I'll get someone on it. Check back in an hour. Are you on your way to Georgian Bay? Do you want me to contact the Provincials?"

"And say what? Not yet. I don't know what you'd tell them."

"Morgan, something else that might interest you. Your friend Alexander Pope — it seems the church property is in his name. He is the registered owner of the crime scene in Beausoleil."

Morgan signed off, his mind racing as he wheeled onto the highway. An oncoming pickup swerved to miss him without slowing down as the driver leaned on the horn. Morgan hardly noticed. He was assimilating the new information into a sequence of probable events, with Alexander Pope displacing Shelagh Hubbard as the pivotal character. Given that her journals were apparently counterfeit, a new possibility pressed inexorably forward. It still seemed likely the Hogg's Hollow murders were Hubbard's project, and it was certain that Rachel was inextricably linked to the revelation of her crimes, but the centre of power was shifting to Pope. He had worked at Renaud's during the period now established as the time when the first set of murders occurred. Although his involvement in Hubbard's murders was peripheral, and his connection with the disposal of her remains was circumstantial, it seemed to Morgan a virtual fact that he was responsible for the deaths in the wax museum and the presentation of his victims on public display.

Trying his best to think and drive at the same time, Morgan wished Miranda were riding at his side. She was better at deductive reconstruction from limited materials. Where, he wondered, would she go with this? How would she fill in the gaps? The narrative demanded a bridge between London and Florence. How did a Canadian on a postdoctoral fellowship who took a hands-on course in London from a Canadian expert in constructural duplicity end up in her instructor's arms, apparently sharing his affection with a younger version of a policewoman from southern Ontario? It had already occurred to him that Rachel was a lesbian or bisexual, even that she and Miranda were having an affair. Were the two women in Florence lovers already, before they got there? Unlikely. The prior connection was between Shelagh and Alexander. There was nothing to suggest Rachel had a history in London, nothing to link her to Shelagh Hubbard before the snapshots in Tuscany.

Suppose, Morgan thought, trying to think like Miranda, the senior two of the threesome had become lovers while she was taking his course in London. It ended bitterly, or perhaps in an aura of doomed inevitability. Pope went to Italy. He had arranged for Shelagh Hubbard to study facial construction in wax simulations at his former employers, perhaps as a parting gesture to assuage his remorse for leaving her behind, or perhaps to ingratiate himself if it was she who spurned him. No, the latter is unlikely, given the eventual course of events.

Passing a couple of trucks, then applying the brakes to keep a third truck between him and a police cruiser scanning for speeders from the side of the highway, Morgan contemplated the brutal irony that Alexander Pope, who elevated fakery to a fine art, should reverse the procedure by transforming the patently unreal effigies of dead murder victims into genuine cadavers. Then, he wondered, suppose in her nocturnal ministrations, cleaning and repairing the wax effigies after their daily exposure to public scrutiny, Shelagh Hubbard discovered his macabre sport? Rather than recoiling, perhaps driven by obsessive love, she was inspired to have found a way back into his heart. She pursued him to Italy, armed with the capacity to renew their relationship on a different and, given their morbid dispositions, ironically revitalized basis.

Why was he in Florence? The answers to that were hanging on the wall in his sanctum sanctorum. He was studying to replicate some of the greatest painters in the Western world, having in effect moved from reconfiguring dead faces of real people to creating authentic reproductions of people long dead. As well as refining his talents with oil on wood and canvas, he undoubtedly studied frescoes. Already an authority on the subtleties of plaster, it would have been impossible to resist the study of tinting techniques at the home of the Renaissance masters.

As for Rachel Naismith, she would have been in Florence to study art in her own right, perhaps under the tutelage of Alexander Pope, an accomplished artist who spoke the same language. Quite possibly. Her talent as a calligrapher, her history at the University of Western Ontario, combined with the irrefutable evidence of her close relationship in Florence with Hubbard and Pope, insisted on her culpability in the subsequent murders. How so, Morgan was uncertain.

What an unholy threesome, he thought, especially appalled by Rachel. Did she know, then, standing arm in arm with her lovers for the snapshot, that the bond between the other two was on the dark side of death? Morgan felt an intense sense of betrayal, and mounting anger for the dreadful abuse of Miranda's friendship. What could have driven Rachel to immerse herself in such malevolence? Was she on the road to depravity from childhood, the victim of a psychopathic mutation in her developing personality? Did her immersion in the dissociative world of Florentine aesthetics somehow exacerbate an already-screwed-up nature? Was the overwhelming time warp of immediate access to the sinister beauties of Renaissance culture enough to make her open to deadly seduction? Did the other two seduce her on the banks of the Arno, or she them? Did she somehow complete their perverse relationship, bringing them closer together, making the banalities of evil seductive? Or did she insinuate herself into the perverse dynamics of their existing affair to feed her own appetites?

Morgan cut north on old Highway 11, the continuing extension of Yonge Street that divides Ontario into east and west, to pick up the most efficient route to the Nottawasaga region of Georgian Bay.

He became aware that he was searching for ways to exonerate Rachel, and recoiled from the creeping sympathy that might compete with his concern for Miranda, who, having displaced Shelagh Hubbard in the unholy dynamics of a new and dangerous threesome, was surely in grave danger. He reached for the radio, determined to contact Peter Singh and ask him to drive over to Beausoleil or, if necessary, to the campground outside Penetang.

Alexander Pope was lounging on the front steps of the church when the women arrived with their camping gear strapped to the back of Miranda's racing-green Jaguar.

"You want to leave your car here?" he asked, unbending his long limbs and strolling to the side of the car. "I've called Tobermory. We're set up with a boat and full gear for you two. I told them we'd be there by a little past noon.

"Thanks," said Miranda. "I've got a lot of work piling up. I think I'd like to head back tonight. What about if you two ride together as far as Owen Sound and we'll drive the rest of the way together? I'll leave my car there so we can cut south on the way back."

"Sounds fine to me," said Alexander Pope. "It will give Rachel and me a chance to catch up on old times."

"Since March?" Miranda exclaimed.

"In detail," said Rachel. "Don't worry, we'll find things to talk about. We'll talk about you."

Miranda smiled uneasily. She suspected perhaps there was a subtext to the relationship between the other two she did not grasp, and ascribed her anxiety to feeling a little left out. On the drive over from Penetanguishene, Rachel had come up with the suggestion, herself, that she ride with Alexander as far as Owen Sound. It had seemed entirely reasonable, but now Miranda felt herself resenting the petty betrayal of her friends. Somehow the three of them broke down into a con-figuration of pairs. They were not all three friends together. Like teenagers, she thought. In any permutation of their affec-tions, one of them was invariably left in the cold.

She had decided early that morning she needed to get back to Toronto. She loved camping and had reconciled her-self to the day's adventure, but she felt an indefinable sense of urgency. Something was not quite right. She suggested they head back after diving. Rachel seemed content with the revised plan.

By the time Morgan reached Peter Singh, he was less than an hour from Georgian Bay. He had anticipated having difficulty explaining what he wanted Peter to do: see that she's okay and stay with her. To Morgan's surprise, this was not received as an unreasonable request. He felt a rising affection for the young officer and told him he'd explain when he got there.

"For sure, Morgan. I will meet you; just say where."

"Wherever you connect with Miranda. When you find her, get back to me."

"I will."

"Good, go for it."

"You mean I should drive to Beausoleil? Why don't you contact her on your radio?"

"She's camping with Rachel — I think you met her. She's not carrying her cellphone. They'll have gone to see Pope, but he's not answering."

"Have you tried the campground?"

"No, I don't know the area. I wouldn't know where to start. I'm counting on you to do that." Morgan's newfound affection was beginning to wane. "I really would like you to get going on this. Call me."

"Where are you?"

"Just north of Barrie."

"You're probably closer to her than I am, but let me see if I can pin her down. I'll get back to you."

The radio went blank, then Officer Singh came on again.

"I was talking to her last night, you know."

"You what?"

"I was talking to her last night. She called from a restaurant in Midland. They were having dinner together — Miranda and Mr. Pope, and Rachel Naismith.

"Why did she call? Was she okay."

"Oh, yes, she was very okay. They were having a good time."

"Why did she call you?"

"Why not? She is my friend. I suppose you would like to be analytic. Possibly she was fulfilling a social obligation, given she's a visitor in my part of the country."

"Did she say where she'd be today?"

"Oh, no, I do not think so. Well, she said if she comes through Owen Sound she would give me another call."

"Why would she be coming through Owen Sound?"

"Goodness, Detective, we'll have to ask her." Peter Singh had lost his sense of the gravity of the situation, in his delight at the possibility of connecting with both of them.

"Peter?"

"Yes?"

"If she calls, let me know."

"Yes, of course. And meanwhile I will call around and see if I can track down her camping ground. I suspect if you cannot reach anybody at the church, they are on their way here. Goodbye now."

Morgan felt the first pangs of hunger since he had left home. It was well past breakfast time and still too early for lunch, so he compromised on a couple of doughnuts outside Midland.

Miranda had to concentrate not to get separated from Alexander Pope's van. She was intent on drinking in the splendour of the countryside, which was at its most lush in June. To one side she could see beyond the gnarled groves of apple orchards the high hills of the Niagara Escarpment creeping along the edge of the coastal plain, and on the other side, beyond orchards and grasslands, she caught glimpses of the lake, dazzling evanescent in the sunlight. Ahead, the blue van snaked through what little traffic there was, and periodically she would rev the Jag and catch up behind them. Pope would honk in acknowledgement and she would honk back. She was more and more looking forward to their adventure.

They stopped for coffee at the Tim Hortons in Collingwood.

"How are we doing for time?" she asked.

"It's too early for lunch," said Alexander. "We'll grab a sandwich in Owen Sound and eat on the way."

"You two finding enough to talk about?" she asked Rachel.

"No," said Rachel. "We don't say a word to each other. It's murder."

All three laughed.

"Let's go," said Rachel. "It's still a long drive. Where are we gonna meet in Owen Sound?"

"At the police station," said Miranda. "We'll leave my car there. A vintage Jag by the side of the road is flaunting temptation. We can pick up some food at the same time."

Rachel and Alexander exchanged looks. He said, "It's okay with me."

Rachel shrugged. "Whatever. See you there."

They pulled out in tandem, coffees in hand.


"Morgan," said Peter Singh. "Save yourself time. I tracked down the campground."

"Good."

"No, not so good. She has checked out."

"Did they know where she was going?"

"The man said she mentioned Tobermory."

"What's in Tobermory?"

"Beautiful scenery, I suppose. Funny rocks with holes in them. A lot of cedar trees."

"Does she have to go through Owen Sound to get there?"

"Yes."

"Where are you now?"

"I am in Owen Sound, at home. I am now off duty, since I talked to you before."

"Where did she call you last night?"

"At home."

"Stay there. She'll call. She likes you."

"I like her, too. Are you coming straight through? I should tell you how to get here."

"Owen Sound's on the map, I've been there before."

"I mean my home. I am looking forward to seeing you."

"Yeah," said Morgan. "Talk to you later."

He looked around. He was driving along the edge of a town. It's big enough, it must be Collingwood, he thought. He pulled into the Tim Hortons for coffee and another doughnut at the takeout window. He thought of a sandwich, but the anxiety running in tremors through his entire body distorted his appetite. Doughnuts fill voids other foods can't even find.

Odd, he thought. Doughnuts and cars. In Toronto he ate the occasional pastry and yet, out here in the country, driving, they seemed as indispensable as gasoline. He looked down at the fuel gauge. He was not used to either doughnuts or cars. His stomach felt bloated and the gas tank read empty.

Miranda ran into the police station and explained who she was — a Toronto detective and a friend of Peter Singh's. No problem, said the woman at the desk. Where was she off to? Miranda explained they were going to Tobermory, and behind schedule. The woman shrugged and waved her away, telling her to have a good day.

On the outskirts of Owen Sound, Morgan got through to Alex Rufalo and pulled over to the side of the road so he could hear better. He had already called Peter Singh, asking him to meet him downtown.

"I've got Officer Naismith's file, Morgan. It looks straight-forward to me. Three years on the force. Good record. Good future. She's got a degree from the University of Western

Ontario, comes from the Chatham area between Windsor and Sarnia. Nothing stands out in her background."

"What's her degree?"

"Honours sociology. Oh, and honours art history. Double honours — very impressive."

"Art history?"

"Yeah."

"Sociology?"

"Yeah."

"Do you have her transcript?"

"Yeah."

"Lots of psychology courses? Courses in deviance?"

"Yeah, not unusual for a cop."

"Art history? Does she have a credit for a course abroad?"

"Double credit. One art, one art history. Universitat degli Studi di Firenze."

"I didn't know you could speak Italian, boss."

"I read it. I don't understand it. What's this all about, Morgan?"

"At this point I'm trying to connect with Miranda. I'm worried about her."

"Anything I can do from here?"

"No, it's okay. I'm closing in. Anything else in the Naismith file?"

"That's about it. Says her parents were undertakers. Don't know how that connects to police work, growing up in a funeral home."

"Undertakers?"

"Yeah. Looks like both parents were in the business."

"Gotta go, chief. I'll call for backup if I need it."

"Good. I'm together with my wife."

"You're what?" Morgan was flustered. Why on earth would the superintendent be telling him this?

"She's a lawyer. We negotiated a settlement. Based on renewing our wedding vows. Thought you'd like to know. Everyone at headquarters has been talking about it for months. So there you are."

"Well, thanks for sharing. I'll get back to you after I find Miranda."

"Morgan —"

"Gotta go."

Past Wiarton the road to Tobermory runs up the spine of the escarpment. On the west side the land falls away gently but to the east it plunges dramatically into the depths of Georgian Bay. Miranda had settled into the back seat and could not hear the sporadic conversation between Alexander and Rachel clearly enough to participate without leaning forward and shouting. The van needed work on its muffler and a good tune-up. Alexander's mind ran to less practical matters.

Miranda ruminated on what she knew about Wiarton. It had the familiar feel of an Ontario town, declaring itself a good place to live through civic pride, with floral displays and refuse containers in abundance. There were numerous signs proclaiming it the home of Wiarton Willie. Pennsylvania has Punxsutawney Phil, Ontario has Willie. Once a year on Groundhog Day, animals otherwise treated as vermin are scrutinized as they search for their shadows to forecast the coming of spring. Every year spring comes, she thought. So far so good.

She turned in her seat to survey Alexander's scuba gear. She had seen compressed-air cylinders in the shed by the side door of his house, but he had only a single tank with him. There was also a box that must contain his regulator and a net bag with his BCD vest, fins, mask and snorkel, and other paraphernalia. She and Rachel had thrown in the gear that was strapped on the back of her car for safekeeping, and they each brought kits with bathing suits and towels.

"Hey, you guys. I've got to stop for a minute."

The van pulled over and she clambered out and disappeared behind a line of cedars. She went through the motions of having a pee, but in fact she had quite suddenly felt claustrophobic in the back of the van and needed to get out for a moment. Rachel poked her way through the undergrowth, coming up beside her.

"You all right?" she asked.

"Oh, yeah, you know, too much coffee."

"Let's go, then."

Miranda watched Rachel as she led their way back to the car. Why was she so abrupt? she wondered. She didn't seem quite herself.

When Morgan pulled into the Owen Sound police station, he was enormously relieved to see Peter Singh leaning against Miranda's green Jag. His heart skipped a beat, however, when he saw the sombre look on Peter's face and realized the young officer was not moving to greet him.

"What's the problem?" he demanded. "Where's Miranda?"

"She was here less than an hour ago."

"She didn't call you?"

"No. The desk officer said she was rushed."

"Damn it," said Morgan.

"How bad is the situation?"

"I don't know. I don't think she's in immediate danger, but she could be."

"Can you explain?"

"Yes. No. Was she with Pope and Rachel Naismith?"

"I think so. Apparently she went off in a blue van."

"Where? Any idea."

"She said Tobermory. She said they were behind schedule."

"Was that her phrase? 'Behind schedule'?"

"Yes, I was told it precisely."

"Let's go! What's in Tobermory?"

"There's a toll ferry over to Manitoulin Island. From there you can drive across to the mainland above Lake Huron. If you want to go to the United States, you can go to the United States."

Morgan's sense of Ontario geography beyond Toronto was sketchy. As they raced from Owen Sound toward Wiarton, Peter Singh laid it out for him as best he could with words and many hand gestures to represent water, shorelines, and the international boundary.

"Why on earth would they want to catch a ferry?" Morgan demanded, as if an explanation was somehow Peter Singh's responsibility as the geography specialist.

"I really don't know. But the ferry does not leave until mid-afternoon. We have plenty of time."

Morgan took a deep breath and slowly exhaled, and another, which came out like a sigh. She should be all right, then. We'll get there, he thought, and bring her back with us. He relaxed a little and let his shoulders drop into a comfortable posture — he had been driving since the middle of the night with them tensed up virtually the whole time. He was exhausted. He pulled over and asked Peter Singh to take the wheel, then he slouched low in the seat and told the whole story, as much as he had figured out.

"Why would Alexander Pope buy the old church?" Peter asked, trying to stitch in a loose thread.

"I've been thinking about that," said Morgan. "He must have known about the frescoes. He would know about Sister Marie Celeste and the pilgrims. He is a man enthralled with the dark side of mystery. My guess is he fully intended to create a miraculous apparition. He would revitalize an old building but, more important, he would control the story. The resurrection of history in a context of fanatical faith. Can you imagine the satisfaction, creating a saint that even the Church might be forced to sanction? Extreme fraud. That's what the man lives and dies for."

"And he substituted Shelagh Hubbard's body for a saint's bones?"

"No, I think that was the work of Rachel Naismith."

"Really?"

"If all three of them were lovers and immersed in passionate depravities, there must have been terrible conflicts among them."

"Why do you assume they were lovers?"

"How else to explain the recurrent connection between Pope and Hubbard? Only love has the capacity to accommodate such sordid desires. You will find, Peter, in our business, where reason fails, love prevails. Sometimes it is the only explanation. And how else to account for the way Rachel was able to insinuate herself between them — proof in the Florence snapshots, proof in the forged accounts of her lovers' atrocities?"

"You think she came between them?"

"Not in Florence, at least not at first. For a while they were probably a charming ménage à trois; she was seduced by the horrific allure of their demonic passion. At some point she had to have discovered the grotesque bond between them. It didn't scare her away — it drew her closer. But life has a way of intruding on romance. I suspect they went their separate ways at the end of the summer. How else to account for the long delay until the Hogg's Hollow murders?"

"Maybe they went about murdering people by themselves," said Peter Singh. "Maybe it was a love game. In the publicity surrounding unaccountable deaths they would recognize each other's signature work. Or they would let each other know, if the murders weren't discovered. It was a way of keeping in touch. It is interesting, you know."

Extreme as the possibility seemed, Morgan realized he could be right. He was thinking like him. "You see, I know how you think," he heard the younger man say, as if he were reading his thoughts.

A little flustered at what seemed an invasive prescience, Morgan silently pursued the notion of unsolved murder as an expression of love. Statistically, it would appear most murders were resolved, but in fact there was no way of being certain. Gangland slayings, domestic homicide, street killings, violent deaths by assassination, by spontaneous manslaughter, were relatively public. But how many murders were premeditated, executed, and never discovered? They happened. They did happen.

"Could it be," Peter Singh continued, "Dr. Hubbard discovered the other two had renewed their relationship? Perhaps that is so, and the result was murder."

"Ultimately her own," said Morgan. "The horrors of the eternal embrace. That was her final love letter — an acknowledgement she knew about their betrayal; a warning, a threat, a farewell gesture. She devised an extravagant drama, intended to be fully accessible only to her former lovers. The headless corpses — another villain would have torn out the hearts, but Hubbard located passion in the brain. The heart is merely a pump to keep the brain flush with lust and the appropriate other bits engorged with blood. Her methods were extravagantly subtle — she knew their discovery would bring Alexander Pope onto the scene. She located the reveal where she could be fairly certain Rachel would be on duty. She revelled in the details."

"She was very good. She knew they would know it was her."

"The ring and the cross, those were for the benefit of the police, maybe for Miranda and me. Could she have known we'd be involved? It's our kind of case. Whether she was thinking religion or Freud, she couldn't resist the ring and the cross. Potent symbols of a romance fated to implode. They invited lovely speculation about motive, so long as we thought it was all in the colonial past. But she needed to have the historical story explode — it wouldn't have worked if we hadn't realized it was a fake. She needed Miranda and me as part of the story."

"But why the next phase? Why would Rachel Naismith kill her?"

"To seize control of the story. Again, literally. Let's say Hubbard's extravaganza had its desired effect and drove a wedge of doubt, or fear, or envy, between Rachel and Alexander. What better way to rekindle a precarious relationship, especially if we're right and he was trying to manufacture a miracle in Beausoleil. Give him a body smelling of violets, the illusion of sacrosanct flesh refusing corruption. The ironies run deep."

"Kill one lover as an act of devotion to the other."

"God forbid if Alexander Pope did not appreciate her efforts. If Pope felt threatened by Rachel's extravagant play for the renewal of his affections, for whatever reason, their love would sour on a cataclysmic scale. Then imagine the two of them vying for the most horrific method of exterminating the other."

"And you think Miranda might be caught between them."

Morgan's silent response chilled the air for a moment, then Peter Singh continued. "What happened to Sister Marie's bones?"

"What?"

"If Rachel Naismith placed her rival in the crypt, what happened to the bones?"

"They haven't turned up. If there was a mouldering body, she might have hauled it away for secret burial. She was experienced with both: secrets and burials. Or she might have ground up the bones and mixed them into Pope's plaster. Saint Marie Celeste literally embodied in her own image. It would be as if Rachel had written her invisible signature across his achievement."

"I think that is unlikely," said Peter Singh. "Perhaps not. In any case, Officer Naismith must have known Shelagh Hubbard's body would be recognized."

"Yes, she would be displacing Alexander Pope's story with one equally as good, maybe better, except this one would be hers. Perhaps meant as a tribute to Pope but taken, I would imagine, as an affront."

"My goodness, competitive psychopaths."

"Psychopathic lovers."

"Deadly."

"Very."

By the time they passed through Wiarton, Peter felt he had a sufficient grasp of the situation to ask, "Can we arrest them?" His voice was tremulous with excitement.

"No," said Morgan. "Not unless, God forbid, they're in the midst of another crime. To make a case, we'll need a warrant to search his house."

"You said you already know what is there, in the house."

"But I am not supposed to know. Meanwhile, if Miranda's okay, we don't want to spook them. Not that there's anywhere for them to run. The easiest place to keep track of fugitives from the city is in the wilderness."

"This is not wilderness, Morgan. It is countryside."

"If you're from the city, it's wilderness."

"The law is a most exciting field of endeavour," said Peter, as if the idea had never struck him before.

"Yes," said Morgan, who had never been in doubt that it was.

# chapter seventeen

## Tobermory

A lexander Pope wheeled the blue van down into the harbour area and pulled up abruptly by the red and white sign in front of the dive shop. There were not many boats to be seen but quite a few tourists were milling about, taking in the nautical ambience. The glass-bottom vessels would be out sightseeing by this time, while the sun was high in the sky and visibility was at its best, and the larger dive boats were out as well. Tied to the wharf across from the shop was a small trawler adapted for diving. It had a waterline platform attached to the transom and rails to hold on to, with a ladder that would flip down into the water at the dive site.

When they entered the shop, a young man greeted them — obviously a diver earning his keep. He glanced at their dive credentials and told them their boat was ready to go.

"You sure you don't want a guide?" he asked.

"I don't mind, one way or the other," Alexander

responded, turning to Miranda and Rachel for input.

Miranda was about to say she would welcome the guide when Rachel spoke up, pleasantly but firmly refusing the young man's offer. "I've been here before. Wrecks aren't a problem. We're not going deep, no penetration. Just give us a good map."

"You look familiar. Not many —." He stopped.

"Not many black women diving in Tobermory?"

Miranda flinched. She had never heard Rachel play the race card before, not so obviously and without even a touch of irony. The young man turned a deep red.

"No," he mumbled. "Police. Not many cops come in here to dive. Usually they, you, make your own arrangements. I remember — you're a policeman."

Rachel thrust her breasts out against the material of her T-shirt until Miranda thought the young diver's eyes would pop.

"Woman," he amended. "Are you all cops?" The question was rhetorical: he was sure Miranda was, and assumed by his imperious bearing that Alexander must be as well. "The gear you'll need is through here. Pay in advance. It's good weather for diving. The trawler over there is gassed up, ready to go."

He was talking to Rachel. When they came in, he had assumed Alexander was in charge. There was no question, now. This was Rachel's show.

Morgan stared out the side window from his slouched position in the passenger seat. He looked at his watch. He gazed at the sky ahead. He turned to Peter Singh. "What time is that ferry?"

"Not for a couple of hours."

Morgan sat up so fast the safety belt wrenched him around in his seat. "Then why the hurry? Why did she say she was behind schedule? What was the rush?"

Peter Singh glanced over at him, then back at the road, then at Morgan again, expectantly, waiting for an answer.

"How far are we from Tobermory?"

"Thirty minutes, maybe forty."

"Let's get moving."

"What are we suspecting?"

"I am suspecting that they are not catching a ferry. They're going scuba diving."

"They are what?"

"They are going wreck-diving, underwater. Scuba, you know?"

"I know what 'scuba' means, I am only surprised that they would be going to do that. Do you think she will be safe?"

"No, I do not."

Rachel cast off as Alexander revved up the engine and Miranda pushed them away from the wharf. Miranda was used to outboards at camp and dive boats in the Caribbean but she had not actually been in a boat this size and was surprised at the stability. It had probably been a saltwater vessel, she thought, retired to a freshwater job that seemed a trifle effete in comparison, after years having decks awash with the guts of innumerable fish.

Although Rachel had never mentioned previously diving at Tobermory, the other two accepted that she was directing their dive on the basis of earlier experience. They had decided on single-tank dives; they had three cylinders of compressed air aboard, including the one Alexander had brought from home. They would pick their site carefully, away from the bigger dive boats. Georgian Bay water was notoriously frigid, even in June, but if they stayed relatively shallow they could dive for an hour, even more if they were exceptionally efficient on air, although even with heavy-gauge wetsuits an hour might be more than enough. If they got too chilled, they could forego the second dive or cut it short.

Once out of sight of the harbour, Rachel directed the trawler toward an isolated area down the coast. Miranda looked back at the shoreline where the Niagara Escarpment, extending from the Falls far to the south, shambled into the bay. It was rugged and elusive, sometimes seeming closer than it was and sometimes farther away. No wonder so many ships met their doom in these waters. In a storm this would be a treacherous place, and even on a placid day in June, the water seemed ominous. Miranda had only been diving in the tropics, where the translucent surface reveals myriad depths of blues and greens. Here, the surface was like polished ebony, as if the bottom were a dark secret. So many have drowned here, going down with their ships, Miranda thought. She was used to diving amidst living coral and bright-coloured fish, not among wreckage haunted only by the drowned ghosts of the dead.

They found a marker buoy flying the diagonal red-on-white flag, and swinging the stern downwind they tied off securely and lowered the ladder into the water. Quietly, they slipped into their gear, helping each other to safety-check valves, regulators, buckles, and BCD vests. *Buoyancy Control Devices*; was there a sport anywhere with more acronyms? Miranda wondered, trying to distract herself. Each checked the others' auxiliary regulators and mouthpieces to make sure in an emergency a buddy could breathe from the same tank. The octopus, she thought. At least *octopus* is descriptive — a metaphor, not an acronym. They conferred about weights, and trusted Rachel's judgment based on her previous experience in fresh water. They needed to dive heavy to compensate for the buoyancy of the thick suits. Better too much weight, she said, than too little. You can increase buoyancy by adding air to your BCD vest, but if you're too light, you'll be fighting to stay down the whole dive.

Rachel had a small dive bag that she attached to her belt, along with one of the flashlights the dive shop provided. Miranda wondered where the bag came from when she saw Rachel take it from her knapsack. They had not come north expecting to dive. "Whatcha got there?" she asked casually, trying not to further arouse the uncharacteristic crankiness Rachel had been showing for the last hour or so. Miranda realized that her friend was likely apprehensive about the dive, just as she was, and that's how she was dealing with anxiety, just as Miranda was coping by being exceptionally quiet.

"Just stuff, don't worry," said Rachel, and she smiled disarmingly.

Miranda felt reassured. At this point in any diving adventure, Miranda found nerves were always a little on edge as the excitement mounted, and a display of companionable affection was welcome. She observed Alexander. He, too, was inordinately quiet. For the moment, Miranda felt a renewed bond with him, perhaps because they both seemed to be enacting a scenario that was primarily Rachel's design.

They stepped down onto the dive platform, moving awkwardly under the heavy burden of their tanks, their limbs constricted by the thick, clammy, synthetic material of their wetsuits. They wriggled into their fins, pumped a bit of air into their vests, adjusted their masks and checked to see their snorkels were in place, slipped on thick gloves, then put in their mouthpieces. Rachel immediately took a broad stride forward and splashed into the water, her head barely going under. Miranda followed and Alexander came last.

Miranda was astonished by the slap of cold against the exposed flesh of her face and even more by the crystal clarity of the water hidden under the dark surface. She felt an icy trickle track the length of her spine between wetsuit and skin, but looking down at the panoramic scene spread out below them in glimmering detail she forgot her discomfort.

Raising her head for the last time in open air, she exchanged excited grins with the other two divers, despite mouths jammed with breathing apparatus, and each diver gave the okay signal followed by a thumbs-down sign. They slowly began their descent along the sloped length of the mooring line. At ten feet Miranda stopped, squeezed her nose through her mask, and blew until a slight popping in her ears relieved the pressure, and then she hovered, surveying the wreck below them. She felt a familiar thrill spread through her body as she slowly descended, pausing periodically to clear her ears, eyes shifting from wonderment at the wreck below to monitor her companions' progress, ensuring that they stayed within easy reach of each other.

Twenty minutes south of Tobermory, Peter Singh asked Morgan, "What is the significance that her parents were morticians?"

"Rachel? I'm sure most kids of funeral directors grow up excessively normal. It's almost *de rigueur*. But it seems likely Rachel was exposed as a child to the arts of embalming and preparing corpses for public display in ways that have shaped her life ever since. She acquired skills and a fascination with death, the way a lawyer's kid will become a classroom advocate and end up as an adult serving hard time for manipulating the limits of power. Or a politician."

"My goodness, I am glad my father was a grocer!"

"Grocers' kids become cops."

"Actually, he was a lawyer, himself, in Punjab, but that is another story." After a few moments, when all they could hear was the hum of the tires on pavement, he asked, "Do you think Rachel could have killed the Hogg's Hollow couple in Professor Shelagh Hubbard's farmhouse? Is there any possibility?"

"Strong circumstantial evidence plus DNA ties Hubbard, herself, to those two. She almost certainly brought the colonial clothes from England; she arranged the corpses just so —"

"Strangers in an eternal embrace. That really is a wicked notion."

"Let's say Rachel and Alexander recognized Hubbard's grisly tableau at Hogg's Hollow as a signature crime," Morgan continued. "They were supposed to. But there was a problem: they would suspect that Miranda and I, and you, might eventually resolve the mystery and find it led back, one way or another, to them — an eventuality they preferred to avoid. So they created the counterfeit journals together. Rachel had the talent — she was a genius with pens and paper. Pope supplied the details of the London murders. He would, of course, know them intimately. And they adjusted the narrative chronology to coincide with Shelagh's tenure at the museum."

"But what about *your* murder?"

"My murder? No, yes, well. The Huron burial site — I think — was legitimate, if incredibly naive. Dr. Hubbard's own genius was nothing if not erratic. It would establish her professional reputation to discover the bones of a Jesuit saint in a Huron grave. I don't think she had any intention of putting me in there at all. But as Professor Birbalsingh said, it was a quixotic fabrication." This pleased Morgan, to think he had not been in jeopardy. Sometimes a sauna is just a sauna. "She must have told Rachel and Alexander about her project, and about my visit. They conflated the two stories and wrote up the third journal as if my death were at the centre of her plans. That would draw our guaranteed attention ... to her alone. Then they killed her. More precisely, Rachel killed her. I'm sure Alexander kept his distance. They both realized he was the more likely suspect."

"Then why not just make her body disappear? Leave it a cold case. Why fake an abduction?"

"They wanted us to think Shelagh Hubbard was at the dead centre of another theatrical contrivance. Letting the scene fade to black would have been anticlimactic."

"But the violets? They expected you to find her body; they practically invited you to find it."

"They couldn't resist a good yarn. They were sufficiently arrogant to believe we'd grow old searching for an explanation. That undoubtedly pleased them."

"Hubris!" said Peter Singh, drawing the word from his sketchy memory of lectures in classical drama. "Seeding the grave of a saint with a fresh cadaver. That opened up a whole new story, in fact."

"Which must have pleased them immensely. Perhaps each in a different way: morbid curiosity, to see how it would all turn out; the thrill of both directing the drama and being on stage. They both knew murders don't just happen — they have lives of their own."

"So to speak."

"So to speak. In subsuming Alexander's saint in a story where she had the power, Rachel would have made sure Pope wasn't compromised — and we had no reason to suspect her. As far as we knew, she was in Toronto, three or four hours away."

Suddenly, they were in Tobermory.

"We're here, Peter. Head straight for the docks. If we're lucky they haven't gone out yet." Morgan could feel his heart thumping inside his chest. He knew how important it was to remain calm, but what started as vague anxieties in the middle of the night had escalated into genuine fear for his partner's survival.

The divers glided away from the cement mooring block and gathered in a hovering conclave just over the rocky bottom beside what remained of an early twentieth-century excursion steamer. The hull, virtually intact, lay heeled over at an angle so that the remains of the superstructure loomed ominously above them. Miranda checked her depth gauge. They were at about sixty-six feet, or twenty metres. Divers are ambi-dimensional. The wreck was down far enough to escape the surge from the wildest of storms, yet shallow enough to be fairly accessible. Apart from layers of zebra mussels and lucent green algae, the steel hull appeared remarkably well-preserved.

With a circular upward sweep of her hand Rachel indicated she wanted to rise partway and circumnavigate the ship in an initial reconnaissance. They swam in a delta formation, with Rachel in the lead. On the upper side they found where the hull had been staved in. From the discrete shape and shear edges of the gaping hole, and the fact that it must have been at the waterline, Miranda deduced the ship had gone down as the result of an offshore collision rather than slamming against the rocks before slipping back into the depths.

She wondered how many had died. Was the sinking ship struggling toward land so that lifeboats could reach the shore, or steaming away to avoid breaking up on the rocks? She wished she knew the history; it felt eerie to be there, not knowing how many lives had been lost and under what circumstances. It made her feel like an invader, not knowing, like a ghoul, exposing open graves to her own invidious gaze.

Once they had circled the ship, Rachel led them up to the wheelhouse, which leaned precariously, and they could see the wheel and the binnacle were intact. Now that the wreck was part of a national marine park, attached artifacts would probably remain in position for the duration. Whatever that meant.

Miranda was relieved when Rachel did not try to enter the wheelhouse but passed up and over the side of the hull, then felt her breath quicken as she realized they were descending toward the gaping wound in the ship's upper side. Rachel hovered over the hole and signalled for the others to turn on their flashlights. Giving them the "okay" sign with thumb to forefinger, she turned and with a slight kick of her fins descended into the darkness. Alexander motioned for Miranda to follow, which she did reluctantly, and he came immediately after. She thought they had agreed there would be no penetration, but these were her friends and they seemed almost casually confident.

Once inside the hull, her eyes adjusted to the murky light. She was disconcerted by the metallic echo of their air bubbling against the steel walls and bulkheads. The rumble of her own exhaled breath as it rushed past her ears was the only underwater sound she was used to. Another sound intruded — an insistent pounding — and she was unnerved to recognize her own heartbeat. Claustrophobia pressed and she pushed back, determined to suppress even the possibility of panic. She focused on maintaining neutral buoyancy. She had fine-tuned the air in her BCD on descent to compensate for the pressure squeezing air out of her 7 ml wetsuit. She carried weights precisely matched to counter body fat. She was pleased — she weighed nothing. Strengthened by vanity, she expanded her mental horizon and took comfort in seeing Rachel immediately ahead and, finding herself a flickering shadow in Alexander's flashlight beam, in knowing Alexander was just behind her.

The three of them edged forward in file, using only the slightest intake or exhalation of breath to modify their relative plane, careful to stir up as little sediment as possible. In the midst of the criss-cross beams of three flashlights illuminating their surroundings, Miranda felt disoriented as she tried to distinguish between ceilings and floors. Structural angles were askew but up and down were more certain, since debris was gathered beneath them and their bubbles rose overhead.

Rachel motioned with her light and they followed her through a door that opened at a crazy slant into a passageway. In file they progressed toward a doorway gaping open at the far end. Rachel veered off and entered as if she knew where she was going. For a moment she was out of sight. Miranda felt reassured as Alexander's light beam cast her shadow into the gloom ahead and a surge of relief when she turned through the doorway and discovered Rachel at the far end of a large cabin with three portholes that previous divers had scraped clear.

The three of them gently manoeuvred until they were close enough to touch. They began breathing in unison, suspended in the middle of this alien world, their bubbles roaring. Miranda could still hear the drumming of her heart against the inside of her skull but the beat was slower, now, and regular. Rachel signalled to extinguish their lights by pressing the beams against their stomachs. Instead of the absolute darkness that Miranda expected, she was astonished by the illumination assaulting the portholes from the ambient light in the water outside, and surprised at how little of that light actually passed into the ship's interior, where she could just barely make out Rachel and Alexander as phantom shapes beside her.

To be reassured it was them, she drew her flashlight away from her body and scanned the beam across their torsos, careful to keep it away from their eyes. Rachel gave the "okay" sign and signalled for a return to darkness. It was as if this room were Rachel's gift and needed to be appreciated in natural light.

Profound gloom, Miranda thought. Still, she pressed the light beam into her stomach and was a little surprised when Rachel reached over and switched it off. She felt she had been admonished, until she saw her do the same with Alexander's. Okay, she thought, it's your show.

Miranda swung slowly on an imaginary axis below her rising column of bubbles and gazed around. The distorted angles of a room out of kilter sorted themselves out as her mind assimilated their defiance of logic. It was an oddly liberating experience and while her heart was slowly subsiding to no more than a murmur she looked for Rachel, wanting to signal her appreciation.

The other two had drifted to the lower side of the room. As Miranda peered at them through eddies of darkness, she was suddenly blinded by a flashlight flaring erratically, filling the chamber with shards of lightning before it went out. Miranda squeezed her eyes shut, veining the absolute blackness with strings of red, then opened them again to gaze through increasing swirls of silt at her friends hovering near the frame of what must have been a built-in bed. Miranda could see their bubbles intertwining in a weird configuration and, for an instant, she felt overwhelmingly lonely. She could hear voices through the water — that strange muffled parody of human speech when divers try to talk inside their mouth-pieces. Then she saw one of them, the smaller, break free and move slowly toward her, coming up from beneath. Alexander on the far side was gesticulating in broad movements but the dark water, laden with particles of sediment, obscured whatever he was trying to express, and his voice seemed to come in disembodied fragments, almost like laughter.

Miranda's renewed apprehension was immediately quelled when she felt Rachel's touch on her ankle, then felt her hand slowly move along her leg as her friend rose up beside her. For a moment they were face to face but the dim opalescence from the portholes made mirrors of their masks and all Miranda could see was the reflection of her own mask, mirroring Rachel's. Rachel pulled away, as if she were trying to find a better angle of light, then took one of Miranda's arms in both hands and give it a reassuring squeeze as she drew closer again, until their merged air bubbles obscured their vision entirely.

Rachel slid her grip to Miranda's wrist to stabilize herself while she adjusted her gear, reaching around and then straightening. To maintain equilibrium, Miranda pushed her friend gently away. She felt her wrist caught and tugged to break free. Whatever the entanglement, it was not an air hose or a BCD strap. She pulled hard and a narrow shackle of metal bit into her flesh through the shank of her glove and there was a slight give, as if she were pulling against a dead weight. She tried to turn on her flashlight but could not do it with only one hand; she tucked it into an armpit and managed to flick the switch so that the beam flared in a haphazard pattern across the upper reaches of the room.

Carefully retrieving the light with her free hand, she shone it down on the manacle around her wrist. She and Rachel were handcuffed together. Bewildered, Miranda followed the beam up Rachel's arm to her face. Rachel's face, even in the glare of Miranda's light, revealed nothing. Miranda shone her light down and across at Alexander. He was handcuffed to a metal bed rail. He did not appear to be struggling, but clouds of bubbles surged from his mouthpiece, making it seem like his head was exploding in slow motion.

Miranda brought the light back to Rachel, tracing down her body until she saw that Rachel's ankle was shackled to another iron rail, effectively enchaining them both to the ship. A series of throttled spasms caught at her throat, yet Miranda's mind seemed clear, as if she were an observer, a sympathetic witness to her own imponderable predicament. She shook her manacled arm and felt a strange surge of affection as she realized Rachel was dying.

Suddenly, her gut seized in a series of lacerating convulsions; a maelstrom of razor-sharp images raked the inside of her head. She too was dying. Survival instinct kicked in and panic gave way to shock and then she felt almost disengaged, again, as if it were all happening to someone else. And again reality took hold and her blood turned to ice, a jagged shaft of pain fibrillated between her lungs and her throat, her jaw and teeth, behind her eyes and into her temples. The pain helped her focus. She let the light zigzag across the bulkhead beneath them and discovered, close together, the other two flashlights, both turned off. Rachel must have intentionally dropped hers, then borrowed Alexander's to retrieve it and, instead, secured him to the wall in the darkness. Miranda had the only light. Clearly, whatever was happening, it was not important to Rachel that they see each other. If this was a tableau of death, it was to be enacted in murky obscurity.

Rachel hovered beside her, very still. Miranda looked again at her face through her mask. There was a flicker of recognition, but neither terror nor pleasure. When Rachel turned to spill the glare from the glass, Miranda could see what might have been tears, and yet her features appeared oddly serene, as if her face were slowly turning into a death mask, changing from flesh into sculptured stone.

Miranda reached for the hose with her gauges attached. Their dive had been almost thirty minutes to this point. More than half her air was gone. She would breathe slowly and eke out the rest as best she could. Then she would die. She was surprised by her own composure. There was nothing to do, there were no options. She was cold. The icy tremor along her spine was a reassuring reminder that she was still alive. She breathed slowly, inhaling long deep drafts, releasing short bursts, a bit at a time until she was depleted, and then again, slowly, and again, and again. She turned out her light. To save the batteries. She thought she would like to have light at the end.

Morgan and Peter Singh stormed into the dive shop. A chill ran through Morgan's entire body when the young man told them three cops had gone out on their own. Grave doubts about Miranda's safety turned to gut-wrenching fear. Without understanding the urgency, the young man scrambled to get Morgan outfitted with dive gear, not even bothering to ask for his certification, while Peter Singh, flashing his Owen Sound Police identification, commandeered a boat from a couple of startled American tourists setting out to go fishing.

"You want me to come with you?" the young diver offered, excited by the prospect.

"No," said Morgan. "Call the OPP, tell them what's happening. Come after us pronto."

"I don't really know what's happening. Is the Coast Guard okay?"

"Do it!" said Officer Singh. "Come out in their boat. We'll need underwater backup. Morgan, do you know what Miranda's boat looks like?"

"Yeah, and what direction it went. Let's go!"

They skimmed over the water in the direction they had been told. There were a number of boats in the offing. They scanned for the trawler, then Morgan realized they might easily have set out in one direction and switched course out of sight of the harbour. He gazed along the coast and in the distance could make out a boat on its own. It was a gamble. If it wasn't them, they would waste precious time, perhaps the minutes of struggle before death. He was certain, now, that Miranda would die if they did not get to her soon.

## chapter eighteen

# The Wreck

---

**M**iranda could feel Rachel floating in limbo at the end of their tether beneath them. She switched on her light and checked her gauges. The pressure-gauge needle was grazing the red zone. She had fewer than fifteen minutes left. She sighed into her mask. The depth gauge remained constant. She was hovering at forty-five feet, fifteen metres; the higher the better, the less air consumed. She smiled to herself, despite shivering from the cold. She struggled to remain fully aware, keeping a delicate balance between panic and shock. She gazed about in the shadowy chambers of her mind but found nothing of interest. Her life didn't flash before her eyes. She felt cheated. She wanted to be solemn, to die with grace and dignity, but small jokes kept intruding.

She lifted her manacled wrist into the murky light in front of her mask. When she turned the flashlight beam toward herself, it was Rachel's hand that dangled lifelessly in front of her eyes. My God, she thought, she's dead! But she could hear the echoing rumble of her breathing beside her. She would finish her air soon. Miranda worked their joined arms around and contemplated chewing through her wrist. Better yet, chewing through Rachel's. Is it cannibalism if you chew and don't swallow? And what if the flesh is your own? She realized that she had not thought about why Rachel was doing this. Rachel was her friend. She couldn't bite Rachel.

Miranda reached about, inside her skull, looking for clarity. It hadn't occurred to her before. There was a dive knife attached to her BCD. She withdrew the knife. It was titanium with a serrated edge. She could saw off her hand. She held the knife out in front of her, then extended her wrist. She would have to cut close to the joint and pry through the cartilage and ligaments. There was no way bone would yield in the time remaining. She tried to think of how she could staunch the blood flow. Tying off a tourniquet might be possible with her remaining hand. She had nothing to use, no accessible strap except for her weight belt and if she removed that, she would soar upwards and maybe be pinioned against the steel overhead. Possibly she could jam the bleeding stump into her BCD harness and bind against it, but then could she swim with sufficient dexterity to avoid getting hung up on or torn apart by twisted railings and shear metal edges?

She could feel Rachel shift her position. She grasped the knife more firmly, afraid Rachel might try to interfere, but then she realized Rachel was leaning down and away and she suddenly grasped what was happening. Even as she felt the clasp of rigid steel around her ankle, she knew it was too late. Rachel had drawn another pair of cuffs from her bag and secured Miranda's ankle to the same iron rail she had shackled herself to Miranda opened her fingers and let the knife slip away. It hit the steel beneath them with a resonant twang. She twitched at the finality of the sound. She shone her light down on Alexander Pope. When the beam caught his eyes, his mask suddenly burst into an explosive balloon of wasted air that immediately expired, drawing a thin stream of bubbles in its wake, and then only a few random beads trickled from his gaping mouth as the mouthpiece fell uselessly into the darkness. Miranda turned her light out, shaken to witness his death, desperate to isolate herself from his hovering body.

The two women swung this way and that, as if they were caught in a haphazard current, but the movement came from their bodies turning gently together against the pain of their manacled ankles. They crashed lightly against a looming bulkhead, tanks clanging, and drifted away, twisting slowly, crashing again. Reverberations like the sound of shook metal filled the room, flooded her head. Miranda, irritated, manoeuvred until they were still, binding against the pain where the cuffs bit into her flesh. She felt Rachel running a hand up the back of her neck. Miranda flinched, realizing it was a gesture of affection. They would die with their bodies conjoined in an enduring embrace.

By the time their commandeered boat pulled alongside the trawler with Peter Singh at the helm, Morgan had set up his regulator and tank, which was large and heavy, attached them to his BCD, and was in his thick wetsuit, with boots and fins on, no gloves — he had come without gloves. Peter tied off to the other boat, then assisted Morgan with the weight belt and gear. Morgan pressed the mouthpiece between his lips and took a test breath.

"Okay," he said, backing against the gunnel so he could flip over into the water as he had done on Easter Island. "Do you see their bubbles?"

"What bubbles?" Peter handed Morgan his mask, which he had thoughtfully spit in and rinsed, as he understood from the movies was required. He then began tugging at the BCD fasteners with meticulous care.

"Damn it, Peter, stop fussing. Look around. There should be bubbles breaking the surface."

"I don't see anything, Morgan. The water's like glass, there's nothing."

"Damn it," Morgan repeated. "Sit tight, I'll be back."

"I hope so," said Peter as Morgan clasped mask to face, regulator to his mouth, and sprawled backward head over heels, disappearing under the surface, leaving his own trail of bubbles behind him.

Morgan dropped uncomfortably fast; he was wearing too much weight. He struggled to get his fins underneath him so that he could slow his descent. Once he had a chance to pop his ears, he looked around, descending through layers of pain, repeatedly blowing into his pinched nose to equalize the pressure in his head. Below him was the wreck, standing clear on its side in the cold pristine water. When he settled heavily to the bottom beside the hull, he unclasped his weight belt and slid one of the lead weights off, dropping it among the rocks, at the same time remembering that his BCD was a flotation vest attached to his air tank, which he could have inflated with a few bursts of air to slow his freefall descent. He gave a brief squeeze to the inflator button and levitated, hovering uneasily just off the bottom. His training was recent; this gear was unfamiliar but the procedures were the same. He deflated a brief burst and sank, then inflated again until he achieved neutral buoyancy.

Even while feeling a certain satisfaction at attaining weightlessness, horror mounted as he realized he had seen no air columns rising while on his way down. The water was freezing against his hands and the exposed flesh of his face, but there was an almost tropical clarity. As he turned a slow pirouette, gazing out in all directions, he saw no sign of their bubbles. Fluttering gently up and over the ship, he looked for bubble traces indicating the divers were inside. Or, if they were, would their exhalations be trapped? He swam the length of the upper side, passing along a series of portholes midship, and down over a gaping hole at the ship's waterline mark, just off the front quarter.

He decided to make another methodical sweep along the uppermost side of the hull. He had turned icily calm after breathing far too heavily, consuming valuable air at a reckless rate. Maybe they had decided wreck-diving was too dangerous. Maybe they were having a recreational tour close by, with no nefarious intent. He would stay close, assuming they would come back to the mooring line before surfacing. Their air must be running low. How strange it will seem, as Miranda swims by, to see me.

Morgan drifted around the stern and back over the upper deck that slanted at a precarious angle against the lucent horizon, gazing in all directions into the distant opacity, searching for movement.

He glanced down as he passed over a row of portholes and caught in one what he took to be a spear of sunlight cast by the prism of a wave overhead. With a slight acceleration he coasted back down over the portholes before passing on to examine the breach in the hull gaping ahead. He directed the beam of his light into the dark cavity in the ship's side.

They must have surfaced — their air supply would be depleted by now. Suddenly, he heard a sharp metallic clanking reverberate from the darkness inside the hull. It was impossible to determine the direction of its source. He remembered the flash against glass like a shaft of sunlight. There were no waves overhead. He withdrew from the cavernous shadow where he had been hovering, bewildered by the sound, and swam back along the side of the ship.

Miranda flashed her light against the glass of the middle porthole and it glared back in a mirror image of their watery crypt. Alarmed by the image, she dowsed the light. And yet several times she repeated the sequence, mesmerized by how the luminescent world outside the ship was extinguished and then reappeared, as if she had transformative powers. Once, she thought a shadow passed by, but when she flashed her light it had vanished.

She inhaled in slow, shallow breaths and slowly exhaled, tilting her head and watching the bubbles rise in front of her mask and gather against the bulkhead above. She switched on her flashlight with the beam directed downwards to soften the glare, and turned her head to see if Rachel was alive. Rachel stared out at her with what Miranda perceived as serenity. Miranda's eyelids dropped interrogatively.

What had Alexander done to deserve such a miserable death? How had Miranda so completely misunderstood their relationship? What terrible things swarmed through a mind driven to murders so contrived and cruel and seemingly arbitrary — without even the satisfaction of knowing her victims understood? Perhaps that is the point, Miranda thought: love as a prelude to death, a prologue to absolute power. Some things are beyond understanding.

Or perhaps Alexander understood his own death. Surely Rachel understood hers. And understanding for Miranda was not important — it would neither console nor redeem, and it would not compensate. Dead is dead. She felt life surge inside her and for the briefest moment she was angry, but anger made her colder. She tried to think of sunlight and fires. But when warmth began to creep through her body, she knew hypothermia was setting in as she shivered in spasms.

Rachel twisted their manacled wrists, and grasped Miranda's hand. She gave it a slow and gentle squeeze — what might have been intended as a meaningful gesture. Miranda turned her light directly on Rachel. Rachel gave an almost imperceptible shrug, then took her mouthpiece from her mouth and held it up over her head.

There was a sudden rush of bubbles, then nothing. Her air was gone. She shrugged again, but instead of inhaling water she seemed to be holding her breath, as if she were determined to be in control to the end, to die by asphyxiation rather than drowning.

Miranda's mask was filling with water, rising above her nostrils and splashing into her eyes. She felt panic tighten inside her. She took a slow breath and, tilting her head upward, exhaled through her nose, feeling the precious air stream out the top of her mask, driving the invasive water with it. Her mask cleared and the panic subsided.

She drew Rachel close. Reaching down to her side she freed up her octopus, which was tangled with her primary regulator hose, and pressed the auxiliary mouthpiece against Rachel's pursed lips. After a moment of resistance, Rachel opened her mouth and grasped it between her teeth, but seemed not to breathe. Calmly, Miranda reached over and pressed the diaphragm on the front of the reg, forcing a burst of air into Rachel's mouth. Rachel took a deep involuntary breath and began to hyperventilate. Miranda pressed against Rachel's chest with her hand, urging her to slow down. They would share her air to the end. Miranda did not want to die alone. But she would prolong the process as long as possible. She would savour every last moment of consciousness.

Morgan swooped down on three portholes that had delib-
erately been scraped clean of algae from the inside. He tried
to peer in but could see nothing. Grasping a steel flange
with his fingertips, he pressed his flashlight against the glass
to eliminate the reflection. He was sure there were human-
shaped forms in the shadowy darkness. He banged on the
window but there was no response. He turned and swam
back to the breach in the hull, plunged into the depths of
the ship, and was swallowed whole, with only the thread of
his light beam to draw him through the bizarre angles of
darkness.

Miranda drew in her last full breath and held it until her lungs
burst and the residual air spewed out in a violent shudder. Her
flashlight was on. She looked into Rachel's mask, surprised to
see fear in her final moment. She shone the light around their
murky prison, calmly conscious of inscribing in her mind her
final perceptions. Overhead, there was a pearly sheen where
their exhaled air had gathered against the steel. She reached
up and discovered she could break the surface and her fingers
disappeared into a shallow pocket of air. She leaned down
and drew Rachel toward her, then stretched upwards, kicking
against the cuff around her ankle, forcing it to slide along the
iron rail to gain a few inches of height.

Arching her neck, her face was less than a hand's width
away from the air. When she grasped to cup air with her hand,
it slipped through her fingers. She needed to press into the
pocket with her lips. Her mask hit steel, she tore it off and
stretched again, until she could feel the flesh of her ankle
break open against the restraining shackle. Still beyond reach.
She dipped her fingertips into the eerily beautiful opalescence

and pulled back to watch as it broke like shattered mercury. Her mind wavered; carbon dioxide tore into the walls of her lungs and trachea and larynx with innumerable edges; her chest and windpipe collapsed in a paroxysm of agony.

As her mask drifted away, Miranda felt the snorkel attached to its band brush against her leg. She grabbed down at it, but it slipped from her reach. Dropping her flashlight, she tore Rachel's mask from her face and, after releasing the snorkel, let her mask drop as well. With a jarring heave she tried to twist the stiff plastic into a straight shaft. Briefly asphyxia took hold and her vision flashed black. She stopped, she clasped the snorkel with her manacled hand, reached out, groping, found Rachel's knife, grasped the release, squeezed, turned the razor-sharp edge against the plastic, incised around the shaft a continuous line. The knife slipped from her fingers. Struggling to remain conscious, she twisted the snorkel with all her remaining strength. It refused, shivered, gave way, the valve end detached and slipped into the murk beneath them.

Miranda pressed the mouthpiece into her mouth and guided the sheared upper end into the pocket of air. She blew out, sucking residual air from cavities of pain to clear the shaft, and took in a slow, deep breath to replenish her screaming lungs.

She took another breath and another, then drew Rachel close, and bending away from her air supply, she pressed her lips over Rachel's lips, forcing them open with her tongue, and blew air into Rachel's mouth. Rachel coughed, regurgitating water into Miranda's mouth. Miranda pulled back, and reached for another breath, then returned and blew more air into Rachel's mouth. Her flashlight beamed from below in wavering swards above Alexander's tethered corpse.

Morgan saw light flashing in fragments against the obscene tilt of the corridor walls. His heart racing, he surged ahead to the open door and swung into a stateroom, clattering his tank against the steel bulkhead, smashing his leg against the door frame. He doubled up in pain and lost equilibrium; he shone his light around, trying to orient himself to the bizarre angles of the room. Immediately ahead was the grotesquely contorted body of Alexander Pope. Above him, the beam shone through the swirling sediment and revealed a strange apparition of shadows and limbs.

As he rose up, he reached out and touched a leg. He recoiled as Miranda screamed into the water. He touched her again, this time not tentatively. He cast his light beam across his own face and then across hers. She had let the snorkel drop from her lips, which were open as she desperately mouthed the water. He released his mouthpiece from his own lips and thrust it between hers. She breathed deeply.

Oh, my goodness, my goodness, he thought. He reached around for his octopus regulator and exchanged it with hers. She took another deep breath and then thrust the mouthpiece out toward Rachel. Morgan grabbed it and forced it between Rachel's lips. There was an interminable pause, then Rachel breathed on her own.

Morgan twisted slowly about and surveyed the situation. His air supply would not sustain all three for very long. Miranda was shaking from the cold but reached for his arm and gave it a tight squeeze through the wetsuit, then made the gesture of pushing him away, but without letting go. He shone his light in the water between them so that they could make eye contact. She rolled her eyes, motioning him to go up. She took the mouthpiece and handed it to Rachel, then, turning back to Morgan, she smiled and blew him an absurd underwater kiss, and gave an abrupt gesture with a jerk of her head. There was no doubt: she wanted him to leave them and save himself. Since he had found her, he understood what was happening. He must — he was here. He was her witness. She felt a great surge of warmth. She was ready.

Morgan wasn't. He released his grip from their convoluted embrace and, handing off his mouthpiece to Miranda, he sank down to examine the handcuffs around the women's ankles. He made a futile attempt to break them free and felt in the darkness where blood from torn flesh seeped through Miranda's wetsuit, warming his hand as he touched her, making him suddenly realize how achingly numb his fingers were, how close to being useless.

He drifted up, took back his reg, and handing Miranda his flashlight he squirmed around to release her gear. She and Rachel were jammed so closely together, and his icy fingers were so clumsy, he could only manage to remove her tank from the back of her BCD, which, when he released it, tumbled with an echoing clang against the steel walls and floor. He struggled to keep her from drifting upward and grasped one of her hands — the other was clutching his flashlight — and pushed it violently against his own chest straps. His fingers flashed white.

She understood, and while Rachel took her turn breathing, Miranda thrust her own fingers between her teeth and, pulling to and fro, peeled off her glove, then reached down and released Morgan's straps. She grasped at his closest hand to warm it. He pulled away, but briefly pumped it against her breast in affirmation. When he dropped his mouthpiece and pulled the octopus mouthpiece away from her, leaving them all without air while he squirmed out of his gear, she was startled, confused, but trusting. Once freed, he handed her the primary mouthpiece and, taking a deep breath from the octopus, he gave it to her for Rachel, then holding on to Miranda with one hand and clasping his gear awkwardly between his knees, he detached his tank and regulator, took another breath from the mouthpiece she held to his lips, then swung around and secured his tank against the back of her BCD. He adjusted her gear and swung around to face her. She seemed overweighted from his heavier tank but when she moved to release her weight belt, he signalled negative and gave her BCD inflator a couple of bursts to increase her buoyancy. He took another long, deep breath from the proffered reg, while clasping her bared hand for a moment in his icy grasp. The gnawing pain reassured him; the pressure of his touch made her feel like a woman blessed.

Morgan let go, intending on searching for the discarded masks in the murk swirling beneath them, and plummeted into the bulkhead below, careening against planes of steel coated with algae, thickly studded with zebra mussels, until he tumbled into Alexander Pope's hovering corpse.

They needed masks and light. If somehow he could free them, it would be difficult to get out if they could see clearly, impossible if they couldn't. He pulled the mask off the corpse and, reaching around blindly, he discovered one of the other masks tangled in the dead man's floating limbs. Sliding sideways he grabbed at Miranda's errant flashlight and looped the lanyard around his wrist. He pushed away with oxygen deprivation tearing at his lungs, and kicked upwards but was pinioned against the steel. His weights! His fingers refused to close around his weight-belt release. Grasping at Miranda and Rachel, he hauled himself upward hand over hand until he reached the air that Miranda held out for him. He drew in a deep breath and could taste her blood, or his own, in the mouthpiece. With a single tug she released his weights. The reverberations as they crashed against steel sent shivers of loneliness through both of them.

Once the masks were secure, Miranda blew hers clear of water. Rachel left hers flooded but continued regular breathing, holding the octopus mouthpiece between clenched teeth. Morgan secured Miranda's flashlight around her wrist, took two deep breaths from the principal reg, then pressed the mouthpiece firmly between her lips, and with a quick parting squeeze on her arm he swam down and over to the door, swimming fiercely but without thrashing. If he could get outside through the hole in the hull, he was certain that he would be able to reach the surface without air.

Miranda succumbed briefly to panic when she realized what Morgan was doing. She stiffened, then slowly relaxed, and breathed deeply, calmly, for his sake as much as her own. Her one hand was still gloveless and it ached; she tried to tuck it between her legs. She tried to pee into the wetsuit and succeeded a little, but not enough to warm her hand. Morgan, one way or another, he would be back. Breathing as shallowly as she could, she struggled to comprehend what was happening. Being captive in a watery grave seemed the inevitable consequence of preceding events, yet it made no sense. Morgan finding her seemed inevitable, as well. She felt a surge of warmth.

Morgan's lungs knotted with pain as he emerged through the breach in the hull into the pellucid water surrounding the ship. He began to exhale a steady stream of bubbles as he kicked slowly to the light, struggling desperately to control his rate of ascent, knowing instinctively that expanding air in his lungs had to be released. He was no use to Miranda if he lost consciousness or succumbed to an embolism or the bends.

As he struggled through the long ascent toward the boats overhead, his mind swarmed with imagery: fragments of banal conversation with Miranda over a thousand coffees, the headless embrace, the radiant serenity of the face when they opened the tomb, the pilgrims like wraiths in the night, the revealed frescoes on the walls of the church. The surface shimmered far overhead. Images turned into walls of black. He kicked with a great surge and in an explosion he breached, heaving for air, and thrashed in the water until Peter Singh's arm appeared within reach, then he collapsed into himself, too exhausted to negotiate the ladder. There was no OPP boat, no Coast Guard rescue vessel, only tourist boats in the far, distant offing.

Peter Singh was distraught as he struggled to haul Morgan up onto the dive deck of the trawler. "Where is your tank? Where is Miranda? What is happening down there?"

"Where's our backup? We need air!" Morgan doubled over to force his diaphragm against his lungs, then straightened abruptly, gasping, twisting his guts into raw knots of pain. "We need air," he repeated. "How long was I down?"

"There are no air cylinders on the other boat. They did not bring extra. Thirty-five or forty minutes, perhaps."

"Which?"

"I don't know. Forty."

"Can you see anyone coming?"

"Maybe over there. They made the same mistake we did and went the wrong way. Who is down there? Is Miranda okay?"

"No, she's bloody not. Find the tool kit — there must be a tool box." As he tried to suppress nausea, Morgan began to straighten and hunch over with slow deliberation, forcing his wracked body into a crude sort of bellows, pumping air into his system. Peter clambered awkwardly about the trawler, tearing open hatches and lockers, and came up with nothing. He climbed into the commandeered fishing boat and found a red tool box.

"Open it. Are there snips, shears, something to cut steel?"

Morgan windmilled his arms, trying to force blood back into his fingers. The excruciating pain was a good sign.

Peter sorted frantically through the box and came up with a rusted pair of cable cutters.

"Good man!" Morgan yelled. "Bring them here."

As he rushed back, Peter stumbled. The cutters skittered across the deck. Morgan lunged for them from the dive platform, tried to wrap his unbending fingers around the blades as they clattered against the gunnel, spontaneously releasing his grasp as they cut open his palm, and watched them slip through the scuppers into the water.

He scrambled to his feet, heaving to take in as much air as he could, and dove after them, sliding his mask into place in mid-air. He kicked savagely to keep the cutters in sight and watched them clank against the hull directly below and slide down past the hole in the wreck's side to the rocky bottom. He could feel his ears throb like bolts of hot steel hammering into his head, he continued his descent, his eyes fixed on the small twist of shadow where the cutters had come to rest. His ears popped explosively, and his vision blurred from the pain, then his eyes came back into focus. He was past the dark opening in the hull. He reached down and managed to clutch the cutters between his frozen hands.

He rose to the gaping hole in the ship's side, unclipped his flashlight, and let its beam lead the way. Within the first chamber he was momentarily disoriented, then found his way through. Careening in slow motion off the angled planes of the corridor, he surged along its length toward the open doorway.

Miranda could see flashes of light and, by their erratic pattern, knew Morgan was on his own. She had recovered her composure, despite shivering bitterly, cold to the bone. She was breathing carefully, ensuring that Rachel was breathing as well. The light beam faltered, stayed ominously still. Dread overwhelmed her. She wrenched violently against the handcuffs on her wrist and ankle, shifting to bang the tank on her back against a bulkhead, sending a thunderous metallic clang resonating through the ship's interior.

The light began to move again. Morgan flailed with his fins against the wall of water behind him and soared ahead, curving through the door and up beside Miranda in a single, violent motion, grabbing at the mouthpiece from her outstretched hand, jamming it between his teeth, wavering into unconsciousness. Miranda shone her light at him. His eyes were glazed, he wasn't breathing. She reached out and pressed the diaphragm on the reg, forcing precious air into his mouth. He didn't respond, and she punched him hard on the chest. He gave a sharp intake of water and air, spat the mouthpiece out, sputtered, and when she replaced it between his lips he drew sweet air deeply into his lungs.

Miranda took a few breaths from Rachel's reg, then returned it. Rachel was compliant but disinterested. Morgan offered Miranda the cutters — she had to pry open his fingers to get them. She took them and grasped the steel links between the blades. With a seesaw motion of her free hand, she worked away, stopping periodically to breathe from the octopus, feeling the blades etch into the steel of the cuffs. Morgan tried to take over but could not get a grasp. Miranda resumed cutting. Suddenly, the steel snapped. Miranda withdrew her wrist in a sudden motion.

Morgan took the cutter, took a shallow breath, and dropped down to work away at Miranda's ankle cuff. He reached twice for air from the mouthpiece she held down to him, and in his third attempt, he gave a mighty heave and the steel broke, setting Miranda free.

Checking to be sure Rachel had a good grasp on her

mouthpiece, Miranda handed off her own mouthpiece to Morgan. Prying the cutters from his frozen fingers she began working through Rachel's ankle cuff, taking occasional shallow breaths from Morgan, knowing her exertion was increasing consumption of their last few minutes or seconds of air. Morgan tried to help but she pushed him away. He was barely conscious, his body still depleted and wracked with pain. She would get him out of here, even if they had to leave Rachel behind.

Everything was upside down. Her heartbeat pounded in her temples; vertigo threatened with nausea, bile, blurring vision. She tried to focus on steel against steel, rocking the blades in a severing motion until suddenly there was an abrupt snap — the cutters fell apart in her hands.

Miranda swung upright and tugged the octopus mouthpiece from Rachel's mouth. She needed the air. She needed to manoeuvre. With Morgan shining the light on Rachel's ankle, Miranda braced against the steel wall with one leg and with the other jammed against Rachel's leg she grasped the cuff in both hands and concentrated all her diminished strength on the cleft in the steel. There was a long moment of unspeakable pain as the steel cut into the flesh of her hands and the water clouded red with her blood. The steel snapped and Miranda careened into Alexander's tangled embrace.

Breaking free from the hoses and limbs, she grasped upward, found her dangling regulator, drew a single breath as she ascended, and put the mouthpiece back into Rachel's mouth. Morgan handed her his. She drew in deeply; there was a rattle and smack as her cheeks collapsed into themselves. Their air supply had expired.

Morgan slid down against the wall as if he were going to take a rest. Miranda pushed against him then swam through the door and drew him abruptly behind her. In the corridor, she turned and, grasping him by the hair, she shook his head violently. He rocked briefly askew, then, righting himself, motioned her to go first. Miranda pushed him past her and reached back for Rachel, drawing her forward. Morgan had dropped his flashlight and she lost hers in the tumble after Rachel's manacle gave way. Rachel had retrieved hers from where she had dropped it — her first wilful act in the last quarter hour — and while its beam flashed erratically as she swam it gave them enough light until they entered the dim aura emanating from the hole through the hull. Prodding Morgan from behind and hauling Rachel after her, Miranda engineered their slow progress through the last of the darkness out into the open.

Morgan drifted free from the hull. Miranda grasped the rough steel edge and tried to pull Rachel through. Rachel twisted to the side and Miranda lost her. Miranda could feel her lungs imploding, her heart thudding frantically. She turned to retrieve her grip on Rachel, but Rachel kicked away and slowly receded into the darkness. For an instant Miranda thought of going after. Morgan was drifting in a stupor toward the rocky bottom, gazing back at her with a vacant stare through his mask, which was filled almost to eye level with water. She turned again and peered into the ship's gaping interior. She saw Rachel move against a shimmer of light and then disappear.

Miranda swooped down to Morgan with a single kick. She still had a tiny reserve of oxygen in her system. She placed her lips over his, prodded between them with her tongue as she had done for Rachel, and expelled a few precious gulps of air into his mouth. He took in the air but did not respond, and settled like a dead weight to the bottom. Miranda shook him and released. If she did not start now, she would never make it to the surface. Instinctively, she kicked away, but

then arced around on herself and grasped Morgan under the
arms, trying to pull him away from the bottom. As she hauled
Morgan roughly against her breast, she could feel the abrasive
material of her BCD scraping the back of the hand that was
still bare. She squeezed the BCD against her body, responding
to its thickness. She had taken in a few extra bursts of air to
compensate for the increased weight when Morgan had given
her his tank. Reaching along the inflator hose, she grasped
the valve with aching fingers and thrust it awkwardly between
distended lips, pressing the deflate button. A rush of air surged
into her mouth. She took a deep breath. It tasted foul but sent
brilliant lights dazzling in front of her eyes as freshened blood
coursed through her body.

She thrust the valve between Morgan's bruised lips and
pressed the deflator button again. Nothing. She squeezed the
BCD material against her body and watched air stream from
his gaping mouth, then his lips closed and she could see him
struggle to breathe. She shifted within the constraints of her
vest to free up her weight belt and let it drop among the rocks,
giving herself a little more air. She took the deflator valve,
drew a trickle of air deep into her lungs, then passed it back,
and pressed the button. A brief burst trickled from the sides
of his mouth, then nothing was left.

Without weights, they were beginning to drift across
the bottom. She drew Morgan to her breast and emptied her
lungs into his mouth. Turning him to face away from her, she
grasped him under one armpit, pushed with a surge against
the rocks, and began to swim toward the two boats overhead,
kicking with all her strength and pulling against the frigid
water with her free arm while Morgan, when he remembered
where they were, fluttered his fins, trying to help as he passed
in and out of consciousness.

As she concentrated on keeping Morgan in her grip,

focused on their upward ascent, Miranda felt lethal waves of euphoria sweep through her. She forced herself to think. Rachel was dead. She knew they would find her body with Alexander, their bodies entwined in a miserable reprise of the eternal embrace — one final dramatic tableau of inspired depravity. It would be the fulfillment of Rachel's desire, although with the wrong partner. Rachel wanted to share death with Miranda and be free at last of her demon lovers. Miranda was sure of that. Nothing was certain. Nothing was sometimes enough.

I hope we live, she thought. He'll owe me,

The shimmering surface spread above them like an enveloping shroud. Blood pounded inside Miranda's head with deafening urgency — suddenly drowned out by an unmistakable roaring. Instinctively, she cringed downward as the hull of another boat slid to an abrupt halt immediately overhead. With a last surge of energy, she pulled Morgan off to the side, then reached desperately upward toward the dive platform. A hand grasped her wrist.

Peter Singh and two OPP officers in full scuba gear dragged both of them onto the trawler deck.

"Miranda," Peter exclaimed in a tremulous voice. "You are rescued. You can release Morgan now." He tried to pull her hand away but she would not relinquish her grip. When he pried her fingers free so the OPP medic could look after him, she rolled on her side and grasped a handful of his hair.

"Miranda," said Peter Singh. "It is all right now, you are rescued. Please release Detective Morgan." He made an incomprehensible gesture of flinging his open palms into the air.

She tightened her grip.

"Damn it, Miranda," Morgan gasped in a faraway voice. "That hurts like hell."

She rolled closer so their faces almost touched. Their noses were running with mucus and blood, their eyes were raw, their lips bruised. Her hands were weeping blood from where the steel had cut into her palms; Morgan's hands bled from being sliced when he grabbed at the cutters. She smiled. Stigmata. Morgan understood; he struggled to keep her in focus, his ears throbbed. He smiled back.

"Hi," she whispered.

"Told you we'd dive together." He couldn't hear his own words over the roar of his blood beating against the inside of his skull.

"Yeah."

"Thanks, buddy." His smile broadened into an awkward grin.

"You too. Buddy."

He closed his eyes.

Miranda watched as he drifted into pain-free unconsciousness. His smile faded and his face relaxed as he seemed to turn into a little boy.

She opened her own eyes wide, brown and green and golden in the slanting sunlight, which seemed to wash the rawness and the red away, then shut them and held them closed as she picked out the familiar sounds of her partner's breathing against the din of rescue activities all around them.

# Also by John Moss

# Still Waters

978-1-55002-790-7 / $11.99

A corpse with a comb-over slowly turns in a garden pond in a wealthy Toronto neighbourhood, leading Toronto police detective David Morgan into speculations about Japanese koi fish, and his partner, Miranda Quin, into a chilling sequence of revelations that nearly destroys her. The real mystery begins not with the dead man but with a stunning woman who, without emotion, declares herself to be the nondescript victim's mistress.

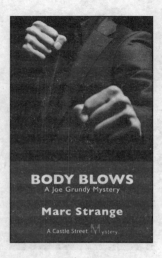

# Body Blows
## by Marc Strange

978-1-55488-390-5 / $11.99

One night the live-in servant and not-so-secret lover of Lord Douglas Hotel owner Leo Alexander turns up murdered and the multi-millionaire becomes the number one suspect. Ex-boxer Joe Grundy must work to get to the bottom of the incident in order to clear the man he's forged a bond with since coming to work for him as head of security at the hotel. But Leo's past serves up more surprises than Grundy bargained for. Another corpse pops up, Leo is arrested and jailed, and Grundy takes more hits to his body and psyche than perhaps even he can handle.

# Outside the Line

## by Christian Petersen

978-1-55002-859-1 / $11.99

Peter Ellis, a rookie probation officer in Interior British Columbia, is saddled with a new client: former NHL player Todd Nolin. The victim is Todd's wife, Marina Faro, who has been badly beaten and feels her estranged husband is bent on killing her. Now Peter must grapple with his need to keep Marina safe while maintaining a rein on his own attraction to her.

Available at your favourite bookseller.

DUNDURN
www.dundurn.com

**Tell us your story!**

What did you think of this book?

Join the conversation at

**www.definingcanada.ca/tell-your-story**

by telling us what you think.